THE INVIVER

KENDALL LESPERANCE

Copyright © 2025 by Kendall Lesperance

All rights reserved. No part of this publication may be reproduced, stored or transmitted in any form or by any means, electronic, mechanical, photocopying, recording, scanning, or otherwise without written permission from the publisher. It is illegal to copy this book, post it to a website, or distribute it by any other means without permission.

This novel is entirely a work of fiction. The names, characters and incidents portrayed in it are the work of the author's imagination. Any resemblance to actual persons, living or dead, events or localities is entirely coincidental.

First edition

ISBN: 979-8-9905684-0-2

Editing by Jessica McKelden

Illustration by Manuel Figueiredo

To those who doubt themselves and their journey. You will get there.

And to my wonderful husband, Zach. You are my light.

Name Pronunciation Guide

People

Kaie *K-AI-ee*
Shayla *SHEY-Laa*
Lorne *Lor-ne*
Rosse *Ro-ss*
Achaius *Aah-KAY-us*
Torin *Tor-in*
Crevan *Cre-van*
Syane *Sai-an*
Haelan *HAY-lan*

Werthall Outpost
Carthan Valley
Scria
The Mists
Fernan Outpost
Riverton
Galicia

CHAPTER I

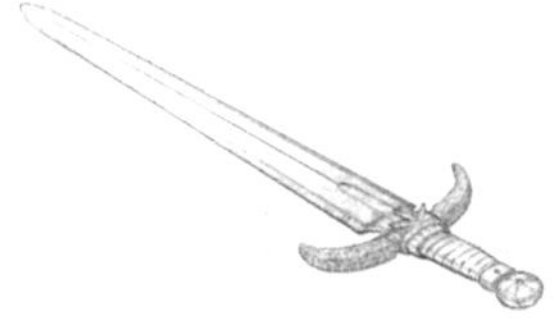

It was a room she did not recognize, the heavy drapes pulled shut with only a sliver of sunlight shining through. The forest-green walls and extravagant trappings did not help with the feeling of foreboding, settling like a stone deep in Kaie's stomach. Across from her, in a bed, a young man around her age struggled to take in air, his breath coming out in gasps.

Slowly, she approached the bed and looked down at him. His face was deathly white, making the dark circles under his eyes stand out even more. Blond hair hung around his face, limp from whatever sickness he suffered from. The minutes painfully ticked by as his breathing grew even worse, the only sound in the room the rasping as he struggled for breath.

Kaie did not know what to do to help him, and only felt apprehension. If she did not help him, he would die, but she was unsure as to what had caused this illness.

Hesitantly, she outstretched her hands towards his shoulders, as if to shake him awake, before pulling back quickly.

Kaie jerked awake, breathing heavily. She fought back the need to vomit, the foreboding and uneasiness she'd felt in the dream not dissipating. On unsteady feet, she got out of bed, softly padding to the kitchen to the bucket of water that had been drawn from the well earlier that day. She splashed it onto her face, hoping to get rid of the feelings left over from the dream. After gulping down a glass of water, she took a deep breath, the panic beginning to fade away.

Unexpectedly, she heard the quiet footsteps of her mother entering the kitchen, a slight glow coming from a freshly lit candle in her hands.

"Kaie? What's wrong? I heard you get up," her mother said, setting the candle on the table. She sat down and patted the empty chair next to her, hoping to comfort her daughter.

"I had a dream," Kaie said hoarsely, coming to sit with her mother at the table.

"Was it another one of... the usual ones?" her mother asked worriedly. "One of your healing dreams?"

The dreams had been happening more frequently, almost always corresponding with someone who would come to visit the young healer in the future. Though Kaie was only sixteen, her abilities had grown by leaps and bounds over the past few years. Word had spread quickly past the nearby town, and many people made the long trek into the forest to find the talented healer.

"Yes," she admitted softly, almost embarrassed about the dream. It always felt like an of invasion of privacy, seeing someone at their most vulnerable. "But this one happened in a nice place. It wasn't here, like the others." Just by seeing the one room, she was able to tell that the person was very wealthy.

"I wonder what that could mean," her mother said softly. She ran a hand through her graying hair and doubled over as a coughing fit overtook her.

Kaie prepared another cup of water for her mother, resting a hand on her back until the coughing subsided. The past few years had taught her it was best to wait until it passed, even if it was agonizing in the moment to do nothing. "Syane is supposed to return with your medicine soon," she said as her mother took a sip.

Syane had been the town healer for years, and Kaie had started informal lessons with her at a young age. As Kaie's skills grew into more than enough to help the townspeople, Syane felt compelled to travel around to other towns to share her services, returning a few times a year to deliver medicine for Kaie's mother. On multiple occasions, she had encouraged Kaie to pursue training with a more experienced healer, but Kaie was needed at home.

Her mother leaned back in her chair, out of breath. The two remained silent for several moments, waiting for her breathing to return to normal.

"What happened in the dream this time?" her mother asked at last, reaching across the table to put a hand on top of her daughter's.

"It was somehow worse than the other ones," Kaie said, working up the courage to elaborate on the dream. Perhaps talking about it would help it make more sense. "I couldn't tell what was wrong with the person, and there was this horrible feeling in the pit of my stomach, a weird mixture of anxiety and concern. Like if I didn't make him feel better, something horrible would happen." Saying it out loud did not help that much with understanding the dream. She frowned slightly. "I don't know."

"Well, if it makes you feel better, in the morning, you can go to the meadow with your sister and get more herbs," her mother said, squeezing her hand gently. "There was talk in town today about someone being ill and I know your supply is getting low."

Kaie nodded and yawned heavily. The dreams never did much to help her sleep soundly. "I'm going back to bed," she said sleepily. "Good night."

"Good night." Her mother came around the table and kissed her forehead before heading back to bed herself. However, she tossed and turned, wondering what could be the significance of her daughter's dream. She did not dare tell Kaie the identity of the sick person she had heard about earlier that day. If the rumors turned out to be true, all of their lives could change more drastically than they could imagine.

***

The next morning, Kaie awakened early despite the night's interruption. She could hear her younger sister bouncing around in the kitchen as always, presumably trying to get their mother's attention as she made breakfast. Already, the scent of porridge wafted through the door to Kaie, making her stomach rumble in hunger. Though she did not look forward to the meal, she was grateful for it.

Despite Kaie's father being a well-paid general in the army, her mother had suffered from a grave illness a few years ago that had dried up most of the family's savings and still had lingering effects on her body. Kaie's healing services helped with the money issues, but there were still nights when everyone went to bed hungry. Her father sent money as often as he was able, but it never seemed to be enough, and the family still had difficulty making ends meet. The medicine her mother needed for ongoing treatment sapped much of their money, and Kaie was unable to forage for the costlier ingredients to make the medicine herself.

Slowly, she got out of bed, putting on clothes that would be suitable to tramp around the forest in. It had rained a few days before and she knew the ground would still be muddy. Not to mention that Shayla always loved to jump in the puddles when she tagged along.

"You're up early," her mother commented when she finally entered the kitchen. "I thought you would have slept late after last night."

Kaie shrugged before walking over to the fire and taking the spoon from her mother to stir the pot. "If what you did hear was true, I figured we better get out early to stock up. There's no point in wasting the day away." She held out a hand for a bowl and began to serve breakfast until the small amount of porridge in the pot was completely gone, then sat down at the table.

As soon as the bowl was in front of her, Shayla immediately began gulping down bite after bite.

"Shayla! Slow down!" their mother admonished. "Eat more slowly. Savor your meal."

The seven-year-old made a face before following her mother's instructions. She kicked her feet under the table, too short to reach the floor. "What are we going to do today?" she asked eagerly, her eyes going to her sister.

"I need to get more herbs and plants for my healing supply," Kaie said in between bites. "So we will be going to the meadow."

Shayla made another face, but said nothing. Though going to the meadow was not her favorite activity, she was happy just to be allowed to spend time with her sister. Lately, with all the patients visiting, Kaie was often too busy to play.

Once breakfast was finished and everyone had pitched in to clean the dishes, Kaie went off to grab her satchel. She returned to the kitchen and looked at her younger sister. "Are you ready to go?" she asked, her eyes brightening in excitement.

"Yes!" Shayla exclaimed, her sister's enthusiasm infectious.

"Be sure to cross at the bridge," their mother warned, leveling them both with a look. "I don't want either of you getting carried away by that current."

Kaie looked to Shayla and rolled her eyes before agreeing. Both rushed out the door, running towards the river. It was great to be outside again after being stuck indoors the past few days due to the rain. Kaie loved the feeling of running, the way her body and muscles responded to her commands, though she had to slow down to ensure Shayla was in step with her. Before long, the two had reached the river.

"Let's cross here," Kaie said.

"But Momma wants us to cross at the bridge." Shayla looked in the direction of the bridge located a few miles downstream.

Kaie turned towards her sister, impatience showing on her face. "But that takes *forever* and we don't have all the time in the world. Come on, let's go. We'll cross at a part where it's shallow, okay?" Her voice left no room for argument.

"I guess so," Shayla said reluctantly, eyeing the river carefully.

"All right then, come on!"

Kaie led the way with Shayla following behind. They stopped along the bank of the river, the water swiftly crossing the rocks and rushing on downstream. The spring wind blew a green leaf from one of the tall oak trees, and it was instantly carried out of sight by the current.

Shayla looked doubtfully after it. "Are you sure this is safe?" she asked tentatively.

"Of course! It's fine. I'll lead the way and you follow exactly in my footsteps. It just looks scary," Kaie reassured her. "This is the shallowest part of the river. We'll be fine."

Kaie's confidence was well-founded, having crossed the river numerous times by herself. A lingering thought nagged at her, saying that she had never crossed in late spring before, so soon after the rainy season. And never with Shayla in tow. But she dismissed the concern. She would help Shayla cross. As she led the way through the river, she almost lost her step, surprised by the chill.

Just a slippery rock. Everything is fine. Don't be such a baby. You're starting to sound like Shayla, she thought to herself.

Shayla slowly followed, trying hard to move against the current like her sister, but it was more difficult. As she stepped on the same rock that Kaie just stepped off, she slipped.

"Kaie!" she screamed, her voice going up in pitch as the current caught her and began to pull her. "Help me! Kaie!"

Kaie turned to reach for Shayla, but the river dragged her just out of reach. Shayla was yanked further downstream as Kaie waded through the water. Panic coursed through her as she pulled herself onto the opposite riverbank and ran after her sister as Shayla fought to keep her head above water. Silently, Kaie cursed herself. She should have listened to their mother. Having crossed successfully by herself numerous times, she had grown cocky.

"Shayla, keep your head above water!" she shouted, watching as her sister got pulled further and further down the river, bouncing against rocks and outstretched trees. "Grab a tree branch if you can!"

Finally, after a couple tries, Shayla was able to grasp on to an outstretched branch. Kaie jumped in and swam toward the younger girl, struggling against the current. The iciness of the water knocked the breath out of her and she struggled to breathe. After what seemed like ages of swimming, Kaie grabbed ahold of her sister before she swam to the shore and pulled them both out. Kaie pulled Shayla away from the water, and they both panted on the riverbank, looking at each other in shock.

"Next time, let's use the bridge," Shayla said, water dripping down her cheek from her hair in little trails.

Kaie brushed Shayla's hair out of her face. "Good idea." She began to examine her sister, already noticing a few bruises starting to form from her journey down the river. Pretty quickly, she found a large gash in the side of her sister's leg, blood mixing with the dripping water.

"This doesn't look good, Kaie," Shayla said in a scared voice. She was starting to panic.

"This is nothing. People have visited with worse injuries and I've helped them." She was trying to keep her sister calm by sounding confident, but Shayla was right—there was a lot of blood. Regret filled her. They should have just crossed at the bridge. "Here." Kaie grabbed a cloth from inside her waterproof satchel, a birthday gift from her father a few years ago, and began to staunch the bleeding. "That should do for now," she said, finishing tying the cloth around Shayla's leg. "Now stay here while I look for something to clean the wound with."

Kaie headed off into the forest to gather some moss to cover the wound. On her way, she discovered some much-needed plants that would replenish her healing supply. There were many of them and she knew that she wouldn't have this opportunity again soon—her mother would not let her and Shayla forage again for a while after this little incident.

Taking note of the location, she hurried along the path to where the moss hung in bunches from the trees. She hastily gathered some, scared that Shayla might have passed out. There had been so much blood.

To her relief, when she made it back, Shayla was pale but conscious. She scooped out some moss to dress the wound with, only to see a thin scratch when she removed the dressing.

Kaie frowned slightly. "That's odd," she said. "I swear this looked worse when I dressed it earlier."

She looked at the cloth in her hand to confirm, and found it was covered in more blood than she would have expected from a scratch. Maybe in the heat of the moment, she had mistaken the injury for more than it was, but instances like that had been happening more frequently. Someone would come in with a grave injury, only for it to recover faster than made sense for the small amount of treatment she had administered. Despite the conundrum, she was relieved that Shayla's injury seemed to be doing better.

"How do you feel, Shayla?"

"Good enough to walk," her sister replied, standing to test out her leg.

"I'm sorry we didn't cross at the bridge," Kaie said after several moments of silence, looking at the river. "I shouldn't have risked it, even if it usually is a shortcut."

As the older sibling, she should have been more responsible and taken Shayla's smaller size into consideration. She let out a huff of frustration at herself, that she had put her sister into such a dangerous situation. They were lucky it had all turned out fine in the end, with no lasting injuries. The image of how badly things could have ended played over in her mind and Kaie shuddered. She patted the ground next to her. She had an idea to distract them both from what had happened.

Shayla sat down as Kaie picked some nearby flowers, weaving them together. The younger girl watched, entranced, until Kaie put the crown on her head. Shayla dashed over to see her reflection in the river before rushing back to her sister's side.

"You're a pretty princess," Kaie said with a smile.

"You need one too!" Shayla giggled gleefully.

Kaie let out a laugh and made one for herself so the two were matching. "Shall we go pick plants then?" she asked.

"Yes!" Shayla squealed.

Kaie took her sister's hand and led her back to where she had found the plants earlier. She stooped down and scooped up the plants while Shayla raced around the clearing, shouting with joy. Kaie held back a laugh. Her sister's actions dispelled any doubts that she was going to have long-lasting complications from their adventure.

Ignoring Shayla, Kaie tried to remember what she needed. She'd already gathered milfoil, black locust, meadow sage, and underbrush, but something was missing, and she could not remember what.

She went over the list in her head. *Milfoil for wounds, black locust for headaches, meadow sage for spasms, and underbrush for rheumatism and gout. But what else do I need?*

Kaie quickly surveyed the meadow, looking for the missing plant, while Shayla continued to shout nearby. Suddenly, she spotted what she was looking for: wood spurge. It was a very useful plant, as it had many healing properties. Breathing a sigh of relief, Kaie grabbed some and tucked it into her satchel.

"It's time to head back," she said to Shayla.

The younger girl let out a groan of disappointment, but followed Kaie.

This time, they crossed at the bridge, which was now only a few hundred yards away, and began the long walk home. The journey back was slower due to Shayla's injuries. Despite the fact that the gash on her leg was now just a scratch and she had been running around, she still complained of the pain.

"How did we get this far?" Shayla asked after they crossed the bridge.

"The river has a strong current. It pulled you far," Kaie said, holding back another shudder at what could have happened. She pulled Shayla to her, as if to confirm that her sister was fine.

"Oh. It was pretty scary, wasn't it?" Shayla said.

Kaie looked down at her sister's frightened face and tightened her embrace. "Don't worry. I won't let anything or anybody hurt you or take you away from me. You're stuck with me," Kaie said.

Shayla looked at her sister with wide, trusting eyes, reassured by her words.

The two gave a sigh of relief upon sighting their house, the aroma from dinner wafting towards them. Light shone through the windows of the small home, but their mother's profile was not waiting in the window for them, as she always did when they were late.

A strange chill ran through Kaie as they approached and saw six horses tethered outside.

CHAPTER 2

Shayla and Kaie paused, exchanging a look. No one ever came this late in the day unless it was a serious injury.

"We've never had that many people visit before," her sister said, her voice signaling to Kaie that she was worried.

"I doubt that they're all sick," Kaie said slowly, not voicing her concerns, which were many. If everyone was sick, how would she manage to heal them all? Not to mention they barely had enough food for themselves. There was no way they could feed this many people.

Slowly, they walked up to the house, pausing before entering the kitchen. The sight inside did little to calm Kaie's nerves. Her mother was pacing while two men sat at the table, and three were standing. All five wore the Galician royal crest and were in perfect health. Kaie's eyebrows came together in a frown. Nothing was making any sense. If there were five healthy men with six horses outside, what did they want?

Suddenly, her eyes widened and her stomach sank as all eyes turned to her and Shayla as they walked through the doorway.

"Momma?" Kaie asked hesitantly. "What's going on? Is Papa all right?" Panic edged into her voice at the thought of anything happening to her father.

"What? Oh, honey, your father is fine," her mother said, coming over to the two girls.

Instant relief swept through Kaie at her words.

"But these men have come to talk to you," her mother continued. "Shayla, we should go outside for this."

Immediately, Kaie's guard was back up as her gaze flew over the men again.

"But why can't I hear what's going on?" Shayla pouted, crossing her arms. She glared at the men, letting them know she was displeased, as her mother ushered her out of the house.

Before her mother left, she placed a hand on Kaie's shoulder and squeezed gently, but that did nothing to calm Kaie's nerves. She watched her family leave before turning to the men in the room.

"Um... so what exactly is going on?" she asked. The relief she'd felt before had completely disappeared. Instead, her stomach churned as she waited for them to speak.

"I'm Sir Lorne Shalane, and these soldiers are part of the King's Guard," a man said, introducing himself. He gestured to an open chair at the table. "You might want to sit down."

He seemed to be the leader of the group, as he had a golden crest on his chest rather than the green the others wore. There was a deep scar along the side of his neck, leading up to his slightly graying hairline, and she knew he was lucky to have survived that injury. His posture was open and relaxed, but his words did nothing to lessen the stone that had sunk to the bottom of her stomach.

"I'm fine, thanks," Kaie said sharply, crossing her arms in defiance. "Now what are you doing here? Clearly none of you are sick."

They all looked surprised at her venom, and it took a couple moments for Sir Shalane to regain his composure. "The king of Galicia's youngest son, Prince Achaius, is gravely ill. He has heard of your healing abilities and thought you might be able to help."

Kaie immediately saw where this was going—she had a view of all the rooms in the house from her position and none were occupied with the prince. "Surely..." She had to lick her suddenly dry lips as the words stuck in her throat. "Surely the court physicians would be able to do more than I can. Why didn't you bring him here? There is more I could have done in person than describing what you should do." She winced slightly at how awkward and ignorant she sounded.

The man said what she assumed he would say, despite her hopes that it was not true. "He was too sick to travel, so we have been sent to bring you to the palace. The court physicians have tried everything, so you're our last resort."

She sat down in the chair he had offered her earlier, her legs suddenly too weak to hold her and her mind swirling in a million different directions.

"Don't you have Invivers?" Kaie asked, frowning. The more she thought about it, the more it did not make sense. "Why can't they Cure him?"

The Invivers were a special group of people, able to Cure others by harnessing their own energy to heal illness and injury. Only the richest of people could afford them, while the only option of the masses was going to regular healers like herself. The king had countless Invivers at his disposal, and even if many were off helping the war effort, a few should have been spared to take care of the royal family in events like these.

The man shook his head. "Unfortunately, everyone has been deployed and there's no one close enough to be of use. You're our last resort," he repeated. "There will be a hefty reward if you do help. And if you refuse..." He trailed off, as if the consequences were too horrible to describe.

"What happens if I don't want to come?" she asked, needing to know the rest of his sentence.

"I'm sorry," he said, his chocolate eyes showing remorse at the words coming out of his mouth. "But if you don't agree to come with, we've been ordered to take you anyway and your family would be imprisoned for your insolence." He saw no reason to hide anything from her. The more she knew, hopefully the less she would fight.

Kaie's face paled considerably at his words. "So I don't have a choice in this?" she accused, her heart sinking rapidly. She clenched her hands in anger, at the threat against her family. "Can't my family come with me? My father is in the army. I can't just leave my mother and sister to fend for themselves!" Her voice rose in a mixture of panic and fear.

"The king has agreed to send your father back home while you are in service to the crown, and your family would be generously compensated. You wouldn't have to worry about him getting killed in battle." He placed a small bag on the table.

From the clinking sound it made, she knew it was filled with coins. Even if it was filled with only copper coins, that amount of money could feed them for a couple months. And based on the compensation promised, she figured it would be enough to cover her mother's medicine for more than half a year.

"This is only a small fraction of what you will be paid for your services."

"Yes, but—"

"You will be taken care of, and we will escort you personally to the palace so no harm befalls you," he added, as if it would do anything to make her feel better about leaving her family.

As the facts washed over Kaie, she knew that she had no choice in this, that she could not put her family's lives in danger. Hating herself for the words that left her mouth, she whispered, "Fine, I'll go."

It was a struggle to hold back tears once the words came out. She looked out the window at where the sun was about to set. During their conversation, the shadows had lengthened, but she had been too caught up to notice.

"When do we leave?" Her voice sounded hollow.

The man looked out the window, as well, as if he, too, was realizing how late it truly was. "We shall leave at dawn," he said. "You can use your remaining time here to pack and say your goodbyes." Without waiting for an answer, he walked to the door, his men following. Opening the door, he allowed her mother and sister back in. "Your daughter will be accompanying us to the palace tomorrow."

Shayla cried out in alarm, a look of horror washing over her face.

Finally, the group of men left the house, leaving the three family members alone. Kaie did not meet her mother and sister's eyes, instead going over to the pot on the fire to stir the soup, which at this point was bubbling furiously. The hunger she'd felt earlier had completely disappeared.

"What happened?" her mother asked when Kaie did not say anything. She had known that the men wanted to take her daughter away, but she had not been told any details.

"One of the princes is sick and the king wants me to heal him," Kaie said, looking away, knowing that if she met her mother's eyes, she would back out of her promise. In the back of her mind, the fact that her family's lives rested on her lingered like a sick bargaining chip.

"Can't you refuse? We need you here!" Shayla sobbed as she attached herself to Kaie's waist, which did nothing to help Kaie's feeling of guilt for abandoning her family. Gently, she patted her sister's head, trying to comfort her, even though she wanted nothing more than to dissolve into a puddle of tears herself.

"No. To refuse a royal order would be unthinkable," her mother said, shuddering at the thought.

"The man said that..." Kaie could not even say what would happen if she did refuse, the words sticking in her throat. She could not mention it with Shayla in the room. The news would only upset her. "He said if I did go, that Papa would be able to return home."

Her mother paled and sat down. "He'd be able to return? Truly?" Suddenly, a rush of color enveloped her face, and Kaie could tell that her mother was as surprised to hear this as she had been.

"We also wouldn't have to worry about money," Kaie added, gesturing to the bag of coins on the table. "And the men will escort me to the palace to make sure I don't get hurt." She thought it would be best to explain everything.

"Your father's been gone too long. Almost four years," her mother whispered as tears glistened in her eyes. "It seems unbelievable that he could be here again." Kaie knew that her father's absence had not been easy for her mother, but she was surprised that her mother did not seem so concerned about her leaving.

"But we'd have to give up Kaie!" Shayla yelled. "How is that fair? Home won't be the same without her." She buried her head into Kaie so her sobs were muffled. Their father had left when she was young, so she barely had any memories of him.

Their mother stood and came over to them, enveloping the two in a warm hug. "Kaie will be back soon. She won't be gone forever," she said softly. "And then we can all be a proper family again." She picked up Shayla, rubbing her back. "We should all go to bed. Kaie, you have a long journey ahead of you tomorrow. I suggest you pack your supplies tonight." Leaning forward, she gave her oldest daughter a kiss on the forehead before taking Shayla to bed, dinner forgotten. The news of Kaie's departure had killed everyone's appetite.

Kaie trudged to her own room and quickly packed her bags, carefully organizing the plants and herbs she'd picked earlier that day. As she fell into bed, her mind spun with thoughts of tomorrow. Slowly, she began to drift off to sleep, only to be awakened by the sound of her door opening and the soft patter of feet. When she opened her eyes, Shayla was standing by the side of her bed.

"What is it, Shayla?"

"Can I come sleep with you? Just like when we were little?" her younger sister asked, her voice still thick with tears.

Kaie moved over and opened her blankets. "Get over here," she said, sensing that her sister needed some comfort as much as she did.

Shayla cuddled up to her, her warm body reminding Kaie of when life was a simpler time—when their family had no concerns, their mother was healthy, and their father was home. Everything had been peaceful, and they did not have to worry about money. Back then, she'd had dreams of a different life, of going on adventures like the stories her father told of his escapades. But never in her wildest dreams had she imagined being forced to leave home, that everything would fall to her.

With those thoughts swirling in her mind, she began to drift off to sleep.

CHAPTER 3

The next morning when Kaie awakened, she held back a forlorn sigh, not wanting to wake Shayla. Carefully, she got out of bed before dressing in a forest-green tunic paired with her fawn-colored hunting boots. Taking one last look at her sleeping sister, she kissed her forehead and left the room. A heaviness weighed on her heart, her satchel of herbs and bag of clothes in her hand.

In the kitchen, her mother stood by the fire, mixing porridge. Through the windows, Kaie could see it was still dark out—the stars had not even left the sky yet. She set her bags on the table before sitting down.

Her mother glanced up at her before turning back to the porridge. "I have a gift for you, a little something to remind you of home." Her voice broke at the end of her sentence as she gestured to a small package on the table.

Kaie ran over to her mother and gave her a tight hug, her throat constricting with unshed tears. "I'll be okay," she said, her voice coming out as a croak. She had never been away from home before and now that she was being taken away, it felt overwhelming. "I'll return as quickly as I can."

Her mother's arms surrounded her, squeezing her back. "I'm sorry for last night," she said. "I wasn't able to process everything properly. But know that I will miss you and I love you very much."

"I love you too," Kaie said. "But dawn is almost here. We'll be leaving soon."

Almost as if on cue, there was a knock at the door, signaling that it was time to leave.

Kaie looked to her mother, face paling in panic. Her mother gave her a final squeeze, tears springing into both of their eyes.

The knock came again, more forceful this time.

"Coming," Kaie managed to squeeze past her clogged throat.

Shayla suddenly burst into the room, sobbing, having just awakened and found her sister gone. Kaie hugged her tightly, barely managing to hold back her own tears.

Her mother answered the door, and the man from the night before, Sir Shalane, stood there waiting.

"It's time to go," he said impassively, taking in Kaie and her sister.

Kaie nodded, grabbing her satchel and pack from the table, biting her lip hard to hold back the tears. Her mother tucked the small package from the table inside her pack before handing her a small loaf of bread and a waterskin for the road—a precious amount taken from their food supply.

"I'm sorry there wasn't enough time for you to have breakfast." She kissed Kaie's forehead. "But these should keep the hunger at bay for the morning."

Kaie wanted to protest at the food, but at her mother's look, she nodded before following the man out the door to the horses.

"Do you know how to ride?" he asked.

Silently, Kaie nodded. She had learned a little from her father.

"These are royally bred and trained horses," Sir Shalane said, gesturing to her horse, a dark-brown mare whose coat matched Kaie's hair. "We will be riding fast and hard to ensure we make the journey in time. To get to the capital, it would typically be a six-day journey, but we will be making it in three—if you can keep up."

Slowly, reluctantly, she got on and settled into the saddle. She clenched the reins, not used to the size of the horse. Despite her father's horse being even bigger, she had only ever ridden with him, not by herself. She gritted her teeth.

She could do this.

Before they began moving, Shayla ran out the door, shrieking, "Kaie! Don't go! You can't go! You promised you would take care of me! You promised, Kaie! You promised!"

Her mother caught Shayla around the waist before she was able to reach the horses, knowing how hard this already was for her oldest daughter. She clutched the sobbing girl to her and motioned for Kaie to go, her face letting her oldest know that Shayla would be fine and it would be best for her to leave.

Kaie took one last look at her sobbing sister before turning to Sir Shalane, her eyes begging him to leave. The man nodded and spurred his horse onwards. Without looking back, Kaie followed, trying to ignore the sound of her sister's screams.

Just as the tendrils of dawn began to creep over the horizon, Sir Shalane led the group out of town to the main road. He set a merciless pace, and Kaie focused on staying in the saddle, her mouth set in a grim line as they rode. The other four in the group surrounded her, one on either side and two behind. By midday, they slowed a bit, enough for the men to start conversing with each other.

The man on Kaie's left was a giant with a ruddy face and white-blond hair, his sea-green eyes twinkling with merriment. "My lady, it is an honor to escort you," he said with an exaggerated nod. "My name is Rosse Swain, and the silent one next to you is my brother, Raven. Perhaps you've heard of us?"

To her surprise, Kaie actually *had* heard of them. The two brothers had risen from obscurity by crashing and winning fighting tournaments. It was a short amount of time—only a few months—before they had gained enough recognition to be invited to join the King's Guard. Their story was regularly told by the traveling minstrels, and they were lauded for their bravery and fighting prowess.

Rosse laughed by her incredulous expression. "I'll take that as a yes then," he said. "Sir Shalane has instructed that we assist you, so let us know if you need anything."

Kaie nodded before turning to look at Raven, who seemed to be the youngest of the group, only a year or two older than her. He was well-muscled, but had more of a quiet strength about him, with midnight hair and a fair complexion. Dark, glittering eyes gave him a mysterious air as he matched her gaze.

"We have food if you need it," he said quietly. "That bread won't be enough, so tell us if you're hungry."

"Rosse, aren't you going to introduce *us*?" one of the men from the back shouted. "Or are you just going to talk about yourself like always?"

Rosse let out a booming laugh. "You never want to miss out, do you, Harbuckle?" He turned back to Kaie. "Those two back there are Ronan Harbuckle and Barra Trisgan. Ronan can shoot like no one's business and Barra is good with a blade."

"Enough chatting," Sir Shalane said. "You're here to do a job, so act like it."

Instantly, everyone quieted and the pace picked up, as if the captain was using speed to discourage further conversation.

As night fell, the group approached a small town, and Sir Shalane led them to an inn.

"We'll rest here for the night," he said, handing the reins of his horse to the stableboy.

Kaie winced as she dismounted, her entire body aching. Riding on horseback all day was not something she was used to. She walked stiffly out of the stables.

Raven approached her, holding out a jar of salve. "This will help with the muscle aches."

"Thank you," Kaie said, opening the jar to sniff at its contents. An acrid smell wrinkled her nose. It seemed to be a soothing balm that would help loosen tight muscles.

"It's not your fault. Lorne always sets a hard pace when traveling," Raven said quietly.

The group headed into the inn and sat down for a meal together. Kaie sat at the end of the table, seated next to Raven and across from Sir Shalane. The men began joking around as they waited for their food. Now at ease, Sir Shalane was full of smiles and laughter, joking around with his soldiers. The difference from his previous stern demeanor was jarring as he roared with laughter.

Kaie remained silent, lost in her thoughts now that she had time to herself. Never having spent a full night away from her family, her thoughts were filled with Shayla and her mother, especially her mother's condition. She hoped there wouldn't be too many coughing attacks until her father returned home. When food was eventually served, she stared at the bowl of stew in front of her, hunger glaringly absent.

Sir Shalane watched her for a few moments while she stirred the stew with her spoon, making no moves to take a bite. "I know your father," he said quietly.

Conversation immediately halted, and the others turned to stare at him and Kaie.

Kaie's head shot up at his words. "You do?" she asked, her face showing her surprise.

He smiled gently. "Yes," he said. "We trained together and joined the King's Guard together. He's a very good friend." His expression fell slightly. "Although I haven't seen him since he was stationed at the Fernan Outpost a couple years ago."

"He never mentioned you." Kaie's tone was clipped. She was skeptical. Her eyes were full of anger and hatred, but underneath, there was a deep fear of him and the power that with one visit, he had been able to uproot her life completely. If the prince was so sickly that they had to bring in a backwoods healer, she was unsure how long she'd be away from home.

Sir Shalane let out a sigh, expecting her reaction. "Kieran Durac is an extremely skilled fighter, a very loyal friend, and fiercely proud of his daughters," he said, hoping to bring down the cold wall Kaie had put up.

His ploy worked. Kaie leaned forward slightly. "What did he say?" she asked.

The man took a spoonful of stew, nodding at her to do the same. After a moment of hesitation, she took a bite. Kaie's eyes widened at the flavor, and she began to wolf down her food, hunger quickly overtaking her. The day of not eating had taken its toll.

A hand reached out and gently restrained her, slowing her down. Looking up, she saw everyone staring at her. Her face colored in embarrassment. They had clearly seen her lack of manners.

"You're likely to choke if you eat too quickly," Sir Shalane said. "There is plenty of food for everyone to eat their fill."

"What did my father say about me?" Kaie asked, eager to move the topic away from her eating habits. She took a small bite, taking her time to chew and swallow to show Sir Shalane that she could eat slowly.

He smiled again. "He would talk about you and your sister whenever there was a spare moment," he said. "About how quickly you picked up what he taught you, how well you took care of your sick mother, and how much he loved and missed you all."

"What else?" Kaie prompted. It had been years since she had last seen her father and even if he did write to them, it wasn't the same.

"Tell her about some of your escapades together," Rosse said, slapping Sir Shalane on the back. "She deserves to hear the tales that we've all heard thousands of times!"

Kaie's eyes brightened, and Sir Shalane nodded. "Very well," he said. "Which one should I tell?"

"The apple cart," Ronan said.

"No, the masquerade caper," Barra said.

"Or the assassination attempt," Raven said.

"Which one?" Rosse asked. "There have been a few attempts on the king's life."

Raven shrugged. "All of them are pretty good stories."

"The masquerade caper is a good one," Sir Shalane said. "This was years ago, when Kieran and I were new on the King's Guard, and there was a masquerade ball that was to take place at the palace to celebrate the eldest prince's birth. Nobility and neighboring royalty were to visit and bring lavish gifts. There were rumors of some infamous thieves who were planning to infiltrate the party, so your father and I were to go undercover to try and catch them. We had to take lessons to learn proper etiquette to not stand out amongst the crowd." He chuckled at the memory.

"And?" Kaie prompted when he paused in his story.

"Come the night of the party, your father gained the attention of most of the young ladies who were attending the ball," Sir Shalane said. "Even with a mask on, everyone could see that he was handsome. He was swarmed by people wanting to talk to him, and he ended up being so popular that he wasn't able to do his job properly. Everything was left to me."

Laughter echoed around the table.

"Luckily, he was able to hold almost everyone's attention so I was able to go around the ballroom without much notice. I was over by the gift table when I bumped into someone accidentally, a visiting prince. He was so angry, he began to loudly berate me, and everyone began to look at us. To get everyone's attention away from me again, Kieran began to juggle, of all things! In the middle of a formal masquerade ball! I was able to slip away with a few apologies."

"What happened next?" Kaie was spellbound by the captain's story.

"The thieves had somehow snuck in and were hiding under the gift table," Sir Shalane said. "By the time I realized what happened, they were running out of the ballroom with jewelry, coins, and other small gifts stuffed in their pockets. So Kieran threw the oranges he was juggling, hitting each in the back of the head. We were able to recover everything and they were arrested."

Kaie's eyes were wide. "He never told me that story before," she said in awe. "I know Shayla would have loved to hear that one."

"Your father is a legend amongst the Guard," Rosse said. "He is so skilled, and Lorne has the craziest stories about him!"

"I had no idea," Kaie said softly.

Her father had kept so much of his life a secret from her, but their time together was always limited before he had to go back to the palace. When Kaie asked if the family could come with, he always said the countryside was more peaceful and he wanted them to enjoy the quiet.

"I miss him. It's been a few years since I've last seen him." She bit her lip, suddenly overwhelmed with emotion. "I even miss the awful jokes he would tell us."

Groans filled the table.

"That's one thing he and Lorne have in common—their terrible sense of humor," Rosse said. "Don't get him started!"

"I'm your commanding officer. You should treat me with more respect," Sir Shalane said. "I may have tried to be the court jester, but I couldn't juggle all that responsibility!"

Kaie groaned along with the rest of the table, holding back a chuckle. That was definitely a joke her father would have told.

"Don't groan. It's not like I'm an executioner—I'm not killing you with humor!" Sir Shalane said with a huge grin on his face.

"I don't know if I would have agreed to come along if I knew I was going to be subject to torture!" she said with a laugh.

"Oh, how you wound me!" Sir Shalane said with exaggerated clutching of his chest.

The whole table burst out laughing at his antics.

As dinner drew to an end, Sir Shalane gave out room assignments. Kaie had a room to herself and as she settled into bed, she thought about how much Sir Shalane reminded her of her father. After his jokes at dinner, she wasn't filled with the same distrust as yesterday.

***

The following morning, Sir Shalane was back to his stoic demeanor, all traces of the jovial captain from the previous night gone. Seeing Kaie's look of alarm, Raven leaned towards her.

"You'll get used to him," he said quietly. "The captain takes his responsibilities very seriously when he's on duty."

Kaie nodded as she mounted her horse—Aira, from what Raven had told her—and they set off at a similar pace to the previous day. Despite using Raven's salve last night before going to bed, Kaie immediately felt sore as soon as she settled into the saddle. It was going to be a long day.

Sir Shalane continued the quick pace and conversation was sparse throughout the day. Once more, Kaie was left alone to her thoughts and she was filled with worry. Her dream about the sickly prince weighed heavily in the back of her mind, mingling with feelings of homesickness.

Halfway through the morning, they passed by an old Inviver outpost. Since Invivers were uncommon, the palace used to send some to outposts scattered throughout the kingdom for the public to receive treatment. But since war began with the Scrians, all Invivers had been pulled to follow the armed forces into battle.

By late afternoon, Kaie felt nauseous from the ride, her legs and back screaming with pain. She shifted atop Aira, but could find no comfortable position. Tears pricked her eyes, but she remained silent, not wanting to halt their progress.

"Sir, we need to stop!" Raven said.

At his words, the captain slowed the group and turned around. "What is it?" he said. "We need to keep moving."

Raven moved his horse next to Kaie's and held out an apple. "Kaie needs a break," he said. "She's not used to all this riding and she needs to eat something."

"I can keep going," Kaie protested, despite knowing Raven was right. She took the apple, and despite the nausea filling her, she took a bite of the sweet fruit.

"We can't continue on at such a pace if she's in so much pain," Rosse agreed.

Sir Shalane rubbed his face. "We need to keep moving," he repeated, though less harshly this time as he saw how gingerly Kaie shifted in the saddle. "Kaie, do you have anything that can help your pain?"

Kaie reached into her pack and grabbed a small bottle of a tincture that she typically used for aches and pains. She had been trying to save as much of her supplies as possible for the prince, but she could not hold the group back. Quickly downing the contents, Kaie felt warmth swiftly spreading to the areas of her body that were hurting.

"I can keep going," she said, finishing the last bites of the apple, then giving the core to Aira. The food had helped her nausea.

"Couldn't we stop at Garbrough?" Rosse asked. "It's a few hours away and we could rest there for the night. There's a great tavern there, and we'll sleep better."

"We have several more hours to go and will make camp outside," Sir Shalane said in a steely tone. "Maybe you would feel more awake if you *didn't* stay out all night."

"Me? Stay out all night? That's only happened three or four times!" Rosse protested.

"You've only been *caught* three or four times," Ronan countered.

Rosse shrugged, giving Kaie a cheeky smirk and wink. "Can you blame a guy for trying?" he asked.

"When you're on duty, I expect you to behave with decorum," Sir Shalane said. "We will continue on. We will not be stopping until it is time to make camp. I want to make it to the palace tomorrow."

As if to make up for Rosse's suggestion to stop, Sir Shalane urged them to travel even more quickly than before. Kaie was surprised at how the horses did not seem to tire; they truly were well-bred for travel.

At last, it was nightfall, and they set up camp for the night. The jovial mood from the previous night was gone; everyone seemed tired and sore. Everyone pitched in with making dinner and Sir Shalane passed out bowls of stew to all the men. When he reached Kaie, she took the bowl from him, eating it slowly. He sat down on a log next to her with a heavy sigh.

Sir Shalane gazed into the fire, taking in the blue of the flame dancing around, creating a mesmerizing sight. It shifted back and forth in a fluid-like dance, the colors blending, merging to make an enchanting display.

"How long have you known my father?" Kaie asked, interrupting the captain's thoughts.

Blinking, he quickly shook himself back to reality, having to force himself to focus despite the fatigue that weighed on him. He looked over to the girl sitting next to him, her gaze focused on him. Kaie's eyes betrayed the sadness she felt and he knew she was missing her family.

"Since before you were born," he said, and her eyes widened. "We both joined the Guard before either of us were married."

"Then you knew him before he met my mother," Kaie said.

Sir Shalane nodded. "Yes, he met her while we were on an expedition around the country," he said. "It was love at first sight."

Kaie's eyes brightened. "I've heard the story of how they met," she said proudly. "At a village festival." Her brow furrowed. "But they never did tell me why they settled in Riverton. I know neither of them grew up there. Do you know?"

The captain let out a chuckle. "While your father enjoys his job, he does not like the bustle of the capital," he said. "And your mother's parents were not pleased with her marrying a soldier. So they picked Riverton to raise you and your sister." He paused. "And there you found a mentor to teach you, so I think they made a good choice."

"Despite that, I don't know how I'm expected to heal the prince," Kaie said softly. Doubt and uncertainty filled her. "There's still so much Syane didn't teach me."

"We'll get there in time," Sir Shalane tried to reassure her. "But everyone needs to rest so we can arrive tomorrow."

Kaie moved away and watched his eyes, gauging if he was telling the truth or not. "Are you sure?" she asked skeptically. Her previous dream weighed heavily on her mind; it did not seem as though the prince had a lot of time left to live.

He returned the stare into her emerald eyes. "Absolutely." His eyes never flickered or gave anything away.

"But why send for *me*?" she asked. "Even if the Invivers were sent away, shouldn't the palace healers know what to do? How to make him better?"

"For whatever reason, the palace healers are at a loss," Sir Shalane said. "They thought bringing you in might help provide a fresh perspective. And you might learn something in the process too."

A yawn escaped Kaie. The day's ride had exhausted her.

Sir Shalane announced it was time to sleep, assigning watches to the men. "We've got a long day ahead of us tomorrow."

As Kaie drifted off to sleep, she imagined she was back home with Shayla snuggling up next to her. She pulled the blankets closer around her in a cocoon. As she slept, a contented smile stole its way over her face as she dreamt of her family.

***

The next morning, the group woke up for an early start. Though there was only one day left before they'd arrive at the palace, Kaie hoped they could move quickly so she could get to the prince in time. She had a feeling that there was not much time left. A foreboding settled deep in her stomach, making it hard to eat any food.

Late that morning, they came upon a road leading out of the forest to the capital, and from that vantage point, the main road to the palace was visible. At the edge of the trees, a group of ten men waited.

CHAPTER 4

"Sir, there are more hiding in the trees behind them," Raven said quietly, breaking the silence. "No more than five men."

"Are you sure? What about the trees on either side of us?"

Raven shook his head. "Just archers in the trees behind them, I'm sure of it. Flanking us on either side would mean the risk of friendly fire."

Sir Shalane let out a sigh, his mouth setting into a grim line. "Very well," he said. "Rosse, you're with me. Put on a mean face. Hopefully that will make them think twice about fighting. Barra and Ronan, you will stay at the back with Kaie. Her safety comes above all else."

Kaie's heart began to pound at his words and how quickly the lighthearted air of the entire group disappeared. They all seemed to feel the same way as weapons were taken out and they prepared for a fight. Soon, they approached the group.

"Good morning," Sir Shalane said casually, though Kaie could tell that underneath his easygoing façade, he was ready for a fight.

"What brings you this way?" the leader asked as he nonchalantly fingered the hilt of his sword. He was a rough-looking man, his face covered with scars from previous brawls. His men looked similar, their eyes harsh and cold, seemingly itching for a fight. Over the group hung an air that reeked of weeks of not bathing, the stench almost enough to make Kaie's eyes water.

"We need to pass through to get to the palace," Sir Shalane said, hoping that by mentioning he was on official business, the men would let them through.

By the gleam that sparked in the leader's eye at this, he knew that he had failed and began to mentally prepare for a fight. There was no way they were getting through without bloodshed. The other guards noticed Sir Shalane's stiffened spine and discreetly readied their weapons as well.

"Well, boys, look at what we have here. It looks like the king's personal guard has come to *personally* escort this young lady to the palace," the man cackled, his evil-looking eyes glittering at the thought. "We could probably fetch a hefty price for her ransom or on the black market somewhere..." He trailed off as Sir Shalane unsheathed his sword, not wanting to hear any more.

"You will not touch her," he warned, his voice dangerously low.

Kaie looked from one man to the other, knowing that a fight was imminent, her heart pounding furiously.

In a blur, the man lunged towards Sir Shalane and the clash of their swords rang throughout the forest. All at once, they were fighting, the smell of blood quickly filling the area. As Ronan used his bow to dispatch the men hiding in the trees, they fell to the ground with shouts of pain. Rosse roared as he swept his broadsword in front of him, taking out several bandits and smashing them to the ground. The remaining guards formed a circle around Kaie, most fighting off two men at once. Raven was quick on his feet, spinning around the bandits and taking them by surprise, while Barra was able to keep a few at bay with his sword. Kaie's head spun around as she tried to watch the fighting, looking for some way to help, but all seemed capable of defending themselves, most already having completely fought off at least one attacker.

In the middle of the fight, a short bandit managed to sneak past the horses. He barreled towards Kaie, grabbing her reins and pulling Aira forward. Clearly, he was expecting her to go quietly. Kaie kicked at him, her foot connecting with the side of his head, and he dropped the reins, falling to the ground in shock. Kaie dismounted and grabbed a spare sword hanging off one of the saddles, turning to face her attacker.

To her surprise, the boy seemed a few years younger than herself. He held only a dagger, his hand trembling. The fighting around them died down as most of the men from the attacking party were wounded. They ran off into the forest, taking their fallen leader with them.

Sir Shalane turned and saw Kaie in a standoff with the young bandit. In a flash, he was at her side, towering over the boy with his sword gripped tightly.

"You dare to attack us?" he shouted as he lunged at the boy.

The young bandit jerked backwards, barely able to dodge the attack. The other guards stood back as they watched their captain fight. Kaie watched in horror as Sir Shalane began to brutally batter the poor boy. From the look in his eyes, he seemed intent on killing him, and the others seemed to be content to let him.

Kaie dashed in front of the boy, lifting up her sword to meet Sir Shalane's. The clash of steel upon steel filled the clearing and her arms shook from the impact. She looked up at the captain, her eyes pleading.

"*Stop*!" she shrieked. "He's just a boy! You can't kill him!"

Sir Shalane shook his head. "He's a bandit, Kaie. If his leader had been successful in capturing you, they would have killed you once they realized you weren't a valuable hostage. The only good bandit is a dead bandit. Trust me."

Fighting back tears, Kaie saw that there was a deep hurt in the captain's eyes, but she shook her head. She could not be responsible for the boy dying. "No! He's practically defenseless!"

Behind her, she heard the boy's footsteps rapidly departing, now that the captain was preoccupied. She let out a sigh of relief. He had gotten away.

Sir Shalane dropped his sword with a scowl. "You let him get away," he muttered.

"He was just a boy," Kaie protested. The look in Sir Shalane's eyes frightened her.

The captain mounted his horse. "Let's go," he snapped at the group.

Kaie got back on Aira, her eyes focused on the horse's mane in front of her. She'd thought the King's Guard had good intentions—Sir Shalane was even a friend of her father's—but she just couldn't get over how easily he was willing to kill the boy. And how could everyone just willingly go along with his decision? Fighting back tears, she clenched Aira's reins until her knuckles turned white.

The group passed in silence through the city outside the palace around late afternoon, their progress slowed by the bustle of the capital. By nightfall, they arrived at the palace gates, the inky night enveloping the riders. Kaie shivered as the wind whipped through her clothes.

All that was visible of the looming palace was the light from the torches sprinkled around the main gate. After stopping within that the circle of light, an armored guard looked Kaie up and down before addressing Sir Shalane. "You were supposed to be here yesterday." His voice was gruff.

"We got a little... held up," Sir Shalane answered. They would have been there earlier in the afternoon if they had not been attacked, but the entire journey had taken longer than he'd hoped.

The guard looked at Kaie. "You'd better hurry. He's not doing well."

Her heart plummeted. "What do you mean?"

"I mean he's near the end. The court physicians have done all they can. You better hurry or he's a goner," the guard explained impatiently. He called out to a nearby servant, ordering him to take Kaie to the prince's chambers.

Without a word, Kaie jumped off her horse and sprinted inside the palace, following the servant's quick footsteps. Walking into the castle, she was awestruck by the decadence of it, pausing slightly as she was spellbound. Large marbled pillars rose to the high ceiling and an intricate mosaic depicting the royal family's crest covered the floor. Lit chandeliers lined the main corridor, a circular rotunda with hallways branching off. It would have seemed welcoming if not for the pristine cleanliness of the foyer.

Kaie was shaken from her surprise when the servant cleared his throat, eager to continue moving forward. She flinched slightly as her footsteps echoed throughout the vast entryway. With the way she was dressed, she felt as though she did not belong, a mere bug waiting to be found and promptly squashed.

Quickly, she was whisked away to another part of the palace, a long hallway that left her too overwhelmed to keep track of directions. Soon, the marbled floor gave way to lush carpeting and she was grateful that her footsteps were now muffled. She walked closer to the walls—moving openly in the vast hallway made her feel exposed and unwelcome.

After turning down numerous corridors, they stopped in front of the doors that led to the prince's bedchambers. The servant knocked on the door before motioning for her to enter, and Kaie hesitated—unsure of what she was going to see. Taking a deep breath, she walked in and gasped at the sight before her.

It was the same room from her dream.

It was nighttime now, instead of day, but just like in her dream, the prince had a sickly white pallor, his long, wavy blond hair limply hanging over his face, almost hiding the dark circles under his eyes. His cheeks were sunken in and each breath rattled in his chest.

Kaie walked over to the bedside and placed her hand on his forehead. It burned to the touch and sweat beaded on his skin. The fever and his breathing could have indicated an ordinary sickness, but his complexion made her think something else was wrong. Gently, she took one of his hands and inspected his fingernails. As expected, they were a light shade of blue. She had seen this combination of symptoms before, but never to this extent.

After making a quick diagnosis, she ripped off the bedcovers, her eyes searching for the injury. His ankle was badly swollen, and upon closer inspection, she found two small puncture wounds on the side of it.

She had barely noticed the two men standing off to the side when she entered, but did now when one of them cleared his throat. She spun around and looked at him.

"How did he get this bite?" she asked softly. She knew what it was, but finding a bite like this was very rare, especially for royalty.

The man stepped forward. He looked to be in his early twenties, his brown hair flopping in his face. His deep-blue eyes were sad, but there were laugh lines around them. He said grimly, "He was out riding a couple weeks ago when he got it. He said it felt like a bee sting and thought nothing of it. None of us did. Over the course of that week, his health has declined. Then we sent for you."

Kaie nodded and turned back to the bed. She pulled a knife out of her satchel and ran it over the flame from a nearby candle, sterilizing it.

Before she could make the cut, the prince moaned and began to thrash around. She looked over to the two men. "Restrain him. I need to drain the wound."

They quickly moved to do as she ordered while she made a potion from some herbs she had brought. Carefully, she poured the drink down the prince's throat, and within a couple moments, the thrashing stopped. The men stepped away from the bed and let her finish her work. Kaie made a connecting incision between the two puncture wounds and held a small bowl under the wound to let it drain. Greenish-yellow pus spurted out, and she gently squeezed the wound to completely empty it. Kaie washed the wound, then spread a paste to help it heal before bandaging up the prince's ankle.

She stepped back and wiped her forehead, not used to the scrutiny from other people. "That's all I can do for now."

The first man nodded and held out his hand, taking hers and shaking it. "I'm Tristen de Galac, Achaius's brother. This is Brayan Merdon, the court physician."

Kaie bowed her head out of respect. "I'm Kaie Durac."

The physician was tall and wore glasses at the end of his nose. He had long black hair and gray eyes that glittered ominously as he stared at her. Brayan nodded politely at Kaie, though there was a small smirk upon his lips that gave her pause.

"What should I do now, Your Highness? Your brother should be fine until the morning at least, but should I stay here to keep an eye on him?"

The crown prince shook his head. "No, I can do that and wake you if there is a change in his condition. I can show you to your room and you can rest. I'm sure you must be tired from your long journey."

It was then that Kaie realized she was not tired at all, though she would have expected the long journey to have exhausted her. "I'm not sleepy. I can watch him and then you don't have to waste time summoning me," she said. "If there is a decline in his health, it would almost be too late by the time I got here. He should be fine, but his condition is very delicate right now."

Prince Tristen walked towards the doorway at her words. "If that is what you think is best," he said. "I'll be checking in from time to time during the night to make sure you're fine." With that, he exited the room, Brayan moving to follow him.

Kaie stepped in front of the physician, blocking his exit. "How did you not recognize a bite from the Erlea snake?" she demanded. The bite should have been easy to diagnose by a capable physician, and should *never* have gotten to this point.

The physician stared down at her, as if she truly was a bug to be squashed. Kaie squared her shoulders. *She* was the one to figure out what was wrong, not him. There was no reason to cower to him.

"I don't acquaint myself with all manner of snake bites from the *southwestern* portion of the country," he said, pushing his glasses up his nose. "The prince was out riding further than expected. That snake is not regional here."

"A competent healer wouldn't let geography get in the way of their pursuit of knowledge. You should want to learn about *every* ailment, *every* injury," Kaie shot back, her pride stinging at his tone. He made her feel like she was dirt. And while her family was poor and her village was not the richest, the people were hardworking and did not deserve to be looked down upon.

Brayan let out a huff of annoyance before pushing past her and rushing out of the room.

Once he was gone, Kaie looked around the room, marveling at how accurately it had been captured in her dream. Now that she had some time to relax, she could observe her surroundings and admire the rich taste of the décor. One thing she had not noticed in her dream were the paintings of branches and leaves on the deep-green walls, reminiscent of the forest. A mahogany bookcase lined one wall, completely filled with books. Kaie walked over and looked at the spines, intrigued by the fascinating titles.

Though she did not have a lot of books at home, Syane had a small collection she was allowed to peruse. Kaie would go to the healer's house most days, and when she wasn't learning from Syane, she read what she could, eagerly devouring the words. One of her favorite titles grabbed her attention, and she carefully lifted it from the bookshelf. She had read the first few pages, a small smile crossing her lips, when she heard a noise.

Quickly spinning around, Kaie saw the prince staring at her with unfocused dark-green eyes. She put the book back quickly and fought back the feeling of panic rising within her. She reassured herself that she had healed many people in the past, and the prince was no different than any of her other patients.

"Is there anything you want, Your Highness?" she asked timidly, taking a couple steps towards the bed.

"Water," Prince Achaius managed to rasp out.

Kaie rushed to the bedside and poured him a glass of water, then supported his head as he drank, water dribbling slightly from his mouth as he drank greedily. He breathed a sigh of relief as he laid back and looked at her, his eyes more focused this time.

"I feel much better. What did you do?"

But before Kaie could give him an answer, he fell asleep again.

She walked over to her satchel and unpacked all her herbs, sorting them into small piles on the table, some unknown feeling telling her that she would need them soon. Once she was done, she sat on a cushioned chair and hugged her knees to her as she waited for the night to pass.

CHAPTER 5

A while later, Kaie was gently shaken awake. Upon opening her eyes, she saw Sir Shalane standing in front of her, a look of concern on his face. She flinched away from him, remembering his previous actions, the way his face had hardened.

"Do you need to go to bed? Prince Tristen said they have a room for you. You'd be more comfortable there."

Kaie edged away from the man, shaking her head vehemently. "I can take care of *myself*, Sir Shalane," she said stubbornly. She did not need help from the likes of him.

The man took a couple steps backwards, mentally berating himself for the day before. He shouldn't have let his emotions get the best of him. "You don't understand. You haven't dealt with bandits before." He tried to repair the damage that had been done. "That boy is going to grow up to be as bloodthirsty as the rest of them." His voice trailed off as she shot him a vicious look.

"And he might decide to go a different way!" Kaie said. "You can't just kill someone because of what they *might* grow into!"

Sir Shalane passed a hand over his face. Neither of them were willing to budge on their position. "They also got in our way yesterday. They needed to be punished."

"Killing that boy would not have made us reach here any faster. As it was, we were lucky to have made it in time. A couple more hours and the prince would have died. No amount of medicine or care could have helped him," she spat out.

Sir Shalane's eyes widened at how close the prince had been to death.

Before he could reply, Prince Tristen stepped out from behind the captain. He had been so quiet and Kaie was too consumed with her anger at Sir Shalane that she had not noticed him before. His face was creased with worry. "Really? He was that bad off?"

Kaie nodded her head. "His illness is a really simple thing to diagnose, and if caught early enough, then it's really easy to treat. But because it was left alone for so long, it's going to take him a while to recover." She paused, frowning slightly. "I'm not sure why your physician didn't realize it before. There's no reason Prince Achaius's condition should have gotten as bad as it has."

She didn't understand how incompetent the court physician seemed. Diagnosing and treating an Erlea snakebite should not have been that complicated. Especially if the prince had known that he had been bitten. Even if the snake was not regional to the capital, it should not have been so easily overlooked.

"How is he?" Prince Tristen asked, ignoring her comment. "Does he seem stable for now?"

"He woke up for a couple minutes asking for water, then fell right back asleep. His fever seems to have gone down and he should be fine for a couple hours at least," Kaie said.

At her words, Prince Tristen's face settled into a grave expression.

"What is it?" she asked, her heartbeat quickening at how serious he looked.

"My father, King Torin, would like to meet you," he said grimly. "We don't have much time to get you cleaned up, so you'll have to hurry."

Kaie was suddenly aware of her dirty hair, travel-worn clothes, and grimy face. She looked down, ashamed of her appearance, and tried not to concentrate on how much she must certainly smell. "I would definitely appreciate the opportunity to clean up," she said.

"Follow me."

Prince Tristen led Kaie down a maze of carpeted hallways, each one resembling the last. Despite being the daytime, flaming torches lit the way, illuminating the painted faces of past monarchs and bringing forth their scowling expressions. Once more, Kaie felt as though she did not belong in the palace, as if she was an intruder.

Upon reaching her room, she had no time to notice anything about it, as she was whisked away by a girl a few years older than her who introduced herself as Farin. She was washed quickly, then guided back to her room, where a forest-green dress awaited her on the bed.

"Who picked this out?" she asked Farin, who had begun dressing her.

Farin motioned for Kaie to turn so she could tie the sash. "Prince Tristen did. He thought it would look good on you."

Looking at herself in the mirror, Kaie thought the prince had made an excellent choice. Never before had she worn anything so lovely. Even when her family had money, they'd never had clothing as refined as this. Reflecting back at her was a beautifully dressed young woman, with a feminine slenderness, her hair pulled back with golden ribbons. It took a moment to register that it was her in the mirror before Farin ushered her out into the hallway, where Prince Tristen was waiting.

He looked at her. "That was certainly quick." He motioned for her to turn, which she obliged, loving the feeling of the skirts swirling around her ankles. "You look stunning. Father shouldn't be too harsh with you looking like that. You look too sweet to warrant his sour attitude. We should hurry or we'll be late."

Offering her his arm, Tristen led her through more labyrinthian corridors.

Finally, Kaie was able to find her voice. "Thank you for helping me, Prince Tristen. It means a lot."

He glanced at her and his gaze softened. "Please, call me Tristen when it's just us. And I'm not the only one who would help you. There are many here who would help. You are so young. Some have tried to help you already..."

His voice trailed off, and Kaie knew that he was speaking of Sir Shalane, but chose not to comment. She felt as though she had trusted the man too easily, given that he was her father's friend. But Sir Shalane was too cavalier about the gravity of taking someone's life. Logically, she knew killing was involved in his line of work—surely her father had killed many men—but the thought that the captain was so nonchalant about killing a boy churned her stomach.

All too soon, they arrived at the throne room, made obvious by the ornate filigreed wooden doors. Tristen escorted her in and she saw the king sitting on a golden throne at the top of a dais. In between her and the king lay a vast expanse of marbled floor that Kaie was not quite sure she would have been able to cross herself if Tristen had not been there. Empty chairs lined the walls where the noticeably absent courtiers normally would have sat.

Tristen gently guided her to the front of the king's throne, prompting a curtsy from her when he bowed to the king. Kaie's stomach somersaulted as she nervously looked up at the king. He had blond hair like Achaius, but his eyes were a deep blue like Tristen's, and were more unyielding than his oldest son's gentle gaze.

The king was wearing an elaborate golden crown, jewels adorning the sides. Overall, his clothing seemed simple, but she could tell even from this distance that they were made from the most elaborate and elegant of fabrics. On his fingers were an array of rings, each one golden and bejeweled. His face held a stern expression, and when he focused his harsh stare at Kaie, her knees began to tremble.

"Your Majesty, I would like to formally introduce Kaie Durac," Tristen said.

At the introduction, Kaie gave another curtsy, this one wobblier than the first.

With a disdainful look upon his face, the king looked her up and down before barking to Tristen, "Is this the healer you told me about?"

Tristen cleared his throat, and Kaie realized he was nervous too. The thought did not bring her any comfort. "Yes, Father. She did a miraculous job. She—"

"Enough!" the king shouted, cutting Tristen off. "I'll have her tell me what she did. Let's see if she really is a great healer or if the rumors have been exaggerated, as they're wont to do."

Rolling his eyes, Tristen leaned towards Kaie and whispered, "He can be short-tempered, but he just wants to test you. Don't let him rattle you."

Kaie nodded slightly, but her spine stiffened when the king directed his attention to her.

"So, young lady, you're the healer we've heard so much about? Nothing about you seems special to me. What have you done to improve my son's condition?" His voice carried throughout the vast space, the bite in his tone as strong in the back of the room as it was where Kaie stood.

Noticing Brayan standing next to the king, a smug smile across his features, Kaie had a feeling that he already told the king what she had done, and somehow, this was a test to see if she really knew anything about healing.

"At first glance, it was obvious that he had received a bite from an Erlea snake. When these snakes bite someone, it seems like a bee sting, but if not treated, the bites can kill a person," she said timidly.

"We already figured that out. What do you take us as, fools?" the king spat out.

Anger coursed through Kaie. If they had known that much, then there had been no reason for her to be torn away from her family. "If you had it all figured out, then why am I here?" she snapped. "Your physician should at least know how to cure a simple snakebite... Your Majesty." Realizing how insolent she sounded, she grumbled out the last bit.

The smirk dropped from Brayan's face, and the king was speechless over the change in behavior. The silence that filled the room was unexpectedly loud and overwhelming. It constricted around Kaie's throat, and when she opened her mouth, no words came out. After a couple moments, she was able to swallow and felt her voice return.

Kaie did not dare look at Tristen's reaction, and instead continued, "In order to get the venom out from a bite that has not been properly treated, it is essential to reopen the wound and rid it of pus, the remnants of the poison that caused infection. Once the pus is gone, the patient can then begin to recover with help. Depending on how long the infection has been left within their system, people usually recover anywhere within a week to a month. In Prince Achaius's case, it might take a little longer since his wound was left for so long without treatment."

The king found his voice again and accused, "Why did you drain the pus in such a violent manner? You surely could have used other methods."

"There wasn't enough time to use any other method. I was lucky to get here when I did. If I had taken the time to use something else, like say leeches, he would have died. By letting the wound drain by itself, I only helped nature along by allowing his body to empty itself of the poison. Again, if your physicians had done their jobs properly, it would have been better for him."

King Torin finally sat back in his seat and said begrudgingly, "Well done. I can tell you know your trade. You will remain here at the palace until Achaius has made a full recovery. But," he warned, "if something bad is to happen, I will hold you responsible and your family will pay the price. You may go now." He waved his ring-laden hand in dismissal.

Tristen led Kaie out of the room. Once the doors closed behind them, Kaie began to violently tremble, and Tristen led her to a nearby chair for fear she would collapse.

"What's wrong? You did wonderfully in there. He's just trying to rattle you. It'll all be fine."

He gave her a reassuring smile, but it was one she did not return. Something odd had happened inside the throne room, but she was not quite able to put her finger on it.

"Why am I here, Tristen?" she asked, looking up into the prince's eyes.

At her question, his face frowned into a quizzical expression. "What do you mean?" he asked. There was a flicker in his eyes that let Kaie know he knew something was going on, but was not going to tell her.

"Never mind," she sighed, slowly standing. "I should head back to check on your brother." Without another word, she headed off in the general direction of Achaius's room.

Tristen watched her walk away, and after a couple moments, followed her.

***

"Is that what you wanted to hear?" The king turned to the wizened old woman who had been standing behind his throne for the whole conversation. She was so tiny and wrinkled that she fit quite easily with no one being the wiser.

She nodded. "The girl seems to know medicine, but I sense the Inviver power within her. We just have to wait for her powers to reveal themselves." She brushed a strand of silvery-white hair out of her face.

"How long will that take?" King Torin questioned.

"That all depends on how your son recovers. But having her join our forces is the only way we'll win this war. We need more Invivers to send out, and powerful ones at that."

"And what if Achaius gets better before she has a chance to demonstrate her supposed skills?"

The woman handed a small corked bottle over to the king. "Then we will need to push her further. If you sneak this into your son's drink, it will be the drastic measure we have to take. It's sure to do the trick. I looked through all her herbs, and she has nothing in her stock to counteract this. If she has any powers, this will push her to use them."

King Torin pocketed the bottle in his robes and sat back. "Now all we have to do is wait." He smiled and folded his large hands together in his lap, content with how things were progressing. With another Inviver, he might finally be able to break the stalemate.

Brayan's features remained neutral at the exchange, but when he at last left the king's presence, he allowed a chuckle to escape. It irked him how he had to pretend to be a bumbling fool, not knowing how to treat a simple snakebite. But all was going according to the king's wishes, and to keep his job, he would endure the misunderstandings of the child. He smirked with amusement, at how gullible the silly girl was.

"She's going to fall right into their hands."

CHAPTER 6

Tristen guided Kaie back to her room, where her freshly washed clothes were waiting for her on the bed. She looked at them before turning to him and cocking her head in a question.

"I thought you would feel more comfortable in those," he said apologetically, noticing how downhearted she seemed on their walk back. His father's words had been harsh.

Kaie nodded, touched at the small gesture. "Thank you for your consideration. I'll change and head back to Prince Achaius's room to check on him."

With no further conversation, Tristen left the room and Kaie changed, needing Farin to dress her since her hands were still shaking. Once dressed, Tristen showed her the way back to Achaius's room. Again, she tried to make sense of the passageways, but the halls were still so confusing that she eventually gave up trying to figure out where to turn. Inside the palace, her sense of direction was failing her.

The prince was sleeping peacefully, and Kaie sighed in relief that all was well. She walked over to her chair and took a seat, settling in to watch over him.

Hours passed, then days, then weeks. She kept a watch on Achaius, periodically having to make him a potion to aid his recovery and changing the dressing on his wound. Despite her treatment, the prince remained unconscious. Kaie did not eat much during those weeks, too worried that Achaius would suddenly take a turn for the worst. The fate of her family and their lives hung over her head, making what little sleep she did receive restless.

Once in a while, Tristen would come and sit with her, trying to engage in small talk, though usually he carried the conversation. Kaie was typically too preoccupied to focus on speaking, or eating during the times he brought food with him. The physician, Brayan, would briefly stop by as well, but he typically left quickly with a frown on his face. It seemed that he only wanted to check on Prince Achaius before leaving. He never spoke to her, not that Kaie minded. Sir Shalane visited as well, but Kaie refused to acknowledge his presence, her gaze always steadfastly focused on Prince Achaius. He would wait for her to speak, but then eventually leave as she maintained her silence.

Tristen came one night and led her to her room so she could finally get a good night's sleep. Over the past few weeks, watching her waste away, he'd grown increasingly worried. Tonight, despite what anyone said, he was making sure she slept in an actual bed for once, as opposed to the uncomfortable chair she had taken up residence in.

Kaie was tired and too confused to realize where they were going until they arrived at her door. "I can sleep in Prince Achaius's room," Kaie argued. "I've slept there for the past few weeks anyway."

"You're starting to look like a raccoon," Tristen said grimly. The circles under her eyes were becoming deeper and darker with each passing day.

"I'm worried that he might relapse and get worse," Kaie said, not sure how else to voice her concerns.

She was not sure Tristen would understand the severity of her situation. Something odd was going on in the palace, but he seemed to be ignoring that fact. The servants whispered among themselves and she always felt as if her movements were being watched. If she stayed at Prince Achaius's bedside, she could ensure nothing bad would happen.

Tristen gently pushed her towards her doorway. "He'll be fine. You've taken good care of him and there's nothing to worry about. If you're needed, then we'll send someone," he reassured her, but her worried expression did not fade.

Kaie fell silent as Tristen shut the door behind him, trying to keep calm. Farin was waiting for her, and helped her get into bed. Before her head even hit the pillow, Kaie was asleep, a soft snore escaping her.

Tristen smiled upon hearing that from Farin and left to spend the night at his brother's side. It was his turn to keep watch. Kaie had already done enough.

***

When Kaie awakened, sunlight streamed through the window. She blinked, adjusting her eyes to the light before getting up to take a nice soothing bath that Farin had drawn up for her. Afterwards, she decided to change into a dress that fit in more with the palace from the giant armoire that was overflowing with gorgeous gowns. It was a soft burgundy, and she braided her hair to match the white braided belt.

After leaving her room and being guided by a servant to Prince Achaius's room, she took a deep breath and walked in, hoping that the prince's condition had not changed. Tristen was standing next to the bed, and she cleared her throat as she entered.

He looked up, his eyes widening when he saw her dress. "Well, don't you fit in now," he teased. A smile spread across his face at the fact that she seemed much more relaxed than the day before. Sleeping well had done wonders for her.

"I thought it would be nice to wear some of the dresses instead of letting them sit in the armoire," Kaie said hesitantly, not quite sure if she had made the right decision.

"That's what they're there for," Tristen said. "I made sure to have them put in your room, we had them sitting in storage. I'm glad they fit."

Kaie walked over to her chair and sat down. Tristen followed her lead, sitting down next to her. They spent the next couple of minutes watching Prince Achaius until Kaie's stomach made a grumbling noise so loud that Tristen jumped at the sound.

"A little hungry there?" he joked.

Kaie flushed with embarrassment. "I guess I haven't been paying attention to how much I've eaten. With taking care of Prince Achaius, I've been too worried and haven't really had the time to be hungry," she said ruefully, realizing at that moment just how hungry she really was.

"We can fix that. Come with me. I'll take you to the kitchen. A servant will get us if Achaius needs you."

Tristen stood, leading Kaie out of the room. She listened as he instructed a servant to come get them if there was a change in Achaius's condition, but she was focusing more on trying to contain the gnawing pit that had taken over her stomach. The intensity of her hunger was surprising in how quickly it had taken over as soon as she realized she was hungry. Tristen walked with Kaie to the kitchen, his hand on her elbow to keep her from falling over.

The kitchen was aflutter with lunchtime preparations, but they took the time to put together a plate for Kaie. Tristen then led her to the dining room, where she ate ravenously, wolfing down the meal.

He laughed. "Slow down or you're going to make yourself sick."

Kaie tried to slow down, but it seemed impossible. The endless pit did not seem to be filling up at all. It felt as though she would never feel full again, that the emptiness would last forever.

Sir Shalane suddenly walked into the dining room and whispered to Tristen, "Your father would like to see you. I'll stay here with Kaie and take her back to Prince Achaius when she's done. You can catch up with us later, but he seemed angry, so you might want to hurry."

Puzzled at what his father could possibly want, Tristen said goodbye and left.

Sir Shalane took his place and sat down. "We need to talk," he said.

The silence from Kaie had lasted long enough and he was not going to put up with her ignoring him any longer. However, she kept eating and tried to ignore him. It had worked well over the past few weeks.

"I need to explain myself," he said.

She finally looked up. "There is no reason for so senselessly taking a human life, Sir Shalane. How can you call yourself a captain if you don't have empathy for others? How can you be trusted in that position of leadership?"

Tears glinted in her eyes as Sir Shalane realized how deeply his actions had cut her. He had been too focused on his past that he had not put much stock into her feelings, her kindness and compassion for others.

"Please, call me Lorne," he said. He closed his eyes, working up the courage to speak. "I once had a daughter like you, who was the light in my life. She always had a way of making me feel like I was the wisest person in the world."

"What happened to her?" Kaie could tell by his tone that something horrible had happened.

"One day when I was out, a group of men came and robbed the house, killing both my wife and daughter in the process. They knew I was in the King's Guard and thought I was paid well so I had valuables to steal. Since then, I've worked hard to defend the public. To save others who are defenseless, as they were."

Kaie's eyes widened in shock, suddenly seeing the man in front of her in a new light. "And that's why you hate bandits," she whispered. "I'm sorry for your loss." She placed a hand on his, understanding his actions now. If her family had been killed, she would have reacted the same as him. She would want to destroy everyone associated with their deaths.

Lorne sighed, happy to have shared the story with her. "I know you miss your family," he said. "But you will see them again."

The gentle tone of his voice and feelings of missing her father caused a tear to slip down her cheek. Lorne stood and came to give her a hug. The absence of close human contact overpowered the strangeness of the embrace and Kaie hugged him back. Lorne then guided her out of the dining room. Instead of leading her to Prince Achaius's room, though, he led her outside through a side door.

Puzzled, she looked at him, not expecting this turn of events. "Where are we going?"

He winked. "It's a surprise."

Soon, they arrived at the stables, to see a small man with sandy hair flitting about as he got a couple horses ready. Eventually, he stopped in front of them and offered his hand to Kaie. "My name is Fyfe," he said with a smile, his hazel eyes flickering. "I'll be in charge of your ride this afternoon."

Lorne laughed at the look of confusion that crossed Kaie's face. "You've been cooped up in that room for weeks. It's time for a break."

"But what if Prince Achaius needs me? I won't be nearby," she protested, though her objections sounded weak even to her own ears. If she was being honest, a ride would do a lot to lift her spirits.

"Already taken care of," Fyfe interjected. "You'll be riding near the castle, just in case they need you."

"Well…" Kaie once more tried to argue, but she eyed the waiting horses with anticipation. She recognized the one she had ridden on the journey to the palace.

"Kaie, just get on the horse. It'll be fine," Lorne promised.

With that, she swung her leg over the horse and settled into the saddle. The animal beneath her whickered and tossed her head excitedly.

"See? She's ready for a ride," Fyfe pointed out. "No one really rides her anymore. The princes have their own horses and they never ride any others. The king has given permission that Aira is now yours."

Kaie was speechless as she gave a thorough look at the horse she had ridden on her previous journey with new eyes. She knew that she was looking at a fine beast, one that was rippled with muscle and filled with stamina. Never before had she owned her own horse, and never in her wildest dreams had she imagined having a beautiful mare, especially one as strong and tireless as Aira.

Her voice was breathless with excitement. "Can I ride her now?"

Lorne was now atop his horse and burst out laughing. "*Now* you want to ride," he said. "It sure didn't take much to get you to agree."

Lorne's horse, Thunder, led the way, starting at a light trot, but Aira kept up easily. After a while, Lorne pushed Thunder to go faster, but Aira still managed to keep up. Kaie loved the wind blowing through her hair and the feeling of being outside after being cooped up for the past few weeks.

Overcome with exhilaration, she shouted, "Race you around the palace!"

He laughed at the challenge. "You're on!"

Both spurred their horses forward, the competition edging them on. Onward they raced, past the training grounds, the gardens, and the stables.

Aira managed to pull ahead until Kaie could no longer see Lorne behind them. She whooped with joy and rode Aira once more around the palace until she came up on Lorne. The sight made her heart stop, and she pulled Aira to an abrupt halt. Thunder stood riderless with his front right hoof raised. Lorne laid crumpled on the ground nearby.

His face was white, and as soon as he noticed her, he shouted, "Go get Fyfe! He'll know what to do. Then get your herbs."

Questions spinning through her head, Kaie wheeled Aira around and headed back towards the stables. Tears stung her eyes as the wonderful break had taken an ugly turn, ruined by her idea to race.

Fyfe came running out when he saw only Aira riding up and Kaie looking distraught. "What happened? Where's Lorne and Thunder?"

Kaie gasped out, "Lorne somehow fell off Thunder and is injured."

"I'll head over. Go get your herbs and meet us back there." Fyfe mounted Aira, saving time instead of re-saddling another horse, and galloped over to where Lorne was.

Kaie raced back to the palace, her braid coming undone. Back inside, she struggled to remember where Prince Achaius's room was, getting caught at a crossroads, unsure of which way to go. A few servants rushed by, ignoring her distress as they hurried on to their duties. Brayan stumbled upon her spinning in circles, apprehension apparent on her face. She seemed on the verge of tears.

"What's wrong?" he asked with a raised eyebrow. It was unusual to see the young healer looking that out of sorts. Whenever he checked in on the prince, she always seemed calm and collected.

A scowl crossed his features, and Kaie knew he was not happy to see her. Thus far, she had been lucky enough to avoid him. A couple times over the past month, he'd poked his head in to check on Prince Achaius, but always retreated when he saw that she was present.

"Sir, would you be able to take me to the prince's room, please?"

His scowl grew. "Why? You should know the way already."

"I may have been here for a month, but I've been cooped up in that room the whole time. I don't know where anything is. Please, take me there. I need to get my herbs. Sir Shalane's been injured and I need to help him," she begged, tears threatening to fall. "Unless you have some that I can use."

Brayan's eyes widened as he heard the news. "The prince's room is closer. I'll lead you there and back, but other than that, you're on your own."

He led her to Prince Achaius's room at such a brisk pace that she had to run to keep up. Once they were there, she pushed all her herbs into her satchel, pausing briefly upon seeing her mother's gift at the bottom of the bag, forgotten during her stay. But now was not the time to open it. She would do so later. As Kaie was about to leave, she looked over to Prince Achaius. He was sitting up in bed, looking at her like he had seen a ghost. His eyes were unfocused once more and his face was flushed with a fever.

She walked over to the bed. "Is everything all right?"

"Mother, how-how are you here?" he stammered. "You can't be here, it's impossible."

Kaie looked over to Brayan for help, confusion written across her features. "What's going on?"

The physician sized up the situation and walked over to the bed. Prince Achaius looked at him, trying to understand what was going on.

"Your mother came home early," Brayan said. "We wanted to surprise you. You should go back to sleep or you won't be able to join your family for dinner."

Prince Achaius nodded and leaned back in the bed, falling back asleep quickly. Kaie turned to Brayan, but he was already leaving the room.

"Wait!" she called, rushing to catch up.

He ignored her, and it was not until they reached the palace entry that she asked him, "What was that all about? Did he really think I was the queen? I don't understand, I thought she died when he was a baby."

Brayan snorted. "I thought you were supposed to be more competent than me?" He took in her bewildered expression and sighed. "He was hallucinating. He started to do that a few days before you arrived. The best thing we've found to do in that situation is to act as if everything's normal. Then he goes back to sleep. He stopped when you arrived so something you've done must have helped him. It should be nothing. Just check back up on him when you're finished with Lorne." He started to leave.

"Wait!" Kaie shouted.

He turned back with an exasperated expression and she knew he was quickly tiring of her.

"Can you look after him until I return?"

The physician gave her such a contemptuous look that she found herself regretting the question immediately.

"I'm sorry, but I don't want him to be alone in case he wakes up again." Remembering why she had called him back in the first place, she said softly, "Thank you. I don't know what I would have done in that situation if I was by myself."

Brayan crossed his arms, but did not move. He did not even bother giving her a response.

Shaking her head at his arrogance, Kaie raced outside, hoping that Lorne was fine. A group of people were gathered around the captain, and Kaie pushed her way through until she was at the center of the circle. Lorne's face was ashen.

She knelt down beside him. "Where does it hurt?"

He was in so much pain, all he was able to gasp out was, "My leg."

Kaie cut open his pant leg, finding that the skin underneath was bright red and swollen. She quickly mixed a paste of milfoil and wood spurge, then spread the paste over the affected area, to help with the inflammation, before giving Lorne a pre-prepared potion to ease the pain.

"It's broken, but that should make it feel better," she said as his face began to relax, her ministrations easing the pain considerably.

Fyfe suddenly appeared at her side, ready to help after he had put Thunder back in the stable. "What can I do?" he asked, eager to help.

"We need to get him back to castle, he's not going to make it there on his own," Kaie said.

Fyfe and another bystander lifted Lorne up and supported his weight between the two of them. Kaie grabbed her satchel and followed behind as they began the trek back to the palace.

"What happened?" Kaie managed to ask.

"Thunder somehow got spooked and reared up. I fell off wrong," Lorne said, wincing as they walked. Though Kaie's aid had helped the pain, it was still an effort to walk all the way back. Beads of sweat dampened his forehead.

"Oh." Kaie's voice was quiet, and it was enough to tip off Lorne that she felt responsible for the accident.

"Kaie, it's not your fault. Thunder was just frightened." His tone was gentle, letting her know that he did not blame her. He stopped for a moment to rest his leg and catch his breath.

"But if I hadn't wanted to race, this wouldn't have happened." Kaie could not meet his eyes, the guilt overwhelming her.

"You don't know that. Thunder still could have gotten startled and I could still be in the same situation. There's no point in blaming yourself over it."

They soon arrived at the side entrance that they had used previously.

Kaie looked at Lorne guiltily. "I need to check on Prince Achaius. I'll finish as soon as I can so I can come check up on you." She looked down at her feet. "I'm sorry."

"Kaie, stop blaming yourself. Just come check on me when you get a chance. Prince Achaius comes first. We both know he's your first priority and you need to make sure everything is fine. I'll be okay until then. Your herbs seem to have done the trick. Fyfe can get me back to my room. I'll be fine," he repeated. Seeing her hesitant look, he added, "Go. Turn right here and you should remember the way back."

Kaie now remembered the way to Prince Achaius's room and reached it easily. When she walked in, there was a group of people waiting for her. King Torin and Tristen were standing around Prince Achaius's bedside. Both had stern faces and Kaie felt a moment of dread as she approached them.

"What's wrong?" she asked apprehensively, a shadow of worry passing over her face. She noticed Brayan standing in the corner of the room, his eyes alight with delight. His joy did not give her any comfort.

"Brayan just told us what happened and how you abandoned Achaius to go help Sir Shalane," the king accused, taking in her flushed face and ruined hair. "You should have stayed with the prince until you were sure he was fine."

"But he was," Kaie protested. "He fell asleep right away. And Brayan said Prince Achaius would be fine until I came back!" She could hear the desperate tone enter her voice, needing the king to understand she had not been slacking in her duties. She looked to the physician, begging him to speak up, but he remained silent.

"If something had happened, by the time Brayan would have sent for you and you had gotten here, Achaius could have been dead," the king said sternly. "Also, why were you with Sir Shalane when he got hurt? You left the prince to go and relax, while he is here fighting for his life!"

"Surely Brayan's presence here was enough, Father. She needed time to eat and rest," Tristen said quietly. Kaie was surprised to see that his jaw was clenched, but she was unsure whether his anger was directed at her or the king.

"Your brother is her responsibility, Tristen! She should not be away from his side for very long until he is better! She's been resting and taking her meals here, and she can continue to do that."

"The prince is well enough that I can leave for a while!" Kaie objected, her voice rising.

"How do you know that?" The king's voice rose in volume to a thunderous pitch.

Kaie flinched at his tone, but her anger had been sparked. First she had been brought here when she should not be needed and now he was questioning her decisions. Once more, the thought crossed her mind that all was not as it seemed at the palace. Something was afoot.

"Because I've been doing this since I was very young! I know the limits people have, and he would have been okay. Besides, did anything happen while I was gone?" Her volume increased to match his.

"No, but what if something had?" the king argued back.

"Nothing did. Just like nothing happened when you called me to meet you. He's tough, one of the toughest patients I've ever had. His condition is stabilized and the best thing for him right now is rest. There's nothing more I can actively do." Kaie could feel her face growing redder the angrier she got.

The king frowned at her words. "Very well. But if something happens to him, I'm holding you responsible. You better hope he recovers soon."

He swished out of the room, his robes swirling behind him. Once he shut the door, he corked a small empty bottle that he had been hiding in his hand. The plan was almost complete.

CHAPTER 7

Tristen shook his head sadly at Kaie. "How could you have left him alone?" he asked. "You were supposed to return after you ate."

Though he knew Kaie deserved some time to herself, the timing of this was most unfortunate. When his father had said he wanted to check on Achaius, both were surprised to see Brayan alone in the room with Kaie absent.

"Lorne said he should be fine and that I needed a break. We didn't ride far," she said, not believing that she had to explain herself to Tristen. She'd thought he was on her side, especially after defending her to the king.

"You still should have checked with me or Father first."

"But I knew he was going to be okay, I gave him a potion last night to help him. His condition is much improved. And like you said, Brayan was here." She turned and shot a look at the physician.

"Fine. Just don't let it happen again." Tristen left the room, leaving Brayan and Kaie alone.

Brayan smirked at the whole exchange, beside himself that Kaie had gotten into trouble. "Well, now that the show is over, I should probably get going." He moved for the door. Now that everything had turned out as he wanted, he did not want to spend any more time with her.

Kaie stepped in front of him, halting his progress. "Why did you do that?"

His smile transformed into an overly innocent one. "Do what?" he asked, his tone mocking her.

"Why did you tell them that I left because of Lorne and spin it that I had abandoned Prince Achaius? You knew he was fine." Kaie racked her brain to come up with a reason as to why he seemed to hate her so much, but could not think of anything.

"They came in here looking to see what you were doing. You weren't in the dining room so they figured you must be here. When you weren't, they decided to wait and see what was so important that you couldn't care for Prince Achaius. You know, the whole reason you were brought here," he sneered. Despite the fact that he was arguing with someone much younger than him, his pride would not let her previous insults go. "He might not be next in line for the throne, but he is royalty."

"Why do you hate me so much?" she asked. "I didn't ask to be brought here." She figured that he held a grudge for being summoned to heal the prince when he couldn't, but she was not in control of the king's wishes.

He stepped closer to her, staring her down. Kaie had never realized how much the man towered over her, but now that he was so close, she could see that he was at least a head taller than her. She forced herself to stand tall rather than back away.

"I had to pretend to be incompetent. I was told to let the wound fester," he hissed. "You weren't needed to heal the prince. The Invivers could have fixed him up quickly, but they wanted to see if all the stories were true. They don't think you can really heal him. You're just here to be the entertainment. The crown prince might not see it that way, but I know what they said about you after you left your counsel with the king."

Kaie gulped, the feeling of dread in the pit of her stomach growing larger. Everything the physician said echoed her worst fears.

"Lorne said all the Invivers had been deployed." Even she could hear the lack of conviction in her words. She'd known from the moment she arrived that something was odd.

He gave a harsh laugh. "And you believed him? Who in their right mind would send away *all* the Invivers and not have a couple stay behind to tend to the royal family? No, this is just a test for you."

"But why?" she whispered. Brayan was confirming all her suspicions that something was afoot and nothing made sense.

"There's a secret plan in place you know nothing about. Just so you know—" his voice dropped to a whisper as he leaned even closer, "—I don't think you have what it takes. I think all those stories about you were made up. I think *you're* the incompetent one." Brayan straightened up and brushed past her brusquely. "Good luck trying to pass the next test that's about to come up," he called cynically over his shoulder, before he slammed the door behind him.

Mouth agape, Kaie stared at the closed door, trying to figure out what his departing comment meant. Her mind whirled with the possibilities of his cryptic answers. Though he had confirmed one thing: all of this was some sort of test. But why would the king go through all the trouble just for her? She was a nobody, a backwoods healer.

A spark of excitement pricked at her heart. Could this mean she was someone special after all? That she had more power than she realized?

Walking over to Prince Achaius's bedside, Kaie observed a glass on the nearby table, coated with a viscous red liquid. The king, Tristen, or even Brayan must have given him something to drink before she came in. Kaie then noticed that the prince's breathing had sped up since she had last checked on him, indicating that something was very wrong. She took a deep breath, trying to calm herself. He had been fine when she had left, but now... there was no time to think of anything else. He had to get better.

Walking over to the table, she pulled out her herbs, searching through them for something that would make him better. There was very little milfoil or wood spurge left, so she tried using black locust. Even though it was used mainly for headaches, she knew it would be fine to lower his fever and hopefully calm his breathing. She mixed the herbs together, then gave the draft to Prince Achaius. Though still asleep, he spat it out, spraying it all over his bedsheets. Finally, she started to allow herself to panic, wondering what she would do if he did not drink it.

She tried giving the potion to him again, and this time, he managed to swallow some of it. His breathing immediately began to slow down, and she felt herself breathe again. Pulling a chair up close to his bedside, she waited for any other signs that could indicate a worsened condition.

As the night passed, Kaie dozed off a bit, but it wasn't long before she awakened to the sound of hoarse coughing. Prince Achaius was coughing in his sleep—not a good sign. Carefully, she elevated his upper body so he could breathe easier. After his coughing had subsided, she checked the liquid inside the glass again. Something was not quite right and it nagged at her.

As she swiped a finger around the edge of the goblet, a gel-like red substance came off. She sniffed at it, and her nose wrinkled at the sour smell. Based on her knowledge of different potions, she figured it contained arrow grass, a type of plant that if used improperly would become a poison. She had some in her satchel, but had not used any on the prince. Knowing that the king would never believe that she had not poisoned Prince Achaius, she worked to repair the damage.

Tristen walked in to her chopping up more herbs in a frenzy. He took in her flushed face, panic-stricken expression, and Prince Achaius's raspy breathing, and came to the conclusion that something was wrong.

"What is it?" he demanded.

"Brayan said something weird earlier about all this being a test. I think whatever was put in his drink earlier has made him sick," she explained cautiously, not sure how he would take the news. A ringing in her ears put her already frayed nerves more on edge.

"Father gave him something to drink while you were gone. What are you suggesting?" Tristen thundered.

Kaie flinched, afraid that he was not going to be on her side. The way he was acting now was nothing like the kind and gentle prince she was used to.

"That's the only explanation I can come up with as to why he is sicker than he was when I left. He should have been awake today based on his progress," Kaie said.

"You need to make him well again or Father's going to—"

"Or I'm going to do what?" the king interjected.

Tristen and Kaie spun around, startled at the intrusion. The monarch towered in the doorway, his blue eyes taking in the scene.

"What—what are you doing here, Your Majesty?" Kaie stammered.

"I was coming to see how Achaius was doing. Not too good, I see," the king observed, his expression unreadable.

"It seems he had something to drink yesterday that has made him sick," Tristen explained, leaving out Kaie's theory that it was the beverage the king had given Achaius.

"Well, whatever it is, you better make him well again or your family will be punished with treason," the king threatened.

Kaie knew exactly what he was insinuating. She gulped—the punishment for treason was death.

"But it's not my fault!" Kaie protested, her voice rising in pitch.

"I don't care," the king said, crossing his arms.

"Can't your healers do anything? Or even your Invivers?" Kaie asked, desperate for any type of help. Deep down, she knew Brayan was right and this was some sort of test, but she refused to believe it. Why would the king risk killing one of his sons just to see what she could do? She was a nobody whose education certainly did not rival that of a palace healer.

"This responsibility was given to you. If you fail, your family will pay the price." With that, the king left the room, motioning for Tristen to follow.

Giving Kaie a sad look, Tristen followed his father.

***

"What is going on?" Tristen demanded as soon as they reached the hallway, the door closing shut behind them. His father's responses indicated that something was amiss. If Achaius was truly near the brink of death, the king would have brought in the Invivers to Cure him.

"This is a test to reveal her Inviver powers," King Torin explained.

"So? We already know that she is a great healer as it is. Why does she have to be an Inviver too?" Tristen was confused. His father was speaking in riddles.

"Listen, I know you may not agree with me, but this is for the best. Your brother will be fine."

"How do you know that?" Tristen asked. He thought back to how his brother looked, and he did not seem to be in the best state. He could not understand how his father was so nonchalant.

"He is sick because of this." The king showed Tristen the bottle he had used to poison his youngest son.

Tristen's eyes widened as he realized what his father had done. "You poisoned him?" he thundered angrily. "Kaie was right!"

"If she can't Cure him, it will put him in a state where it will only *seem* as if he is dead. I blame her and send her home. The Invivers come in and Cure him. It's foolproof," the king explained. "Maeve senses Kaie's powers, but we need them to fully manifest. And Kaie can't know anything about this until we get confirmation of her powers." King Torin frowned as his son looked back towards Achaius's room. "You are not to tell her about any of this, do you understand?"

"Achaius has been sick and in pain for weeks!" Tristen exclaimed, not believing what he was hearing. "Why would you want him to suffer for that long?"

"It's something that needs to be done if we are to know her true potential."

***

Now panicking even more, Kaie chopped at the herbs vigorously. She made a quick drink out of them and attempted to give it to the now writhing prince. His breathing was now rushed and his face was bright red. She slowly administered the drink, praying that he would not spit it out. Upon swallowing, he immediately slumped in her arms, but his symptoms remained the same.

Kaie collapsed in her chair. There was nothing else that she could think of to do and if she did not act quickly, he would be dead and her family would be killed. Fury rose up within her. There was no way the king's healers should be unable to help the prince. Why was she, a mere teenager, in charge of his health to begin with?

Either way, it did not matter. The king was going to kill her family and there was nothing she could do about it. His mind seemed made up. She tried talking to the prince, to at least make his last moments more bearable for him and herself, though he probably could not hear anything.

"It's going to be okay, you'll be well soon." She tried to persuade him to get better, to lessen the guilt of just giving up on him even though she knew it was a fruitless pursuit. "I've done everything I can do. It's all up to you now."

Kaie waited a couple minutes, the only sound in the room Prince Achaius's rushed breathing. The ringing in her ears grew louder. Suddenly, she grew angry at the unfairness of the situation.

"Fine, if you want to give up on a perfectly decent life, that's not my fault," she snapped, taking her anger out unfairly on the prince. "I've tried everything I can think of. Just think of how *I'm* feeling. My family will be killed if you die. How would you like that, hmmm? You're responsible for killing innocent people just because you're selfish enough to give up. It's *my* family and now they'll die because of you."

She stood up and paced next to the bed hysterically, her repressed feelings and all the unfairness that she had felt over the past weeks pouring out. The shrill sound echoing in her ears drove her anger.

"Wake up! Do you hear me? Wake up! My family doesn't deserve to die just because you can't pull it together. You can't do this to me. You're letting all the time I spent on you go to waste! What is wrong with you? A normal person would be over this in a couple weeks, but no, you have to take almost a month and pretty much die so you can feel all special. Well guess what? I'm not letting you take the easy way out."

She leaned forward, about to take Prince Achaius's shoulders to shake him awake, her anger rising to a peak. The moment she touched his shoulders, a huge shock passed through her and a bright flash of light burst from her hands. Immediately, the shrill pitch stopped. That was all she had time to take note of before she blacked out.

CHAPTER 8

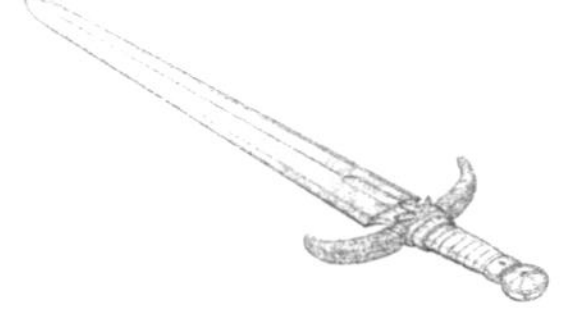

Kaie slowly opened her eyes, her head and body throbbing. The room was pitch black, with only a sliver of the moon shining through the curtains onto the bed. After a couple moments, she recognized her bedroom at the palace, but she had no memories of how she'd arrived there. The sudden recollection of what last happened with Prince Achaius propelled her out of bed and onto her feet. She stopped as dizziness overwhelmed her, body swaying.

Focusing on her ghostly reflection in the mirror, Kaie noticed that she was dressed in a pale-pink nightgown that draped down to her ankles. From what she could tell, her face was extremely pale and slightly gaunt. Stumbling over to a nearby chair to grab the robe hanging there, she put it on and walked unsteadily to the door, struggling to remain upright.

Trying to catch her breath from the exertion, she leaned on the door and tried the knob, hoping that it was not locked. She let out a relieved exhale when it turned in her hand, slowly opening the door to look into the candlelit hallway. No one was around as Kaie walked down the hall in the direction of Prince Achaius's room, the memory of where it was located slowly coming back to her. Her hand brushed along the wall to keep her balanced, and she stumbled over her feet a couple of times, almost falling over in the process.

Concentrating on trying to stay upright, she missed the sound of footsteps coming behind her. At first the person seemed hesitant, but picked up speed when they realized who was out walking so late at night.

Kaie managed to stifle a scream when she felt a hand on her shoulder. She spun around, putting a hand to her head from dizziness. When she saw who it was, she flinched.

Tristen stared at her with an unreadable expression. He peered into her pale face, his brow furrowing in concern. She stumbled back a couple steps, trying to sort out everything in her mind, but she felt sluggish, unable to connect the dots. Tristen reached out a hand to steady her when it looked like she would fall.

She managed to speak first. "Tristen, what are you doing here?" she asked, her voice barely above a whisper. Her throat felt scratchy as she spoke and she was surprised at how hoarse she sounded. It was a struggle to get the words out, so she cleared her throat.

His eyebrows rose. "I live here," he pointed out, a small smile crossing his lips.

Kaie quirked a smile to match his. "I meant, what are you doing out of bed at this hour?" she rephrased.

"I could ask you the same question," he said. "You should be resting."

"I need to find out if Prince Achaius is okay. I don't know what happened." Kaie frowned at the gap in her memory. The time that was missing after the flash of light mystified her.

"This should probably wait until morning. It's too confusing to explain it all. Why don't you go back to bed? It's late enough as it is." He gestured back towards the direction of her room.

The need to see Prince Achaius grew. She felt as though Tristen was trying to distract her. "But—" Kaie started to protest.

"Kaie, please go. It'll make more sense tomorrow."

"Can you at least tell me he's all right?"

Tristen hesitated over how much to tell her. After all, she had been through a lot and his father had ordered that she wasn't to be told anything. Seeing her look of desperation, he took a deep breath. "He's fine."

"Really?" Doubt crept into her voice at his words.

"Please just go back to sleep. You used up a lot of energy trying to heal Achaius," Tristen said gently. "Just go to sleep. It'll all make sense in the morning and we'll tell you everything then. I'm not at the liberty to explain anything right now."

"What do you mean by 'trying to heal'?" Kaie picked up on Tristen's mistake.

"I meant... I'll tell you tomorrow. Just go to sleep," he said hurriedly, ushering her to her room. After they arrived at her chambers, he stayed to make sure she went back to bed.

Once he closed the door, Tristen muttered to himself, "That was close."

He did not fully understand the need for secrecy, but decided he would not risk his father's wrath by spilling anything to Kaie. With a slight headache coming on, he headed off to his room to get some more sleep and prepare for the next day.

***

Early the next morning, Kaie awakened to the sound of birds chirping. Astounded that she had been able to get any sleep after last night, she slowly got out of bed, remembering how dizzy she had been the night before. To her surprise, she felt much better today.

She took her time getting ready, slipping into the green dress Tristen had picked out for her for her first meeting with the king. Thinking back to last night, she was curious about all that had happened recently, Tristen's cryptic remarks baffling her. After getting dressed, she slowly pulled her chestnut hair back into a long braid down her back, taking a cursory glance at her reflection in the mirror.

Almost as soon as she was done getting ready, Farin entered the room, surprised to see that Kaie had gotten dressed without any help. "Prince Tristen mentioned you woke up last night. They're waiting for you now," she said after a moment of awkward silence.

"What happened?" Kaie hoped Farin would share details with her.

"I'm not at liberty to say, miss." The maid bowed her head.

Kaie let out a sigh. "I figured, but thought I would ask anyway," she said quietly.

Farin led Kaie to the throne room, motioning for her to go in. This time, Kaie realized that she would have to enter by herself. Tristen would not be there to help her across the room. Taking a deep breath, she pushed the doors open and walked in.

The sun shone through the stained-glass windows and reflected an array of colors and designs on the floor. Unlike last time, courtiers filled the chairs, their eyes trained on her. Keeping her head tall, she walked towards the king deliberately, looking only at him and ignoring the prickling of stares.

When she reached the open area in front of the throne, she curtsied, her heart beating furiously. As she stood, the king began to clap. Everyone in the room joined in a round of applause as she looked at all of them in confusion. There were many people that she had never seen before and there was one person who looked very familiar, but she could not place who he was.

The young man sat next to Tristen amongst the courtiers closest to the king, and while he was dressed in rich-fabric clothes that fit in with the palace finery, they seemed too plain for him to be high ranking. His wavy blond hair was pulled back into a short ponytail and though he was whispering to Tristen, his deep-green eyes studied her. Tearing her gaze away from the young man, she looked at the king, waiting for him to speak.

Once the applause had died down, the king's booming voice filled the room. "Kaie Durac, you have gone above and beyond what I have asked," he began. "Not only have you done your duty, but you have shown us who you truly are while managing to keep your head throughout the circumstances that we placed you under. Well done."

Kaie frowned as she tried to interpret what he was trying to say. He was as good as Brayan at talking in riddles.

Seeing her confusion, the king continued, "You have done a marvelous job healing my son, Achaius." He motioned to the young man Kaie had noticed earlier.

It sunk in that she had healed him. He looked very different now that he was no longer ill. The prince's color had returned, his cheeks were no longer gaunt, and his eyes were sharp and studious.

"Even at a risk to your own health. I appreciate all that you have done and I know that I did not make it the easiest task in the world. However, there was a reason for my gruffness. We needed to see if you were an Inviver, and you have shown us that your healing abilities are far stronger than we could have ever imagined."

Kaie's eyes widened as she realized what the king was saying, her mind whirling at the announcement she was an Inviver. She looked over to Tristen, her lips widening into a smile. He returned the smile, his eyes reflecting the confidence and belief he had in her. The king began to speak again, so she turned her attention back to his words.

"Now that we have all that out of the way, we have another matter at hand. I will let Maeve explain everything to you."

An old woman, possibly the oldest Kaie had ever seen, stood up and walked towards her with the help of an oak cane. She motioned for Kaie to follow her out of the throne room. "We need somewhere more private to talk," she explained.

Kaie followed, but glanced back to everyone else and saw them dispersing. She took one last look at Prince Achaius and still could not believe that he seemed so healthy, remembering how sickly he'd looked when she'd arrived. Seeing her look back, he gave her a nod and a chilly smile. Confused by his reaction, she turned and followed Maeve out of the room, her attention back to the woman in front of her.

Maeve led Kaie outside, where it was warm and sunny. They walked around to the garden, filled with beautiful, blooming flowers. When they came upon a bench, Maeve sat and motioned for Kaie to sit next to her.

Looking out at the roses, Maeve began to speak. "You must have many questions, I am sure," she said. "I am the leader of all the Invivers of Galicia, so it falls to me to explain everything to you. Where do you want to start?"

"How do you know if I am an Inviver?" Kaie was still doubtful, but was willing to hear what Maeve had to say. "I'm only sixteen." The Invivers she'd heard about were all well into their adulthood when their power manifested.

"You are an Inviver from birth, it just takes time for the power to reveal itself. And sometimes it's even longer before someone recognizes their abilities. My powers revealed themselves at seventeen, making me the youngest Inviver in history, but now you hold that title. It's a great honor to be added to our ranks."

"How did you find out about me?"

"It started when we began to hear stories about your abilities—your mentor talked about you a lot when she visited the capital, and her words eventually reached our ears. When the prince got sick, it seemed like the perfect opportunity to test you. Once you Cured him, there was no doubt for me or for any of the other Invivers that you are one of us."

Maeve could tell Kaie was still skeptical. She knew she had to ease the young Inviver into things, but she knew without a doubt that the girl was one of them.

"How could you tell?" Kaie was growing increasingly confused.

"You Cured him," Maeve said, not quite sure where the disconnect was happening.

"And how did I do that?" Kaie was now lost, the mechanics of Curing unknown to her.

Maeve's eyes widened, realizing that Kaie did not know anything about Curing. "When someone is injured, an Inviver is able to transfer some of their energy into that person, which forces their body to heal itself. Since Achaius was dying, you were able to give up some of your energy to replenish his." Maeve paused, then continued, "Well, you gave him more energy than you should have, so you fainted. Normally, you would feel weak or lightheaded if you had given a smaller amount, which you have probably experienced when you were working on other patients. Now that you know what you are, you will be able to better control the energy you give. It shouldn't explode like that again."

Kaie thought back to before she passed out, and remembered the flash of light. "What was that light that appeared?" she asked.

"When Invivers Cure others, sometimes it takes the form of light if you use a lot of energy. What you did was no easy feat. You have the ability to become one of the most powerful Invivers in history."

Kaie remained silent for several moments, trying to gather her thoughts. She immediately thought of her mother. "Can Curing work on illnesses too? Not just injuries?" She was anxious about the answer. What if she had been able to Cure her mother this whole time?

Maeve clicked her tongue. "Illnesses are a lot different than injuries," she said. "In some cases, you can Cure a sickness, but it depends on how severe it is and what bodily systems are affected. Injuries are usually straightforward and easier to figure out where to Cure. Since illness can be caused by many things, it takes more energy and effort to Cure, if you can at all. Some illnesses are too big for us to handle, and the best we can do is help alleviate some of the symptoms, but even then, it's only a temporary fix. Curing is not an answer to everything." The Inviver paused, knowing why Kaie was asking. "You would not be able to Cure your mother's sickness."

"Oh."

Hearing the answer, Kaie felt a rush of relief, then immediately felt guilty. It would have been better if her mother's illness was completely curable by her newfound abilities, but the fact that it was not and she had not figured out her powers sooner made her feel better. She thought back to the times her mother had coughing fits and whenever she touched her, the coughing had subsided considerably. But they always came back.

"Sometimes people would come visit with serious injuries and I wouldn't have to do much before they got a lot better," Kaie said slowly, remembering previous patients. "It never seemed like the amount of help I did matched their recovery. Do you think that was me Curing them?"

Maeve nodded with a smile, glad that Kaie was a quick learner. "Yes, those were the instances your mentor spoke of that caught our attention," she said. "With training, you can learn how to properly harness your powers."

"But there aren't any Invivers back home for me to learn from." Kaie was being deliberately obtuse, seeing where the conversation was headed.

The old woman shook her head, knowing what Kaie was doing. "You may pretend to be ignorant, but I think we both know what I mean," she said. "Now that you know you are an Inviver, you have a choice to make: stay and train with me, or return home. If you stay to train, I can show you how to better use your powers, to help you better control your energy and hopefully increase your limits. Without proper instruction and usage, your powers would eventually dwindle and disappear." Maeve looked into Kaie's eyes, trying to impart the seriousness of her next words. "Unlocking your potential as an Inviver is a wonderful gift. It will be lonely for you at first, but you learn to fight past that. We are at war, and we need many more Invivers than we have right now." She sighed heavily. "We need you."

Kaie's heart thundered at Maeve's words and thought back to her family. She had been busy these past weeks with Prince Achaius's recovery, but she still found herself missing them. She ached to give Shayla a hug and to see her father again. She wanted to see if she could Cure her mother. Despite Maeve saying it would not work, she had also said Kaie had the potential to be one of the greatest Invivers. Maybe Kaie could surpass the known limits.

"I'm not sure what to do," she admitted. "I recognize that this is an amazing opportunity to grow my skills, but I do miss my family."

"You do have the option to train with us for a while, and then if you want to, you can go home. I will warn you that there will come a point of no return. Once you reach this point, if you decide to continue, there is no turning back."

"What do you mean by that?"

"You would have to stay to complete your training and go to the front lines until the war is over," Maeve said. "You wouldn't be able to see your family until then."

"I can't visit them? Couldn't they come live in the capital?" Kaie asked, trying to hold back the sudden grip of panic. No one knew when the war would end; it could be years until she saw her family again. From her father's letters, she knew that the Scrians had initiated the conflict and the Galician soldiers were holding their invasion at bay. But he'd never mentioned *why* they had attacked.

Maeve shook her head. "It is better to not deal with the distraction of family," she said. "The king would prefer to force you into training regardless of your opinions, but I pushed to give you the choice to learn from me."

"Would you say that leaving your life behind was worth it?" Kaie was still mulling things over, overcome by the huge decision in front of her. Even the hope of Curing her mother would make the time away from her family worth it. She felt a rush of gratitude that Maeve fought for her to choose her path forward.

Maeve nodded. "Yes. It was absolutely worth everything I left behind, even though it wasn't much. I am glad that I didn't give up when I got discouraged. It's a difficult life, but very rewarding when you are out there Curing others. When you complete your training, we will need you to go to the Carthan Valley, where the main siege is occurring, and you won't be able to return home until the war is over. We are currently at a stalemate with the Scrian forces."

Kaie thought for a few moments. "I would like to do the trial period, to see if I'm cut out for this type of work," she said, trying to ignore the feelings of homesickness that suddenly filled her. She reminded herself that this was for her family.

A part of her, deep down, felt a little guilty at the excitement she also felt. At last, she was going to have a formal education centered around helping others—Syane's teachings, while informative, were still guided by Kaie's eagerness to learn rather than an official curriculum. Kaie would now have proper guidance rather than figuring out everything for herself. Not to mention, the idea of Curing held its own intrigue.

Maeve smiled and stood up, waving for Kaie to follow her back into the palace. When they arrived at the throne room door, Maeve gestured for Kaie to enter.

"You must tell the king of your decision—he's very invested in you and your education. I will go talk with the other Invivers about your trial period. We'll start your training soon."

With that, she left Kaie in front of the doors, alone. After a deep breath, Kaie pushed them open and entered the room. The crowd that was previously present had thinned considerably. The only people left were the king and his sons. She walked forward and curtsied once more, the magnitude of everything starting to weigh on her.

"Have you made a decision?" the king asked. Though he was trying to hide it, Kaie could tell that he was eagerly awaiting what she would say.

"I'm still mulling things over, but Maeve was kind enough to let me have a trial period for training," Kaie said. "After that, I'll decide if I will continue or not."

The king frowned at her response. "That wasn't what we talked about," he muttered, drumming his fingers on the throne. "Just be sure that you make your decision soon. We need to know if we can count on you as another Inviver to help with the war effort or not."

Kaie nodded. "I will let you know as soon as I make a decision." Her stomach grumbled so loudly that it echoed through the throne room. "I guess I must be hungry," she said sheepishly. She suddenly realized that she had no idea what happened after she had Cured the prince. "How long was I unconscious for? It seems like I haven't eaten for a while."

The king knew exactly why she was asking—Tristen had filled him in that morning on the nighttime encounter. "You were unconscious for a week," he said matter-of-factly.

The answer flabbergasted Kaie—she never had imagined such a long amount of time. Mouth agape, she managed to say, "Thank you."

She turned to leave, trying to act as calm as possible, her ears filled with a rushing sound. The ground swam in front of her and she walked on unsteady feet out of the room. Paired with all the information she'd received so far, this news pushed her emotions over the edge.

Everyone knew that the answer stunned her, and once the doors closed behind her, the king motioned for one of his sons to follow and make sure she was fine. Today, a lot of information had been dumped on her. It was enough to make anyone, let alone a young girl, feel overwhelmed.

"I'll go," Tristen said, immediately heading towards the door.

Achaius moved to follow his brother, wanting to see Kaie up close for himself.

Tristen stopped and held up a hand. "You should stay here, you might overwhelm her," he countered. Tristen was not sure how Kaie would react to Achaius at the moment. He could tell she was distraught when she left the room and already had a lot on her mind.

"She has already seen me," Achaius said, crossing his arms.

"She's been through a lot," Tristen argued.

"You both can go," the king said, shaking his head at the two of them. "She'll be fine."

Looking at each other, the two brothers nodded and walked into the hallway together. They looked around for Kaie, but were unable to find her immediately. Then Tristen spotted her, sitting in a chair in a nearby corner with her head in her hands.

"There she is," he said, walking over.

Kaie's shoulders were shaking. The sounds of soft sobs reached them, and both brothers became alarmed. They approached her cautiously.

"Kaie, what's wrong?" Tristen asked, his voice filled with concern.

She lifted her tearstained face. "It's a lot to take in," she said. "First, I find out I'm an Inviver, then I'm expected to go to war... And I didn't even know that I was out that long." Once more, she collapsed into sobs. "I'm just one person, Tristen. How is it so much is expected of me so soon?"

"It's all going to be okay," Tristen said calmly, moving to sit next to her. His presence brought her an overwhelming sense of comfort. "You just need to take it one day at a time."

Kaie took a deep breath, trying to calm down. "I just... I saw the way your father and Maeve looked at me. They have high expectations. And even without all that, it's scary to think that just from Curing someone, I could be indisposed for a week."

"See? This is why I didn't want to tell you last night. I was afraid of your reaction." Tristen took out a handkerchief and handed it to her.

"But you still should have told me." Tears continued to stream down her face as she wiped them. The ache in her chest began to intensify and she held back a sob.

"I didn't want to worry you," Tristen said kindly. "You still needed to concentrate on getting better. I'm sure that as you train, the limits of what you can Cure will expand, and this amount of Curing won't have the same effect on you again."

Suddenly, Kaie became angry. Jumping up, she faced Tristen and said accusingly, "You had no right to keep that information from me. It's my responsibility to decide how I deal with the information, not yours. You should have told me last night. This is all your fault."

"My father wanted to be the one to tell you. I was not supposed to say anything," Tristen said delicately. Truth be told, he did not understand the whole reason behind keeping her in the dark, only that his father had ordered it.

Remembering that the king had orchestrated everything, Kaie's anger found a new target. "He had no right to do that!" she said, clenching her fists.

"He's the king. He has every right to do whatever he wants," Tristen said softly. He took one of her hands and squeezed it gently. Kaie looked at him and unclenched the fist, taking his hand in hers. "You'll find that he likes to do things his way and you won't always understand why. But despite whatever schemes he has going on, you have people in your corner."

Kaie's anger faded away as quickly as it had begun, feeling as if all her energy had been sapped. Her heightened emotions and adrenaline dissipated, leaving a deep exhaustion in their wake. She returned to her seat.

"You didn't think I could handle it?" she asked, her voice heartbroken.

"Based on your reaction just now, I would say you didn't handle it too well," Tristen admitted, giving her a small smile.

"I'm sorry." Kaie looked at Tristen ruefully. "I'm upset at how long I've been away from my family. And it's all so much information to take in. I've been kept in the dark about so many things."

Tristen gave her a gentle hug, one that she welcomed. "It's all right. You've been through a lot this past month and it hasn't been easy for you." He suddenly remembered something. "There is someone who has been wondering where you've been this past week. He has been filled in on what has happened, but he has missed you terribly."

Kaie knew exactly who he was talking about. "I almost forgot about Lorne! I promised him that I would look at his leg after..." She fell silent as she realized Prince Achaius was present. Her cheeks flushed—she was still unsure how to act around him. With Tristen, she could let her guard down, but she had not really interacted with the younger prince to know how to behave. And already, she'd made herself look like a fool with her outburst.

"Let's not keep him waiting then," Prince Achaius said nonchalantly, attempting to cover up her obvious discomfort.

He led the way to the captain's room. After knocking, he opened the door and let Kaie in. Lorne was propped up in bed and his face lit up as soon as he saw his visitor.

Kaie ran over to the bed and gave Lorne a hug as best she could.

"I've missed you," he said as he returned her hug.

"I've been... preoccupied this past week," she said.

"So I've heard. You're an Inviver now, huh?" he asked, an eyebrow raised.

"Apparently. Not everything is clear to me, but that's what I've been told." She fidgeted with the frayed edge of the blanket and looked down at his broken leg. "I could even Cure your leg now, or at least I hope I can. Maeve said I should be able to control my powers a little better." Kaie brightened at the idea of Curing him and making him whole again. The tiredness she felt earlier weighed on her, but she wanted to heal the captain.

"You shouldn't strain yourself. You've been out for a while," Lorne said. "It sounds like you've woken up recently, based on what I've heard."

"That's a pretty stupid idea," Prince Achaius said, and Kaie turned to look at him. He crossed his arms, a disdainful expression upon his face. "Curing him after you've just woken up? You don't have all your strength back and you haven't even started your proper training yet."

Kaie's mouth dropped open at his words, shocked that he was being so rude. She'd saved him and this was his thanks?

"Achaius, mind your manners!" Tristen hissed before turning to Kaie. "While Achaius could have phrased that better, he's right. You shouldn't do anything until you've recuperated some more and received training." He took a step forward, holding up his hands to stop her. He knew enough to know that if she collapsed again so soon after waking up, his father would be furious.

"I'm fine," Kaie protested. "Besides, it's my fault he's hurt anyway. I need to fix what I've caused. It shouldn't take up too much energy anyhow."

"Kaie, don't waste your energy on me. Save it for your recovery," Lorne said sternly.

Her head whipped back towards him. "No! I'm going to fix it," she said firmly, a stubborn frown on her face. Though she did not know how to harness her powers, she had done it before and was determined to do it again.

"Kaie..." Lorne was not sure what else to say to dissuade her. The look she gave him reminded him of his daughter.

Despite his protests, Kaie put her hand on Lorne's leg, right where the broken bone was located. Now that she had awakened her powers, she could feel an undercurrent of energy flowing through her. She took a deep breath in concentration, and as she exhaled, energy released from her hands through his leg. She felt her strength begin to leave her, and her arms sagged as Lorne's leg began to heal.

Lorne could feel her energy seep into him, the bone reconnecting itself. As the light began to dim, he sighed as if a great weight had been lifted.

Kaie took her hands away when black dots spotted her vision, and Tristen managed to catch her as she staggered away from the bed, helping her sit down in a nearby chair.

Kaie was barely able to stay conscious as Lorne swung his legs off the bed and tested his newly Cured leg. After a couple of tries, he was able to stand and walk around the room. Then he came to Kaie and knelt in front of her. He was beaming with pride, but there was an air of worry in his expression.

"You shouldn't have taken that risk. Look at how weak you are now," he said.

"It was worth it." She smiled, satisfied by her accomplishment. Despite the exhaustion creeping into her limbs, there was also a feeling of pride.

Her stomach began to gurgle again, notifying the room that it was hungry.

"Sounds like you need to eat," Tristen said. "Do you think you can make it all the way to the kitchen?"

Kaie nodded, and Lorne helped her up. The group walked slowly, keeping to Kaie's labored pace as she forced herself to remain conscious. Lorne guided Kaie to the dining room, where she collapsed into a chair with a sigh of relief. He sat next to her while Prince Achaius slouched in a corner, keeping an eye on the events in front of him. Even though he did not seem to like her, the younger prince obviously did not want to miss out on what was going on. Kaie was surprised that he did not gloat on the way to the dining room that she had overdone it.

While Lorne was getting her settled, Tristen went to the kitchen to give the servants directions on what to make her. When he returned, the older prince took a seat opposite her.

More quickly than Kaie thought possible, her food came out: a warm, steaming bowl of chicken broth.

"I thought it would be best to start you out with something light," Tristen explained, seeing her brow crease in disappointment at the simple meal.

She tried to pick up the spoon, but was so weak from Curing that it clattered back onto the plate loudly. "Sorry," she mumbled, her face heating in embarrassment. She noticed Prince Achaius rolling his eyes, and ducked her head in shame. Why did he have to be present for her humiliation?

"It's quite all right," Lorne said as he picked the spoon up and began to feed her.

"I can do it myself," Kaie protested, despite her prior attempt proving otherwise.

Lorne gave her a stern look, but his eyes were lighthearted enough that Kaie knew he was just trying to help. "You're too weak to do anything right now. After you eat, you're going straight to bed."

Realizing that she would never make it through the soup by herself, Kaie nodded and allowed Lorne to feed her. Halfway through the meal, her exhaustion overcame her and she fell asleep. Before her bobbing head could fall into the hot soup, Tristen safely maneuvered the bowl out of her way. All of them exchanged glances with each other and Achaius let out a sound of disapproval.

"I'll take her back to her room," Lorne said as he gently picked her up. "You two should go talk to your father. I'll meet you in a few minutes."

"What does he need us for?" Achaius said, his tone argumentative.

"He didn't ask to see us," Tristen added, not wanting to go see his father. Most meetings with him were fairly unpleasant.

Lorne looked at the two princes and knew from their expressions that neither of them were looking forward to seeing the king. "No, but I'm guessing he will want to talk to all of us regarding Kaie's training. And yes, I do mean *all* of us," he added, seeing Achaius open his mouth in protest. "I'll meet you there."

CHAPTER 9

On the way to their father's quarters, Achaius kept up his petulant attitude.

"It was such a stupid thing to do," he muttered under his breath.

Tristen gave his brother an exasperated look. "Knock it off. She's the only Inviver I've ever heard of who could Cure a broken bone so soon after her first bout of Curing and not pass out immediately after."

"There are the other Invivers who can Cure too," Achaius pointed out.

"They're all so old that what she's been through would have them in a coma for months," Tristen said evenly.

"But Maeve's really good," Achaius said defensively, a frown crossing his face.

"In case you haven't noticed, Maeve is no spring chicken. She'd be out of commission for the whole week doing what Kaie just did."

"Well, Kaie's out for the rest of the day," the youngest prince said stubbornly.

"She's still recovering from Curing you. You might be nice enough to cut her some slack. She did save your life after all," Tristen said. He did not understand why Achaius was so set on being insolent.

"*You* don't cut me any slack," Achaius retorted, his scowl deepening.

"You've never Cured anyone before. You don't know what it's like," Tristen said patiently, trying to keep a lid on his growing irritation. He knew he had to keep a calm demeanor as the eldest and not let his brother get under his skin.

"Neither do you," Achaius countered.

"That's true, but you didn't seem to notice how tired she was after she Cured Lorne." Tristen's face told of how weary he was growing of the conversation.

"I did notice, but I just don't see why she bothers to push herself further when she's already worn out," Achaius said with a sneer on his face.

"She's trying to find and understand her limits. With any luck, she'll be able to expand them. Now this little talk is over." Tristen's tone conveyed he was finished with the conversation and would not be speaking any more on the subject.

When they reached their father's study, Achaius's face shifted into a deeper sulk. After a moment of hesitation, mentally preparing for the upcoming conversation, Tristen nodded to the guards, who pushed the doors open. Straightening his shoulders, he entered with Achaius trailing behind.

King Torin sat behind an ornate desk that matched the décor of the throne room. Every piece of furniture in the room had been handcrafted with emerald and gold accents, the colors of the family crest. Colorful tapestries hung on the walls, and candlelit sconces illuminated the room. In front of the desk were two couches and a table. Torin was reading a report from his generals on how the war was progressing. By the look on his face, the news was not good, and Tristen's heart sank.

The king looked up as his sons entered the room. "What do you want?" he growled.

"I take it we aren't doing so well?" Tristen asked, choosing to ignore his father's tone as he sat down. He was only here at Lorne's request and because he cared about Kaie's future—that was all. It was not out of any loyalty to his father that he was here right now.

"No, we're not. We need ten times more Invivers than we have, but if Kaie starts her training soon then we may be able to turn the tables. Maeve said she could be one of the best in history," Torin informed his sons, his eyes gleaming at the possibility. "If she's as powerful as Maeve suspects, that could change everything."

"We came to talk about her training. Sir Shalane will be here any minute." Tristen's voice was clipped.

"I'm right here, Your Majesty." Lorne's voice came from behind them as he walked into the room. He bowed as he came to stand in front of the king.

"How's Kaie?" Tristen asked. Achaius stood off to the side, barely inside the door, not willing to step a foot further into the room.

"She's fast asleep. Farin will come get us if she wakes before morning," Lorne said. He had made sure Kaie was well taken care of before leaving her in Farin's care.

King Torin looked Lorne up and down. "I see you're all better," he observed. "No doubt the girl Cured you and then wore herself out in the process."

Lorne nodded at his words.

"Why didn't you do anything to stop it?"

"Father, we tried, but she was too stubborn. She felt responsible for Lorne's injury and felt like she needed to fix what she'd caused," Tristen explained. A surge of anger filled him as he could tell by his father's face that the older man was going to be critical of Kaie.

"Such a foolish thing to do," the king muttered under his breath.

Tristen clenched his jaw to keep from bursting out.

"That's what I said!" Achaius said indignantly, a glow of victory in his eyes. He took a few steps forward, thinking he'd found an ally in his father.

"You *what*?" Torin's face filled with a shadow of anger.

"I told her that it was ludicrous to Cure Lorne when she was still recuperating." Achaius missed the warning signs of his father's anger and smiled smugly, glad that his father agreed with his earlier sentiments.

Tristen could see the storm brewing, having had years to learn the way his father's jaw ticked, an expression that only appeared when he was extremely angry.

The king stood, his face bright red in anger. "You will *not* meddle in this. Even if it was foolish, it is not your place to tell her so. It is up to Maeve or another Inviver to tell her these things. Do you understand?" he shouted.

"Yes, but I don't see what the big deal is," Achaius grumbled, pouting that he had been harshly scolded. He retreated back to his spot by the door.

"If you keep doing this, she'll be thinking of your opinion every time she's about to Cure someone and that would be detrimental to her progress. If you keep this up, you will be forbidden from continuing your healing lessons." A sudden silence followed the king's ultimatum.

After a couple moments, Achaius broke the quiet. "But I need those lessons! How else am I supposed to learn?"

"Figure it out yourself. Right now, we have more pressing matters at hand. Has anyone summoned Maeve? She needs to be here to discuss Kaie's training." Torin sat back down, rubbing his forehead in frustration.

"I asked one of the Invivers to fetch her," Lorne said. Ever the soldier, he was always thinking two steps ahead of what needed to be done.

As soon as the words left his mouth, Maeve walked in the room and bowed her head towards the king in respect. "Greetings, Your Majesty." She came to sit next to Tristen, letting out a sigh as she sat down. Her eyes flickered to Lorne, widening slightly upon seeing him standing, and pursed her lips.

"Your newest student will need to learn when an injury is beyond her limits," King Torin said.

"So I see," Maeve said in a clipped tone. "Her education is going to be of the utmost importance to winning the war. With enough instruction and practice, I think she'd be able to Cure a great many soldiers in one sitting."

"What do you have in mind for her training?" Lorne asked.

Tristen could tell by the way the older man was shifting on his feet that he wanted to take the focus away from Kaie Curing him.

"I will be starting her off slowly, to make sure she understands what she's getting herself into. But I can't reveal too many secrets to her until she decides to go through with her training. We can review the things she already knows, see how her education has been so far, and then right before she has to make her decision, we'll take her to the Mists. After that, she'll want to train with us. No Inviver can resist the Mists—they're too enticing and hold too many secrets." Maeve's eyes glinted at the possibilities of what the future could hold.

"Is there anything we can do to speed up her training?" the king asked, impatient with the amount of time everything would take. If the report he had on his desk was any indication, they needed help sooner rather than later.

Maeve thought for a moment. "She should probably learn to fight, as it will help her expand her limits. The more strength and endurance she has, the more she'll be able to Cure."

"Is learning to fight wholly necessary?" Tristen asked, a note of concern in his voice. He knew going to the front lines was dangerous, but thinking about Kaie fighting against the Scrian forces sent a shiver down his spine.

"We also sometimes get attacked during battle, so she'll need to learn how to defend herself if she'll eventually be sent to the front." Maeve's voice was sharp.

"I can teach her, but I'll need some people to help her practice. Raven and Rosse Swain should be able to assist," Lorne said musingly. What Maeve was saying was true—if Kaie was going to be sent where there was much fighting, it would be better if she knew how to defend herself.

"Then it's decided," the king said. "Kaie will practice with Maeve in the mornings and train with Lorne in the afternoons. The evenings will be her own and she can do whatever she likes. It would probably be better to not start her out too hard too quickly. Achaius," he directed the conversation to his youngest son, "you will train with Maeve and Kaie to continue your studies. They shouldn't be covering anything outside of what you can do right now. Even if you aren't an Inviver, this is still valuable information you should learn."

"But I don't want to train with Kaie!" Achaius wailed.

Tristen let out a small chuckle at his brother's childish behavior.

"You either train with Kaie or you don't continue with your education. It's your choice. Remember, if you say anything to discourage her, your studies will be discontinued immediately. Maeve will be giving me a report each week on your behavior." Torin turned and directed the conversation back to Lorne, effectively dismissing Achaius. "Does she have a sword to practice with?"

"As far as I know, she does not," Lorne answered. "But she can use one of the practice ones."

The king frowned slightly. "If she is truly going to be sent to Carthan Valley then we'll need to fix that—I will not have a future Inviver sent off with a mediocre weapon. Can you make sure she has a sword made for her?"

Lorne nodded. "I'll talk with the blacksmiths so they can get her measurements. She'll just need to use one of the smaller practice ones for a while."

The king nodded. "I think we have everything settled so all we must do is wait for Kaie to wake up. Once she becomes a fully trained Inviver, we can send her to Carthan Valley and our position in this war should change. We might have a chance after all." With that, the king settled back into his chair, signaling that the meeting was over.

Everyone started to leave.

"I hope she's up to this. She has very high expectations set upon her shoulders," Tristen whispered to Lorne. The journey ahead was a heavy weight to bear.

Lorne smiled at the younger prince's concern. "She can do it, I have no doubt. Kaie has enough power that she'll probably give us all a run for our money."

"Kaie has quite the promising start as an Inviver," Maeve agreed. "I'm sure she'll complete her training in record time."

CHAPTER 10

The next morning, Kaie woke up, confused by her surroundings. The last thing she remembered was eating in the dining room, and she had no recollection of how she'd ended up in her own room. She got up, determined to find out what had happened. After dressing herself in a simple blue gown, she left the room, but was stopped by Farin, who was waiting outside the door.

"Wait here," Farin said. "I need to go get Sir Shalane."

After several minutes, Lorne came sprinting through the hallways.

"Why did I have to wait for you to come?" Kaie asked in confusion.

"Sorry I took so long," Lorne gasped, trying to catch his breath. "I was outside training new recruits and we didn't know when you'd wake up." He took a couple more moments to get his heart rate down to a normal pace before speaking once more. "We need to talk about your training. The king has outlined what your schedule will look like during your stay here. He wants Maeve to explain everything. Please follow me."

Soon, they arrived at the king's study, and Kaie was in awe of how regal it was.

The king sat behind his desk, and looked up as she entered. "The guest of honor has arrived," he said dryly. "I believe Sir Shalane has informed you of the purpose of this meeting?"

Kaie nodded at his words, her eyes still darting around the room, taking in the opulence.

"Maeve will explain everything."

Maeve was standing in the corner of the room, but she had been so quiet and unassuming that Kaie had not noticed her at first. "We have many details to discuss," she explained to Kaie. "Since you won't be training full time, I will teach you in the morning and you will train with Sir Shalane in the afternoons."

"What will I be doing with Lorne?" Kaie was not sure how he fit into the picture.

"He will be teaching you to fight," Maeve answered.

"Why?" Kaie asked. She wanted to spend her time studying. The sooner she finished, the sooner she could go home.

"We need you to be stronger than you are now. You're a skinny thing," Maeve said as she pinched Kaie's arm to prove the girl did not have much muscle. "You will be learning how to fight properly with a sword, and how to use a bow and arrow. This is not open for discussion," she added, seeing Kaie open her mouth.

Lorne stepped in. "Through my training, we'll be expanding the limits of what you can Cure," he said.

"How?" Kaie asked.

"With physical training, your strength will grow, and when that happens, your limits will start to increase. You'll be able to Cure more," Maeve explained.

"I think I get it. When do we start?" Kaie asked, eager to begin.

"As soon as you change clothes. A pretty dress like that is not suitable for training. Change into something more like what you wore when you arrived," Maeve said. "When you're finished, meet me near the garden. The guards will be able to tell you where that is if you get lost."

Kaie headed back to her room, where she changed into her tunic and trousers. They felt like an old friend, a second skin. Her whole body relaxed, everything feeling just like it used to—everything except that her family was not there. She wished they could be there to celebrate the moment with her, that she was an Inviver. Her mother and Shayla would have been busy in the kitchen baking one of her favorite desserts while her father would congratulate her on her newfound abilities, then share stories from his time on the battlefield. Trying to overcome the wave of sadness that overwhelmed her, Kaie sat on the bed for a moment.

Suddenly, she remembered that her mother left something for her in her pack. Since arriving at the palace, she'd had barely any time to do as she pleased. Taking a couple moments for herself, she rushed over to the closet and pulled out her rucksack. Digging to the bottom of it, her hand closed on the small package that her mother had tucked away.

Kaie pulled out her hand and opened the gift to see that lying inside was a small, leaf-shaped locket. Her eyes teared up as she realized the significance of her mother's gift. She had always admired the locket since she was a little girl, one of the few things in her mother's very small collection of jewelry. It was the one piece she had always wished was hers, and now it was.

As she reached to put it on, she noticed a piece of paper stuck inside the box. Puzzled, she pulled it out and unfolded it, realizing that it was a letter in her mother's handwriting. Her heart beating loudly, she began to read.

My Dearest Kaie,

I know this will not be the easiest journey for you, but you must prevail. Remember that your father, sister, and I will love you no matter what happens. I cannot even begin to express how proud I am of you.

Hopefully this token will remind you of us and our love for you. There are so many things that I should have told you when you were younger, but now there is no time. All I will say is this: I know what you are. I have known since you first started healing. Hopefully, at the palace, the Invivers have explained more, but know that you have a gift and you must use it to help others and us to win the war—the Scrians will tear this country to the ground if they succeed. This may be confusing for you right now, but remember that your family will always be here to support you when you need it.

Help can be found in the least likely places. No matter how it seems, hope is never lost, not if you look for it hard enough. I know this won't be the easiest path, but there will be people to help share your burdens. If you ever feel homesick, just read this letter and it will hopefully remind you of our unconditional love for you.

With all my love,

Mother

After reading the heartfelt letter, Kaie folded it back up and wiped the tears away from her eyes. Slowly, she opened the locket to see two locks of hair inside—Shayla's and her mother's. Another tear escaped as she closed the locket and put the letter back in the box, closing it.

Remembering that she had a lesson to attend, Kaie fastened the locket around her neck and left in a rush. After making a couple of wrong turns, she finally arrived at the side door. After asking the pair of burly guards at the door where she needed to go, she stepped out into the dazzling sunlight. It blinded her for a moment, but her eyes quickly adjusted.

Kaie went around the side of the castle and spotted the herb garden, filled with numerous healing plants that she recognized. Prince Achaius was standing near an empty garden plot, a scowl on his face when their eyes met. To try and ignore him, Kaie looked around the grounds. Lorne was practicing with a group of soldiers. She watched them for a while, weaving in and out of different routines, their swords a blur of metal in the sun. Achaius cleared his throat to try and get her attention, but Kaie ignored him, caught up in the exciting, dangerous dance.

Achaius cleared his throat again. When this did not work, he called to her. "Kaie, I... um." He trailed off as she gave him a scornful look. "I wanted to apologize for yesterday," he said in a rush.

Tristen had lectured him last night on his behavior and he wanted their training to go well. If she complained, his father might decide to remove him from lessons even if he was on his best behavior.

"What I said was completely out of line. I don't want us to start out on the wrong foot since we're going to be training together."

"We're what?" she said incredulously. Never would she have thought that her Inviver training would include Achaius.

"We're both learning from Maeve together. Didn't my father tell you?" he asked.

"No, all he said was I'm training with Maeve in the morning and with Lorne in the afternoon. Are you an Inviver too?" she asked. Excitement crept into her voice at the thought of training with another Inviver her age. Even if it was Prince Achaius.

"Well, I... uh... No. No, I'm not," he said, blushing from embarrassment. He clenched his fists. He did not like being reminded of how powerless he was.

"Then how can these lessons be of any help to you if they're for Invivers?"

"First, we'll be learning stuff that I can do. Then, if you decide to continue with your training and you start to learn more about Curing, I'm going to continue with lessons on my own." He looked down and kicked a small rock.

"Oh." This new information surprised her. The idea of sharing lessons with Prince Achaius was not a pleasant one for Kaie. His attitude so far had not been that welcoming and she was not sure how she was going to survive lessons if he was to learn with her.

Before the conversation could get any more awkward, Maeve appeared. "Enough chitchat. We have work to do."

When Kaie and Achaius moved to stand on either side of her, Maeve explained what some of the different plants could be used for. "Remember, in a battle, if a soldier gets wounded, to spread some milfoil paste around on the wound. It's important to keep your head during these times. It can be very tricky to figure out what type of plant or herb a soldier needs during a battle. There's not much time to dillydally. Every second counts."

She continued on for a while longer about different plants, information Kaie already knew. "We need to bulk up our medicinal supply. It's important not to run out, even if we have Invivers. Your job today is to plant these seeds about an inch apart. Around midday, Kaie, you can head over to Lorne to begin your training. I will be checking on you both periodically, so I better see some progress." With that, she left them to plant.

The work was difficult. After a couple hours, both Kaie and Achaius ached from the effort of being hunched over in the glaring sun and using muscles that were not often utilized. Maeve checked in on them occasionally, giving direction from time to time. After a couple more hours, Kaie tried to break the silence.

"So... how did you become interested in Curing?" she asked awkwardly.

"It's always been something that intrigued me," he said. "Being able to help anyone with my own power, that would be fantastic. But no matter how much I study, I will never become an Inviver." There was a note of bitterness in his voice.

"There's still a lot you can do with plants and medicine," Kaie said, finally understanding where his resentment was stemming from.

"It's not the same," Achaius said, scowling at the seedling he was planting. "You and I both know it."

Kaie was stunned into silence at his response and turned back to her own seeds.

At that point, Lorne came over. "Sorry to steal your planting buddy, Prince Achaius, but Kaie needs to work with me for now."

"It's fine. I can manage on my own." Achaius continued to focus on planting, ignoring Kaie.

Lorne led Kaie over to the spot where he was practicing with his new recruits. "I just want to get a general idea of your existing skills," he said. "I want to see what your father has already taught you and what we need to improve on."

"All right, but I'm not that good," she said uncertainly. She could feel the eyes of the other soldiers on her, curious as to what she could do.

"I understand," Lorne said. "But don't worry about that. That's why you're getting lessons—to be better than you already are. Go ahead and pick out one of the swords from the rack. We'll be getting a custom one made for you eventually."

Kaie walked over to the nearby rack of swords and picked one out, weighing it in her hand. It was off balance, so she put it back to select another one. This one felt fine, and she figured it would have to do.

Finally ready, she turned to face Lorne. Doing her best to ignore the other men watching her, she crouched in a ready position. Almost in a blur, Lorne lunged at her. Barely able to dodge his attack, she somehow managed to bring her sword up to meet his.

The clang of metal on metal was enough to grab everyone's attention on the grounds. They all turned to watch as a sixteen-year-old girl attempted to defend herself against one of the best sword masters in the castle. She tried to fend him off, though she could tell he was going easy on her, trying to test her defenses and get an idea of her skill set. Although her father had taught her some form of defense, she felt out of sorts going up against Lorne. The blade she was holding felt awkward and stiff in her hand.

Soon enough, Kaie's arm started to feel like lead from fighting, the clanging of the swords reverberating up to her shoulder. Sweat dripped down her face and she knew that her arm would give out soon. She could tell what Lorne's next move was going to be, but she was too tired to bother to try stopping him.

Lorne could see in Kaie's eyes that she had given up, so he moved in for the final blow. He hooked his sword under hers and sent it spinning out of her grip. It landed harmlessly in the grass nearby. Kaie was panting, trying to catch her breath, but Lorne looked as if he had barely broken a sweat.

"Good job, Kaie," Lorne congratulated her. "You did very well. Your father has set you up with good foundational work."

Kaie rubbed her arm, trying to return the feeling back to it. "I didn't stand a chance against you," she said, feeling a little discouraged.

Lorne came up and patted her on the back. "You have a very good start," he encouraged her. "We just need to work on building up your muscles."

"You're so much bigger and stronger than me. I'll never be able to beat you."

Lorne looked at her, a grin spreading across his face. "Rosse!" he called out to the giant man who was running the soldiers through some exercises. "Come here."

The man jogged, an easy smile on his face. "Very nice to see you again, my lady," he said with a bow.

Kaie nodded.

"You and I are going to spar," Lorne said. "I will be teaching Kaie that size and strength don't mean everything in a fight."

Rosse laughed and took out his broadsword. "Very well," he said, giving Kaie a wink.

Kaie took several steps back as the two men circled each other, the recruits coming to watch as well. Lorne's stance was loose, but she could tell he was waiting for Rosse to make the first move.

The giant lunged with a yell, bringing his broadsword down. Lorne met his sword with a clang and shifted his weight so the attack went to his left. Quickly, he spun, aiming for Rosse's left, but the big man moved to block. When Rosse attacked again, Lorne went for the base of his broadsword and pushed Rosse's weight off kilter. When the man stumbled slightly, Lorne set off a barrage of attacks, pinpointed to keep Rosse off balance. As Rosse moved to get back on the offensive, Lorne used well-placed jabs to keep him defending himself. After several minutes of this, he finally spun around Rosse and held his sword to his back.

With a sigh, Rosse dropped his broadsword. "You win," he said with chagrin, breathing heavily. He looked to Kaie. "The man is a monster."

Lorne's breathing was slightly labored, but he looked to Kaie with a smile. "Just because someone is bigger or stronger or *younger* than you doesn't mean the fight is hopeless," he said. "Now shall we get started?"

***

For the rest of the afternoon, Lorne worked Kaie on some different strength and stamina-building exercises. She ran sprints until she was gasping for breath, and pulled empty barrels up and down the training ground until her legs felt like rubber. But Lorne pushed and encouraged her to keep going. Finally, she collapsed on the ground, out of breath and spots dancing in her eyes.

"You've done a lot of work for your first day of training," Lorne said, coming to sit beside her.

"This is torture," she gasped. "What do you even expect from me?"

"With time, this will get easier," he said. "We all have to start somewhere." He then noticed that her locket had fallen off during her training. It glinted on the ground in the fading sunlight. "Where did you get this?" he asked, picking it up and examining it.

"It was my mother's. She put it in my pack before I left. I just remembered it today and found it," Kaie said, looking at the locket as well. It seemed that she had not fastened it correctly, and with the intensity of her training, it had slipped off.

"It's very pretty," Lorne remarked, placing it in her hand.

"Thank you." Kaie glowed at the compliment and was able to refasten it around her neck, correctly this time.

The two got up and headed back towards the palace, training completed for the day. Achaius followed them inside, having just finished his planting. He had spent the afternoon lost in his thoughts, about how harsh he had been with Kaie when she did not deserve it. Seeing how hard she was working made him realize how seriously she was taking everything.

"That was intense training you had today," he said to her. "Lorne's working you to the bone."

"Kaie exceeded my expectations for today," Lorne said. "She did an excellent job. I wonder what other secrets she's hiding from us," he teased.

"I'm not hiding anything. All you have to do is look," she countered. As they walked inside, Kaie nodded to the other two. "I'm going to wash off and I'll meet you for dinner," she said before running to her room.

Earlier that day, she had been informed that she was expected to attend dinner with the royal family, an honor only a few were privileged enough to partake in. She wanted to be clean before dining with the others.

"Lorne, can I ask you something?" Achaius said as they watched her go.

"Sure, what's on your mind?" Lorne could hazard a guess as to what the youngest prince wanted to talk about, but he wanted Achaius to say it out loud. He knew there was some tension between him and Kaie.

"I know I haven't treated Kaie the best, but I can't seem to stop myself from being rude. And if I keep this up, she's going to resent me. Do you have any ideas on how I could work on that?" Achaius wrung his hands as he spoke. Asking for help was not something he was really used to. Especially not emotional guidance.

"Well, you could remember that she's been taken away from her family and that her abilities don't have anything to do with you. She didn't ask to be an Inviver, so you shouldn't take out your frustration on her." Lorne knew what Achaius was upset about. "There aren't many people around here her age. She could use a friend."

"Do you think it's too late?" Achaius asked. For most of the morning, the two had worked in silence. And the one time she'd tried talking to him, he'd been rude.

"Well, you haven't made her feel welcome and she's not the type to forgive easily. Believe me. But if you keep making the effort, I'm sure she'll see that you're sincere," Lorne said kindly.

"I guess it's worth a shot," Achaius answered. He had been hoping for a quick and easy solution.

"It's worth it. Having her as a friend would be a hundred times better than having her as an enemy."

Lorne thought back to when Kaie had been angry with him. She definitely knew how to hold a grudge—Kaie had refused to speak to him for a whole month—but if Achaius showed her that he was sincere, he had no doubt she would warm up to the youngest prince.

CHAPTER II

With Farin's help, Kaie washed and dressed for dinner. The two of them decided on a pale-blue dress with deep-sapphire accents and elaborate navy embroidery on the bodice. After several minutes of brushing, the maid recommended that Kaie leave her hair down because the light playing off the subtle waves in her hair was pretty.

Farin had offered to take her to the dining room, but Kaie insisted she could find it herself. After all, she had been able to return to her room with only one wrong turn that afternoon. On her way to the dining room, Kaie came across a huge room filled with books. It was even more impressive than Prince Achaius's collection, as there were three walls of shelves bursting with books. The only wall that did not have bookcases had a huge window that looked out into the softly lit garden.

Unable to tear herself away from the magnificent sight, she walked over to a bookcase and picked out a book at random. Soon, she was engrossed in the text, sitting on one of the nearby couches, her feet tucked underneath her.

Half an hour later, Tristen found her, having been sent on a quest to fetch her for dinner when she had not shown up. "There you are. I've been looking everywhere for you."

Startled, Kaie looked up. "I'm sorry. I got so caught up, I didn't realize what time it was."

"It's not a problem, but dinner's getting cold. We should hurry." He held out an arm to escort her.

She put down the book reluctantly and followed Tristen out of the library.

He noticed her forlorn expression and reassured her. "You can come back later to finish your book. It's not going anywhere."

"I know. It was just so engaging, I didn't want to put it down." Kaie bit her lip and looked behind her, as if the book was calling out to her.

"They say that's the sign of a good book."

"I'd say it is."

Their conversation ended as they reached the dining room.

"I found her," Tristen announced to the room.

The king was sitting at the head of the table. Prince Achaius and Lorne sat on either side of him, and there were two empty seats for Kaie and Tristen.

As they sat down, Tristen said, "She was in the library with her nose stuck in a book."

"I'm sorry, Your Highness, Your Majesty," she said sheepishly, bowing her head in apology. "I lost track of time. I was amazed at how many books were in there."

"Very well," the king said. "How did training go today?"

"It went well, but I still have a lot of work to do."

Kaie tried not to feel overwhelmed by the amount of work she would have to complete before being ready for battle. Her road to becoming a decent fighter was going to be a long one. Despite the massage Farin had given her after her bath, her limbs and back still ached from the day's activities.

"Don't sell yourself short," Prince Achaius said.

Everyone turned to stare at him, surprised that he was offering her a compliment.

"You did a great job at your exercises today," he continued. "You put in a lot of work."

"Thank you," she said. "But I still wasn't very good. I'll need to practice harder if I'm to improve."

"It will get better as time goes on," Lorne added.

The food arrived, hot and steaming from the kitchen. Everyone turned their focus to the delicious meal. The jokes and banter made Kaie relax and feel more at home in the palace than ever before. From the sound of things, the captain of the guard was a close friend to the royal family in addition to being in charge of their protection. Kaie could tell it was not a normal arrangement, but one that seemed to suit everyone just fine. All too soon, the meal was over. Everyone stood and prepared to go their separate ways.

Lorne, Tristen, and King Torin needed to discuss the war, leaving Kaie and Prince Achaius alone at the table. Neither knew what to say, and silence descended upon them. Prince Achaius opened his mouth a couple times to say something, but no words came out.

Eager to escape the uncomfortable silence, Kaie said, "I'll go finish my book now. Good night." And without another word, she disappeared before Achaius could call her back.

"That was smooth," Achaius muttered to himself. "You wanted to talk with her, and instead you clam up." He stood to follow her. Maybe he could work up the courage to have a conversation with her.

***

Back in the library, Kaie settled back into her seat and was whisked away into another world by her book. She did not notice Prince Achaius walking in, trying to act nonchalant by stopping beside a bookcase and pretending to search for a book.

His cheeks were burning, so he faced away so she would not see how red he was. After a while, he heard her giggling. Thinking she was laughing at him, he turned, ready to snap at her, his temper flaring up. What he saw surprised him—she was intently reading, but she was laughing so hard that tears were running down her face.

Summoning up the courage, he finally asked, "What's so funny?"

Startled, Kaie looked up. Her eyes widened as she realized who was asking her the question. "Oh, I didn't realize you were here, Prince Achaius," she said. She moved to stand. "I can leave so you can read in peace."

"There's no need for that," he said. "And you can call me Achaius if you want."

Kaie sunk back into the couch and looked at her book, pondering the prince's sudden change. Maybe he was warming up to her after all. "Tristen said the same thing," she said, smiling brightly. "I'll try to remember."

"So what was making you laugh?" he asked.

"It was the main character," she said. "He's so oblivious to everything around him. A con man has come through twice and robbed him of all his money, using the same scam both times. I suppose unless you've read it, it doesn't sound that funny, but the author does a good job of showing what a fool the guy is."

"I think I've read that before." Achaius walked over and looked at the title. "Yeah, I read that a couple years ago. It was a really funny book."

He quoted several passages from the book by memory, using an outrageous voice for the main character. The two burst into laughter until both of their stomachs ached, gasping for breath.

Tristen happened past the library to see them both laughing. Pleasantly surprised, he walked in, curious to find out what Achaius had said that was so funny.

When Kaie saw him, she immediately stopped laughing. "Is there anything you need, Tristen?" she asked, a wide grin still on her face.

"I was not expecting to see you getting along so well," he said, a smile crossing his face. "It's nice to see you two having fun."

"Why wouldn't we?" Achaius asked, prickling at his brother's insinuation.

"You were very harsh with her yesterday. I'm just surprised at the sudden change," Tristen said innocently. He was having fun riling Achaius up. His brother usually fell for his tricks.

Achaius scowled, and Kaie eyed him cautiously. "Well maybe I'm trying to make up for that," he snarled. Tristen always knew how to pick on his shortcomings.

"It's fine," Kaie said quietly, unsure how to remove the growing tension in the room.

Tristen immediately realized his mistake, that he was making Kaie uncomfortable. Even if he enjoyed teasing his brother, he did not want Kaie to feel awkward. He sat on the other side of her. "I'm sorry, Kaie," he apologized. "I just wanted to tease Achaius a bit."

"Well, you didn't have to make fun of me to get your laughs," Achaius grumbled.

"I don't know of any siblings who *don't* tease each other. That's part of the fun," Kaie said, chuckling softly. Her mind briefly turned towards Shayla.

"I bet you and your sister have all sorts of fun teasing each other," Tristen said. Seeing her face suddenly drop, he knew he had made a mistake. "I'm sorry, you probably miss her a lot."

"Yes. Her and my parents. It's hard to be away from them this long." Kaie looked at the ceiling, willing the tears that entered her eyes to go away. She did not want to cry in front of the princes.

"You've never been away from home before?" Achaius asked.

"I've been away for a night when I was out getting plants or medicine, but never for this long." A tear slipped down her face, and she attempted to discreetly brush it away.

"You'll be back home before you know it." Tristen knew he'd messed up and now did not know how to fix his mistake.

"That's what Lorne said, but if the war is doing as poorly as the king indicates, I might not see them for a long time." A couple more tears slipped down her cheeks and her voice choked up. She turned her face away, trying to rein in her emotions. "And Maeve said that I can't see my family until it's over."

"Father just likes to worry. If he's not worrying about something, he's not happy," Tristen tried to reassure her. He cursed himself internally for bringing up this topic of conversation.

His words did nothing for her. Realizing that she might not see her family for a while was enough to make her start sobbing, all her earlier happiness gone.

Seeing that he had upset her, Tristen reached for a handkerchief, but Achaius beat him to it.

"Here you go," he said, handing his own to her. "It's okay to cry."

Tristen was both surprised and proud at how gentle Achaius was at that moment. He seemed surprisingly grown-up, especially considering how he'd acted the day before.

"Thank you." She took the handkerchief and wiping her eyes. "I'm sorry, I didn't mean to ruin our conversation."

"It's my fault, Kaie. I shouldn't have said that," Tristen said, gently rubbing her back.

"I wasn't expecting to react like that." Kaie bit her lip. She suddenly stood, grabbing the book she had been reading earlier. "I'll get your handkerchief cleaned and returned to you, Achaius," she said. "But I think I should head off to bed now."

"Kaie, wait!" Tristen could tell that she was still upset and trying to hold back more tears. "You don't need to leave on our account. We can leave if you want to be left alone."

"I'm fine, Tristen," she said with a smile that did not reach her eyes. "But I'm really tired. Good night."

After she left the library, Achaius hit Tristen on the arm. "Why did you bring up her family?" he hissed. "Of course she misses them!"

"I know," Tristen said miserably. "I need to figure out how I'm going to make it up to her. I should have known better." He looked at his younger brother. "But you handled that situation very well. I'm proud of how well you did consoling her."

"Well of course I did," Achaius grumbled, trying to hide a small satisfied smile at Tristen's compliment. "We can't all be as emotionally obtuse as you."

Tristen let out a small chuckle before starting to leave the library. "Good night, Achaius."

Back in her room, Kaie let out a shaky breath. Remembering her book in her hand, she found she did not feel like finishing it anymore. What had turned out to be a page-turner no longer had the appeal it had earlier in the evening. Instead, she tossed it on the nearby desk and got ready for bed.

As she slid under the covers, she took a close look at the locket that was still around her neck. A tear slowly slipped down her cheek as she whispered, "Good night, Shayla."

CHAPTER 12

The next morning before lessons, Kaie took out a sheet of paper to write to her family. Last night had highlighted how much she missed them all and she hoped that writing to them would help lessen the feelings of homesickness.

Dear Shayla, Momma, and Papa,

I miss you all so much and hope you are doing well. Hopefully you've been told that I am an Inviver (even if Momma already knew). Momma's letter gave me the strength and courage to feel comfortable with agreeing to training. Unfortunately, that means I won't be able to see you as soon as I would like. Even if we'll be apart, I am excited for Curing lessons and I hope you're excited for me as well. The head Inviver here, Maeve, has said that once my training is finished, I'll be sent to Carthan Valley to help with the war. But I'm receiving swordsmanship lessons, so please don't be worried about my safety.

I hope that you are all healthy and safe. Momma—please make sure to take your medicine. Shayla—don't get into too much trouble. Please know that I love you all. Give Shayla lots of hugs from me and please tell her I'm sorry I won't be home as soon as I had promised. I hope to hear from you soon.

Love,

Kaie

She sat back with a sigh and took a look at what she had written. It was enough for now. The pain she felt last night had settled into a dull ache. She folded the letter and put it in her pocket before heading down to the garden. Maeve and Achaius were waiting for her.

Kaie approached Maeve, holding out the letter. "I wrote a letter to my family. Could you make sure it gets to them?"

The Inviver looked at her for a moment before taking the letter. "I will pass it along," she said, tucking it away. "Now today, you're going to do more planting."

Kaie frowned. "Will you be teaching us anything else?" she asked in confusion.

"Planting first. Make sure you rip out any weeds on this bed," Maeve said, gesturing to the right plot. It had been worked on earlier in the season and already had some sprouts and weeds growing. There were still bare spots where the two could plant seeds. She pointed to the plot they worked on yesterday. "Ignore the other one." before heading back inside the castle.

"I don't understand how this is supposed to help my training," Kaie grumbled as she knelt on the ground to beginning planting once more, vigorously ripping out a nearby budding weed. "I already know about all these plants. I thought I would be learning something new."

"Maeve has to have some reason for us doing this," Achaius said, moving to work beside her.

The two worked in silence until Lorne retrieved Kaie for her afternoon lessons. Once more, he ran her through stamina exercises until she was drenched in sweat and ready to collapse. That night, she went to bed right after dinner and fell asleep immediately.

By the end of the week, Kaie could not take it any more when Maeve said they would be planting again. Even Achaius was starting to complain about the work and repetition.

"How is this supposed to help?" she asked the older Inviver. "I already know about all these plants and how to care for them. What am I supposed to be learning?"

She had barely started her official training and already she was tired of the busywork, tired of reviewing everything she already knew. Kaie had planned to bring up her frustration calmly, but she was irritated with how coy Maeve was acting.

Maeve smiled mysteriously. "What is the difference between these two beds?" she asked, pointing to the two that they had been working on all week. One was thriving, all the weeds plucked and sprouts were pushing up from the soil. The one she'd had them ignore was filled with weeds and no sign of any growth.

"Well, the one we've been taking care of looks great," Kaie said. "The other one looks terrible."

"Exactly," Maeve said with a nod. "This is to demonstrate how, with care and effort, your powers will grow and flourish. If you neglect your studies—" she pointed to the overgrown bed, "—then your powers will suffer for it. Whatever amount of work you put into yourself will determine how successful of an Inviver you are."

"Couldn't you have made that analogy without all the work?" Achaius asked, rubbing his aching neck.

Maeve's smile widened. "The work still helps," she said. "I wasn't lying when I said we needed to bulk up our plant supply. Follow me." She led them to other flowerbeds that had more plant growth than what they had been working on, the plants more easily identifiable. "You will go through all the plants in the garden and write down what each one is used for. If you *both* get all of them correct, we'll start on something more 'useful' tomorrow." She pulled out two small notebooks, handing each to Kaie and Achaius. "Make sure you get none wrong," she called as she left.

"What was that about?" Achaius asked once Maeve was out of earshot.

"What do you mean?" Kaie began writing down information on the plant nearest to her.

"I mean you getting angry. I know we're both frustrated, but you don't usually let your emotions spiral like that. What's wrong?"

"I was just sick of relearning everything that I already know. I know how to plant all of these, all the special techniques you need to use. We've wasted a week on planting for an analogy! I need to learn something useful," she answered, moving on to the next sprout. "Have you learned about all of these plants?"

"Yeah, we covered them about a month before you got here. Do you want to learn new stuff or is it just so you can go home sooner?" Achaius pried.

"I want to learn new stuff, but going home sooner is just a bonus. I want to be the best I can be, but if she moves at a glacial pace, I won't learn anything by the time the war's over." Her tone indicated that they should work, and Achaius took the hint.

For an hour, they combed the garden, writing down their notes as they went. After they both finished, they compared answers.

"No, underbrush is used for rheumatism, not headaches," she corrected one of Achaius's answers.

"Oh, right. I forgot," he said sheepishly, fixing his answer. He was impressed by her breadth of knowledge. They were around the same age, but he knew she had not had the same educational opportunities he'd had.

"Did you finish?" Maeve's voice came from behind them.

"Yes," Kaie said, holding her notebook out.

Maeve took it, leafing through her answers briefly.

"Here you go," Achaius said.

Maeve did the same thing, browsing his writing. "Very well," she said, closing both notebooks with a nod. "Tomorrow, we will get more serious with your education. Achaius can show you where the classroom is and we will meet there in the morning."

"Thank you," Kaie said.

That afternoon, there was a renewed vigor in her movements as she ran through the same exercises with Lorne. Unlike with planting, she could feel small changes in her body and knew she was improving. Not to mention, Lorne switched up her exercises enough to keep things interesting.

***

The next morning, there was a knock at her door. Kaie finished braiding her hair before she went to open it. In the mornings, Farin would wake her up, but she preferred to get dressed by herself. It still felt awkward having someone take care of her, but she was typically so sore in the evenings that she allowed the maid to help more.

To her surprise, Achaius was waiting for her. "I figured we could head to lessons together," he said. "I didn't get to show you where the classroom was last night."

He was right. After dinner, she had returned to her room to write another letter to her family. She was excited to share that she was going to be learning something new and that her training with Lorne had been going well.

"I'm sorry about that. I wanted to write another letter," she apologized. "Thanks for coming to get me this morning."

The two had struck up a tenuous friendship, still trying to figure out the other. Kaie had not forgotten how he had treated her after she had woken up and was wary of his new attitude. But as long as he remained friendly, she would follow in kind.

Achaius led her to a tucked away corner of the palace, to a small room with a couple desks. At the front of the room was a chalkboard and a table with some unfamiliar equipment on it. Maeve was already waiting for them.

"Good morning. Are you two ready to buckle down?" she asked. Immediately, she launched into a lecture about the different energy levels an Inviver could use to help others.

"As each level gets used up, it takes longer to replenish," she explained, drawing a bar on the chalkboard to illustrate the different energy levels. "When you start to use up those higher levels more frequently, your limits expand and they become quicker to replenish in the future. Your limits are like a muscle—if you don't use them, they will atrophy and you'll only be able to Cure a small amount. But if you use your Curing at those higher levels, it becomes easier to do over time."

"What about increasing your physical endurance? You said that was going to help too," Kaie said.

"Yes." Maeve nodded. "Another way to increase your Curing limits is to increase your strength and stamina. The healthier and stronger you are, the more you would be able to Cure. It is a safer way to expand your limits when you are just starting out."

"What energy level did I use up when I Cured Achaius?" Kaie asked. Maeve had been very encouraging of asking questions throughout her lecture.

"It's difficult to tell, but since you gave up so much energy at one time and were out for a week, I would say it was one of the highest ones," she answered. "You have to remember that he was near death and that always takes more energy to Cure. You released your power like an explosion." Maeve paused, pursing her lips. "As you practice your Curing, you will better be able to control the amount of energy you give out. You'll be able to feed your power to another person as you would a fire, building it up slowly rather than exploding all at once. Your technique on larger injuries needs work."

"I'll be able to practice Curing?"

Achaius could see that Kaie was excited by the prospect. She was practically bouncing with energy.

Maeve smiled and nodded. "Yes, you'll be able to practice after we go over the more technical side of Curing," she said.

Kaie beamed. At last, she would be able to put her powers into practice—to take the next step to becoming the strongest Inviver in history. Though the expectations placed upon her weighed in the back of her mind, she was eager to see what the future held.

CHAPTER 13

For Kaie, the next few weeks passed in a blur, as she followed the same schedule day after day. In the mornings were lessons, Maeve continuing to teach them about the Curing energy levels. Kaie found that she enjoyed the hands-on approach and Maeve even allowed her to Cure minor injuries of the soldiers who came to the infirmary. What Maeve taught stuck in her brain, as if she had known this information all her life and it just needed to be unearthed. And even though she'd asked, there were still no letters from her family. Kaie tried to tamp down the disappointment every time and instead focused on learning.

In the afternoons, Lorne had her running drills, sprints, and practicing different sword techniques. At the end of every training session, Kaie felt wobbly, her limbs turning to jelly, but as the weeks passed, she could start to see the improvement. She was able to last longer and take on heavier weights. Typically, she could barely stay awake at dinnertime, and afterwards, she would immediately slip back to her room to crash into bed, sleeping deeply until the next morning.

After about a month of training at the palace, Lorne finally moved on to exercises with a practice sword, tweaking her form as she went along. Her strength had drastically improved since she had arrived, so it was easier to hold the sword now, and her arms did not shake as she continued the drill.

"I think by the end of the week, we'll be able to have you start sparring with Raven," Lorne said, beaming with pride at her progress. "You've done very well. Your father gave you a good foundation to build off of."

Kaie smiled, remembering the times she'd practiced with her father. He had made training into a game with her and it was something that she'd always had fun with, coming at him with a wooden branch that he had whittled down to look like a sword. Gently, he had helped her with her posture and had given excellent tips on how to injure an enemy enough to run away. She looked up to him, a picture of strength and protection, and when he had left, she had done her best to emulate him, to take care of her family in his absence. When her mother grew sick and they had to sell most of their belongings to pay for her treatment, he had already been sent off to the war. Through infrequent letters, they had been able to communicate, and he never forgot to mention how proud he was of her.

She sighed, her voice wistful. "I miss him. It's been too long since I've last seen him."

Lorne patted her back. "I know," he said gently. "I know he's been gone for a long time, but you'll see him again."

She nodded, looking at the horizon off in the distance, the late afternoon sun was burning bright. "I should probably get ready for dinner," she said, clearing her throat to fix the croak in her voice.

Her mentor dismissed her for the day, his heart aching for the young Inviver. It had been a couple years since he had last seen his friend as well. But the whole time he'd known Kieran Durac, the man had boasted about his two young daughters. Based on Kaie's skill, it was obvious that it wasn't just fatherly pride. His daughter was truly talented. Lorne was looking forward to what other skills Kaie would learn under his tutelage.

***

On her way to her room, Kaie ran into Achaius. He fell into step beside her and they walked together down the hallways.

"How was training today?" he asked.

Kaie shrugged. "I think it's going fine," she said. "Lorne said by the end of the week, he thinks I should be able to spar with Raven."

"He's an excellent fighter and a good person to practice with," Achaius said. "You'll learn a lot sparring with him."

Kaie paused in surprise. From her limited experience with Achaius, he was sparse with his praise of others, but based on his words and stories of the Swain brothers, Raven really was a great fighter. The fact that Lorne was having her learn from Raven meant he thought she was ready to move forward in her training. She hoped she did not disappoint him.

"I'm looking forward to learning from him then," Kaie said. "I just hope I can keep up with everyone's belief in me. There's still so much I don't know and yet everyone has these high expectations for me."

"The fact that you Cured me and Lorne shortly after regaining consciousness proves that you have the talent to do so," Achaius said with earnest. From what he had seen and heard from other Invivers, she was already showing such promise. From time to time he was still pricked with guilt about how he had initially treated her.

"I never asked to be taken away from my family though. I'm not old enough to be sent to try and save the war."

Achaius gave her a surprised look. He had heard that his father was planning to send her to war once her training was finished, but there had been no mention about her saving the country.

"What?" she asked at his shock. "I know the king is sending me to the front lines after I complete my training. We aren't doing well, so he must be planning on sending me to go do something that the other Invivers can't, right?"

A familiar voice came from behind them, startling the two. They had been so engrossed in their conversation that they had not noticed anyone approaching.

"That's none of your concern at the moment. Your only job right now is to focus on your training. You can worry about everything else later," Tristen said. "Just focus on enjoying what you have right now, while you have it. Don't go looking for things to upset the balance you have."

Kaie chuckled. "If only I had done that when I was still at home. I spent all my free time daydreaming about when I could leave to travel the world and help people. Now that it's happened, I can't wait to go back home." She paused before adding, "I will try to enjoy my time here though."

"It's understandable," Tristen assured her, patting her shoulder. "It can be easy to focus on what you wish things could be like, rather than how they are."

As they approached her corridor, Kaie slipped off to her bedroom. For once, she felt invigorated after training rather than exhausted. Farin was shocked to see Kaie return with a bounce in her step, as usually the young Inviver collapsed on her bed the moment she came back. She helped her change into a green and gold dress, bringing out the elaborate gown in celebration of the Inviver's energy boost.

"I think that I'm starting to get used to this," Kaie said excitedly as Farin braided her hair. "This past month has taken a lot of getting used to, but I think I'm starting to get a handle on things. Sir Shalane has mentioned he's going to step up my training soon."

"That's great to hear," Farin said, glad that the young girl was doing so well. During the first week, Kaie had cried frequently from missing her family. Seeing her start to flourish was encouraging.

"And my training with Maeve is going well too. Everything seems to be going so well." Kaie frowned slightly after she spoke, something bothering her. "I've written a few letters to my family, but I haven't heard back from them yet. I wish they would respond and tell me how they're doing."

Farin was silent for a moment, then looked up, seeing Kaie's eyes on her. "Why not write them again? I'm sure they enjoy hearing from you, even if they aren't able to respond," she said, sensing that the young Inviver was seeking some guidance.

Kaie thought for a moment. "But what if something's wrong and they can't tell me?"

"I'm sure the king would share important news with you," Farin said. "If something was wrong, he would tell you. Or you could ask one of the princes if they've heard anything."

Kaie considered the suggestion and nodded. "I think I'll ask Tristen," she said. "He meets frequently with the king." She examined her hair as Farin finished it. "Thank you, Farin, I appreciate your advice." She smiled at the maid before leaving the room.

Initially, she started heading for the library, but quickly turned in the opposite direction, deciding to explore the palace instead. Kaie had not taken the opportunity to look around other than the areas she already frequented.

After a while, she discovered another room stuffed with books. This one was smaller than the library and filled with thick, fat books covered with dust. She pulled one off the shelf and blew the dust off the cover, spraying particles all around that made her sneeze. Walking over to the only table in the room, she set the book down and opened it carefully. Her eyes widened at what she had discovered.

"This is amazing," she whispered as she read the fading words. She flipped through the pages, absorbing the maps and diagrams carefully drawn out by hand so long ago. Looking at the shelves in wonderment, she went to another book and took it off the shelf. She skimmed through it as well, confirming the contents of what she thought the room was: full of history.

Kaie stayed there for an hour, learning about Galicia's past and the different kings, queens, and wars. Surprisingly, there was more information about Scrian history than she expected. The conflict between the two countries spanned generations, back to even before the countries were formed. There were even details about Invivers and the role they'd played in the founding of both kingdoms—how Invivers had used their powers in the wars to Cure soldiers to continue fighting. Based on what she read, it seemed that the Galician Invivers had focused on helping the citizens with their powers, while the Scrian Invivers had fixated on new discoveries and knowledge. It seemed most conflicts were centered around Inviving secrets, with the Scrians continuously trying to figure out what the Galicians were learning.

She did not notice the time passing by, not even as the room grew darker and a servant came in to light the candles. Due to her mother's illness, her education on the country's history had been very limited. She could recall some of the stories her father had shared, and what little her mother had been able to remember. Really, the only history she was aware of was the more current events. And even then, the cause of the current war was not well known. The general population just knew that the Scrians had attempted another invasion while the Galician army held them at bay.

"Trying to hide out here?" Tristen asked when he found her in the room.

Startled, Kaie immediately stopped reading and stood to face him. "No, I just... was exploring," she tried to defend herself, stumbling over the words. Her face reddened. She wasn't sure if she was allowed in a place like this, with old and expensive books. Carefully, she closed the book she was reading and moved to put it back.

Tristen chuckled. "You're not in trouble. You're allowed to be here," he said. The panic on her face had been easy to read.

She nodded silently, still embarrassed to have been caught unawares.

"Would you like to take a walk with me?" he asked kindly. "Dinner will be starting soon."

"I would like that very much," she said, following him out of the room.

After walking for a couple steps, he said, "I didn't know you were interested in history."

"I liked it when my father told me stories, usually of his escapades. I had no idea what was in that room. It seemed quiet and cozy, and was quite a surprise," Kaie said. "Unfortunately, I was unable to receive much of a formal education growing up. I know how to read and write, but we never had money for books."

"Well, I could teach you more history if you want," Tristen said. "Part of being the crown prince is learning the nation's history and that of other countries as well. I have a wealth of knowledge to share."

"Really, you would do that?" she asked, her eyes brightening at the idea. When he nodded his head, she exclaimed, "That would be wonderful! I've always wanted to learn more since Father left."

Tristen chuckled at her reaction, her excitement infectious. "I would imagine, with your attitude, that you would pick it up very easily. I can teach you in the evenings, after dinner."

"I would like that very much," Kaie said earnestly.

They walked in silence for a couple moments before Kaie spoke up. "Did you enjoy learning about history growing up?"

"It was the first thing I ever showed interest in as a child. My mother thought it would be best to encourage me to learn more to help run a kingdom, but my father thought I should spend more time learning to fight with sword. I had time for both, so Mother got her way after all." He smiled at the memory, though Kaie could sense a hint of sadness in his voice. It was common knowledge that the queen had died years ago, and it must be painful for Tristen to think about her death.

She took his hand and squeezed it gently. "Your mother sounds like she was a lovely person," she said.

Tristen nodded. "She was," he said. "And she would have liked you." He paused as they heard a clock chiming in the distance. "Sounds like it's time for dinner," he said, turning to lead them to the dining room.

"Do you think Achaius will be mad?" Kaie asked, suddenly worried about angering the other prince. In the evenings, he always asked if she wanted to go to the library or the gardens, but she was usually too tired to agree. The friendship she had grown with him was delicate and she did not want to upset the balance right now. Achaius was finally starting to *not* get on her nerves.

"He'll only be mad that I found you before he did. Unfortunately for him, I'll be teaching you about Galicia for the rest of the evening, starting at the founding of the country," he said, the edges of his mouth twitching into a smile.

Kaie smiled back. "I guess it does help to start at the beginning." She paused for a moment, her eyes brightening. "Do you think we'll get through the whole roomful of books?"

"Maybe." Tristen slowed as they reached the dining room, hearing the voices of the king and Lorne talking. It seemed as though they had arrived before Achaius. Tristen led Kaie to her seat before sitting next to her.

"Where is your brother?" the king asked as Tristen started to fill his plate.

His eldest son shrugged. "Probably looking around for Kaie. But she's going to be spending the rest of the evening with me learning about the history of Galicia."

The king scowled. "You know I don't want you focusing on that anymore," he said. "You have more important duties now."

"It is the only connection I have to Mother. She's the one who taught me everything. It's the least I can do to pass on her knowledge," Tristen argued.

"There are other things you should focus on. You need to spend your time learning how to run a kingdom."

King Torin and Tristen glared at each other, daring the other to back down first.

"It *does* help," Tristen said through clenched teeth. "We need to learn from the past to not make the same mistakes in the future. My free time in the evenings is to do what I please. I will do what I want." His tone made it clear that he was going to fight this point until the king backed down.

Torin glared at Kaie as if his son's behavior was her fault. "Very well. I will let you teach her until her training starts to pick up. Once it does, these lessons are over and I don't want to hear of this ever again."

Kaie's gaze dropped to her plate, where she picked at her food, her appetite suddenly gone.

Tristen noticed the change in her and argued even more. "I want to teach her and she's willing to listen to me. That's more than I can say for *you*!"

"My plans for this war are none of your concern. I'm doing what is right for this country and you do not have the authority to question me." King Torin's eyebrows lowered into a scowl.

By now, both men were standing and shouting at the other.

"I do if I'm to take over the throne someday," Tristen countered.

"I do not have to explain myself to you," Torin roared, spit flying from his mouth.

"Then how do you expect me to understand your decisions? You just make them and expect me to follow you blindly! I'm not a puppy!"

The king's voice turned to a dangerous whisper. "Then after dinner, you and I will be meeting with my advisors to talk in depth about the war," he said. "And this discussion is *over*." With that, he left the room.

Slowly, Tristen sat down, shaking with rage. Even if his father was willing to bring him into more discussions, he hated how the older man disparaged his hobbies. For a while, he remained silent, the only sound in the room was Kaie and Lorne pushing their food around their plates.

Finally, Lorne spoke up. "It's not your fault, Tristen. He's been moody all day."

"I shouldn't have brought up the history lessons." Tristen pushed his brown hair away from his face, his muscles clenched. "I knew it would bother him, but that's probably why I did it. When Mother was alive, he was fine with it, but since she died, it seems like he's trying to get rid of every little reminder of her. But you can't squash memories. The past will always affect us," Tristen said, his eyes glistening.

Kaie was at a loss for words. She looked to Lorne, begging him to say something. Seeing Tristen this upset was something that almost frightened her. He was usually so optimistic and positive. But the man in front of her seemed broken.

Taking the hint, Lorne tried his best. "Tristen, it's nice that you're trying to keep your mother's memory alive through the history lessons, but it's up to your father whether he can handle it or not. Don't let this bother you. At least he's letting you teach Kaie."

The prince nodded at his words, seeming to take some comfort in them.

"Now, you'd better go before he loses his temper again. I'm guessing you aren't too hungry after that."

Tristen sighed heavily, knowing that the older man was right. "Very well," he said. "Kaie, I'll try to make this meeting brief, but I make no promises. I think we'll have to have our first lesson tomorrow night instead."

Kaie nodded, trying to give the prince a smile of encouragement before he left.

After a few moments, Kaie knew that she was not going continue eating either, her appetite completely gone. "I'm done," she announced to Lorne. "Do you think I can ride Aira before bed?"

Lorne nodded. "It should be fine as long as you stay within the palace grounds," he said.

"Then I'll go now. When should I be back?"

"Around the time they start to light the torches outside. You should be able to get an hour in," he said, glancing to the windows to see the dusky sky.

"I'll hurry so I can get in as much riding time as possible. Aira probably thinks I've forgotten her." Kaie dashed out of the dining room, running into Achaius.

"Where have you been?" Achaius said accusingly, bad tempered from trying to find her. He had been searching for her since he heard she was exploring around the palace from one of the servants.

"I was reading about Galician history," she said defensively, frowning at his tone. "I'll be learning everything I possibly can every night with Tristen until my training gets more rigorous."

"What?" Achaius asked in shock. "I'm surprised Father is letting him teach you."

"They just had a big fight over it. But you better head in for dinner. It won't last much longer. The servants are going to take it away soon." She raced outside before he could question her further, the eagerness in her escape apparent.

As he walked into the dining room, Achaius muttered to himself, "I thought she was warming up to me. What was that about?"

"It's because you come across as overly eager. You're still allowing your emotions to get the best of you," Lorne said, having heard the end of their conversation. "If you tone it down a bit, she might be more willing to spend time with you. You just need to be yourself."

"How do you know this?" Achaius asked. Deep down, he knew what Lorne had said was true. He was laying it on too thick to get on Kaie's good side.

"I don't. But she gets along well with Tristen because he doesn't try so hard," Lorne explained. "He lets her take the lead when they spend time together. He doesn't push her to talk or do anything."

As Achaius seemed to process this, the older man smiled and left the room. Now it was time to see how Tristen and the king were faring in their conversation.

***

As soon as Kaie reached the stables, she noticed that they were deserted. Fyfe was nowhere to be found, so she walked over to Aira's stall and let her out. To do without the hassle of saddling her up, Kaie put on the bridle and decided to ride bareback. She had loved riding bareback on her father's horse when she was little. Too late, Kaie took notice of the extravagant dress she had on, a brief worry crossing her mind that she might ruin it.

Aira whinnied in anticipation, and that spurred Kaie to ignore her concerns and get on. Once the girl was seated securely, the mare took off. Kaie's braid soon came undone and her hair whipped behind her as Aira galloped onward. A shout of laughter escaped her, and quickly, she was caught up in the moment. What seemed all too soon, the guards started to light the torches, bringing the evening escapade to an end. Reluctantly, Kaie led Aira back to the stables. As she approached, Fyfe came out.

"I saw that you had taken her out. I was worried for a moment when I didn't see her," he commented.

"Yeah, it had been a while," she said, breathless.

"Hopefully you had a good time, but you better hurry before they close the doors for the night. I'll put Aira away for you."

She handed him the reins and raced back inside, just as the guards were about to lock down the castle.

"You almost didn't make it, missy," one guard said jovially. "Let's not cut it this close in the future, understand?"

"Sorry, I lost track of time," she replied, smiling ruefully.

Once inside the palace, her heart sank as she noticed that her dress was ruined. The golden fabric was visibly dirty and parts of the skirt were ripped from her ride. Tomorrow, she would ask Farin for tips on how to fix the dress.

CHAPTER 14

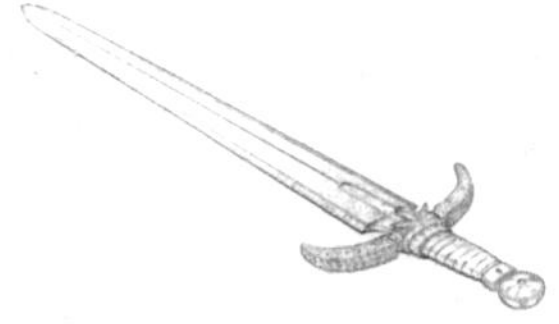

Kaie awakened early the next morning, a couple hours before Farin usually came to her room. After deciding to try to fix the gown now, she dressed quickly in her tunic and headed off to where she last remembered the sewing room to be from her earlier explorations. On her way, she bumped into Tristen.

"What are you in such a hurry for this early in the morning? Breakfast isn't even ready yet!" he exclaimed.

"I, uh, I have things I need to take care of today before training." She struggled to think of an excuse. It seemed irresponsible to have ruined such an extravagant dress that the royal family had so kindly lent her.

Noticing the dress in her hands, Tristen took it from her and shook it out. "What did you do to this? It's almost completely ruined!"

"I went riding last night and I forgot to change. One thing led to another, and it got wrecked. I'm going to fix it though," she added hurriedly.

"It's Catriona's favorite dress," he murmured sadly. "How could you do such a thing?" he demanded.

"I'm sorry. I didn't do it on purpose. It can be fixed." Even though the family had been generous, Tristen's outburst seemed to be a bit of an overreaction.

"This is not just any dress. It was Catriona's favorite! And now you've ruined it." The eldest prince continued to look over the dress, despair written across his face.

"Who is Catriona?" Kaie said, surprised by Tristen's violent reaction. Except for arguments with his father, she had never seen him act like this, especially to her.

"Catriona was my sister." His voice slipped to a whisper. "She died five years ago. Come with me." He walked off, still holding the dress in his hands.

Feeling intrigued and a little guilty, Kaie followed. After taking a couple confusing turns in the maze of hallways, Tristen stopped and faced the portraits that hung on the wall. Confused, Kaie looked at the paintings, too, two immediately popping out at her. One was of a sophisticated woman with mahogany hair and dark-green eyes that mirrored Achaius's. She wore an emerald dress that matched her eyes. To the right of that painting was one of a young girl with matching hair, but instead, she had deep-blue eyes like Tristen. In the painting, she was wearing a similar dress to the gold and forest-green one that Tristen was holding.

Kaie's eyes widened as she realized who these two women were.

"When I was three," he began, "Mother gave birth to Catriona. Everyone was happy, but there were... complications, and she almost didn't survive. The Invivers told us that she would not live through another birth. Then she became pregnant with Achaius. When the time came, things went smoothly, at first. Then something went terribly wrong, I'm not quite sure what, but she didn't survive." He took a deep breath and continued, "Her death shattered our lives. Father still hasn't gotten over it, but at least he's better than he was at the beginning. Catriona took it harder than any of us. Even though she was only five, she and Mother were very close.

"Then it got even worse. We weren't getting along too well with the Scrians to begin with, but after that, things went to pieces. When Catriona was ten, Father went to go make a peace treaty with their king. When he came back, he told us that when Catriona turned eighteen, she would be wed to the prince of Scria in an arranged marriage. Now, Catriona was very stubborn and didn't like to be told what to do—kind of like you." He smiled gently, and Kaie knew that he did not mean this as a rebuke. "She was furious over this. Amazingly, after a while, she calmed down and got used to the idea. But fate wasn't on our side again."

"What happened?" Kaie asked softly when Tristen paused.

He closed his eyes before continuing. "One day, Catriona went for a horseback ride outside the palace walls. She snuck away and no one could find her. Father sent the guards out, frantic." Tristen broke off for a moment, trying to build up enough energy to relive that day. "They were able to find her body, slashed and bloody. Bandits had found her, and once they'd realized that she had nothing worth stealing, they'd killed her. She was only sixteen. After the Scrians found out, they decided to go to war. They were convinced that we were going to marry her off to another kingdom—a ridiculous idea, but they were certain." He stopped, unable to continue.

Kaie now understood who all the dresses belonged to and why they fit her so well. Catriona must have been the same size as her. "Is my room...?" She was not able to ask the full question.

"Catriona's? Yes, it's hers. You two are so alike, it's amazing. You would have been great friends," he said.

"Is that why you took such a liking to me when I first met you?" Kaie did not know why, but the thought that Tristen only viewed her as only a replacement for his sister bothered her deeply. She wanted him to view her as her own person.

"That, and you just seemed so vulnerable when you first came," he said. "It was hard not to be drawn to you."

The sun started to peek through the window, the beams shining on the paintings, giving them a cheerful glow.

Tristen sighed and said to Kaie, "We should go to breakfast. I'll take this to the seamstresses. They'll be able to fix it."

Together, the two headed off to breakfast. No one else came, so they finished and headed off to their respective duties.

Maeve took Achaius and Kaie outside to the palace gardens, which Kaie had not gotten a chance to explore yet. The older Inviver wanted the two of them to sit in the garden and listen to the sound of the earth for the morning.

"Close your eyes and listen," she said. "Feel yourself rooted to the ground. Stretch out your senses to feel the plant life around you."

"What is this supposed to do?" Achaius asked.

"As Invivers, we receive our power from Mother Nature," Maeve said. "Every being is tethered to the earth and therefore when we are healthy and well, our energies are in alignment with that of the earth. There are some Invivers who can distinguish this energy—whether it's a sound, a smell, or color—and thus, make it easier to Cure others. Injuries or illness can cause our energy to become out of sync with the earth. Invivers are able to correct that and bring them back into alignment."

"Can all Invivers do this?" Kaie asked.

"Not all Invivers can distinguish this energy, but that doesn't prevent them from Curing," Maeve said. "But for those who can, it makes Curing easier. It helps to follow the direction of the misalignment and uses up less energy when you can pinpoint the exact spot that is causing the disharmony."

Kaie's eyes widened. "Right before I Cured Achaius, I heard a screeching sound," she said. "Is that what you're talking about?"

Maeve nodded. "It could be," she said. "Now sit down and close your eyes. Focus."

Kaie settled on the ground to follow Maeve's instructions and heard the Inviver walking back into the palace. She tried to focus on the noises of the garden, of the bugs and animals nearby. But try as she might, she could not hear the "sound of the earth" Maeve was talking about. And she could not hear any sounds similar to the screeching.

Achaius let out a heavy sigh a while later. "I don't get what we're supposed to do," he said.

Kaie cracked an eyelid to look at him. "We're listening to the 'sound of the earth'," she said, mimicking the way Maeve said it.

Both burst into laughter.

"Yeah, but how are we supposed to do that?" Achaius asked.

She shrugged. "I don't know, but I somehow did it before so I should be able to do it again, right? Come on, let's try concentrating some more."

She closed her eyes once again and attempted to focus, but could hear Achaius moving about. Despite his noisiness, she tried to listen to nature, to focus on the sounds she heard. But Achaius's movement kept her from focusing on any one sound for too long.

"What are you doing?" she asked in exasperation after several minutes of him rustling around.

When she opened her eyes, she struggled to hold back a snort of laughter. Achaius had taken two sticks and put them behind his ears and somehow managed to make a beard of leaves. He was crouched in front of her making a silly face.

"I'm of the earth," he said before they both dissolved into giggles.

"We're supposed to be taking this seriously!" Kaie protested between bouts of laughter.

"Yeah, but it's so *boring*," Achaius said.

Just then, a droplet of rain fell onto Kaie's head. "Uh-oh. Looks like the earth did not enjoy you making fun of it," she said as it began to pour.

They exchanged another look before laughing once more.

The two raced inside, but not before getting soaked. Their hair was plastered to their heads, their clothes soggy from the rain.

A deafening crack of thunder made both Kaie and Achaius jump.

"I wonder what I'll be doing this afternoon for training if we can't go outside," Kaie said.

"Oh, we have a separate arena for indoor training for situations like these," Achaius said.

"Where is that located? I haven't come across a place like you're describing when I've been exploring," Kaie said.

"Follow me." Achaius led her back outside, both racing to get out of the rain. Behind the barracks and the training grounds was an unobtrusive building that she had not noticed previously. The building was surrounded by trees, making it easy to overlook.

Stepping inside, her eyes widened at the space. Two walls were covered in weapons, while the other two remained bare. Lorne was in the middle of the arena with a group of soldiers, running them through drills. The pounding sound of the rain could barely be heard here, but the grunting of the men overshadowed it. Kaie's nose wrinkled as the stench of the men hit her nose. She guessed they had been training all morning. At least when training outside, there was more room to spread out, and usually a breeze to waft away the smell.

Achaius laughed at her reaction. "It can get a little ripe," he said. "But after a while, you become nose blind to it." He bid her goodbye and raced back to the castle.

"I sure hope so," she muttered under her breath as she watched him go.

After a couple moments, Lorne noticed her and motioned for his men to take a break. Walking up to Kaie, he said, "I hoped you'd be able to find us."

"Achaius had to show me," she said.

"Today, Raven is going to work with you," Lorne said, motioning for the young man to approach. "I need to focus on these men today."

Kaie looked at the group and recognized most of them from her time training. "Why? I thought they already knew how to protect the palace."

"They do, but not enough about fighting in battle." He saw her look of astonishment. "That's right, the king will be sending them off in a couple weeks to go fight at Carthan Valley. Only a few are staying behind to help train the new recruits."

Raven appeared next to Lorne, brushing black hair out of his face. "Today we're going to spar," he said, crossing his arms with a kind smile on his face. "Put all those drills into practice. Go pick out a sword and we can get started."

Kaie nodded, walking toward a rack of weapons nearby, where she took her time picking her sword. She could feel the prickle of eyes on her back as she examined the weapons until Lorne called the men back to continue their drills. After careful consideration, she picked out a long, thin sword and walked over to Raven.

He bent his knees and held his sword up, an easygoing smile spreading across his face. "Are you ready?" he asked.

"No," she answered honestly.

This was the first time she had faced an opponent since her test over a month ago with Lorne. Since then, they had been working on drills and technique. A surge of anxiety flared up, mixed with excitement.

"But I might as well try."

In an instant, the clash of swords rang through the arena. Kaie clenched her teeth as she could feel Raven's strength pushing back against her. He pulled back and she moved forward, using one of the techniques Lorne had constantly put her through. Raven's smile widened when he recognized the movement, and swiftly moved to block her, flicking his sword under hers. With much effort, Kaie was able to keep her weapon from spinning out of her hands.

"Good job," he said, nodding before going on the offensive.

He moved slower than he usually would, giving Kaie a chance to block and counterattack. Her eyes widened as she realized what he was doing, and instead dodged the attack, bringing her sword up to attack from the side, which he was able to block at the last minute.

They continued to spar for a few minutes, weaving and jabbing at each other. Kaie could tell Raven was giving her the chance to use her drills in a practical setting, but wanted to surprise him. Her arm was starting to leaden and she knew that soon, he would knock her sword away. In a move of desperation, she jabbed her sword forward, hoping to catch Raven off guard. To her delight, her ploy worked, and he staggered backwards in surprise, not expecting her ferocity. She pushed her advantage, continuing to swing at him until he eventually fell against the wall, held at sword point. A look of astonishment crossed his face as he took in her shocked expression, knowing that this turn of events stunned her as much as him.

"Looks like Lorne's exercises have paid off," he said. "I wasn't expecting that last move from you." A sly smile crossed his face. "Let's see if you can do that again."

Without another word, he lunged at her, hoping to take her by surprise. With much effort, she was able to deflect the attack, feeling the reverberations of the metal through her arm. They continued clashing swords and Kaie could tell when Raven wanted her to use more of the moves she had practiced during her drills. It was obvious he was still going easy on her, but a few minutes later, Kaie's arm gave out, almost taking a serious blow in the process.

"Do you need a break?" he asked, lowering his sword in concern.

"A short one," she panted, rubbing her arm.

After a quick break, the two continued to work on different attacks for the rest of the afternoon, going in depth on every movement of each technique. Raven also showed her common reactions fighters used against the moves, as well, and offered tips on how to take an opponent by surprise. The day finished with a quick sparring session, ending in Raven's victory.

"All right, you can go now," he released her. "Good work today."

Exhausted, Kaie headed back to the castle with aching arms and a throbbing head. Luckily, the rain from earlier had stopped and she was able to slowly trudge back inside. On her way to her room, she ran into Tristen.

"What's wrong?" he asked, taking in her tired appearance.

"Training wore me out today. It hurts to move."

"Why don't we start our history lessons tomorrow?" he asked.

Kaie nodded gratefully. "I'll see you at dinner," she said.

Farin was waiting for her, a bath already drawn up. Kaie soaked in the hot water, her aching muscles savoring the heat. Afterwards, Farin once more massaged her arms and back, taking great care where Kaie's muscles were knotted. During the massage, the young Inviver drifted off to sleep, exhaustion from the day overwhelming her. Quietly, Farin left the room and sent a message to the eldest prince that Kaie was sleeping peacefully and would not be coming to dinner.

CHAPTER 15

The next morning, there was a new face at the front of the classroom with Maeve. She was an exceedingly beautiful woman with flowing red hair. She seemed as though she should have been wearing a noblewoman's gown at court instead of the plain linen dress she wore.

"This is Avalon Hertaag. She will helping with your lessons," Maeve said, gesturing to the woman.

Kaie was immediately intrigued. The other Invivers she had met at the palace had all been older, though not as elderly as Maeve. This was the first young Inviver she had met.

"That's a Scrian last name," Achaius said with a slight frown.

Avalon smiled, her entire face lighting up. "You're very astute, Your Highness," she said with a nod of her head. "I am indeed originally from Scria."

"What are you doing here?" Achaius asked, crossing his arms.

"Achaius, be nice," Kaie hissed to the prince. "She's here to teach us."

Maeve rapped her cane on Achaius's desk. "You will mind your manners," the old woman chastised him. "Or you will be thrown out of lessons."

"I don't mind answering his questions, Maeve," Avalon said. She turned back to Achaius. "To put it simply, I defected from the Scrian forces. As you know, Scrian and Galician Invivers take different approaches to Curing. I could not stand by and be indifferent at the techniques our commander was using on Invivers."

"Like what?" Achaius asked, his eyes growing wide.

"That's a story for another time," Avalon said. "But His Majesty and Maeve have heard details about my time at the Scrian camp and trust my motives for defecting."

"And Avalon's specialty is what we'll be working on next," Maeve said.

"What is that?" Kaie asked, practically rising out of her seat in excitement.

"In addition to Curing, Invivers also are able to implement Calming," Avalon said. "It is more of a mental ability than physical—we are able to influence the mind, to some extent. And in battle, it can be extremely useful to raise the spirit of the soldiers."

"How does it work?" Kaie asked.

"The person, or people, you're trying to Calm must be receptive to it," Avalon continued. "It isn't impossible to Calm someone who is resistant, but that does make it a lot more difficult. As Invivers, we are able to amplify or dampen people's emotions."

"What use is that?" Achaius asked.

"Calming is a bit of a misnomer. Before a battle, we can use this ability to invigorate the soldiers, or we can ease anxiety and agitation. On the battlefield, Invivers can be used as a source of morale—depending on how skilled you are, your sphere of influence grows so you can boost more soldiers." Avalon exchanged a brief look with Maeve, but Kaie could not interpret the expression. "Calming is more difficult than Curing as you don't have the same visual cues that it is working. It can be easy to expend too much energy and not receive a lot of return for it."

The rest of the morning was spent discussing the values of Calming. Achaius and Kaie both had many questions about the newfound ability, which Avalon was happy to answer with a gentle smile.

***

Kaie raced outside to training that afternoon, invigorated by the new lesson. The day was bright and sunny, the warmth of the sun splashing on her face. She walked over to the training grounds where Lorne and Raven were talking.

"Good afternoon," she greeted both, noting the smiles the two were trying to hide.

"We have some good news for you," Lorne said, looking past her towards something.

Kaie turned. Her eyes widened as she saw the blacksmith approaching with a long slender package in his arms. A giddy feeling rose in her stomach as she could guess what it was. He had taken her measurements ages ago and she had purposely avoided asking about her sword, not wanting to rush him.

"I finished your sword last night," he said proudly, presenting her with her new weapon. "It's custom-made just for you."

Carefully, she pulled it out of its black leather sheath, admiring the craftsmanship. The silver blade glinted in the sunlight and she could feel the weight of the weapon. To her surprise and delight, the curved cross guard was decorated with metal vines wrapping around the quillons, giving the sword a more feminine look. The pommel was inset with a circular bright green gemstone and Kaie was shocked such an expensive looking jewel would be used for her. As her hand encircled the hilt, she could tell that the sword was perfectly balanced and made for her smaller stature. Taking a couple steps away from the men, she tentatively slashed the air, enjoying the feeling of the sword in her hand. Never had she imagined having a sword all her own.

"It's beautiful," she whispered, turning to the blacksmith with sparkling eyes. A large grin crossed her face. "It's absolutely stunning."

The blacksmith smiled at her obvious delight. "It's the best I've ever made," he said. "I'm so glad you like it."

Kaie turned eagerly to Lorne and Raven, excited to use her new sword. Both were smiling at her reaction.

"Let's see how well you handle it," Lorne said. "Raven will be practicing with you today."

***

For the rest of the day, Raven continued to work with her on framework and different attacks to help in battle. There was a heightened thrill of injury with the sharpened blades—which most recruits used—but typical injuries on the training ground were easy for the palace Invivers to Cure and were most of what Kaie practiced on during her morning lessons.

At the end of the day, as the sun started to set, Kaie felt disappointment rising within her that training for the day was over. She was in awe of how the sword felt like an extension of her arm compared to the dulled practice swords. Never before had something felt so right in her hand and she was looking forward to practicing more.

Upon her return to the castle, Kaie was ambushed by Achaius.

He blurted out, "I have a really interesting book I want to show you."

Kaie took a step back in alarm, taken aback by Achaius's enthusiasm. He quickly realized his mistake and took a couple steps away. Silently, he cursed himself. He'd come on too strong again.

"I'm sorry, I just really think you're going to like this," he said apologetically.

"Well, let me change and then we can go," she said.

Kaie quickly changed into a white dress with an azure sash, specially picked out by Farin. By the time she was done, Achaius was waiting expectantly outside her door, his hands hidden behind his back. There was a skip in his step that she had not been expecting, but she was curious to see why he was so excited. Once in the library, he immediately walked over to a shelf and pulled out a thick, black book. On the cover was silver curly writing, but the letters and words were in a language that Kaie did not recognize.

"What is this?" she asked, curiosity piqued.

"It's written in the ancient language of the Invivers. You'll probably be learning how to read and write it soon," Achaius said. "Maeve taught me some, but there are still several parts I don't understand. It contains the history of how the Invivers were created and what their duty is."

Carefully, he opened the first page, yellowed with time. The curvy writing continued on each page, and drawings took up most of the pages. For some inexplicable reason, she felt drawn to the book, as if her body recognized and craved the knowledge inside.

"Here's where it starts. Supposedly, it was written by the first Inviver," he said quietly, solemnly. Then he began to read.

Mother Nature created the Earth. When she created humans, there was peace at first. But soon, a tyrant rose to power, subjugating all those beneath him. Revolution had begun and people were dying by the thousands. The rivers ran red with blood. Mother Nature soon became angry at the violence. The balance of the Earth was shifted. Her solution was the creation of Invivers to stop the bloodshed. Out of the Earth came those who could stop the wars, who could Cure others without harming themselves. They helped overthrow the tyrant and gained freedom for the rest of mankind. For a time, there was peace and harmony throughout the lands.

But the tranquility was not to last. Instead, people thought to use Invivers as weapons, to gain more power over each other. The Invivers separated into factions, some wanting to keep power, while others wanted to help people. Our power was used for terrible purposes. The conflict caused a vast amount of suffering that soon became too much for the Invivers to bear.

Mother Nature again stepped in. She gave them a weakness: every time they Cured, part of their own energy was given out. If they gave too much, they would faint or die. They could only restore their own energy as they slept.

The different factions eventually separated into the kingdoms we know today. We are now at peace, but those of us who know well enough, know that it will not last.

But there is one hope for us: Mother Nature has promised that when violence threatens once again, she will send an Inviver who will finally stop the worst bloodshed, the misunderstanding, once and for all. With this Inviver, the kingdom who uses this power for good or evil has the power to change the fate of the world. If used for evil, the world will collapse into an age of darkness.

I leave this warning to my fellow Invivers: Find the one who has been promised, and protect them from those who would use them for evil, and from those who seek to harm them. Protect this Inviver from themselves. The fate of the world could depend on it.

Achaius stopped reading and looked at her.

Kaie sucked in a breath, having been entranced by the words and his voice. As he'd read to her, a weight had felt like it was slipping over her shoulders.

"Do all Invivers believe this?" she asked softly, feeling the need to keep her voice quiet.

"I once asked Maeve that same question, but she gave me a very vague answer. I would imagine they do, but I don't know what would happen if that Inviver was ever found," he answered honestly.

A fleeting thought passed through Kaie's mind that it could be her. But that was too fantastical to believe, and she squashed the notion. Being praised by Maeve and everyone else was clearly going to her head and boosting her ego. She needed to stay grounded.

"That story didn't take up a lot of the book. What else is in it?"

"Different advice on what your powers can be used for. I've read some of it, but it never was as interesting to me as the story was, since I can't Cure anyway. Once you learn how to read it, you could know everything there is to know about your powers. But there *is* a section that no one is allowed to read."

Achaius flipped to another part with different writing that looked coarse and wicked compared to the previous curly writing. The hair on the back of Kaie's neck stood up and she felt queasy just looking at it.

"One time I was looking at this when Maeve walked in and she almost took my head off," he said. "All I know is that it's all the bad stuff that the first Inviver was talking about. In addition to Curing and Calming, there's a third ability that Invivers have: Killing. But most Invivers don't really talk about it."

Kaie gulped, her nausea increasing. She closed the book. She didn't want to know more about her third ability.

She changed the subject. "How can this be written by the first Inviver? All the history seems to spread over generations."

"Supposedly, he lived for a really long time. It was his 'duty' or something to pass on his knowledge about the clans to future generations. I guess with your powers, you could unlock the secret to immortality. He says something about it in here about how the tyrant and later kings forced the Invivers to find a cure for death. Maybe he uncovered the secret."

Kaie's eyes widened. "Does anyone know who the first Inviver was?"

"You'd have to ask Maeve that. I haven't found anything about his identity," Achaius said.

Kaie noticed then that the candles had been lit in the library. The two had been so engrossed in the text that they had not noticed the servants coming in. It was time for dinner.

"We should go eat," she said, standing to leave. "The others will be waiting for us."

"Yeah," Achaius said, following close behind her. He watched the way her russet hair glimmered in the candlelight and was glad he had been able to share something new with her.

***

After dinner, history lessons began. Kaie felt renewed from the meal and walked with Tristen to the history room. He'd stopped by earlier and laid out several books on the table.

"This specific book helps explain everything I don't cover," he said, pointing towards the large tome closest to her. "I can test you as we go along to see how well you're retaining information throughout our lessons."

Kaie sat down, and the lesson began. Almost immediately, she struggled to remember which dates corresponded with which people as Tristen started with the beginning of the monarchy. A couple hours in, he asked her a question, which she struggled to answer. Based on his expression, she knew she had answered incorrectly.

By the time the candles had burned low, Tristen was able to sense her frustration at not being able to remember names. They had covered a lot of information and he wondered if he should change up his teaching style. He was only modeling how his mother and tutors had taught him, but it seemed Kaie did not learn the same way.

"Let's end here for today. You need to go to sleep," he said.

"All right," she said, relieved that the painful lesson was over.

It was quite different from her Curing lessons—though the only facts she was able to retain pertained to the Invivers. She had learned that within the last few generations, the Galician kings had pulled all the country's Invivers into their service rather than letting them roam the land helping the public. Nobles who had pleased the king were assigned an Inviver to stay at their estate to tend to their family and townspeople.

The new system the past kings put into practice grated on Kaie's nerves. Like Syane, she thought that medicinal skills should be shared with the general populace, not hoarded among the nobility. Kaie decided that when she was finally able to go back home, she would go around helping others. She would refuse to be handed over as a prize. People like her family—like her mother—should not be punished based on their situation in life. But she remained silent as Tristen had spoken, unsure how to voice her displeasure at the current state of things. Or if he would agree with her sentiments. Even if he was her friend, she had not forgotten that he was to be king one day.

CHAPTER 16

Over the next few weeks, Kaie began to learn more about the theory and mechanics of Calming from Avalon, and Maeve continued to have her Cure minor wounds on the newest group of soldiers. Fighting lessons continued to increase in difficulty as she improved, a sense of pride growing within her when she could see the marked difference from where she'd started. Now she could even hold Raven off for several minutes without getting tired, and she beat him during their sparring matches on a regular basis.

In the evenings, she continued to learn Galician history with Tristen, though she still struggled to keep all the information straight. He was extremely patient and went over the information as many times as she needed.

One night, Brayan's cryptic comments that had bothered her a few months ago became so overwhelming that she could no longer keep them to herself. After her lesson with Tristen, Kaie wandered to the infirmary looking for Brayan. Usually when Maeve brought her to Cure the soldiers, he would leave in a huff.

"Can I ask you a question?" she asked when she finally found him.

As soon as the words left her mouth, his face darkened. "I suppose," he said, crossing his arms. She was blocking the doorway and he could not leave without making a scene.

"Do you remember that day I Cured Achaius and you said there was a plan in place I knew nothing about?"

"I suppose." The physician shrugged. "What about it?"

"How did you know he was going to get worse? What did you overhear?" Her voice grew low. She knew that he knew something; he had insinuated as much that day. "I know he was given something."

"I don't remember," he said while staring her down, daring her to call him out on his lie. Even if he did not like her, he knew that the revelation would still come as a shock. Not to mention, he didn't necessarily want to get on Maeve's bad side when she found out he'd told Kaie. The old woman could be scary when she wanted to be.

"We both know that's not true. Tell me," Kaie pressed.

Brayan did not answer and began to put away his supplies for the day. It was late enough that he should go to bed.

Knowing that he was the only one who could answer her question, she blocked his way. The physician sighed heavily and knew that she would not leave him alone until she received answers.

"What did you hear?" she demanded, giving an edge to her voice that let Brayan know that she would make his life miserable if he did not tell her.

"I overheard the king and Maeve talking about the prince's recovery," he said tiredly. "They talked about poisoning him so they could unlock your powers."

"*What?*" Kaie backed away from him, her face paling in horror. "What kind of person is the king? He almost killed his son just to add another Inviver to their ranks?"

"The poison would have only put him in a deathlike state. Once you thought he was dead, the Invivers would have taken care of everything." Brayan watched the young Inviver's reaction, knowing that there was nothing he could do to blunt the blow he'd just dealt to her. "The king is willing to do anything to help us win the war. Just remember that you're only a tool to him."

"No... you're wrong," Kaie said in a heartbroken tone. There was no way Maeve would had deceived her like this. She leaned against the wall, her mind swirling.

Now that she had her answers, the physician left the infirmary, rubbing his head at the sudden headache that had started. The Inviver certainly had a way of making his life more difficult. He was positive Maeve would visit the infirmary some time tomorrow to yell at him.

In a daze, Kaie returned to her room and cried. She was terrified to think of what else the king was capable of, unable to believe his cruelty in offering up his son as a sacrificial lamb. And what of Tristen and Achaius? Were they only using her as well? Conflicting thoughts filled Kaie's mind, making her second-guess every moment of warmth and kindness she had been shown. More than ever, she missed her previous life, the simplicity and warmth of her family.

***

Kaie awoke in the middle of the night with such a strong feeling of homesickness that she could not breathe. Immediately, she jumped out of bed and raced for the door, the walls closing in on her. Soundlessly, her feet padded through the palace as she let them lead the way. Her heart constricted painfully, and she tried to concentrate on moving, breathing shallowly as she tried not to focus on the pain. Kaie's mind whirled as she sprinted through the castle, trying to flee the panic following her. Suddenly, she found herself in the ballroom which looked out to the garden, gasping for breath as the tightness of her chest slowly lessened.

A few candles were lit, casting gentle light throughout the room. Kaie went to the window and looked out, her wide-eyed reflection staring back at her. She took a few deep breaths, trying to calm herself down. Experimentally, she shifted her weight to her toes and spun, remembering when her father had taught her some of the court dances before he had left.

The day had been full of laughter, spinning around as her father whisked her about the floor. She closed her eyes, lost in the memory, the homesickness lessening just a bit. Slowly, she raised her hands, imagining her father as she began to go through the moves, gracefully gliding over the floor. The song her father hummed played in her mind and softly, she sang it under her breath. It was a slow dance, one that required precision, and she knew with each turn what was coming next, her nightgown swirling around her ankles. A lone tear trickled down her cheek as she thought of her family and how much she missed them. Dancing was one way to soothe her aching heart.

She had been dancing for a few minutes when she heard a noise. Opening her eyes, Kaie flushed when she saw Tristen staring at her from the doorway. His expression was unreadable as he watched her movements, his eyes following her hands as they fell to her sides.

"What—what are you doing here?" she stammered, embarrassed because she did not know how long he had been standing there. Fear pricked at the corner of her heart. She did not know if she would be in trouble for her late-night escapade.

"Farin checks in on you during the night," he explained, walking towards her. "She woke me when she found you missing. It was better than waking up the entire palace for a search party." He was now standing right in front of her. "Did you have a bad dream?"

Kaie shook her head, feeling extremely foolish. "I... I felt homesick," she admitted softly. "And I found myself here. My father taught me some court dances before he left... It helps... a little..." She trailed off, unable to say more.

The thought crossed her mind that Tristen might have known about Achaius's poisoning, but she remained silent. She could not stand more disappointment tonight. At the moment, it was easier to shove all doubt aside. If she received confirmation that Tristen knew, she would fall to pieces.

"Well, it looks to me as if you need a dance partner," Tristen said, smiling as her head shot up to stare at him in surprise. He offered her his hand. "May I have this dance?"

Shocked, Kaie took his hand as he led her into a waltz, moving slowly and twirling her around. The dance felt so much better with a partner, and he was an excellent dancer, making it easy to follow his lead. Tristen was amazed at how easily she moved, how fluidly she danced, and knew he should not be surprised based on how well Lorne commented on her progress. Dancing and fighting required a similar fluidity and quickness to react to the other person. Kaie possessed both these skills and executed them perfectly.

Once the dance was done, Tristen led them into a gavotte this time, another slow dance. Kaie vaguely remembered the steps and willingly followed Tristen's lead. With each step, she felt her homesickness lessen until it was a dull ache once more, no longer a sharp, stabbing pain.

"I think it's time for you to head back to bed," Tristen said gently as they both stopped.

He noticed how she'd relaxed the more they'd danced, all traces of tension gone from her face. As soon as he had entered the ballroom and saw her dancing, he'd known something was wrong, but she had looked so peaceful that he'd hated when she'd stopped and looked towards him in fear.

Kaie was surprised at how sleepy she suddenly felt. She nodded. "That sounds like a wonderful idea," she said, and Tristen led her back to her room. She stopped in the doorway. "Thank you, Tristen, for the dance," she said hesitantly. "I'm sorry that you got woken up tonight."

"It was a pleasure dancing with you," Tristen said. "And if you ever feel homesick, I will gladly do it again, if that's what you want."

She smiled up at him, a warmth filling her heart at his kindness. "I'd like that."

She got into bed, and before her eyes fully closed, she whispered under her breath, "I've always wanted an older brother like Tristen."

Sleep came swiftly.

CHAPTER 17

Dear Shayla, Momma, and Papa,

I miss you all so much. Prince Tristen and Prince Achaius have been very kind to me. My Curing lessons are going well and I've been making a lot of progress in my training with Sir Shalane. I can't wait to show Papa my new techniques when I come home! I spar with one of the soldiers on a daily basis, Raven, and I can sometimes beat him now!

Are the apple trees full now? I wish I could have a slice of Momma's apple pie. The chefs here are wonderful, but I wish I could have that taste of home. Eating her pie was always one of the highlights of the fall. I hope you all are doing well and I wish you would write back to me. I want to hear about everything that's been happening since I've been gone.

Love,

Kaie

She took the letter with her to the classroom to give to Maeve to mail. As usual, she asked if there was a response from her family, and like always, her teacher said no. But Kaie still held out hope that her family would write back. She wanted to hear from them and read their words.

Before the lesson began, Kaie wanted to talk to Maeve before Achaius arrived.

"Is it true you poisoned Achaius to unlock my powers?" The words came tumbling out.

Maeve gave her a startled look. "What makes you ask such a thing?"

"Brayan hinted at something back then that didn't add up. When I questioned him about it yesterday, he told me what he'd overheard. I want to know if there's any truth to his words." Kaie crossed her arms, daring the elder Inviver to lie to her.

Maeve looked at her before speaking, carefully choosing her words. "Yes, the king wished to poison Achaius to activate your powers. He's a very impatient man. You'd have to discuss the matter with him to know his reasons."

Kaie's face paled at the confirmation of the poisoning. For some reason, she had not doubted Brayan's claims, but to hear Maeve corroborate everything was still a shock.

"My father did *what*?" Achaius's horrified voice came from the doorway.

The two Invivers turned towards him. Kaie's heart clenched at the look of anguish on the prince's face.

"Achaius, you have to understand," Maeve began. "We had to find out if Kaie—"

"Was there no possible way to figure out if she was an Inviver other than poisoning me?" Achaius interrupted, his voice rising in anger. His hands were clenched into fists at his sides.

Kaie bit her lip, suddenly second-guessing her decision to dig into the secret, but knowing deep down that Achaius deserved to not be kept in the dark. She knew firsthand how much it hurt for others to keep secrets. She only wished that he'd found out a different way.

"Why don't we skip today's lesson?" Maeve suggested. "We can continue tomorrow." The Inviver quickly left the room, not wanting to answer any further questions. She had to go talk to Brayan.

Achaius turned to Kaie. "How did you find out about this?" His voice was terse, and she could tell he was trying not to yell at her.

"Brayan mentioned something," she said quietly. "I was trying to ask Maeve about it before you got here. I'm sorry you found out this way."

"Would you have eventually told me?" Achaius asked.

Kaie nodded. "After I figured out how to tell you," she said. "I know what it's like to be kept in the dark."

Achaius turned to leave.

"Where are you going?" Kaie asked, rushing to follow him.

The prince began to walk in the direction of his father's study. "I'm going to get answers about what's really going on around here," he called over his shoulder, his angry steps falling heavily on the stone floor.

***

Without even knocking, Achaius entered his father's study, slamming the door open.

The king looked up calmly from his desk, taking in his son's rage-filled face. "Ah, my youngest son. I thought you had lessons this morning?" he remarked evenly as Achaius stormed up to his desk.

"They were canceled based on some information that came to light," Achaius said through clenched teeth. "Did you poison me to find out if Kaie was an Inviver?"

"Who told you that?" the king gasped, his face paling.

"Kaie found out from Brayan and Maeve. Now tell me why."

Seeing that he had no choice, the king sighed resignedly. "Yes, I did poison you, but if anything had happened, the Invivers would have fixed everything. It was a test to see if our suspicions were correct."

"You were willing to risk my life based on a suspicion?" Achaius's voice rose in pitch.

"Relax. It was all under control. Besides, if we had not tested her, she would not be here now. Is that what you really want?" Torin had noticed that both his sons were enraptured with the Inviver who had wormed her way into their lives. It was at their behest that he'd allowed her to attend meals with the royal family.

"No, but—"

"See? It worked out for everyone." Torin's tone stated that the matter was settled.

"How did you even hear about her?" Achaius flopped into a chair, staring at his father. The older man seemed unflappable, so nonchalant that he had poisoned his own son.

"Despite being talented, she somehow slipped through our radar in scouring the country for Invivers. Her fame for healing had spread through the neighboring towns, but we had not heard anything. It wasn't until her mentor was traveling through the capital, bragging about her, that we took interest. She had mentioned that Kaie sometimes seemed to heal people instantly. As soon as Maeve heard that, she recognized the signs of an Inviver."

"And when I got bitten, it was the perfect opportunity to test her." Achaius finally understood his father's thought process. It did not make amends for him being in agony for a month, but he knew better than to expect warmth and compassion from his father. Anything to do with the war, and his father seemed to lose any sense of emotion.

"Exactly. Now if you'll excuse me, I need to get back to this military report."

"What's it about?" Despite still feeling hurt, Achaius was curious. His father only talked about the military reports with Tristen or Lorne.

The king frowned as he read. "It's from the Fernan Outpost. They seem to have plenty of supplies, but things have started to fall apart since I sent Kaie's father back home. He was the commander there for the past few years."

"I had not realized he was so highly ranked," Achaius said.

"Yes, he used to work as one the guards here for many years. Probably one of my best generals," the king said. "It was part of the deal that I send him home if Kaie came here."

"So what's the problem?"

"The new general doesn't seem to have a grip on things there. The men don't respect him and treat all his orders like they're a joke. He formally requests that I send more men." The king sighed and put a hand to his head.

"Will you do that?" Typically, Achaius would not ask his father questions, but he was encouraged that his father had not kicked him out of his office yet.

"And how will that help? So even more men can act like spoiled children? No, I'll do more than that. I'll send Rosse Swain down there to whip them into shape. He's done a good job helping Lorne with the troops here. Go find Sir Shalane and tell him to come see me. If you run into your brother, I need to see him too."

Achaius nodded before following his father's orders. It was still morning, so Lorne would be at the training grounds.

To his surprise, Lorne was overseeing Kaie and Raven's sparring session. It seemed that when Curing class was canceled, she'd come early for her lesson. The older captain whistled as he saw Achaius approaching. Raven and Kaie stopped at the signal, both dripping with sweat.

"The king requests your presence to discuss the Fernan Outpost. He would like to send the elder Sir Swain to go keep things in line there, but wants to talk to you first about her training." Achaius nodded his head towards Kaie. "If you come across Tristen, he wants him too."

"Very well," Lorne sighed, looking at Kaie and Raven. "You two can take the afternoon off. You've done enough for today."

Achaius watched as both lowered their weapons and Kaie sheathed her sword before Lorne left.

Raven approached Achaius. "He's thinking of sending Rosse to the Fernan Outpost?" To Kaie's surprise, Raven sounded angry.

"Yes, apparently the men there need more discipline than their current commander can provide," Achaius said, crossing his arms.

"I haven't seen Sir Swain around lately," Kaie said. When she had first started training, he had been helping Lorne train the troops, but over the past few weeks, she had not seen the giant man. Her main interactions with him had been on the journey to the palace.

"That's because King Torin has him running around, disciplining the new troops so we can win," Raven said mockingly. He rolled his eyes with a scoff—his brother's skills would be better used than babysitting a bunch of soldiers.

"You don't know what he has in mind for us to win. I doubt you are involved in discussing war strategy," Achaius said, his voice heated. Even if he didn't particularly like his father, he wouldn't stand for a soldier ridiculing him.

"Well, it sure doesn't seem like *you're* doing anything to help."

"Settle down, you two. It's not a big deal," Kaie said, trying to calm both down as the tension between them grew.

"No big deal? *No big deal?* My brother is getting sent to the most dangerous outpost in history! They get ambushed almost every other month there. He raised me. What will I do if something happens to him?" Raven cried, fear evident in his voice.

"My father was the general at that outpost. I know what you're going through," Kaie reassured him. "But your brother is a great fighter from what I've seen. Don't you trust his abilities?"

"Well yes, but I still worry about him! Didn't you worry about your father even if he is *the* famous General Durac?"

"Always," she said in a soft voice. Achaius immediately picked up on her turmoil. "I always think about my family and their safety."

"See? So even if I know Rosse can handle himself, I still worry—" Raven cut off as Achaius nudged him, nodding towards Kaie, who had a tear running down her cheek. "Kaie, what's wrong?"

"Nothing," she sniffed, wiping away the tear. "I'm fine. If you don't mind, I'm going inside. It's gotten chilly." She rushed inside before either one could ask her more questions.

Achaius rubbed his arms as well, realizing that the air had gotten a chill to it. Looking out to the palace trees, he realized that the leaves had already lost their emerald hue and were fading into crisp reds and oranges. Autumn seemed to have arrived without warning.

"What was that about?" Raven asked, staring after Kaie.

"She misses her family," he said, still surprised at the season change.

"I hope I didn't make her too upset," Raven said worriedly.

"Don't worry about it. I'm sure she'll be fine tomorrow," Achaius said, before following Kaie inside.

CHAPTER 18

Kaie wiped the tears from her eyes as she tried to stay out of sight in one of the more deserted hallways. Despite being so busy, she still missed her family. She continued to write to them, even if they never responded. Most of the time, the ache of loneliness assailed her at night, when she had time to herself, but over the past few days, it had grown stronger. During the day when she was distracted, the loneliness sometimes disappeared, but now it was back, as if to make up for being gone. And with the revelation of all the secrecy within the palace, she felt more alone than ever.

Tristen came upon her as she started to sob, the pain in her chest overwhelming her like a bursting dam.

"What's wrong?" he asked, putting a gentle hand on her shoulder.

"It's nothing." She turned away from him to hide her tears, shrugging his hand off of her. He could still be pretending to be her friend. What she could easily ignore the previous night was glaring at her, daring her to ask if he knew about all the secrecy.

"Really? Because last time I checked, nothing didn't mean you were crying." He crossed his arms in front of him, determined to find the underlying cause of her pain.

"A lot has come to light recently. Your father poisoned Achaius on purpose, everyone seems to be hiding something... It's just all too much."

"Ah."

Kaie looked at him, examining his neutral expression. "Did you know?"

"Only after the fact," Tristen admitted with a look of remorse. "I yelled at my father. I told him it wasn't okay to sacrifice Achaius like that, to allow him to suffer. But at that point, it had already been done and was too late."

"How can you just accept that?" Kaie asked in horror.

"Despite the fact that he can be a callous monster, he does have the weight of the entire kingdom on his shoulders," Tristen said, his mouth settling into a grim line. "And one day, I will bear that burden. I try to view things through his eyes and it's... difficult. But I know he's doing what he believes is best for the kingdom and our people."

"There's been so many secrets and lies about how I was brought here," Kaie whispered. "How do you expect me to believe anything anymore?" Tears glistened in her eyes. "I haven't even heard back from my family. They haven't written to me at all. How can I trust that my letters are truly reaching them?"

"Even if my father is capable of doing terrible things for the sake of the kingdom, I don't see a reason why he would hide letters from you," Tristen said.

"Do you really believe that?" Kaie asked. She would never dare ask the king to his face if he was hiding her letters.

"I honestly do," Tristen said, putting a hand on hers. "Now what else is bothering you?" He could tell that she was still holding something back.

"Why do you... how are you..." Kaie floundered her words. "Are you being nice to me because you actually want to be my friend or is this all just a front so I join the war effort?"

Tristen's mouth dropped open at her question, flabbergasted that she would ask it. Though with the recent revelation of his father's schemes, he should not be surprised at her doubt.

"Kaie, I promise you that I never approached you with ulterior motives in mind," he said, staring deep into her eyes. "I know so far the royal family has not given you much reason to believe our intentions, but please believe me when I say that I only want to be your friend."

The prince's words seemed so sincere and heartfelt that Kaie nodded, the vice around her heart lessening a little. "With everything, I just don't know what to believe anymore," she said, wiping away a tear. "I just still feel so alone."

"Well, you have Achaius and I close by," Tristen said. "I know we aren't your family, but we can distract you as best we can. And I'm sure it doesn't help that your birthday is soon."

She looked up, her tearstained face shocked. "How did you know?"

He smiled. "I've heard from some very reliable sources. Are they correct?"

"Yes. It's in six days. I'll be seventeen, you know."

"I do know. In fact, I have a gift for you, but you need to come with me now so I can at least get it ready." He started to walk away.

"What is it?" Curious, she followed him. The prospect of a surprise helped to ebb the flow of fresh tears.

"Some dresses of your own. I'm sure you're getting tired of wearing all of Catriona's old ones. I have a dressmaker who's going to make some for you."

He led her through a door, where the dressmaker was waiting, then left her there to be measured while he went to plan for their history lesson.

***

On the morning of her seventeenth birthday, Kaie awakened to the sound of geese making their trip to the south for the winter. Her room was chilly. The small fire Farin had made the night before had gone out, leaving an empty black hearth in its place. There was a soft knock at her door, and after she threw on a robe, she went to answer it.

Achaius stood there sheepishly, looking at his feet when he realized that she was wearing her nightclothes. "Maeve wanted me to tell you to dress warmly today. I guess we're going exploring or something. We'll meet at the training grounds. Anyway, it's chilly and all, so you best be prepared." He turned to leave as a blush of red covered his cheeks.

"Thank you," she said.

He turned back. "No problem. Oh, and happy birthday." He smiled.

Kaie closed the door to change into her old clothes, fingering her necklace for a moment, her thoughts focused on her family. A lump rose in her throat and she fought tears as memories of previous birthdays assailed her. Even when they did not have a lot of money, her mother had always tried to scrimp for birthdays to be able to buy ingredients to make a cake or pie. Kaie's favorite was always her mother's apple pie, as apples were an easy ingredient to get around her birthday. During the last birthday her father had been home, he had gone into town, returning with a bag of boiled sweets and a small plate of sweetened fried bread. Shayla had bounced around the house from all the sugar, making everyone laugh at her antics.

Shaking the thoughts from her head, Kaie raced outside to see what her lesson was to be today. A thrill of exhilaration filled her. Exploring with Maeve and Achaius sounded fun, a different pace from their usual lessons. She remembered the last time Maeve didn't have them stuck in the classroom or infirmary—the "sound of the earth" exercise several weeks ago—and she held back a chuckle. She hoped today's lesson was as memorable as that one. Even if they got distracted, the day had ended with laughter and fun.

Maeve and Achaius were waiting next to the training area, and Lorne was standing with them, Kaie's sword in his hands. She slowed, surprised that Lorne was not training with the recruits.

"Here you are," he said, handing her the sword as she approached.

"What do I need this for? Are guards not coming along with us?" It did not escape her notice that Achaius also had a sword strapped to his waist.

"Where we are going is not necessarily the most peaceful place to get to and one that is not open to outsiders," Maeve answered. "You'll also need this. Those clothes will not be enough for warmth." She handed Kaie a travel-worn cloak.

"Thanks. Is Avalon not coming?" Kaie asked as she strapped on the sword and put the cloak on, the heaviness of it immediately warming her.

"Not for this excursion," Maeve said.

"Where exactly are we going?"

"It's a surprise. You'll see soon enough," Maeve answered cryptically. "Now, we must go before the sun reaches any higher. We need to be gone before it passes the tree line."

The trio left through a side entrance, that way anyone watching the front would not be able to see them leaving. Their breath billowed out in front of them, like a cloud of smoke, and despite her cloak, Kaie still shivered. This early in the morning, the capital was eerily silent, with only a few people walking about. Most shops and houses were still dark, but the scent of fresh bread wafted from a nearby bakery—someone was up early preparing for the day.

Quickly, they were able to reach the forest, with Maeve setting a rapid pace despite her age. The frost on the grass and trees gave the forest a surreal quality, as if everything had been frozen in time.

When they reached a few miles in, the branches of the trees curled over them, creating a passageway. Maeve stopped, holding out a hand to prevent Kaie and Achaius from moving forward. They looked at her in question, keeping silent as she held a finger to her lips.

The old woman whispered, "We must be quiet now. This is the most dangerous part of our journey." She inched forward, walking on her tiptoes.

Kaie followed, glad that she had worn her old boots and that she knew how to be quiet from all her escapades in the forest. Fifteen minutes later, Achaius stepped on a twig, its snap echoing throughout the forest. Maeve and Kaie froze before turning back and looking at him.

He smiled sheepishly. "Sorry," he whispered.

Maeve looked at them both. "If we get ambushed, just run," she told them. "Don't try to fight them unless you have no other option. I don't want you two getting hurt. It's dangerous enough taking you out here with me."

As soon as the words left her mouth, a small bird cried a sharp warning call and flew overhead, its flock close behind.

Suddenly, Kaie's keen eyes saw the flash of a blade in the thicket and she held her hand up in warning. Maeve and Achaius froze for a moment, but as soon as she made the gesture, the bandits who had fanned out in the dense forest attacked. Maeve and Achaius ran for it, while Kaie stayed back to make sure they escaped safely, despite Maeve's warnings. She unsheathed her sword, its blade glimmering in the early-morning sun.

The bandits stopped for a moment, allowing her to get a good look at them. Her eyes widened as she recognized the leader. They were the group that had ambushed her and the guards on their way to the palace.

The leader's scarred face broke into a sinister grin. "Well, well, boys, look what we have here. It's that girl that they brought to the palace months ago. What are you doing out? Did they let you off your leash?"

He menacingly stepped forward a couple of steps, underestimating Kaie's abilities. Since that day all those months ago, her fighting skills had improved immensely.

She backed up a couple of paces, and when he lunged at her, she brought her sword up and slashed at his face. When he stumbled back howling, she made a run for it. One of his men darted forward and grabbed her leg, bringing her crashing to the ground. She lashed out with her sword, trying desperately to escape as another man approached her. There was a yell as she made contact, and the hand on her foot loosened. Quickly, she scrambled away.

Kaie ran for a few minutes, and once she was sure that no one had followed her, she leaned against a tree to catch her breath. A scream abruptly left her mouth as a hand stifled it.

"It's just me," Achaius hissed. "Be quiet."

He released her when she nodded. She spun around to look at him, her heart beating like a frightened rabbit's.

"What did you think you were doing?" he demanded. "Maeve specifically told us to run, not stay and fight."

"I wanted to make sure you two got out all right," she said.

"Well, you look terrible. You've got blood on you. Did you get hurt?" he asked, a look of concern on his face.

"No, I don't think I got cut. I was too busy trying to escape," she reassured him, holding out her stained cloak as proof.

"Good. Because if anything happened to you, I'd..." He trailed off, a flush covering his cheeks.

At that moment, Maeve walked up. Achaius turned away, grateful to have an interruption to the awkward silence.

"Where were you?" she hissed at Kaie. "I told you to run, not be a hero."

"I'm sorry," Kaie mumbled. "I wanted to make sure you two were all right first before I got out."

"Who cares about us?" Maeve snapped as she pointed at Kaie accusingly. "If anything happened to *you*, this war would be all over and we'd be on the losing side of it. Now, we must be moving on before we get ambushed again. The place isn't too far away. Come on."

After ten minutes, they came across a sudden wall of mist. The back of Kaie's neck prickled. She innately knew this was not a natural occurrence. Without hesitation, Maeve stepped into the mist, quickly disappearing from view. Kaie and Achaius glanced at each other before following their mentor. After a quick moment of panic at not being able to see anything, Kaie flailed her hand about until it caught Achaius's, and he held on tightly. She looked at him, and he gave her a wavering smile. The mist was disorienting for them both.

After several yards, the mist swiftly dissipated and they arrived at a rocky hill where Maeve was waiting for them. The Inviver placed her hand on the cold, gray stone as Kaie and Achaius watched in confusion. After a few moments, part of the hill moved away, leaving a stone staircase leading downwards in its place.

"Come," Maeve said. "This is an important part of an Inviver's journey."

She went down the staircase, leaving Kaie and Achaius no choice but to follow her into the unwelcoming darkness. Once they were inside the cavern, Maeve took a torch off the wall and lit it before pressing a section of the wall next to her. The doorway closed, leaving them all bathed in the light from the torch.

Maeve led them down another staircase. At the foot of it, a huge cavern sprawled before them. Every inch of it was covered in glittering crystals, illuminated by some external source. Stalagmites rose up in small groupings all around the room, creating a little walkway for them to weave around. Stalactites protruded from ceiling, some extending all the way to the floor, creating shimmering columns. The ceiling of the cave looked like a fantastical chandelier made of ice due to the dripping stalactites.

Maeve went around lighting each torch that was mounted on the walls around the cave. In the middle of the space was a shallow pool, illuminated by the light from the torches. The bottom glistened, an opal-like substance reflecting the light on the ceiling. Some small, opalescent fish were swimming to and fro, excited at their presence. Around the rest of the cave, there were other passageways leading to mysterious areas, and on the back wall was swirling writing, much like the letters in the book Kaie and Achaius had looked at together.

"What is this place?" Kaie whispered in awe as she took in the sight, her face glowing with excitement. It almost seemed like there was a deep heartbeat within the cave, and she felt a peace wash over her.

"This is a secret, reserved only for Invivers to see," Maeve said.

"What about me?" Achaius asked.

"You're the exception. Since you are so passionate about Curing, if you were an Inviver, you would eventually see this place. This is as close as you'll get to being one," Maeve answered.

"Why'd you bring us here?" Kaie asked.

"This is where Curing was created," Maeve said. "The calm waters make it easier to Cure because they help us concentrate better. It also can act as a conduit to connecting with the earth."

"What about the wall of mist outside?" Achaius asked.

"That is a protective barrier," Maeve said. "Only Invivers or those with pure intentions can enter. Anyone else either gets lost in the mist or is unable to enter."

Kaie shivered. "It's really cold in here." Her breath billowed out in front of her when she spoke.

Achaius moved closer to offer her his cloak, but Maeve said, "Come to the pool and stick your feet in. It will warm up your entire body."

Kaie walked over, took off her hunting boots, and stuck her feet in the clear water. The fish swarmed around her toes as a sigh escaped her and she started to relax as warmth encased her entire body. "Achaius, you have to come over here. The water's so nice," she called, slipping off her cloak.

Achaius walked over, upset with Maeve for helping Kaie before he could. He sat next to Kaie and followed her example. As his feet entered the pool, all his resentful feelings melted away as the magic water drained his anger.

"This is nice," he murmured in agreement, trailing his feet through the water.

Kaie sighed. "I wish we could come here all the time."

"Kaie, what's wrong with your arm?" Maeve asked when she approached them. "Are you bleeding?"

Kaie and Achaius looked down at her arm where her sleeve was ripped. Before she could do anything, Achaius slowly moved the fabric away, revealing a long, slim cut across Kaie's arm. Blood trickled down, staining the fabric.

"I thought you said you didn't get hurt," Achaius said accusingly.

"I didn't think I did. I can't believe they actually got me," she said.

"Maeve, can you Cure her?" Achaius asked.

"No. Invivers cannot Cure other Invivers—that's another weakness we have," Maeve said. "She'll have to Cure herself, or you might be able to, since you're in the pool."

"What does the pool have to do with anything?" Achaius said.

"If you're in the pool with another Inviver, you might be able to harness some of their power and Cure someone. Now, I need to go check on something. You two stay here," she said, walking towards the back of the cave, where writing covered the wall.

"Where are you going?" Kaie asked. She felt drawn to the back wall, somehow knowing that it held more knowledge. An unnamable yearning filled her.

"To a secret of a secret. Only fully realized Invivers can go through this door. If you finish your training, you will be able to come here to learn more about our past."

Maeve put her hands over the writing and began to mumble in another language. The letters began to glow a pale-blue light as another door revealed itself. She opened it and walked through, but before closing it, she leveled the pair with her eyes.

"I expect you two to behave yourselves while I'm in here. This is a sacred place. Don't make me regret bringing you here." She disappeared, and the door closed with an authoritative click, letting them know that it was locked.

By now, Kaie's wound had begun to sting and she gave a quick intake of breath as the pain intensified.

Achaius looked at her, concerned. "Can I try?" he asked Kaie, longing clear in his voice. He had always wanted to Cure someone, and now that the chance had presented itself, he was especially glad that the someone might be Kaie.

Seeing how much this meant to him, she nodded.

He gently moved a finger over the wound, tentative at first about touching Kaie's soft skin. He only used the pads of his fingers, but soon, he gained confidence and he focused his attention on her torn flesh. He took a deep breath then exhaled, a soft glow emanating throughout the cavern. The water in the pool began to pulsate with energy as it drew on Kaie's power and transferred it into him. As the light faded, he felt energy rushing out of him. Once the light had disappeared, the wound had vanished.

He let out a triumphant cry. "I did it!" he shouted, his joyful voice ringing throughout the cave.

"Great job, Achaius! I can't feel a thing. It's all gone," Kaie congratulated him, as she clasped his hands in hers.

"Thank you so much for letting me try this on you. I can't tell you how much it means to me," Achaius said.

Overcome with emotion, he leaned forward and embraced her. Her eyes widened with surprise, as he had never hugged her before, but after the initial shock, she returned the gesture. Taking this as a good sign, Achaius turned his head and kissed her on the cheek. Kaie's heart began to beat faster as she felt the butterfly-soft kiss against her skin, but her face remained motionless. She was not sure on how to react.

When he saw her expression, he winced. "Sorry. I don't know what came over me. I guess I was just so happy that I'd actually Cured someone that well... you know," he said, blushing.

Kaie remained silent, her face crimson, still shocked over the kiss.

"Um, I better go see if there are any other secret places in here," he said, rushing to put on his boots to try to forget about what happened.

Why do I have to ruin everything? he thought to himself. *I could have just kept it to a simple thank you, but no, I had to ruin it by kissing her. Although... it was kind of worth it.* He started to run off.

"Achaius?" Kaie's voice stopped him.

He turned and looked at her, his expression unsure. "Yes?"

"I... I want to thank you for... everything. I'm glad that you had a chance to see what Curing is like," she said. Her face was unreadable.

"No problem." He nodded and raced into one of the passageways.

A few moments later, Maeve exited the secret room and closed it off, double-checking to make sure that it was sealed properly before joining Kaie in the pool. "What's wrong?" she asked, seeing Kaie's expression and her flushed cheeks.

Kaie stared into the water, watching the fish dance around. "Nothing. I'm fine," she said.

Maeve raised her eyebrows, but did not question her. "Where has Achaius gone to?"

"He went to look around. He Cured me," Kaie explained.

"Good for him. He's always wanted to be an Inviver, you know," Maeve told her. "He bothered me so much about it when he was younger that I once tried to pass some of my powers on to him, but I was unable to do so. It's extremely rare that Invivers are able to do this, but it is up to the Inviver whether they want to or not."

"If an Inviver has the ability to pass on their powers, shouldn't they pass them on to as many people as possible? That would help with the Inviver shortage," Kaie said.

Maeve shook her head. "Our powers are not a limitless supply," she said. "Passing Curing powers to one or two people would not affect the original Inviver's abilities, but as they shared more of their power, it would eventually dwindle until there was nothing left. And whatever power is passed on will never be as strong as the original Inviver's."

"Oh." Kaie nodded; Maeve's explanation made sense. "But isn't it possible that the Invivers with the transferred powers could grow their abilities and limits like I'm doing? So they could eventually surpass the original Inviver if they tried hard enough?"

"Excellent question."

Kaie beamed at the praise.

"But unfortunately, no. Transferred powers don't work the same as ours. Because the powers did not naturally manifest, there is a limit to how powerful that Inviver can become."

"So if an Inviver transferred a lot of their power to a bunch of people and became weaker, each subsequent Inviver they created would be weaker too," Kaie said.

"Exactly. And that also causes problems if they become too injured past their own abilities, since Invivers can't Cure other Invivers." Maeve let out a sigh. "It would be easier if we didn't have these stipulations, but Mother Nature knows best and we must respect her decision."

The two drifted off into silence. Kaie swirled her feet in the pool, enjoying watching the fish chase her toes. After a few minutes, Maeve broke the silence.

"We better go find where Achaius has gone off to," she said.

They both stood up, and as Kaie put on her boots and cloak, Maeve went to find Achaius.

Her boots back in place, she looked at the pool, watching the fish dart around. Just as they were settling down, Maeve and Achaius reentered the cave. Before they left, Maeve put out all the torches, and they headed up the stairs to leave. Kaie was the last one to exit, and she looked behind her to get one last glimpse of the cave, to try and imprint it in her memory. As she gazed at the back wall, the unnamable yearning filled her once more. She wanted to know what secrets the hidden room held.

When they reached the outer door, Maeve motioned for Kaie and Achaius to leave before sealing it shut.

"We must be careful. Those bandits aren't going to give up that easily," she whispered, before they headed back into the mist. "Kaie, just run this time.

Don't worry about us if we get ambushed again." When Kaie nodded, she said, "Let's go."

As they approached the tunnel of trees, Kaie had an uneasy feeling. Before Maeve and Achaius started to enter, she said, "Wait! Something's not right here."

They both turned to look at her as she looked around for a clue to indicate that something was out of place. Her sharp eyes looked at the shadows, trying to see through them. She unsheathed her sword, ready for the unexpected.

"All right, let's go. There's nothing we can do if they do decide to attack. Is there another way to get back?" she asked Maeve.

Maeve shook her head. "No, this is the only way to return. The Mists are located in such a way to keep it safe from prying eyes. However, it does leave us vulnerable for ambushes."

"If we hurry, we might be able to take them by surprise," Kaie said.

They all ran through the trees, each one silently hoping that they would not get attacked again.

CHAPTER 19

Kaie heard the ambush a moment before they attacked. A leaf crunched, giving them away, and she spun just in time to defend her face.

The head bandit grinned as he saw her astonishment, his newest injury bandaged up to stop further bleeding. "Surprised to see us so soon?" he laughed. "You didn't think we were going to give up on you so easy, now did you?"

Maeve turned and yelled, "Kaie, just run! It's not worth it!" before a couple of the bandits attacked her. She pulled out a hidden knife, ready to kill anyone who got in her way. "Come and get me!" she shouted, trying to draw the attention away from Kaie.

"So," the leader said to Kaie, "you seem to be pretty important. This time, you are coming with us. We are ready for you."

He lunged, hoping to catch her by surprise, but danger had heightened Kaie's senses. She dodged the attack easily and turned to run, but was stopped when she realized she was surrounded by bandits. They did not attack, however, and she realized that the leader wanted to beat her by himself. She saw Achaius through the wall of bodies, standing still, not yet involved in the fight. She could see by his face that he was unsure of what to do.

"Just run!" she called to him. "I can handle this bunch by myself. Go back and get Lorne. He'll come and help us!"

Achaius nodded and sped off through the forest.

The leader gave a shout of anger as he dove at her. "Go get the boy, you fools!" he bellowed at the others. "I'll handle the girl. Whatever you do, make sure he does not arrive at the palace."

The men hastened to follow his orders, running after Achaius with surprising speed, given their size.

"*No!*" Kaie screamed.

Her only chance of helping Achaius was to beat the leader.

She turned and faced him resignedly, ready for the fight of her life. She could still hear Maeve fighting off the other two bandits, but tried to concentrate.

The bandit smiled as she raised her sword. He could see the determination in her eyes.

"Kaie!" Maeve yelled. "Just run! Just—" She was cut off as another bandit slammed into her from the side, knocking her unconscious.

"Maeve!" Kaie turned and tried to run towards her mentor, but the leader's voice stopped her.

"If you want your friend alive, you'll fight me here and now, Kaie Durac." His coarse voice gave away his amusement at her distress.

An icy shiver ran down her back at the fact he knew her full name, but she shoved it out of her mind at the sight of one of the men lifting Maeve up and holding a knife to her throat.

"Now that we have your attention," the leader said. "If you beat me, we will let you and your friends go. However, if I beat you, you come with us and your friends will live. If you don't fight me, your friend here will die. Understand?"

"Fine," Kaie spat out, knowing that if she did beat him, his men would just attack anyway, but she did not see any other alternative. "But you seem to know my name and I don't know yours. It hardly seems fair." She hoped that if she won, Lorne would be able to find him later and take care of him.

He laughed, sensing her reasoning behind this. "Very well. My name is Revelin," he said grandly, bowing slightly with a mocking smile. "But now that you know that, I have to tell you that you will not be leaving my sight so you can go tell your precious guard all about this." His smile grew as he saw his men come up behind her.

She turned, her heart sinking as she saw that they had Achaius with them. His head was bleeding profusely and he was unconscious. "What did you do to him?" she whispered.

"Oh, they just roughed him up a bit," Revelin answered with a sneer.

"But... he could die from that wound." She started to panic, knowing that the wound was likely a lot worse than it looked from a distance.

"Maybe. Too bad you can't do anything to stop that," he said, underestimating her again.

"Can I take a look at him first? Before we start this?" Her thoughts were consumed with Achaius's welfare.

"No."

"But I won't be able to focus as well. Don't you want to beat me fair and square?" She turned to face him, knowing somehow that even though he was a thief, he did not want to cheat to beat an opponent he desperately wanted to defeat.

He thought for a moment. "Very well," he said at last. "You may look him over for one minute." He motioned for his men to bring Achaius forward.

She looked at Achaius's head wound, knowing that what she was about to do could be very risky in the presence of the bandits. As she probed the wound gently, Achaius let out a moan. A high-pitched buzzing sound filled her ears, reminding her of when she heard the screeching before she Cured him for the first time. After a brief inspection, she knew that Achaius would die from blood loss if she did not Cure him soon. By the time they reached the castle, he would already be dead, even if they escaped quickly. Kaie set her hands gently on his head and took a deep breath. The familiar tingling spread through her arms and light began to glow from her hands. The bandits watched in astonishment as the wound began to disappear. With it, the buzzing faded.

When the light vanished, Achaius awakened and looked at Kaie. When he saw their surroundings, he groaned. "What did you do?"

Kaie was lightheaded, but managed to answer, "I had no choice. You would have died."

Revelin came up behind her and demanded, "What did you do?"

"I Cured him," she said softly, realizing how much trouble she was in.

"You're an Inviver?" Revelin was fascinated with Achaius's Cured head, probing around and looking for any sign of the previous wound. Achaius stayed still, but his face let Kaie know that he was not happy.

"Yes," she said in a clipped tone, knowing that she had to keep as much information to herself as possible.

"Does this mean you could Cure the wound you gave me earlier?" he asked, eager to know all about her power.

"Yes, but it's not a good idea."

"Why not?" His voice took on a threatening quality, and he raised his sword just an inch.

"It can get dangerous if I Cure too much. I start to feel faint," she said reluctantly.

"So you're saying that now I can beat you?" he asked, inching closer towards her.

She remained silent until he leapt at her, then she brought up her sword quickly, barely managing to dodge the attack. Achaius watched worriedly as they attacked and dodged, attacked and dodged each other. Soon, Kaie became weary, her body weakened from Curing Achaius, but she was able to summon enough energy to launch an offensive attack, making Revelin stumble back in surprise, shocked by her ferocity.

Kaie's arms were sore, and every time her sword clashed against Revelin's, it was all she could do to not drop it. Finally, Revelin caught her sword with his and spun it out of her grip. He held her at sword point triumphantly.

"I win," he said.

There was a brief moment where he seemed to contemplate killing or maiming her, but a short figure darted from the edge of the surrounding bandits. The boy Kaie had convinced Lorne to spare leapt in front of her, blocking her with his body.

"Joran! Get out of the way!" Revelin hissed.

"She saved my life," Joran said. "Let her and the others go."

"But she could be the biggest payday we've had in years!" Revelin said.

"To get to her, you'll have to go through me." The boy stepped forward until Revelin's sword was touching his chest. From her vantage point, Kaie could see that he was trembling.

Revelin's expression was conflicted and Kaie sensed his reluctance to go against the boy, much to her surprise. As she was contemplating what to do next, she heard horses' hooves approaching, and immediately, the clashing of swords filled the area.

As she turned her head to see who had come to help, she recognized Thunder wading through the bandits towards her, Lorne's sword flashing as it cut down bandits on either side of him. Thunder galloped towards Revelin, who dove towards Joran, rolling them both out of the way. Quickly, he got up and dragged the boy back to the trees. The other soldiers who came with Lorne were already winning the fight against Revelin's men.

Upon seeing Revelin's retreat, the bandits all fled back into the forest. Lorne's face was furious and he looked like he would kill Revelin if he got the chance. Instead, his focus was on Kaie and getting her to safety.

As he disappeared into the trees, Revelin shouted to Kaie, "You may think this is over, girl, but you'll see that we will find you again. You can't hide from us forever!"

Kaie shivered as his voice faded through the trees.

"Thank you for saving us," she said, turning to Lorne and grabbing her fallen sword.

Lorne jumped off Thunder and enveloped her in a hug when she stood. "I was so worried," he said softly as Kaie hugged him back. "Someone saw Achaius running out of the forest, but Revelin's men grabbed him before we could help. We knew immediately that something was wrong and came as quickly as we could. You were so brave." His voice was choked and his hold on Kaie tightened a fraction more before he stepped back and wiped his eyes, trying to hide the display of emotion in front of his men.

The soldiers averted their eyes, knowing that their leader would want some privacy, but they knew that if something had happened to Kaie, they would never have forgiven themselves for letting harm come to her.

Lorne gave the order for Achaius and Maeve to be taken back, and only a few men stayed to return with him and Kaie.

"I was worried about what was going to happen. He might have killed me if that boy hadn't stood up to him. The one you spared—he stood up for me," Kaie said. "I was so glad to see you, you have no idea. Revelin was the one who ambushed us, attacked us when I first arrived at the palace. He seemed to know about me. And you."

"That's… surprising. I wouldn't have expected one of his men to stand up to him," Lorne said seriously as he offered her a hand. She took it, and he swung her up onto Thunder. "We'll need to head back and tell the king about this. Hold on," he called as Thunder galloped off back to the palace, the rest of the men following behind.

***

That night, after debriefing the king of the attack and dozing off in her history lesson, Kaie dreamt of the back room in the cave that Maeve had gone in.

She walked confidently towards the back wall of the crystal cavern. The fish swam curiously through the water, their sleep disturbed by her entrance. The torches were already lit, their flames flickering, creating mysterious shadows on the back wall.

She peered at the runes, trying to make out the strange language in the shadows. Somehow, she immediately understood the writing that she had been unable to before. She read a brief line, the instructions for opening the door:

Chun an doras a oscailt, a rá go simplí, "Oscail."

To open the door, simply say, "Open."

Taking a deep breath, Kaie prepared herself to enter the room.

"Oscail," she whispered.

The door clicked open, revealing a light-filled room. Blinking in order to see, she entered and was immediately filled with joy. The light became brighter and brighter until she blinked—

She was back in her room, sunlight streaming through her windows.

Saddened by this turn of events, Kaie tried to remember what was in the room, but was unable to remember clearly what she'd seen before the bright light.

"Oh well," she sighed. "I might be able to dream of this tonight and remember tomorrow."

Kaie got up and started to write a letter to her family, to tell them of the previous day's events and of her dream. It had only been a few days since her last letter, but she wanted to share what happened, while downplaying the bandit attack. She was still writing when Farin entered the room to help her get ready.

"Writing another letter?" the maid asked.

"A lot happened yesterday," Kaie said with a nod. "I wanted to tell them."

Farin grabbed Kaie's clothes and ushered her to get ready. "You'll be late if you keep dawdling," she said. "You can finish writing to them later today."

When she got to her Inviver lessons with Maeve, she was delighted to find the old woman conscious and well. "Achaius told me what happened. That was very dangerous," she scolded. As Kaie hung her head, she said, "But I appreciate what you did."

Kaie smiled, knowing that she was off the hook.

***

The following weeks passed quickly, and fall soon gave way to winter as Kaie's head was filled with knowledge. Maeve began to teach her how to read the language of the Invivers, and she eagerly soaked up every bit of knowledge that she could. Each night, she dreamt more of the mystical cave, and longed to return with every fiber of her being. She was so caught up with her training that she did not realize it was a week before Yuletide until Maeve gave her and Achaius a week's break from lessons.

Servants were busy flurrying around the palace to prepare for a ball to celebrate the holiday. It was a highly anticipated event for the country's nobility and everyone took part in the preparations. Kaie did not expect an invitation, but the two princes insisted that she come and have a fun night filled with extravagance.

Farin even began giving her extra etiquette lessons in preparation when there was a spare moment.

"When you go to get food, make sure you don't fill it all the way or pile your plate high," she warned. "And you can't go back too many times."

"Why?" Kaie asked. She was confused. If the food was good and she was hungry, why couldn't she eat as much as she wanted?

"The nobility try not to eat a lot in front of each other," Farin explained. "It's a stupid custom, but no one wants to look like they're gorging themselves. They will judge you if you eat too much."

"Oh." Kaie was disappointed. She was looking forward to trying all the food.

"I'll make sure you have a plate of goodies waiting for you afterwards. That's a benefit of staying here," Farin said with a grin.

"That would be wonderful!" Kaie said, brightening immediately. "Thank you so much!"

***

A few days before Yuletide, instead of their usual history lesson, Tristen led her towards the sewing room. When he threw open the doors, she gasped, for nothing could have prepared her for the rows of multicolored gowns standing before her. The rich fabrics took her breath away and she stood in awe.

"I'm sorry I'm late. It's been a couple months since your birthday," he said. "But as you can see, there was a lot of work for the seamstresses to do."

"They're beautiful," she said. "Tristen, thank you. This is the best present anyone has ever given me."

He laughed at her reaction. "I thought you might like them. Why don't you try one on? I have the perfect one in mind for you." He went to the end of the first row, where a light-green silk gown hid behind many dresses. He plucked it out and handed it to her. "I'll wait out in the hall for you."

As the doors whisked shut behind him, Kaie looked at the beautiful dress. The embroidery was stunning—it swirled and weaved over the bodice, making an intricate pattern. The rest of the dress was simple, and she immediately fell in love with it.

Within moments, she was in the dress and found a mirror, admiring her reflection. The skirt billowed out at her waist, and for the first time, she noticed that the embroidery matched the design of her locket. It was then that she recognized the significance of the dress—of the details Tristen had put into the design. A lump started to rise in her throat, but she quickly forced it down. Kaie took her hair out of its braid, allowing it to flow over her shoulders.

She exited the room to where Tristen was waiting.

He smiled at her obvious joy. "That looks wonderful on you. Do you like it?"

She nodded, unable to say anything at first. "Yes. I especially like how the details match my locket." Her fingers moved to touch the necklace.

"I knew you would like it. That one is my favorite out of all the others. It looks very becoming on you." A brotherly pride rose in Tristen's chest as he took in how well the dress looked on her. "Now you have something to wear to the ball."

Kaie threw her arms around Tristen and hugged him tightly. "Thank you so much. This is the best birthday gift ever."

***

Yuletide morning came with a thick blanket of snow. Kaie awoke to Farin adding more logs to the fire in her room.

"Happy Yuletide," she greeted the maid.

Farin jumped and looked at her, a startled look on her face. "Happy Yuletide," she said before going to the closet to pick out one of the new dresses.

It was a festive gold and green dress modeled after one of Catriona's old dresses, and Kaie smiled at the selection.

"I think this one would be a good choice today."

"I think so too," Kaie said before climbing out of bed to get ready. "I have a present for you. It isn't much, but it was all I could come up with." She handed the other girl a small Yuletide bouquet of holly, ivy, and a snow rose that she had been able to prepare a couple days before. It was a tradition her mother had started when they were low on money. They would forage for plants to make winter bouquets for the house. It helped keep the holiday spirit alive when there was no money for presents. "I'm sorry I don't have anything else."

"Thank you, this is lovely," Farin said, accepting the gift graciously. She helped the younger girl get dressed, then brushed her russet hair until it shone, pulling part of it back from her face.

Kaie gathered the remaining bouquets into a small basket before heading to the dining room. She left the basket by the doorway, not sure when the royal family exchanged gifts, but was positive it would be after breakfast.

"You look beautiful today," Tristen said when Kaie entered the room. He noticed the basket, but kept quiet.

"Thank you. Happy Yuletide," she said to everyone before sitting down. Lorne was noticeably absent.

Achaius smiled at her, but King Torin just stared around the room, as if trying not to see her. Kaie's smile faded slightly before she began to help herself to the breakfast feast. There was a large assortment of pastries and meats, and everyone piled their plates high with a little bit of everything. Before long, Kaie was stuffed from all the food she had taken. The cooks had outdone themselves with the meal, and it had all been delicious.

A lull entered the conversation as everyone finished their plates. Kaie took this opportunity to fetch her basket.

"I made presents for everyone," she said, pulling out her bouquets. "They aren't much, but I hope you like them." She went around the table, handing everyone a bouquet.

"It's lovely, Kaie. Thank you," Tristen said, giving her a big hug.

Achaius thanked her as well, graciously accepting his present.

"Here you are, Your Majesty," Kaie said, giving King Torin a bouquet.

His expression changed to one of shock before slipping into a scowl. After a moment of hesitation, he took the bouquet before standing and sweeping out of the room without a word.

Kaie bit her lip before turning to the brothers. "Did I do something wrong?" she asked. The king had seemed distracted and insistent on not looking at her ever since she had entered the room.

"No, it's just..." Tristen trailed off, not sure how to tell her this. "In that dress... with your hair... you look so like Catriona. And during the holidays... it can be difficult sometimes. For all of us."

Kaie flushed, not realizing what an effect her clothing would have on everyone. She knew that her earlier borrowed dresses were the princess's, but had not realized how her presence itself could be a painful reminder of what was.

She looked down at her hands. "I'm sorry," she said softly. "I had no idea." Tears filled her eyes at the pain she may have caused the family, especially after they had worked so hard to make her feel welcome. "I'll just... I'll go so your father can come back. This is a time for family, after all."

At saying that, an ache entered her chest so strong that she almost choked on the words, immediately regretting eating breakfast as it churned in her stomach. Her throat quickly closed, a painful lump preventing any deep breaths. The intensity of the feeling reminded her of the night she danced with Tristen.

Tristen could see the emotion pass over her face and knew what she was feeling. He stood and walked to her, putting a hand on her shoulder before she could flee the room. "You don't need to leave," he said quietly, moving to wipe away a tear that had fallen down her cheek. "This is a time for family and *friends*, and to count our blessings. We are lucky to have you with us this year." He held out a hand. "Will you dance with me?" He knew that would help with her homesickness.

She looked up at him with wide eyes, the tears still there but none threatening to fall. His actions surprised her, but she was also relieved at the same time. Spending today alone would have been too overwhelming, and much of it would have been spent in tears.

Slowly, she took his hand and smiled. "A dance sounds lovely."

The three of them walked to the ballroom and Kaie's breath caught at how festive everything was decorated. Garlands hung from the windows and a giant tree stood in the center of the room, glittering ornaments and colorful paper hanging from its branches. She had not been in the room since that one night with Tristen and could not believe the transformation. It was completely covered in decorations for the Yuletide ball that evening.

Tristen spun her around the ballroom in a faster dance than before, trying to keep her mind off his father. Kaie forced herself to focus on the steps and enjoy herself, loving the swirl of colors as she twirled. Though she did not know this dance very well, Tristen made it easy for her to follow and decipher which move he was going to do next. By the end, both were panting slightly from the exertion.

"Thank you," Kaie said, dropping her hands.

"I didn't know you could dance," Achaius said when the two stopped.

Kaie turned to him and shrugged. "My father taught me a little bit." She froze as she noticed the king standing in the doorway, staring at her with a strange look on his face. "Your Majesty?" she asked, stepping away from Tristen.

At once, his expression hardened. "Get out," he hissed through clenched teeth.

Both his sons' expressions showed the shock they felt at his words.

"Father, that's uncalled for," Tristen warned.

"Why would you say that? She doesn't have to leave," Achaius protested loudly.

"Your Majesty?" Kaie asked once more, confusion entering her features. Her heart began to pound at the look of hatred that spread over his face.

"You aren't her. You never could *be* her," he said, walking towards her. He gripped her shoulder painfully before pushing her towards the doorway forcefully. Kaie stumbled a few steps before turning to look at him. "You are not a part of this family. Go!" he shouted when she hesitated.

Kaie flinched at the volume of his tone before running out of the ballroom. She turned randomly through the hallways, the king's expression of pain and anger etched in her mind. Her footsteps rang throughout the halls, each step taking her further and further away from the royal family.

Eventually, Kaie found herself in the library, the room warm with a blazing fire. Slowly, she walked towards a shelf and reached to pick up a book, stopping in surprise when she saw her hands shaking. She brought her hands back to her body and stared at them, willing the trembling to stop.

"He's wrong, you know," Lorne's voice came from the doorway.

Kaie spun to face him, surprised to see him. What she did not know was that he had heard the entire exchange and followed her. She'd missed him standing outside the ballroom when she fled.

"You've become a part of their family in the short time you've been here. None of you have had an easy life."

"He hates me," Kaie said. "I can feel it. Because I look like her... like Catriona." The name fell from her lips and she flinched.

Lorne walked over to her and gently put his hands on her shoulders. "The holidays have always been rough on him," he said quietly. "And now with you here... it changes things a little. But he does not hate you."

"Yes, he does," Kaie argued, looking up at the captain. "I saw it in his eyes. He resents that I look like her." A tear fell down her cheek. "How can I expect him to behave rationally when he holds this against me? How do I know he won't send the order to kill my family on a whim?"

Lorne hugged her, a surge of fatherly compassion filling him. "He would never dare to do such a thing," he said. He felt her arms move to hug him back.

"Why?" she asked quietly. She missed her family dearly, but Lorne's hug helped her more than he knew.

"The king would never kill a man who saved his life, or kill his family."

"You've mentioned that before," Kaie said, pulling away. "What happened?"

"An assassin snuck into court," Lorne said. "This was back when there were multiple balls a month and the noblemen stayed at the palace for months at a time. Back before... everything fell apart."

"Before..." Kaie could not force herself to say the words, but she knew Lorne meant before the queen and princess died.

Lorne nodded somberly. "Yes. Your father kept watch over him from the moment he arrived, but I didn't believe him that someone would send an assassin. It was too foolish of an idea to even consider at the time. One day, a man got unusually close to the king and was about to stab him when your father lunged in front of the blade. That's how he got the scar on his shoulder."

"Oh." Kaie was shocked to hear the story. Her father had never answered the questions she'd had about his shoulder—she'd had plenty when she had first seen the scar when she was younger—but he always found a way to speak around the subject. "Because of that, you think my family is safe?"

"Absolutely," Lorne said.

Suddenly, they heard footsteps running down the hallway towards the library. The two turned to the doorway and saw Tristen enter the room, out of breath.

"Kaie, there you are," Tristen said in relief when he saw her and Lorne. "We've been looking for you everywhere. Are you all right?"

She nodded slowly. "I'm fine," she said, glancing at Lorne.

"Will you join us for the rest of the day?" he said hesitantly, knowing that it would be a tense time. "We were going to exchange gifts soon. There's a couple for you."

Kaie shook her head and smiled sadly. "Your father has had a tough enough day already. It would be for the best if I wasn't there."

"But Kaie... it's Yuletide," Tristen protested, looking to Lorne for help. "You deserve to be there."

She walked over and put a hand on his arm, wanting him to understand. "Trust me, I'll be fine." Kaie went on her tiptoes and kissed Tristen's cheek. "Thank you for the dance, Tristen. It meant a lot to me." She left the room before he could protest.

Tristen turned to Lorne. "You understand, don't you?" he asked. "Why she should be there?"

"I do," Lorne said. "But she also doesn't want to torture your father any further today. I don't think you realize how much he sees Catriona in her and how that brings back the painful memories."

"I understand all that—we all see it in her—but why can't he look past her appearance to see the person inside?" Tristen demanded. "She's young, vulnerable... She shouldn't be alone today, not without someone there for her."

"You've come to protect her like you did with Catriona," Lorne observed quietly. "But you can't push her like Catriona, Tristen. She's different from your sister. You need to be gentle, especially concerning her family."

"She's become like a sister to me," Tristen said. "Can't you talk to her? She looks up to you. Get her to join us for dinner tonight, at least. She doesn't even have to attend the ball if she doesn't want to."

"You overestimate my influence on Kaie," Lorne said. "And I don't think today is the day to push her to do something she doesn't want to do. Especially involving the king. She's convinced he hates her."

"That's not true!" Tristen said vehemently. "He's just... confused."

"I know, but— Tristen, listen to me," Lorne said, putting a hand on the younger man's shoulder when he saw that the prince was not going to listen. "Kaie will take this at her own pace. Let her do that. If you push her to do something she's not ready for, it will end badly. I will go talk to her, but don't expect us to join you for dinner. I'll see if I can convince her to still attend the ball. For now, go enjoy the time with your family."

The eldest prince gave Lorne one last look before doing as the older man suggested.

Lorne took a deep breath and then followed after Kaie, knowing that she was going to spend the whole day holed up in her room unless he intervened.

CHAPTER 20

"What's wrong?" Farin asked when Kaie entered her room. She paused in her duties from dusting to look at the young Inviver as she collapsed in a chair. "I thought you were going to spend the rest of the day with the royal family."

"The king does not appreciate my presence at this time," Kaie said quietly.

Though she had started to feel better after her talk with Lorne, all the anxiety and guilt came rushing back. She bit her lip, trying to hold back the homesickness that crashed through her again. It was as if Tristen's dance had done nothing to help at all.

"This time is about family, and if he does not want me to join the celebration, then I will respect his wishes."

Farin knew Kaie was upset and could easily guess the reason why. She had worked in the palace when Catriona was alive and could see the similarities between the princess and Kaie. She put down the cloth and walked over to kneel in front of the Inviver. "It's hard for him," she said softly. "But do the princes not want you there as well?"

"No, they want me there, but... I don't want King Torin to be upset," Kaie said. "He doesn't deserve to have his holiday ruined."

"But you do?" Farin gently pushed. "I can already tell you're not going to be happy for the rest of the day."

"I don't know what to do," Kaie admitted, looking at the maid. "I miss my family more than I can say, but I can't join the others. What would you have me do?"

"I—" Before Farin could respond, there was a knock at the door. She went to answer it, and found Lorne.

"May I speak with Kaie?" he asked her, peeking around the door. "Farin, you can take the rest of the day off if you would like."

Farin moved out of the way and left the room, sensing the dismissal. There was a slight skip in her step, as she was never afforded many days off from her duties. Being a shopkeeper's daughter, she was already lucky enough to get a job in the palace.

Kaie looked up at Lorne and watched as he grabbed a chair to sit across from her. "What is it now?" she asked tiredly. "Did Tristen send you to convince me to come back?"

Lorne smiled at the question. "No, although I'm sure he would like that very much." The smile faded slightly. "What are you going to do for the rest of the day?"

Kaie looked out the window, at the snow-covered view that lay beyond the room. "I'm not sure," she said. "I suppose I could read..." She trailed off, knowing that it would do nothing to distract her from her feelings.

"Well, if you don't have any other ideas, I would love for you to spend the day with me," Lorne said.

She looked at him in surprise. "Really?" she asked. "Don't you get tired of seeing me every day?"

"Like you said before, this is a time for family," Lorne said. "Right now, neither of us has our families, so why don't we spend the day together?"

A smile slowly spread over Kaie's face at the idea. "That sounds wonderful," she said, jumping up to join him.

For the rest of the day, Kaie was glued to Lorne's side. The whole morning, they rode their horses around the palace grounds, Kaie's face flushed from the exhilaration and cold. At midday, the two of them went to the kitchen to warm up, and grabbed some leftovers from the dinner preparations before scurrying outside once more. This time, Lorne took her to the palace greenhouse to see the blooming flowers. Inside, it was warm, and Kaie enjoyed listening to Lorne tell her all about the different types of plants, even the ones she already knew.

Despite the absence of her family on Yuletide, Lorne helped ease the ache she felt. She felt cherished and loved. Spending time with him made the day feel special after all.

***

Kaie sighed as they began to head back to the palace. The sun had gone down over an hour ago and they'd remained inside the greenhouse. But now it was time to go back inside the stone structure, where an angry king did not want to see her face.

"What's wrong?" Lorne asked, knowing that something was on her mind.

"We have to go back for the ball, don't we?" she asked, looking at the brightly lit windows of the palace. From a distance, she could hear the laughter of the nobles who were beginning to arrive for the festivities.

"We don't have to do anything you don't want to," Lorne said. "However, if you were to go, I think you would have a fun time. There will be enough people there that you can easily avoid the king. What do you say? May I escort you to the ball this evening, my lady?" He bowed dramatically, making Kaie giggle.

"I suppose it would be a shame to let all of Farin's hard work go to waste," she said hesitantly. "She's worked for weeks teaching me etiquette so I can attend and not make a fool of myself."

Together, the two walked in through a side door. Lorne promised he would come get her in a little bit, then she headed to her room, where she'd get ready for the Yuletide ball that she wasn't sure she even wanted to attend.

Kaie quickly changed for the ball, slipping into the light-green dress that Tristen had shown her days ago. For one of the first times since she had arrived at the palace, she did her hair herself, opting for a simple updo with some strands of hair framing her face. Afterwards, she admired herself in the mirror, wishing not for the first time that day that her family was present. A lump rose in her throat. Her mother would be fussing over her and Shayla would gush about how pretty she looked.

A knock on the door interrupted her heavy thoughts, and she went to open it, revealing Lorne dressed up in his navy-blue dress uniform. Many medals adorned his chest, a few she recognized from her father's own collection.

"You look lovely," he said, pride shining in his eyes. "I'm glad you decided to go tonight. I think you'll have a wonderful time." He offered her his arm to escort her down.

"I am a little nervous," Kaie admitted, "being around so many nobles."

"Just stay by me and no one will bother you," Lorne said as they walked towards the ballroom. Already, there were sounds of music and laughter. The party had started.

Kaie gasped as they entered the ballroom. Though she had seen it earlier that day, it seemed magical at night, alight with what must have been thousands of candles. Music drifted over those on the dance floor, and colorful gowns swirled across the floor. The giant tree in the center of the room was now decorated with lit candles, the most elegant tree she had ever seen in her entire life. Tables along the walls were filled with mouthwatering food and drinks. Never had she ever expected to see, let alone attend, such an extravagant event.

Lorne chuckled at her reaction, leading her to the side of the floor to observe the dancers. Kaie's eyes darted from couple to couple, observing their graceful movements.

After a few songs, Lorne asked, "Would you like to dance?"

Kaie's eyes sparkled at the question and she nodded enthusiastically before Lorne escorted her onto the floor. A waltz began to play, and Lorne led her through the steps. Beaming the entire dance, Kaie kept time as they twirled around the giant tree. As the waltz ended, she thanked him.

"Never in a million years would I have dreamt of dancing at a ball," she said, her cheeks pink with exhilaration. She glanced around the room briefly. "I don't see either of the princes though."

"The royal family makes an entrance after the party has started," Lorne explained. "They should be arriving soon."

As soon as the words left his mouth, the arrival of the royal family was announced with fanfare. When the king and his sons entered the room, everyone bowed to show their respect.

The king immediately went to sit on his throne, while many nobles stopped to wish him a happy Yule. The princes were quickly surrounded by eligible noblewomen, each vying and hoping for a dance. The music started to play once more and people returned to the dance floor.

"Would you like to dance again or get some food?" Lorne asked.

"Another dance." The words were quick to leave Kaie's mouth.

Lorne once more escorted her to the floor and they danced again. As she spun around, Kaie accidentally made eye contact with the king. He stared at her, his expression immediately turning to a scowl. Her hand tightened in Lorne's and he took a quick glance to see what had happened.

"Just ignore him," he whispered, leading her to the other side of the tree, out of King Torin's sight.

Kaie did as Lorne asked and focused on dancing. She stumbled slightly, but was able to recover quickly. For the rest of their time on the dance floor, Lorne kept them on the opposite side of the tree, as far away from the king as possible.

When the dance ended and Lorne led her off the floor, Tristen was there on the sidelines waiting for them. He looked handsome in deep green with a gold sash, and on his head was a golden circlet.

He stepped forward and offered a hand to Kaie. "May I have the next dance, my lady?" he asked, bowing slightly.

"I would be honored, Your Highness," Kaie said, curtsying deeply. There were whispers as he led her to the floor.

"You're going to cause rumors and your father won't be happy," she said quietly as the music started.

"I don't care," Tristen replied with a cheeky smile. "It's Yule, and if I want to dance with my honorary sister, then I will."

Kaie's eyes filled with tears at his words. "That means a lot," she whispered hoarsely.

Tristen kept them away from King Torin's gaze, dancing out of sight at the other end of the giant tree. "I missed you today," he said, his eyes reflecting the sadness he felt.

"I missed you too," Kaie said, her voice tight. "But I don't want to make your father suffer by my presence." She sighed. "And I didn't want to worry about him glaring at me all day. Out of sight seemed to be the safest."

"Well, I'm glad you decided to come tonight," Tristen said, his eyes sparkling. "I wish we could dance all evening, but *that* would start rumors."

Kaie smiled. "I'll take what I can get. One dance with my honorary brother is a wonderful gift."

Tristen gave her another smile before twirling her. As the two glided around the floor, Kaie's heart was light.

When the song ended, she curtsied once more. "Thank you for the dance, Your Highness."

Tristen kissed her hand, an action that set off another flurry of whispers. "The dress looks lovely, Kaie, and I hope you have fun tonight," he whispered before leading her back to Lorne. "Keep the vultures away," he said in a low voice to the older man before walking off to dance with someone else.

Noticing all the eyes that were suddenly on her, Kaie put a hand on Lorne's arm. "I want to get some food," she said quietly, eyes darting around at all the people.

Lorne looked to see where her gaze was directed and nodded, realizing that she wanted to get out of the spotlight. Her expression reminded of him of a lost and scared puppy. "Come with me," he said, placing her hand around his arm as he led her to the tables.

There, Kaie filled a plate with all sorts of pastries, meats, and desserts. She tried to stick to Farin's advice, but everything looked delicious. Lorne grabbed a plate, as well, taking half the food off her plate and putting it on his before grabbing them both glasses of lemonade. She flushed slightly, knowing he was trying to save her from the embarrassment of taking too much. Then he led her outside to the empty terrace where torches were lit, casting away the cold.

The two ate in silence for a few moments, Kaie breathing more easily now that no one else was around. She stared at the snow that had begun to slowly fall from the sky, adding more to the already blanketed ground.

Lorne watched her pick at the food on her plate. "Are you having a fun time?" he asked hesitantly. "If you're having second thoughts, we can always leave."

Her head shot up at his question. "I'm having a wonderful time!" she insisted. "I loved being able to dance with you and Tristen." She paused slightly, lowering her gaze. "I just don't like all the attention, all the whispers about me."

"That sometimes comes with the territory," Lorne said. "The princes are very popular with the nobility and while you were introduced to the court after Achaius was Cured, no one really knows who you are. Everyone is curious who has captured their attention."

"Despite that, I'm glad I came," she said. Her voice turned wistful. "I wish my family could be here. Shayla would have loved to see all the pretty ladies and we could see our parents dressed up and dancing." She paused, allowing herself a moment to wallow in sadness before brightening up once more. "But this is a nice distraction and I know it will be a wonderful memory." She began to eat more of the food on her plate.

"I'm sure they miss you too," Lorne said gently. "Have you contacted them since you arrived here?"

She nodded. "I've sent them multiple letters telling them how I'm doing. I've shared about how I'm doing at lessons and training, about everyone here." Her expression fell. "But they haven't responded. Knowing my father is back home taking care of Momma and Shayla helps ease the anxiety, but I wish they would write back."

Lorne's heart pinched upon hearing her words and heartbroken tone. "I'm sure they're just busy and don't want to distract you," he said. He looked at her empty plate and changed topics. "Would you like to go back inside?" he asked. Upon spotting the occupied doorway, he smiled slightly. "I think there is someone else who wants to dance with you too."

Kaie frowned in confusion before turning to see who he was looking at. "Your Highness!" she exclaimed as Achaius approached them, remembering at the last minute to use his title. "What are you doing out here?"

"I could ask you the same thing," Achaius said as he came and sat next to her. His outfit was deep blue and he was wearing a silver sash. Rather than a golden circlet, like the one Tristen was wearing, his was silver.

"I needed a break from all the staring," she admitted. "Dancing with Tristen put a lot of attention on me."

Achaius looked disappointed. "Does that mean you don't want to dance with me?" he asked, his voice sounding sad. "I—I was looking forward to dancing with you tonight. It looked like you had a lot of fun dancing with Tristen."

Kaie looked to Lorne briefly for encouragement before nodding. "I... I suppose a few more dances wouldn't hurt," she said, steeling herself for the attention that was sure to be on her.

A smile crossed Achaius's face as he held out a hand. "Then, may I have this dance, my lady?" he asked, bowing to her. The tips of his ears were red, and Kaie had to fight the urge to tease him for it. He was trying.

"I would love to, Your Highness," she said, standing to go back inside.

Achaius gently squeezed her hand before they reentered the ballroom. "Just keep your attention on me," he whispered. "Ignore everyone else."

Her face flushed slightly at his words as they entered, but she pushed her shoulders back. She fought with a sword on a daily basis—the stares of others were nothing compared to that.

It was not long before the whispers started again, everyone's eyes focused on Achaius and Kaie. Ignoring them, the prince confidently led her to the dance floor. When he settled his hand on her waist, his cheeks flushed, causing Kaie to suddenly become overly conscious of where their points of connection were. Their hands tentatively clasped together and he pulled her closer than they had ever been before. A romantic waltz began to play, and he led her into the slow, swirling dance.

"Did you have a nice day?" he asked, his face still red.

Kaie could feel her own face flushing to mirror his. "I did," she confirmed. "Lorne spent the whole day with me. He showed me the greenhouses this afternoon."

"I hope that my father's behavior…" He trailed off, stumbling over his words. "I hope he didn't ruin your day." When his eyes met hers, she could see how sincere he was being. "You… you deserve a good holiday too."

"Thank you," she said softly.

Though Lorne, Tristen, and Achaius had expressed similar sentiments over the king's behavior, it was Achaius's that warmed her heart the most. The coarse, brusque prince that she'd met when she had first arrived had melted into the gentle young man dancing with her now. For some reason, the memory of their time in the cave entered her mind, of the kiss he had placed upon her cheek, and her face flamed further.

Achaius led her skillfully around the dance floor, surprising her with how deftly he navigated around the other dancers. It also did not escape her notice that he purposefully kept her on the side of the tree furthest away from his father.

"You are a magnificent dancer," she said, and his face flushed further at the compliment. She felt a thrilling enjoyment at that fact.

"Thank you," he said. "You dance wonderfully too. If I had known you enjoyed dancing this much, I would have asked you to dance much earlier."

"Tristen found out months ago," she said. "He found me one night in the ballroom when I couldn't fall back to sleep. It helps with the homesickness."

"I'm glad he was there to comfort you," Achaius said, twirling her in a circle. "I know your stay here hasn't been what you expected, but please believe me when I say that we are all blessed to have you here."

Kaie was at a loss for words. Never before had Achaius said something so elegant and sentimental. "I'm glad to have met you too," she said, tears of happiness pricking her eyes. Lorne had been right—the two princes did care about her.

The two lapsed into silence for the rest of the dance, unable to come up with any other topics of conversation. But when the dance came to an end, Kaie was surprised to find herself saddened that she would no longer be dancing with Achaius.

He offered her his arm and escorted her back to Lorne. In another surprising move, he took her hand and kissed it when they reached the captain. "Thank you for the dance, my lady," he said softly.

"Thank you, Your Highness," she said, trying to ignore the newest flair of whispers.

Lorne stifled a chuckle as he watched the youngest prince head to the other side of the ballroom, then looked down at Kaie, noting her reddened cheeks. "Did you have a fun time?" he asked her.

Wordlessly, she nodded, her gaze still locked on Achaius. There were a few other young men Lorne could see already looking at Kaie with interest. When they met his eyes, Lorne stared icily until they looked away.

"Could I interest you in one last dance?" he asked, leaning down to look at Kaie. He could tell that she was getting tired. "Then we can leave and you can go to sleep."

"One more dance," she said, her tired eyes brightening.

As the two took to the floor for their final dance, the orchestra played another slow song. Lorne twirled her around the floor, making sure to spin her frequently, enjoying the little giggles she let out as she spun. He could feel the eyes of the bystanders on them, but focused instead on Kaie's happiness. She was radiating joy. For not the first time, he felt fatherly pride towards her and was glad that her first Yule away from her family had been a happy one.

CHAPTER 21

A few days following the ball, Maeve entered the classroom with an unusually serious look on her face. "We need to talk," she said.

"What's wrong?" Kaie asked, turning to look at Achaius to see if he knew what this was about.

He shrugged at her, just as in the dark as she was.

"We've come to a turning point in your training," Maeve said. "You have been to the Mists and started to learn the Invivers' language. You can either go home or you can continue. A decision does not need to be made right now," she added as Kaie opened her mouth to speak. "We will give you five days to decide. Until then, your training is postponed. This includes your lessons with Lorne as well." She walked off, leaving Kaie to process this information.

Kaie slowly sat down, stunned at this new revelation. "What do I do?" she whispered.

Her mind spun. On the one hand, she could continue learning about Curing, a subject she was passionate and excited about. Or there was the option to go home and see her family, who she had not seen in months. The thought of not seeing her family until the war was over hurt her heart.

"If you ask me, you should continue," Achaius said, his voice quiet. The thought of Kaie suddenly leaving panicked him. He might never see her again. "We could still learn together."

"What do you mean 'we'? You're not an Inviver. Only I would continue," she snapped. Suddenly angry, Kaie stomped out of the room.

***

That night, Kaie could hardly focus on her history lesson, having more difficulty than usual, and Tristen knew the reason why. During one particular section of reading, no matter how many times she read it, the material did not want to stick with her. After reading the same paragraph for the tenth time, she smacked the book shut in disgust, the force of her frustration knocking it onto the floor.

"Your mind is elsewhere tonight," Tristen observed, leaning over to pick up the book, gently setting it on the table. "What's wrong?"

"I don't know what to do about my training," she said, holding back tears. She put her head in her hands, the situation spiraling about in her mind.

Tristen thought about it for a moment, his expression unreadable. "You've mentioned that you have dreamt a lot about the cave lately. Perhaps it's a sign you should keep going?"

"But I haven't seen my family in months. What if I don't want to continue?" she asked in a small, sad voice.

"Then go home. However, I think you *do* want to continue, but you feel guilty, like you're giving up on your family in the process." He watched her closely for her reaction, knowing deep down that he was right.

"You don't know how I feel!" she cried, letting Tristen know that he had hit a nerve.

"I don't?" he said, his voice raised, suddenly angry since she had been in a mood all evening. Dinner had been a tense affair, with Kaie avoiding looking at Achaius while providing one-word answers to any questions directed her way. During their lesson, she had been moody towards him too.

"When Mother and Catriona died, I had to get over their deaths somehow. When I finally found an outlet, I felt like I was giving them up, that I was choosing something over remembering them. So don't tell me that I don't know how you feel!" His clenched hands pounded the table in front of him.

"My sister is waiting for me, believing that I'll be coming home soon. I know that, and I promised her I would. You didn't make any sort of promise like that to Catriona. She's *dead*!" The words fell like weighted barbs from her lips. As soon as they left her mouth, she gasped, wishing she could take the harsh words back.

"We are done here," Tristen said quietly, in shock over what she said. Even though he knew she was only letting her emotions get the best of her, he'd never thought she would say something like that. "Lessons are over. For good. I've taught you enough and if you'll be leaving soon, what's the point of continuing?" He walked swiftly towards the door, his shoulders hunched under the weight of her words.

"Tristen... I... I didn't mean it," she said, realizing just how deeply her words had cut him. What she said was unforgivable, no matter how high her temper had risen. "I'm sorry. It just came out."

He paused at the doorway, about to say something, but changed his mind and left.

Shame filled her, and Kaie paused, trying to rein in her emotions. Knowing that she had hurt one of her best friends, Kaie raced after him, only to find the hallway empty, the prince already gone.

She walked back to her room and cried herself to sleep.

***

The next day, Kaie wandered the hallways until she stopped by the classroom. To her surprise, Avalon was inside reading the Invivers' book. She looked up as Kaie entered the room.

"Ah, Kaie. What can I help you with?" Avalon smiled warmly, nodding towards a chair.

Kaie sat down and fiddled with her hands. "I... I was wondering if you could tell me more about why you left the Scrian army," she said. Maybe hearing from Avalon would help make her decision.

Avalon's smile faltered for a moment, and she slowly closed the book, clearing her throat. "As I mentioned before, the Scrian commander was using techniques on the Invivers that I didn't agree with."

"Like what?" Kaie asked when Avalon paused.

"He would work us to collapse, barely treating us as human," Avalon said. "Despite the fact that Invivers cannot Cure each other, Crevan would injure or maim us past our abilities to see if there was a way to bypass that." She raised her sleeve and showed Kaie a thin scar encircling her entire wrist. "He had worked me to the point of collapse before cutting off my hand," she said, and Kaie covered her mouth in horror. "Luckily, I had just enough energy to Cure myself, but not completely. It still aches during bad weather."

"That's awful," Kaie whispered.

"He's cold and calculating and will stop at nothing to push the bounds of Curing. He also had us try different Curing and Calming techniques on the soldiers as well." Avalon gulped, reliving the memories. She shuddered.

Kaie put a hand on hers. "It's okay if you can't say it. You don't have to tell me," she said.

Avalon shook her head. "You deserve to know what you're going up against if you continue your training," she said. "He found a way for us to use our powers to essentially brainwash the soldiers and make them mindless killing machines. To push past their mental barriers and bend their mind to your will. Though not many Invivers were able to do that, that task mostly fell to me as I was the best at it." She closed her eyes and grimaced. "Being in their minds and knowing I was the one sending them to their deaths was awful. I always vomited afterwards. The feeling of crawling in their minds like that was disgusting, like being covered in a sticky sludge that would never go away." She shuddered.

Kaie gasped. She'd never imagined that Curing and Calming could be used for such horrible means. "And that was your breaking point?" she asked.

"Yes," Avalon said. "After sending an entire battalion to the slaughter, I could not take it anymore."

"Why not use your powers to Kill him?" Kaie asked, remembering what Achaius had mentioned months ago.

Avalon's face turned white, and there was a noise at the door. Both turned to see Maeve rushing in. She ran to Kaie's chair and put her hands on the younger Inviver's shoulders.

"Where did you hear that technique?" Maeve asked, her panicked face inches from Kaie's. "What do you know?"

"Achaius mentioned that's what is in the forbidden section of the book," Kaie said, taken aback by Maeve's reaction. "But I don't know anything other than that."

Maeve's eyes searched hers for answers before nodding, concluding that Kaie was telling the truth. "Very well," she said with a sigh, pulling back to lean against a desk.

"What's so bad about it?" Kaie asked. "I mean, obviously killing someone isn't good, but why are you reacting so harshly?"

Avalon and Maeve exchanged a look before Maeve spoke. "Killing is very serious," she said. "Unlike when you kill a person without your powers, Killing them with your abilities takes a toll on the body. To do something like that, to use your powers in the exact opposite way that Mother Nature intended, does have a cost. Each person you Kill makes your lifespan significantly shorter." The old woman's eyes looked pained, as if she was remembering something.

"But if this commander is truly that terrible, isn't it worth the cost?" Kaie asked.

"He did force a few Invivers to Kill people. I saw the aftereffects firsthand," Avalon said. "To die from a shortened lifespan is excruciatingly painful. I can still hear their screams." She looked at Kaie and leaned forward, as if to impart the importance of her words. "You must never try to Kill another living being unless you are fully prepared to deal with the consequences. Understand?"

"Well I don't know how to even do that, so I don't think there's an issue with that," Kaie said. She nodded solemnly. "But I won't ever do such a thing."

"Good," Maeve said. "Now go on. You aren't supposed to be getting lessons anymore."

Kaie bade the two goodbye before leaving the room, alone with her thoughts once more.

***

Over the next few days, Kaie and Tristen's relationship was strained. They refused to talk to each other and everyone could tell they'd had some sort of falling out, although no one knew the details. The atmosphere between the two was tense. Kaie locked herself away in the library, barely speaking to anyone, while Tristen threw himself into war-planning sessions with his father. At meals, they studiously avoided looking at each other, the strangled silence over the table making everyone flee as soon as the food was finished.

On the third night at dinner, King Torin made an announcement, gently tapping his spoon to his glass to gain everyone's attention. There was a glint in his eyes that gave no one any comfort. "Tristen, you are going to the front lines, to Carthan Valley, this week," he said.

Kaie looked in horror at the king, her heart skipping a beat in terror.

"Fine," Tristen said noncommittally.

He had been as affected about his argument with Kaie as she was. Nothing interested him after the fight, her words cutting him more deeply than he had realized. At his father's announcement, he felt nothing.

"Wouldn't you like to know why?" The king tapped his fingers together, slightly disappointed that Tristen would not give him more of a reaction.

Tristen rolled his eyes and let out a sigh. The old man always wanted a reaction to his schemes. He would take the bait and ask. "Fine. Why?"

"I need someone at the front who understands where I want to go with this war, to help us get past this stalemate. Since we've been discussing strategies, I feel that you realize what I want to get done. I need a general who will take command confidently and I need to know that he won't lose his head during battle. This means you."

"Why does *he* have to go?" Achaius asked, voicing everyone's unspoken question. It was almost unthinkable to send the kingdom's heir to the throne to the most dangerous battlefield.

"Because it is time to trust him with this responsibility. If he's to be king one day, I need to know that I'm leaving the kingdom in capable hands." King Torin's eyes went from face to face, taking in everyone's reactions. His gaze lingered the longest on Kaie as he watched her stare at Tristen in panic. However, his oldest son just looked at his plate, moving some peas around it.

"He could get hurt," Achaius objected. It was a thought that was running through everyone's mind. "Why would you send your heir to such a dangerous place on purpose?"

"We have plenty of Invivers there. It's nothing they can't take care of," the king said.

A sob escaped Kaie's throat, and she raced out of the room as tears sprung to her eyes, her emotions overwhelming. The lid she used to keep her emotions at bay sprung open.

"Now see what you've done," Tristen muttered, setting his fork down and staring at his father.

"What are you talking about?" King Torin asked in mock confusion.

"Using me in your sick plot to make her continue training," Tristen said. He was used to his father's tactics, so he knew when he was making decisions in order to manipulate someone. "I'm out of here." He threw his napkin on the table and left. He wished to find Kaie and was ready to listen to what she had to say, hoping that they could go back to the way things were before he left.

Upon reaching the main foyer, Tristen looked around, searching for any sign of where Kaie might be. The side door was slightly ajar, the freezing wind making Kaie's cloak on the nearby rack rustle back and forth. He sighed as he put on his own cloak, and then grabbed hers before following her into the chilly night.

Outside, the blast of cold air made him shiver. A few yards away, he could see Kaie in the garden, staring into an empty fountain that was blanketed in snow. Her arms were wrapped around her body, her back turned to him. He walked over and gently draped the cloak over her shivering form, to which she jumped in surprise, spinning to face him.

Tristen looked down into her eyes, unsurprised to see tears streaming down her face. Despite her words a few nights ago, he knew she cared about his well-being.

"Tristen, I'm sorry for what I said earlier. I was just so upset and I don't know what to do, and I said things that I didn't mean. Even though we haven't been talking, I don't want you to leave." She broke off, sobbing, unable to continue. Ever since the king's announcement, a pit had settled in her stomach. But she did not want to express her worries to Tristen. He had enough to worry about.

He reached over and hugged her, doing his best to comfort her. Kaie wrapped her arms around him and she buried her face in his chest as she cried harder.

"Shhh. Shhh, it's all right. There's nothing to be sorry about. We were both upset that day," he comforted her.

She looked up at him. "What were you upset about?"

"I heard from Maeve that you have to decide what to do next and knew that Achaius wouldn't be of any help. I wasn't sure how to give you advice without pushing my preference for your decision. I let my emotions get the better of me." His lips came together in a thin line. He was the adult—he should have been able to provide her comfort when she had obviously needed it.

"What is your opinion?"

"I know that you miss your family but would like to continue training," he began. "It's your choice and..."

"Tristen, just tell me. Please," she pleaded.

"To be honest, I see you as my sister. You've started to fill up the hole that Catriona left. You'll never be able to fill it completely, but you're creating your own little space in my heart. I couldn't bear the thought of losing another sister," he said, his eyes glassy. "But it is your choice and I didn't want to impress my reasons on you like Achaius. You've had enough pressure already from him without my opinion weighing in."

"Thank you," she whispered. "I appreciate that. It seems like I've been here forever and that the people here are slowly replacing my family. Lorne is like a second father to me and you're the older brother I've never had. It almost feels like—"

"Like you've just given up on them?" Tristen guessed.

"Yes. I don't even remember what my father looks like. I haven't seen him for over five years. When I try to remember what he looks like, all I can picture is Lorne's face." She stopped, unable to continue talking.

"I know you haven't given up on seeing them again," he said, putting an arm around her. "You're much too strong for that. Now come on, let's go inside. It's pretty chilly out here." He headed back towards the castle, but her voice stopped him.

"Tristen, I'm glad you came out here. I feel much better now."

He nodded, and they headed back inside.

Kaie let out a large yawn, and Tristen smiled.

"It is time for you to go to bed," he said gently. "I'm guessing that I will probably be leaving in a few days, so we can talk more tomorrow." He took her to her room and had Farin tuck her in.

***

The next morning Kaie was awakened by a flurry of servants rushing past her door, the shouting and movement too loud to sleep through. With growing confusion as to the commotion, she put on her green dress before looking at her reflection in the mirror. Satisfied with her appearance, she opened the door and stopped short as a servant flew by her.

Farin noticed the young Inviver and came to her. "I'm sorry I did not wake you this morning, but as you can see, we've been swamped with work to take care of."

"What's going on?" Kaie asked as she watched the bustle of activity.

"Prince Tristen is leaving with many of the soldiers at midday today," Farin said. "We are rushing to get everything ready for a comfortable journey."

Kaie felt as if she had punched in the stomach and her face paled. She raced out of her room to look out of a nearby window, ignoring the other servants rushing past her. In the courtyard below, Tristen seemed to be in a heated discussion with his father. An idea hit Kaie, and she raced downstairs, hoping to catch the king before he disappeared.

She flew into the courtyard, just in time to hear the king say, "Look, Tristen, I know we haven't seen eye to eye on a lot of things, but you have to trust that I know what I'm doing."

Tristen opened his mouth to reply, but stopped once he spotted Kaie. "What are you doing here? I thought you'd still be asleep," he said. The night before, she had been exhausted.

"The noise woke me up," she said before addressing the king. "Your Majesty, is there any way I can change your mind about sending Tristen to Carthan Valley? If I decide to finish my training, would you reconsider?"

As she spoke, both men's eyes grew wide. Tristen's face paled at her words and he shook his head vehemently. Kaie noticed that a small smile crossed the king's lips. At least one of them was pleased by her offer—the one who controlled Tristen's fate.

"You need to continue training because you *want* to, not to save me from going," Tristen said, putting a hand on her shoulder. He did not want her to sacrifice her happiness just to save him. "I thought you wanted to see your family?"

"But you're *also* my family. And I don't want my family to be taken away again." A tear slipped down her cheek and she felt ashamed over how much she had cried during the past few days.

Tristen gently wiped the tear from her cheek. "Don't worry," he said. "We'll see each other again. Even if it turns out to be longer than we expect, we will see each other again."

"Promise?" She could barely keep her voice from breaking. Another tear fell.

He nodded and looked straight into her eyes. "I promise. Now think carefully about your decision. I don't want you making any rash decisions on my account."

"But—"

"Kaie, why would you risk the chance of not seeing your family for a long time just to get Tristen out of going to Carthan Valley?" King Torin interrupted, questioning her.

She looked at the king before answering. "I have a feeling that something bad will happen." She could not explain further, but it was lodged deep in her heart, a panicky feeling that had not gone away ever since the king's announcement the night before.

"We have Invivers there to watch out for him. He'll be fine," the king reassured her. "I'll leave you two to say your goodbyes. Tristen, you'll have to leave soon." He headed back inside, giving the two of them their privacy. He knew that this would be a big change for the both of them and that they should properly say goodbye. Despite knowing that his plan had worked, he did feel a twinge of remorse at using his son as a pawn.

After the king was gone, Tristen watched Kaie, who was trying to avoid his eyes. "Kaie, I guess this is it. We should—"

"No. No goodbyes," she pleaded, finally looking at Tristen. "It sounds too final, like we'll never see each other again."

Tristen sighed, seeing how she had come to feel this way. "Very well. Then you might as well come with me while I get my horse ready. By the way," he added, "I'm glad to see you are wearing your dress. But you should be wearing a cloak. It's cold out."

"I was in a hurry. I didn't have time to grab my cloak on the way out."

"You should be more careful in the future," he said, sweeping his own cloak around her so they were both protected from the cold. "I want you to know that I appreciate what you did to try and get me out of leaving, but Father has had his mind set on me leaving for a while. You still have a couple more days to decide. Will you promise me that you'll think carefully about making a choice?"

Seeing how much this meant to him, she nodded. "Yes, I promise to think about it, Tristen."

"Good," he said, pleased that she was going to think seriously on her decision. "Now come on, we have to go see Fyfe."

Both walked towards the stables slowly, for making it there would mean Tristen would need to leave. Once they reached the stables, Kaie saw that Fyfe was scurrying about, getting most of the horses ready for the departure. A few of the stable boys were helping him as well.

Fyfe looked up as they approached. "Your Highness, your horse will be ready in a few minutes, so I'll bring him out when I am done."

Achaius and the king arrived soon after, just as Fyfe brought out Tristen's horse, a big black charger. Most of the other soldiers were already mounted and ready to go, and a few were saying goodbye to their loved ones who'd come for the final send-off. Tristen turned to the small group and went down the row, shaking Achaius's hand and encouraging him to look out for Kaie while he was gone.

When he reached Kaie, he hugged her. "I know you don't like goodbyes, but I need to say it. Goodbye. I'll be careful, so don't worry."

She clung to him, unwilling to let go, but when he started to pull away, she released him.

Tristen nodded to his father and mounted his horse. He looked back for a moment, straight into Kaie's eyes. She bit her lip, willing herself not to cry, and clenched her jaw tightly to prevent the tears from falling. When he turned to leave, it was all she could do not to run after him, begging for him to come back. Remembering how horrible she felt when Shayla did that, she resisted, not wanting to do the same thing to Tristen.

King Torin went inside after a few moments, but Achaius stayed with Kaie, sensing that she needed him. Kaie stood motionless, watching Tristen's back as he left with the men through the castle gates and off into the northeast towards the mountains.

Snow began to fall, and Achaius lightly draped his cloak over her shoulders, but the action did not register. She watched the horses until the last man sitting tall and proud had disappeared over the crest of the hill, toward a future that neither she nor anybody else could predict.

Kaie blinked, shaking herself from her daze as she realized that tears were streaming down her face. Achaius was looking at her in concern and she smiled to reassure him, wiping the tears away. Without a word, she headed inside, the prince following closely behind. Kaie handed Achaius back his cloak and headed off towards the library.

Achaius watched her leave, sensing that she needed to be alone.

CHAPTER 22

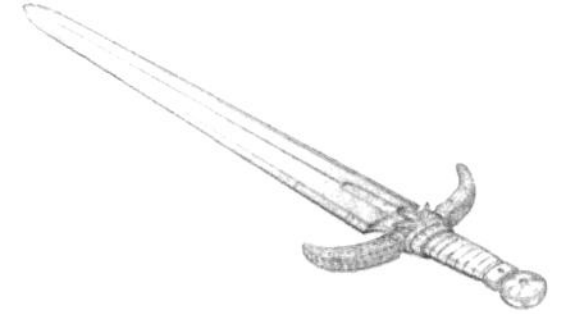

That night, while sorely missing Tristen, Kaie thought carefully about her training, just as she'd promised. She even skipped dinner with the royal family, not feeling very hungry after the day's events. Farin brought up a tray of food, but she barely touched it, thinking over her options. After much deliberation, she finally came to a decision.

The very next day, she sought Maeve out and told the older Inviver, "I'm going to continue. It's the only way I'll be able to help Tristen in the war and stop their commander's horrible acts. It's what I really want to do."

Maeve nodded, and they got to work. Despite the demanding and hard work of training, the next few weeks passed slowly for Kaie as she increasingly felt Tristen's absence. Achaius was now no longer included in lessons as Kaie worked to master different techniques, like being able to Cure at a distance and trying to diagnose without seeing the injury. Kaie found she was able to hear the sound of injuries a lot more often, but as much as Maeve talked about the sound of the earth, she never could hear the evasive noise. Maeve and Avalon also focused on Calming more—the technique was especially elusive to Kaie if she was not in the correct mindset. More often than not, she ended up making the soldiers feel more anxious than calming them down.

After lessons, she would go to the library and stare into space. Everyone knew she was severely unhappy. At mealtimes, she would eat, but mostly, her food remained barely touched. Achaius tried to help her—he felt Tristen's absence too—but she mostly remained quiet. Finally, he decided to approach her about her sorrow.

He walked into the library one day and found her staring blankly at a book. "Kaie, can we talk?" he asked, coming over to sit next to her.

She looked up at him and set the book down. "What is it?" she asked wearily. Her training was exhausting, and with Tristen gone, she felt like the color had been sapped out of her life.

"Your attitude. I know you miss Tristen, but it's time to accept that he's gone right now. He'll come back, but it's best for you to just try and get over his absence." Achaius did not know how else to better word his concerns, but it was obvious that Kaie could not go on like she had been the past few weeks. She had been walking around the palace like a widow—all vivacity and life in her had disappeared.

His words sparked something in her—anger. Kaie's eyes flashed as she snapped, "Well, I might not have known him as long as you have, but I seem to be the only one who misses him. You're off doing your normal shenanigans. You don't seem to care at all."

She turned to leave, but Achaius grabbed her shoulder and turned her to face him. "Just because I don't show my feelings doesn't mean I don't miss him," he said, his voice dangerously low. "He's just had to leave for a little while. He's not dead, so don't mourn him."

Kaie shook his arm off and stared at him defiantly. "I've essentially been cut off by my family and now Tristen gets taken away from me too. Can't I have some time to get over his absence?"

"Of course, but he's not gone forever. Why don't you write to him like you have been with your family?"

"I haven't heard from them at all!" Kaie screamed. "At this point, I don't even know if my letters are being delivered or withheld! That seems like something your father would do. He was willing to poison you—hiding my letters would be child's play!" The silence from her family was glaring and made her feel even lonelier.

Achaius gaped at her. "You still haven't heard *anything*?" he asked. "I thought at least for Yule they would..." He trailed off upon seeing her glassy stare.

"I thought they would write too," she said, a tear spilling down her cheek. "For my birthday or for Yule... anything. It's like they've forgotten about me."

Achaius moved towards her and put his arms around her. To embrace her was instinctive, and once he had done so, his mind caught up with his body. His cheeks burned. Maybe she didn't want him to touch her at all.

But Kaie leaned into him, crying into his chest as her arms softly encircled his waist. The prince's actions warmed her heart and she knew Tristen's leaving was the catalyst for all these mixed-up feelings. If he hadn't left, she could still pretend that her family was too busy to write. But now that another familial figure was gone, everything was staring at her, asking her to examine the truth.

"We can go talk to my father," Achaius said quietly when she began to calm down. "Make him answer your questions."

Kaie pulled back. "Do you really think he'd answer honestly?" she asked, biting her lip. The king always seemed cold with her and had pulled a lot of tricks. She doubted that he would tell the truth.

Achaius shrugged. "Then we can say we've tried," he said. He took her hand. "Come on."

The two walked to the king's study, and Achaius folded his arms, waiting for the guards to knock. When they were allowed entrance, the king looked extremely annoyed, his pen tapping impatiently on a stack of papers.

"What is it?" he asked.

"I'm sure you know that Kaie's been sending letters to her family," Achaius said. "Why hasn't she received any responses back?"

The king narrowed his eyes at his son's insolent tone. "Why do you expect I would know anything about that?" he asked, his eyes flicking to Kaie. She shrunk back behind Achaius, remembering his explosive reaction during Yule. So far at dinners since then, he had ignored her.

"We all know that you're capable of scheming," Achaius said. "Keeping hold of her letters is something you would do."

"Despite your lack of faith in me, that is not the case," the king said. He put his hands together and focused on Kaie. "Maeve has told me of your concern for your family," he said. "I did send a rider prior to Yule to check on them. Everyone is fine and well. It seems your mentor has returned home with more medicine for your mother. While her illness isn't gone, her symptoms are much improved."

"Then why haven't they written?" Kaie demanded.

"Maeve sent a letter when you first began training explaining your decision and how important it was that you stay focused on your lessons," the king said. "Your family merely didn't want to distract you."

While his words seemed true enough, Kaie still had doubts. "But I ask them to write back every time I send a letter," she said. "Surely they would respond to that?"

"They want you to succeed," the king said. "But they do enjoy your letters and hearing how you've been doing. Is that all you came to discuss?" He looked at the door behind them pointedly.

Achaius looked at Kaie, and she silently nodded. "Thank you, Father," he said, bowing his head slightly. "Good night."

Kaie curtsied before following Achaius out of the room.

"Is that enough of an answer for you?" he asked as they walked towards her room.

"For now," Kaie said, biting her lip. "I still wish they would respond, but the king's answer makes sense. If Maeve did tell them to not send any letters back, it would make sense that they wouldn't. Even if I want to hear from them." They had reached her door. "Thank you for asking for me, Achaius. I appreciate it."

As she went to sleep, she mulled over the king's words. She would still continue to write to her family, even if they didn't respond back. The best she could do was keep the lines of communication open and await a reply.

***

The next day, when Kaie sparred with Raven in the indoor arena, she decided to ask him a question. "When Rosse left, how did you get through it?"

Raven lowered his sword, as he knew the source of her question. "Loving someone means trusting their decisions and that they'll be fine without you. I still miss him, but I find that if you keep yourself busy, the loneliness starts to fade. Work on learning more about history, then you'll have something new to show him when he gets back."

Kaie nodded thoughtfully, showing her understanding.

For the first time since Tristen left, she went to dinner in a happy mood. It was as if a heavy fog had lifted from around her to expose some of her radiance.

CHAPTER 23

"**C**ome on, Kaie. Concentrate," Avalon encouraged the young Inviver.

Kaie's frown deepened. "I'm trying," she said, a bead of sweat popping on her brow.

A small group of soldiers stood in front of her, waiting. Kaie was attempting to use her Calming powers to influence all of them to fight in battle. Over the past few months, she had successfully mastered Calming one person, but a whole group still eluded her.

"Okay, close your eyes," Avalon instructed. Kaie did as she was told. "Now, reach out and try to feel their energy. Like when you're trying to connect with the earth."

"You know I still struggle with that." Kaie focused on the sounds around her, trying to connect with the men in front of her. The spring wind gently blew her hair and the birds nearby were chirping. As she concentrated, she was able to pick up a deep hum, and a feeling of peace and safety washed over her.

Finally, I've got it.

Slowly, she followed the sound, focusing on how it flowed to the men. Their sounds were not in sync with each other, each comprised of a plethora of tones. She frowned slightly.

"You have it," Avalon said quietly. "Now try and bend them all to match, to energize them."

Kaie's mind reached out and played with the sounds, trying to align them all. The soldiers let out a groan of pain.

"Not like that," Avalon said quickly. "Be gentler. Ease them into what you want."

Once more she tried, with smaller movements this time, and Kaie let out a breath when the sounds began to align with each other. She pushed some of her energy towards them, focusing on them fighting. The sounds rose to a triumphant roar, and when she opened her eyes, the men were breathing heavily, their eyes alight with energy. They were ready for battle.

"You did it! That was excellent for a more expansive Calming attempt," Avalon exclaimed. She turned to the soldiers. "You may go see Sir Shalane for training."

The men let out a yell of victory and raced off to spar.

Kaie's shoulders slumped. She was suddenly drained. "That took a lot out of me," she admitted.

"Well, you did expend a lot of energy doing that," Avalon said. "We might need to work on how to optimize your output and focus. But for now, that is enough for today."

"I wish I could take a nice bath and then my history lesson," Kaie lamented.

Over the past few months, Achaius had taken up Tristen's mantle, going over the history books with her, further explaining historical battles, and expanding upon knowledge not found in the literature. He took a different approach from his brother, using figurines and maps to explain the mechanics of the different battles. To her delight, Kaie began improving with remembering dates and details. Achaius really brought the stories alive when sharing them with her.

Spending time with the young prince made Kaie see him in a different light, no longer did he seem arrogant and hot-tempered. He was so patient with her, gently guiding her when she made mistakes. His over-eagerness from when they were first getting to know each other had lessened and she felt more comfortable with him the more they were together. From time to time, she would be struck by how handsome he was, noticing the way the candlelight glinted off his golden hair, the brightness of his emerald eyes. In those moments she would have to put extra effort into focusing on the lesson. But she also noticed the secret glances he cast at her when he thought she wasn't looking. A warmth filled her in those moments.

"If you keep training even when you're exhausted, it helps your limits expand," Avalon reminded her.

The two walked towards the training grounds, arm in arm—Kaie still had archery practice in the afternoon. Training had moved back outside a few weeks ago at the beginning of spring, and she was finally getting the hang of archery. Lorne had left most of her lessons up to Raven, but occasionally joined them.

"How did you get so good at Calming?" Kaie asked.

"It's always come naturally to me," Avalon said. "Similar to how Curing comes to you. Each Inviver has their own specialty when it comes to their powers. Even if you haven't mastered Calming, Maeve won't delay in finalizing your training. Your Curing powers are more than needed at Carthan Valley."

"But won't Calming help too?" Kaie asked. "Why wouldn't I try to master that before going?"

"Because your Curing powers are needed more than Calming, especially against Crevan's forces," Avalon said. "And I think Calming can be something you work on at the front lines. There will be more people for you to work with than there are here."

"That's true." Kaie paused. "Do you think I'll ever be able to hear the sounds of the earth without going through the full exercise every time?"

Avalon thought for a moment. "Possibly," she said. "But not everyone learns or connects the same way. You are a very hands-on learner; that's why Curing comes so easily to you." When Kaie's shoulders slumped, she patted the young Inviver's back. "But you should be proud of how much you've accomplished in such little time. Kaie, I don't know if I've ever seen someone with Curing powers like yours. You have the possibility of becoming a very powerful Inviver. Don't give up just because you need to work harder at this one aspect of it."

Kaie nodded. "I'll keep on working at it," she said.

***

Raven was waiting with a bigger bow than usual. "You're going to shoot with this today," he said.

Kaie let out a groan. She was already exhausted from Calming earlier and knew her arms were going to be aching by the end of the day. At the other end of the field, she saw Lorne running the men she'd Calmed through drills, trying to burn off their excess energy.

"Remember to just pull the string back gently. Keep your arm straight," Raven said before helping her guide her arm into place. "Now, aim and let her fly!"

The arrow whizzed from the bow, but landed on the outside of the target, almost missing it completely. Kaie's face fell in disappointment.

"That's all right. You're not used to the tension on this one," Raven said. "By the end of the day, you'll be shooting like a pro."

Kaie blew a stray strand of hair out of her face, trying to ignore the half circle of recruits watching her. "I wish they'd go away," she whispered, annoyed at the attention. She felt the prickle of their gazes on her and shuddered slightly. A line of sweat trickled down her back and she was unsure if it was due to the men or the rising temperatures.

Raven smiled as he heard her remark. "They just admire you," he whispered as he handed her an arrow.

"But I can't concentrate."

"You need to learn how to shoot with distractions," he told her.

She huffed, and he smiled at her annoyance.

True to Raven's word, by the end of the day, Kaie was shooting arrows as if she had been doing it her entire life. Near the end of the lesson, she could even hit moving targets.

As they walked back to the castle, Kaie asked Raven, "Why do most of the recruits stare at me when I'm training?" Lately, the men had not been at all discreet with their gawking.

Raven remained silent for a few moments, trying to gather his thoughts. He was not surprised that she noticed the attention, but he was surprised that she did not know why. "I think it's probably because they find you attractive," he said.

"Attractive?" The word caught her off guard. "Me? But I'm almost always dressed like this, in my tunic and trousers."

"To some men, that doesn't make a difference. You're a skilled fighter and an Inviver, not to mention, a beautiful girl. To most men, you're quite a catch."

Kaie gave him a wary look. "Do *you* think I'm beautiful?" she asked, surprised to hear the words that had come out of his mouth. She hoped that Raven did not think of her the way those men seemed to. He was a friend, and that's all that she wanted from him.

He sighed. "Yes, I think you're beautiful," he said, causing her eyes to widen. "But you're a good friend to me and I don't think of you that way," he rushed to reassure her after he saw her expression of panic.

"Achaius kissed me on the cheek once," she said softly, slowing to a stop. Though it had been months, memories of the kiss had been popping into her mind more frequently lately. "Do you think he had more than friendship on his mind?"

"I don't think he would do anything to jeopardize your friendship."

Raven had noticed the difference in Achaius's attitude towards Kaie once they'd returned from the Mists, how much nicer and gentler he was with her. But he knew if Kaie knew about that, she would only push the prince away. She did not seem ready for anything other than friendship with anyone at this point. Her sole priority was to train and become a better Inviver.

Satisfied with his answer, Kaie thanked him and went off to get ready for dinner. However, her mind was spinning at the new information, and Farin noticed how unfocused Kaie was while getting ready.

"Is there something on your mind? You're very distracted tonight," she asked the younger girl.

Kaie looked into the mirror at Farin, who was brushing her hair. She blushed with embarrassment. "I am thinking about something," she said slowly, unsure of how much she should divulge. Though Farin had become a close friend over the past months, she still felt awkward bringing up this topic.

"I am here to talk whenever you would like," Farin said. "I will be discreet with any information you share with me unless it directly involves your welfare."

"Well..." Kaie paused, and her blush deepened.

Farin smiled, easily guessing what was bothering the young Inviver.

"Lots of people have been paying a lot of attention to me lately."

"The young soldiers in training?" Farin easily guessed.

Kaie nodded. "Yes," she said. "Raven says it's because I'm beautiful and... a while ago—on my birthday, actually—Prince Achaius... he kissed me on the cheek."

Farin tried to keep her expression neutral, deducing that the girl did not want her to make a big deal out of things. "And... how do you feel about that?" she asked, keeping her tone even, focusing on brushing Kaie's hair.

"The attention from the soldiers bothers me," Kaie admitted, "but as for Achaius..." She trailed off as she thought through her words. "I didn't mind the kiss." Her words were almost a whisper. "And I enjoy the attention I get from him."

The maid smiled softly. "And what's bothering you about that?" she asked. She pulled up a nearby settee to sit next to Kaie, who turned to look at her.

"I don't know how to do this," she said. "I don't know if I like him the same way he likes me. And what if I do? What do I do then?"

Farin gave Kaie an impossibly kind look, reaching a hand up to stroke her cheek. "You don't need to make any decisions right this minute," she said gently. "If you decide you do like him the same way, then just act in a way that feels natural to you. Based on how he acts towards you, he certainly wouldn't reject your advances."

"Are you sure?" Kaie asked, her voice small. "He's a *prince* and I'm just... a nobody." Even though the king had gone to such lengths to bring her to the palace and she was receiving an education from the head Inviver, she did not see herself the same way as everyone else seemed to. At times, she still felt like a backwoods healer.

"You saved his life and you are the youngest Inviver in history," Farin said firmly. "And your father is a distinguished general. You are not a nobody."

"But we're poor," Kaie pointed out.

"Despite that," Farin continued, as if Kaie had not interrupted. "That does not mean anything when it comes to matters of the heart. Prince Achaius—or any man—would be lucky to have you on his arm. Remember that." She glanced at the clock and pulled Kaie up. "Now, you need to go to dinner or you'll be late."

Kaie stopped at the doorway and turned to Farin. "Thank you," she said, giving the maid a wide smile. "Your words helped."

CHAPTER 24

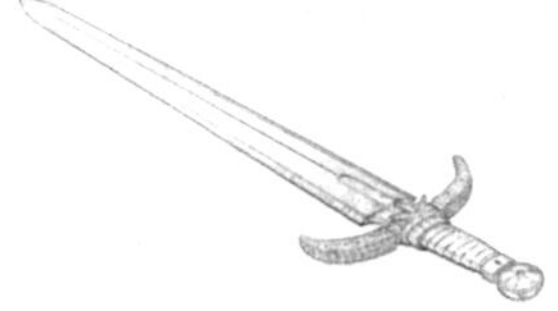

Dear Momma, Papa, and Shayla,

I'm told my training should be coming to an end soon. Lately, I spend most of my time in the infirmary Curing. Maeve even made the palace Invivers leave everything to me. I've come a long way from when I first started—I can now Cure over two dozen injuries before feeling tired! Calming is still tough for me, but Avalon says it's different for each Inviver and my main focus should be Curing. I try to spend time each day listening to the sound of the earth, and that seems to be going better—I think with spring, everything is waking up again. The other day, I heard a deep thrumming! Maeve says that's what she's talking about, but I still can't figure out how to align the sound with a person's injuries, only when I'm Calming. Which she says isn't necessary to become a full Inviver, but it would still be nice to be able to do...

Despite that, Maeve says that I will have completed training faster than any other Inviver in history! After this, I think I'll be sent to Carthan Valley. Sir Shalane has also complimented my shooting—Papa, he even says I might be able to outshoot you! Personally, I think he's exaggerating, but the compliment was nice to hear.

Shayla's birthday is coming up, and I hope she enjoys the necklace I'm sending with this letter. Please let her know how much I wish I could be there to celebrate in person.

I love and miss you all so much. I know that Maeve doesn't want me to be distracted, but please respond, even if it's a short letter. I just want to hear from you.

Love,

Kaie

Kaie let out a sigh as she folded her letter, dropping it and the silver necklace into the envelope. A couple weeks ago, she and Farin had received approval to go outside the palace to do some shopping, Kaie had specifically wanted to get a birthday present for her sister using some of the money the king usually sent to her family. When she saw the small leaf pendant, she knew that was the perfect gift—it reminded her of her locket.

"Any letters from my family?" she asked as she handed Maeve the envelope.

The older Inviver frowned slightly as she felt the unexpected weight of the necklace. "What's in here?" she asked.

"A necklace for my sister," Kaie said. "It's her birthday next week."

"Ah." Maeve tucked the letter in her pocket. "No letters for you, I'm afraid," she said.

"So what are we doing today?" Kaie asked, trying to tamp down her disappointment. Despite not expecting any response back, she was still surprised at how sad she was at the silence from her family. "Will we be going to the infirmary again?"

"Actually, you're all done," Maeve said with a smile "You have learned everything I have to teach you."

"Really?" Kaie's mind suddenly went blank.

The day was finally here, everything she had been working for. Maeve had given no indication that she was nearing the end of her training so soon. A weight unexpectedly descended upon her shoulders. Now she would be expected to go to Carthan Valley, to stop the war. During the past several months, Avalon's stories about the enemy commander, Crevan, grew her determination to aid in his defeat. Different soldiers returning from the battlefield also told her stories of the enemy forces and how they became injured. Kaie knew she would be able to make a difference one she was out there. But the tales of Crevan's cruelty also frightened her. And now she was going where he was located.

She wrung her hands. Despite being eager to do her part in the war effort, she was filled with anxiety. "Are you sure? This is happening so fast."

"I am sure." Maeve chuckled. "You have enough knowledge and power to do well. The king is planning to send you off at the end of the week." She came forward and gave the young Inviver a bony hug. "Congratulations, my dear."

With suddenly nothing to do, Kaie went to the library to read for the rest of the day, enjoying the unexpected lull. Since Tristen had left, she'd been busy with lessons and training, and she missed reading for enjoyment. She got halfway through a short romance novel filled with daring rescues and sweeping declarations before it was time to get ready for dinner.

Farin insisted that Kaie dress up in one of her fancier gowns, a purple velvet dress with lavender accents. Even though she had owned the dresses for many months, she still had not gotten the chance to wear all of them yet.

"This one is so pretty, it's a shame to just have it sitting in the wardrobe," the maid said when Kaie expressed doubt at wearing such a lovely gown.

"I suppose it wouldn't hurt," Kaie said. Farin's enthusiasm was infectious.

The maid arranged Kaie's hair in a sweeping updo, one involving many more pins than usual to keep it in place. At the very end, she spritzed a floral perfume on the young Inviver.

"What's all that for?" Kaie asked with a laugh.

The maid's smile widened as there was a knock at the door. "Go and open it," she said with glee.

Achaius was dressed in an outfit similar to what he wore to the Yuletide ball, only in a dark-green that matched his eyes rather than blue. He looked very handsome. In his right hand was a pink flower, which he offered her eagerly.

"What are you dressed so nicely for?" Kaie asked, laughing at how formal he looked.

"May I escort the lovely lady to dinner?" Achaius asked gallantly with a slight bow.

"Very well, kind sir," Kaie said, curtsying and giggling before taking the arm he offered her. She took a quick glance back at Farin and saw that the maid looked very pleased with herself. Apparently, Farin had known about this plan the whole time.

Walking into the dining room, Kaie saw that Maeve, Avalon, Lorne, Raven, and King Torin were all dressed up for the event as well. Achaius led Kaie over to a chair, pulling it out for her.

Kaie smiled at the special attention. "What is this all about?" she asked the group.

"To celebrate your accomplishment," King Torin said, smiling at her. Over the course of her stay, he had slowly warmed up to her. It also helped that her training was almost finished—she could finally be useful with the war.

Dinner was filled with all her favorite foods, and at the end of it, more surprises awaited Kaie. King Torin stood and approached her, his sword strapped to his waist.

"Please kneel," he said solemnly.

Kaie gulped and did as the king commanded. He removed his sword and placed the flat of his blade on her right shoulder.

"With this, I induct you into the Galician forces," he said. He moved his weapon over to her other shoulder. "May you find courage, safety, and loyalty amongst your new brothers and sisters. I hope you return to us safely."

Once more, the unseen weight on her shoulders grew heavier. Kaie bowed her head, knowing a response was expected of her. "I pledge my loyalty and services to the King of Galicia," she said softly.

When she looked up, King Torin nodded with a smile, motioning for her to stand. As soon as he sat back down, a small group of musicians entered the room and began to play.

Quickly jumping up, Achaius walked over to Kaie. He bowed and offered his hand. "May I have this dance?" he asked.

She laughed at his unusual behavior, but accepted, taking his outstretched hand. Tonight, the prince was certainly acting strange, but she enjoyed the special attention.

"Very well," she said. "I would like that very much."

When the new bar started, they began to dance. Achaius whirled her through various steps, ones she did not know, but somehow she was able to keep up. The colors spun before her as she concentrated on keeping in step and in tempo. Soon, she gave up and lost herself in the music. The others watched as she gracefully maneuvered through the steps, keeping up with Achaius. Lorne noticed that it was like her sword fighting—she could anticipate the next step before Achaius led her through it. A smile crossed his lips. She certainly had grown from the shy, trembling girl who had arrived at the palace almost a year ago.

A slower dance started, and to Kaie's surprise, Achaius showed no signs of letting her go. He twirled her before pulling her close once more. Her cheeks flushed at the closeness.

"Are you enjoying you the party?" Achaius asked, stepping on Kaie's toes for the third time. The slower dance gave him more opportunity to overthink, to make mistakes. He had danced a lot better at Yule and was hoping his errors were due to nerves. Being this close to her was very distracting.

"Yes, it was a lovely surprise. Who came up with all of this?"

"I did. But I let Lorne convince my father to go through with it." Achaius grinned.

Kaie chuckled. "Well, I appreciate it. It's a wonderful party."

Her voice communicated her gratitude, and Achaius leaned forward, wanting to kiss her. At that moment, he felt a tap on his shoulder. He turned, seeing Raven standing behind him.

"May I dance with Kaie?" Raven politely asked.

Achaius nodded, but his eyes were like ice. Kaie did not notice the look that passed between the two as she took Raven's hand. The dance turned to a very slow waltz. and Kaie talked to Raven to keep the silence from becoming too awkward.

"Have you heard any news on the war?"

She knew that he was able to find out information that was normally kept secret. All her knowledge had come from the soldiers who came back to the palace.

"It seems to be going well. Prince Tristen has led us to several victories."

"I've been reading up on some other wars that we've had with the Scrians and Achaius has been helping teach me," she said. "Did you know most of the wars have been fought over Invivers? They want to find out our secrets. You'd think they'd want to foster peace rather than letting lives be lost."

"Some people would rather take by force," Raven said. "If they could defeat us, then they would have unfettered access to our records. Otherwise, we could still hide some of what we know from them."

"It still seems like a waste of life," Kaie lamented. "On both sides."

"Well, you'll be going to help with that soon," Raven said. "I know that the soldiers will appreciate your skills and—" He was cut off as there was a crash behind them.

Both turned to see the remnants of the main course overturned on the table. Achaius looked sheepish.

"I'm sorry, I was trying to get some more food," Achaius said. "I bumped the platter and it fell."

"Let the servants clean it up," King Torin said, waving at Achaius to be silent.

The rest of the night passed smoothly, and when it was time to go to bed, Kaie regretfully left the festivities. Dancing all night had thoroughly worn her out and she was expecting a restful slumber as she drifted off to sleep.

Despite the delightful evening, a nightmare plagued her dreams.

CHAPTER 25

An unnamable dread filled Kaie as she approached a tent, her steps filled with caution. Inside, she could see the shadows of three figures kneeling around a thrashing figure on the ground.

"Hold him down." The voice came from within the tent. "The more he thrashes, the sooner the poison will reach his heart."

The other two attempted to do as instructed, and Kaie watched as they tried to save the poisoned man's life. Paralyzing fear encompassed her as she realized who the poisoned man was.

The man on the floor stopped thrashing and laid still.

The first figure spoke. "I've done all I can, but I'm afraid he's gone. I got here too late."

A scream escaped Kaie's throat, and she yelled Tristen's name before jolting awake. Her legs were entangled in blankets and she was covered in a cold sweat. Like the nightmare she'd had prior to being summoned to the palace, she had the premonition that the dream could happen in real life.

Scrambling out of bed, she stumbled to the closet to check her pack to ensure her supplies were ready. It had been months since she had last looked in her pack and she was relieved to see almost everything she would need was tucked away. Even though it was spring, the mornings were still chilly, but she paid no mind to the cold as she scurried around in only her nightgown.

Farin entered the room, surprised to see Kaie awake so early and looking so frantic. "What's wrong?" she asked, watching as the Inviver got dressed in a heavier tunic and trousers. "Why are you in such a rush?"

"Something's wrong," Kaie gasped, pulling her bag of Curing supplies and her satchel from home out of the closet. "I had a nightmare." She pulled out a dagger that matched her sword—Tristen's Yule present to her—before strapping it to her waist.

"It was just a dream," Farin said, coming forward and putting her hands on Kaie's shoulders. "That doesn't mean it's going to come true."

"This happened before too," Kaie said, her face pale. "I dreamt that Achaius was sick, and later that day, Lorne showed up on my doorstep. Something is wrong, Farin. I think Tristen is in trouble."

"What are you going to do?" Farin said. "Go to the king with your concerns?"

"I... I don't know," Kaie admitted. "I don't know if he'd believe me. At the very least, I want to make sure I'm ready to leave right away."

"I can finish packing your things," Farin said, gently taking Kaie's bags from her. "You go get some breakfast. Maybe you'll feel better when you don't have an empty stomach."

Slowly nodding, Kaie went to the dining room, where Achaius was already seated. Distracted, she picked at her food before leaving the table, unable to stay still. Her entire body itched to get moving.

Achaius looked at her with concern before following her out of the room to the main foyer.

Kaie left the palace, standing at the main entrance, chewing on her lip, her eyes darting around the grounds. Her foot tapped rapidly as Achaius came alongside her, troubled by her nervous energy.

"Is... everything all right?" Achaius asked tentatively.

Her eyes flicked over to him before sweeping the grounds once more. "No." Her answer was short and clipped. "I had a dream last night, similar to the time you were ill."

"You had a dream I was sick?" Achaius's voice could not hide his incredulity.

Kaie nodded. "I had that dream the night before Lorne came to get me. It was similar to the dream I had last night."

"Is it Tristen?" he asked.

"I think so."

Kaie's face paled at the sound of thundering hooves. A messenger was approaching the palace, and as he neared, he vaulted off the horse, handing the reins to a nearby guard before rushing inside. Kaie briefly recognized the man as Barra, one of the men who had escorted her to the palace, and swiftly followed him as he rushed towards the king's study. The guards on either side of the door refused her entry, closing the door swiftly after Barra entered.

"I need to see the king," Kaie said desperately.

"You have not been summoned," one of the guards said.

"We demand to see my father," Achaius said. Kaie turned to see that he had followed her. "Is that a problem?"

The guards exchanged a look before one went inside to speak to the king. Several moments later, he exited. "You may enter," he said, holding the door open.

Kaie rushed inside, stopping short upon seeing Barra's bowed head and the king's anguished face. Maeve, Lorne, and Raven had already been talking with the king prior to Barra's arrival, and they looked pained as well.

"Your Majesty, what's wrong?" she asked, dread settling in her stomach.

"It seems that Tristen has been seriously injured. None of the Invivers can help him. They're too exhausted from the past few weeks of continuous fighting. Tristen won't hang on much longer, and he's too weak to be moved. You're our only hope. Please help my son," the king whispered, his eyes pleading with her to help him fix his mistakes. He had been too arrogant sending his eldest son to the front lines.

In his look, there was an apology for the way he had treated her, pleading with her not to hold that against him. In an instant, all of his anger had fallen away, leaving behind a vulnerable man wracked with grief over his dying son.

Kaie fought back tears at this information, despite having expected some news of this sort. "I'll do all I can," she choked out.

"I know this is happening sooner than expected," Maeve said. "But you can do this, I believe in you. Don't let the other Invivers underestimate or undermine your skills or confidence." She came forward and pinned a starburst brooch to Kaie's chest. It was silver, with the language of the Invivers engraved onto its surface—an Inviver prayer of protection. "This will show the camp Invivers that you are one of us," she said softly before kissing Kaie on the forehead, dismissing her.

"Raven and Lorne, you will accompany Kaie to the battlefield," the king said before she could leave. He glanced to Achaius and saw his son's expression, knowing that he was going to go as well, even if he had to sneak out. "Achaius, if you wish, you may go. I would prefer you to stay here, but you're old enough to make your own decisions."

Achaius came forward to hug his father goodbye.

"Just be careful," Torin whispered as he watched his son leave his study.

A dark feeling settled deep in his heart, already knowing it was going to be difficult. Having his remaining child go to a deadly place was a foolish decision, but one he did not have the heart to go against. If Tristen died, it was only fair that he had his loving brother by his side.

CHAPTER 26

Swiftly, the small, somber group left the capital, heading northeast towards the mountains. At Kaie's desperate urging, they rode all through the night, hoping to make it to Tristen's camp before the next nightfall. Not far into their ride, the terrain grew rocky, slowing down progress. At dawn, it was clear that they had been ascending up the mountains throughout the night. The rest of their journey would be downhill.

"Once we pass into the Carthan Valley, we can stop at an inn, then continue on," Lorne said.

Around midday, they neared the base of the valley and were greeted with the sight of a small inn, smoke rising from the chimney. The weather on this side of the mountain range was warmer, causing the group to shed their heavy cloaks.

"We don't have time to stop," Kaie snapped as everyone dismounted at the stables. "We need to keep moving. You said it yourself before, the horses can take it."

"*We* need to rest," Lorne explained tiredly, glancing at Achaius, who was practically falling off his horse in exhaustion, his eyes struggling to stay open.

"I can keep going," Achaius protested.

"You can meet me at the camp, but I need to go. I'm the only one who can help Tristen." Desperation cut through her voice. "I can't wait."

Lorne paused, looking over at Achaius. He was worried about Tristen as well, but needed to take the younger prince's well-being into account. He could not continue riding at their current pace.

After a couple of moments of deliberation, he nodded. "You and Raven may go, while Achaius and I follow behind. We will catch up with you at camp."

Kaie looked at Raven. "If you can't keep up, I'm leaving you behind," she said in a serious tone.

"I understand." He steeled himself for the rest of the journey ahead.

They both set off, their only comfort being the thundering of hooves on the path, hoping that they would make it on time. After a few hours of intense riding, they arrived at the center of the valley, where the Galician army kept the Scrians at bay. Kaie could see a field with many tents clustered on the south end, with an opposing set of tents on the northern end. Based on the colors of the flags, she could tell the further camp was Scrian forces.

Before entering the clearing where the camp was set up, Raven instructed, "Pull your hood up. The king doesn't want the enemy to see your face."

The two rode into camp unchallenged. Enough soldiers seemed to recognize Raven that they let the two pass by without confrontation.

After dismounting and walking towards the largest tent, they were finally stopped by a male Inviver.

"What do you want?" he demanded, a frown on his face.

"I'm here to help Prince Tristen," Kaie said, moving her cloak to show her brooch. "Maeve gave me this to prove my identity."

The Inviver looked at her in shock, surprised by both the brooch and how young she sounded. "Follow me." He escorted them into the tent.

***

Across the field, the commander lowered his spyglass. He stood under a wide tent marked on either side with the blue flag of Scria, having been constructed as a vantage point. It was a lavish tent with multiple tables strewn with maps and various weapons, one end laden with wine and a roasted pheasant.

"I don't believe it," he said. "They are bringing in someone else to help their fallen prince. No matter. They cannot beat this poison, am I correct, Fallon?"

"Yes, my lord," Fallon said nervously while clutching the empty vial in his pocket. "It's filled with a mixture of venom from the Erlea snake and the nightshade plant. It's impossible to Cure."

"For your sake, I hope so," Commander Crevan said, fingering a nasty-looking dagger.

Fallon gulped, knowing that it would not be difficult for his greedy commander to carve a few lines in his face for making a mistake.

"We'll see who this new Inviver is, one way or another."

***

Kaie gasped when she entered the tent, not believing the sight before her eyes. Tristen laid on a bed, with two Invivers nearby who were discussing what to do. His body was covered with festering sores, his breathing ragged. As Kaie leaned in to see the sores more closely, the rancid smell of decay permeated the liquid oozing out of them. When Tristen opened his eyes, she was dismayed to see that his usually kind blue eyes had turned completely black.

"What happened?" she demanded to the nearest Inviver as she threw off her cloak and unloaded her satchel.

"He was shot in the chest a few days ago. The arrow was poisoned and we didn't realize it. That's where the damage is the worst. We Cured the wound, but that doesn't stop the poison. We don't know what else to do. We've tried everything," the Inviver babbled in panic. His thinning gray hair was mussed, as if he had been running his hands through it.

Kaie ripped open Tristen's shirt and gasped at the sight. His entire chest was bright red, the wound where the arrow hit still swollen and bleeding despite all the bandages. Now that she was nearer, she picked up on a high-pitched sound. She winced at the noise.

"Kaie?" Tristen whispered her name, his eyelids fluttering. "Can you fix me?"

She cupped his face in her hands. "I'm going to try my best."

"I was so stupid... I fell right into their trap..." He gasped for breath.

"Shhh, I need you to be quiet. This might hurt a little."

Kaie reached into her satchel, pulling out an herbal mixture, and began to rub that on his chest wound. To her dismay, it did nothing to staunch the bleeding.

He began to thrash, moaning in pain.

"Hold him down," she ordered. "The more he thrashes, the sooner the poison will reach his heart."

The two Invivers followed her instructions, doing their best to keep the prince still. Tristen's breathing only became more labored, and she knew he would die if she did not Cure him. Kaie placed her hands directly on the wound, ignoring the protests of the other Invivers.

"We tried Curing him already," the older one said. "It didn't work."

"You'll only make yourself tired," said the other, a younger man with mousy brown hair.

Tristen took a shuddering breath and fell still. The ear-splitting shriek stopped.

Kaie's breath caught in her throat. She could no longer feel Tristen's heartbeat beneath her hands. "No," she whispered, tears pricking her eyes. Without his heartbeat, his body was just a shell. A lump rose in her throat, threatening to choke her.

"What is it?" the younger Inviver demanded.

Kaie echoed the words from her dream, realizing the full extent of what it had signified. "I've done all I can, but I'm afraid he's gone. I got here too late." The words came out strangled.

"No, he can't be dead." The Inviver shook his head.

In a last moment of desperation, Kaie placed her hands on Tristen's chest. Maybe she could bring him back. She *had* to bring him back. She refused to accept that this was how Tristen died. Despite the sound being gone, she could still sense the poison coursing through his veins. Maybe she could remove it.

"It's too late," one said, reaching forward to stop her.

As she exhaled, the familiar feeling of energy leaving her passed throughout her body, channeled through her hands. Her power trailed through his veins, purifying the poison, and raced towards his heart. Kaie's mind was focused on Tristen, but she briefly registered that she did not feel as tired as she usually did. A blinding flash of light burst forth from Tristen's chest, swiftly fading as he inhaled again.

Kaie and the other Invivers watched in amazement as the sores on his body disappeared and his chest wound closed up. When the light completely faded, Tristen opened his eyes and looked at Kaie, the black reverting back to their original deep-blue hue. Dumbfounded, the Invivers watched as Tristen sat up.

Mouth open, Kaie looked at Tristen as he smiled. "I did it," she whispered, tears of happiness streaming down her face. The tight knot that had been constricting her heart since the nightmare the previous day was finally starting to loosen.

"You sure did. Thank you." He embraced her, and she clutched him tightly as if to ensure that he actually was alive.

"But how?" the gray-haired Inviver asked.

"There is no way that should have worked. He was gone," the other said.

"Gone? What are they talking about?" Tristen directed his question to Kaie.

"Your heart stopped beating. You were dead for a couple moments," Kaie said. "I was desperate, so I tried to Cure you anyway."

"Have you read the book?" the brown-haired Inviver asked her, a dark expression on his face.

"Yes, Maeve taught me to read it," Kaie answered slowly, unsure of where the conversation was going.

"What about the Dark Curing Secrets? Did you read those?" he continued to press further, his brown eyes darkening with anger.

"No, I've never read that section—Maeve said it only contained secrets about Killing. Why?" she asked.

"If you've been using the Dark Secrets, then we would be forced to take your power away."

"I'm not sure what I did," Kaie said, shrinking back against Tristen. He put an arm around her, as if to protect her from the Invivers.

"I suppose it's possible," the older, less aggressive Inviver said, "that she's able to bring people back to life if their body is still warm. It would be as if their soul hasn't left their body yet."

"Evidian, we'll need to contact Maeve. If the girl can do this, then we may be able to win this war. Come on." The younger Inviver stood, leaving the tent with Evidian following in his footsteps.

Kaie breathed a sigh of relief, her body sagging as the tension in the tent immediately dissipated with their exit.

Tristen had many questions about his death, but could tell now was not the time for any of them. "While I'm sure they're glad that you came in to save the day, you've given them a lot of questions they don't have answers for." He looked at Kaie, as if he could not believe she was there. "It's wonderful to see you again," he said, pulling her into a hug once more.

Kaie relished the embrace and buried her head against his chest. "I missed you so much," she said. "The palace was so quiet without you."

"This isn't how I expected our reunion to go. Thank you for saving my life," Tristen said. He'd thought he was going to die, so suddenly being rescued was something he could not wrap his mind around.

"By the way, I'm officially a full Inviver now." Kaie beamed with pride. "We actually celebrated my completion last night."

"That's amazing!" Tristen shouted. "Does that mean you'll be staying here?" Nothing in his father's missives had mentioned Kaie's progress, so he had not been expecting her so soon.

"Yes," Kaie said. "We'll be able to see each other every day, just like before."

"I'm sure the Invivers will be thrilled to have you," Tristen said.

"How many do you have here?" Kaie asked.

"Around a dozen now that you're here," Tristen said.

"Any women Invivers?" she asked. In Kaie's experience at the castle, the women were more likely to listen and give her guidance. They would actually listen to her, and based on what she had just encountered, the male Invivers were going to give her problems.

"The king sends them to other areas that are less dangerous," Tristen said. "We have a few cooks in the camp that are women, but otherwise, it's just all the soldiers."

"I guessed as much." Kaie made a face of discomfort.

"Why? What's the problem?"

"The male Invivers back at the palace wouldn't really listen to me unless Maeve made them. I'm afraid the same thing will happen here."

Tristen pursed his lips, silently agreeing with her. The Invivers tended to be overconfident in their abilities and could be pig-headed. Having a young woman outshine them wouldn't be easy on their pride. "It might not be the easiest, but if you ignore them and show them your skills, they'll have no choice but to listen to you. Let your abilities do the talking. And if anyone is giving you problems, let me know. I can set them straight."

A soldier entered the tent. "Your Highness, your brother has arrived."

The prince looked at Kaie in surprise. "Achaius is here?"

She shrugged with a smile. "He wouldn't be left behind. You know how he is."

"Let's keep the whole me dying thing from him for now, okay? I don't want him worrying too much."

Kaie nodded. "I won't tell him," she promised.

Tristen scrutinized her for a moment. "Was that the most Curing you've ever done before?"

"Yeah, why?" She frowned at his question.

"You don't seem as tired as you usually do."

"I guess not," she said. "But I've been working hard while you've been away. My limits have improved."

"That makes sense. Are you ready to head out and show everyone how amazing you are?"

"I suppose so." Kaie stood and followed Tristen out of the tent, remembering at the last minute to pull her hood up to hide her face.

***

"What?!" Crevan let out a shriek of rage, stabbing his dagger into the table as he saw Tristen walking around, as healthy as ever. "Fallon, I thought you told me that no one could Cure the prince?"

"No—no one can, sir," Fallon stammered, fearful of Crevan's wrath.

"Really? Because to me, it looks like he's walking around, better than ever. What do you see?" He handed the telescope to Fallon to peer through.

Fallon paled. "That's not possible," he whispered. "All the subjects we tested the poison on were unable to be Cured."

Crevan jerked the spyglass back, spotting the new Inviver, their face hidden by the cloak. "It must be that boy," he snarled. A thought hit him, and a smile crossed his face. "No matter. He may be just what I'm looking for. We'll just need to convince him to come to our side then." He turned to Fallon. "I'll give you one more chance to redeem yourself. If you don't..." He trailed off, leaving the unspoken threat hanging in the air.

CHAPTER 27

Upon spotting his older brother, Achaius exclaimed, "Tristen, you're all better!" He raced forward to hug his brother, practically knocking Tristen over in his enthusiasm. "I knew Kaie could do it!"

Kaie blushed at the compliment, but only Tristen was in the position to notice her flushed cheeks. He raised a curious eyebrow, meeting Raven's eyes. The younger man gave him a shrug and knowing smile.

"It's great to see you too," Tristen said with a laugh, pulling back from the embrace.

Tristen turned, coming face to face with Lorne. A smile broke out on both their faces before they began to laugh, clapping each other on the shoulders.

"What's so funny?" Achaius demanded.

"We both knew that Kaie had it in her to be powerful, but sometimes she can be insecure with her abilities," Lorne said, leveling Kaie with a pointed stare. "Hopefully she knows her own worth now."

"I didn't believe Lorne at first, but when I left, he said Kaie would follow just to take care of me, like a mother hen. Very interesting to think about these past few months," Tristen chuckled.

"Apparently, you can't function without me. You have to go and get shot, then I have to come save you," Kaie said sarcastically, rolling her eyes. Now that

Tristen was alive and well, all the tension had slipped away. "You obviously need me to protect you."

"I was fine for a while," Tristen countered. "I led us to more victories than we've had in a long time."

"You've had some of Sir Swain's help for that," Lorne said, causing Tristen to groan at his blown secret.

"Rosse is here? Where is he? I thought he was stationed at the Fernan Outpost." Raven perked up at the mention of his brother.

"He was transferred here a little while after I arrived. He's probably near the armory tent. He's almost always there when he has free time," Tristen said.

Without another word, Raven ran off to find his brother.

"What have you been up to?" Achaius asked. "You've barely written to us."

"It's been a busy time," Tristen admitted, gesturing for them to join him in his tent.

For the remainder of the evening, the group caught up on the escapades of the past season. They talked late into the night, until Kaie began to yawn.

"You'd better head off to bed," Lorne said. "You've had a busy couple of days. You need your rest."

"I can stay up longer," she protested. "Tristen, can't you—"

"Lorne's right," Tristen agreed. "You look exhausted, and you need to rebuild your strength. We'll catch up more tomorrow at breakfast. Lorne set up your tent earlier. He can take you to it. And I'm nearby if anything happens." Seeing her crestfallen look, he added, "Don't worry, I'm sending Achaius off to bed soon too. I'll see you in the morning."

Lorne led her outside, past a few tents, before coming upon a smaller one sandwiched between two hulking tents. "Here we are," he said, gesturing between the two giant tents. "This one's yours. Mine's on the right and Raven's is on the left in case anything happens. Raven will be bunking with Achaius. Consider yourself lucky—the rest of the Invivers have to share tents, but Tristen insisted you have your own."

"Probably because they're all men," Kaie grumbled. Then she spoke more softly. "Thank you for accompanying me these past couple days, Lorne. I really appreciate it."

"That's my job," he said, wrapping her in a quick hug. "I'm just glad you made it in time."

***

Early in the morning, Raven came to fetch Kaie. "Tristen wants to see you," he said, a big grin on his face.

"I take it you found your brother?" Kaie asked.

"Yes, and—" He cut himself off, his grin widening. "Oh, I better not ruin the surprise."

Curious, Kaie followed him the short distance to Tristen's tent. Upon entering, she saw a group of men circled around a map. All their heads swiveled towards her when she entered.

Tristen beamed when he saw her. "Kaie! Come sit here." He patted an open spot next to him. "I just need to finish up this meeting and then I have a surprise for you."

Kaie walked past the men, lowering her cloak as she took a seat. She studied the map of the battlefield, drowning out the conversation around her. Almost everyone's eyes were on her, astounded at her youth and of how much she had accomplished. Rumors of her Curing Tristen had spread throughout the camp overnight, invigorating the soldiers. If she was able to bring him back from the dead, the tides would surely change now.

The meeting ended quickly, with a plan in place to seize the hills from the Scrians in an attempt to gain the upper hand. Currently, that vantage point at a higher elevation was causing issues and was one of the reasons Tristen had been shot.

"We can continue this discussion later," Tristen eventually said, ending the meeting.

The men left, except for Lorne, Raven, and Rosse.

Kaie turned to Tristen. "What's the surprise you wanted to show me?"

Tristen's face broke into a mischievous grin. "It's more of a test," he said. "I want you to fight against Rosse."

"Really?" Kaie remembered all those months ago when Lorne had demonstrated how strength and size didn't mean everything in a fight. She hoped to make him proud with her skills.

"Well, Raven and Lorne have been bragging about how much you've improved," Tristen said. "I want to see for myself."

"What about my cloak?" She had not forgotten Raven's warning from the previous day.

"That's part of the challenge—you have to keep it covering your face."

Everyone let out a laugh when she groaned in protest.

Once outside, Kaie unsheathed her sword and faced Rosse. His size and strength would make him a tough opponent to beat, but she hoped that her speed and dexterity would help her last through the fight. She took a moment and stretched out her mind, trying to sense him. Before she could fully grasp his being, Lorne clapped his hands to start the sparring match, and she was reminded of her previous fights with Raven. Rosse jabbed his sword at her, but she deftly moved away and it did not even snag her clothing.

Again, Rosse jabbed, and again she moved away. Despite her focus being on the fighter in front of her, she could still sense his energy and movements before he attacked. The back and forth continued before he suddenly struck at her head, missing as she quickly ducked, anticipating his move. Soon, a small group gathered to see which fighter was the best.

Kaie held off his attacks as she concentrated on his sound. Sweat beaded on her brow as she attempted to manipulate it, and Rosse stumbled as she tugged too hard.

"What are you doing?" he asked with a gasp as he swung towards her again.

She dodged the blow and adjusted the sound to make him sleepy. The Inviver did not want to injure Rosse, but make him too tired to fight. Rosse's feet stumbled on themselves, as if a weight was dragging him down.

Seeing Rosse's energy beginning to flag, Lorne motioned for Raven to join the fight. Raven eagerly jumped in, and Kaie was almost thrown off balance in surprise. She was able to hold off the two brothers with difficulty, continuing to move backwards to force them to step forward. Rosse's sword eventually collided with her cloak and she scrambled to keep her face hidden, reduced to fighting with just one hand. Already, her energy was sapping from her Calming on Rosse and she did not dare try it on Raven.

Raven gave a triumphant smile as he moved forward to attack, growing cocky now that she was distracted. Kaie jumped forward, jabbing at an opening, throwing Raven's sword out of his hand—mimicking Lorne's move of using his opponent's strength against him. She quickly spun to block Rosse's next attack, sliding her sword down his, creating an unpleasant screech. His strength was starting to overpower her so she ducked and somersaulted under his legs, holding her sword at his back.

Against all odds, she had won.

Tristen began to clap as she panted for breath. "Well done," he told her. "Your skills have certainly improved since I left. You managed to beat them and not reveal your face."

She smiled at his praise as the crowd dissipated.

"What was that?" Rosse gasped, sheathing his sword. "I feel so heavy."

"I used Calming on you to make you feel tired," Kaie said.

"You couldn't beat me without resorting to tricks?" Rosse asked. He gave her a cheeky grin. "I expected better from you, my lady."

"I used the skills I have at my disposal," Kaie said.

Raven walked up to her. "Just so you know, I was just going easy on you," he said. "I demand a rematch."

Kaie grinned, knowing he had not gone easy on her. "Just tell me the time and the place." She shot a look at Rosse. "I promise not to use Calming on you again."

***

Commander Crevan lowered his telescope. "Amazing. He was able to take down those two without a single scratch to himself. Not only is he a very powerful Inviver, but a great fighter as well. It is decided. I must meet this remarkable boy." He licked his lips, he wanted to engage the other Inviver, to use his powers. Just the idea of having the boy switch sides was enough to make him salivate. Crevan enjoyed the challenge.

Fallon had noticed something during the fight, but did not want to completely bring it to Crevan's attention. He also had been around his commander long enough to recognize when Crevan was becoming obsessed with a new toy. "How can you be sure that's a boy, Commander?"

"Because, Fallon," Crevan spoke slowly, as if to a child, "they send all their female Invivers to other parts of the country. They think this area is too dangerous for women. This logic is what makes *me* commander and not you."

CHAPTER 28

It did not take long for Kaie to fall into a new routine. After Curing Tristen, she was expected to stay to help with the war effort. Despite Tristen's protests, Achaius insisted on staying by her side. Every day, Lorne ran her through drills, always with the order to keep her cloak hood in place.

One night, Tristen pulled Kaie and Achaius aside, sensing the rising tensions. Earlier that day, from across the field, Crevan had been heard screeching at his soldiers, which usually resulted in a battle the following day. Whenever he was angry enough to yell for hours, it meant his usual short temper was even more volatile. It seemed as though only battle could calm down his rage.

"I want you to stay by my side during the battle," he directed Kaie. "The other Invivers can handle the smaller injuries, but we can't give them the chance to capture or injure you. If you get separated from me at any time, find Lorne, Raven, or Rosse, and stay close to them. Do you understand?"

Kaie nodded, and he turned his attention to Achaius, who had done an excellent job of laying low over the past week. "For the last time, could you please go home?" he begged. Every night at dinner, he'd had the same request for him.

"As long as Kaie is here, I'm staying," Achaius said, crossing his arms. "I can help, Tristen. I'm a good fighter. I trained under Lorne too."

Tristen passed a hand over his face. Every night, it was the same argument, and even Lorne could not convince the younger prince to return. Not to mention, they could not spare the soldiers at the moment to force Achaius to go back home.

"At least stay out of the way," he said. "There will be a group at the back of the battle. You are to stay with them, out of harm's way."

"I can fight!" Achaius said, leaning forward.

"You are not getting hurt on my watch," Tristen said through clenched teeth, his eyes flashing in warning. "You will stay where I tell you to. If you disobey me, I'll have you restrained and send you back hog-tied."

Achaius's face flushed in anger, but he sat back, remaining silent.

"I wish Father hadn't sent you," Tristen said quietly. "Between the two of you, I have a lot to worry about."

"My fighting has gotten better over the past year. I'm better able to defend myself," Kaie said, not wanting Tristen to spend extra effort worrying over her. "And the whole point of my training was to come here to fight!"

"I have no doubt of that, but I still don't want to take the chance. This is your first battle," Tristen said grimly. "Now go to bed. Someone will fetch you in the morning."

The two left after saying good night, and Tristen turned to Lorne. "Is this what it feels like to be a parent?" he asked hoarsely.

Lorne nodded his head. "You just try to keep them alive as best you can, even when it seems they're trying to kill themselves," he said solemnly. "But we'll do our best to keep them safe."

"I hope tomorrow goes well," Tristen said quietly. "I don't want either of them to get hurt."

***

At dawn the next day, the battle commenced, the sound of a bugle across the field heralding the oncoming bloodshed. Achaius was already tucked away within his squadron while Kaie was positioned next to Tristen up on a nearby hill, surveying the battlefield on horseback.

The Galician army was split into eight regiments of three hundred men, and each of the men from the meetings with Tristen over the past week led a regiment. Archers stood near the back of their force, ready for the order to fire, while the infantry at the front prepared to make way for the cavalry.

Across the field, Kaie could see the Scrian army in position, as well, their blue uniforms standing out against the forest surrounding the field. Rosse and Raven rode up to position themselves next to Kaie.

"What are you doing here?" Kaie asked. "I thought Tristen would have you protecting Achaius."

"He has others handling that job," Rosse laughed. "It wouldn't be a good idea considering—"

The sound of the bugle spread across the field, announcing the movement of enemy forces. They marched forward toward the Galicians, and Kaie gripped her reins tightly to stop the trembling in her hands. Both sides seemed equally matched in terms of manpower, but she was not looking forward to the upcoming cries and screams.

"Kaie, just remember what I told you," Tristen said, his face stony. "Just—"

"I remember," she interrupted, anxious for this to be over. She did not like the change that had come over her friend. Rather than his usual cheerful self, a serious and grim mask had descended upon him.

Tristen signaled to his generals, and their troops began to advance. Swiftly, both sides met each other in the middle of the field and the bloodbath began.

From her vantage point, Kaie could see the other Invivers running around the field, Curing most of the fallen soldiers. A chosen few Invivers held back near the rear to disperse their Calming influence across the battlefield, to invigorate the soldiers to fight. Her entire being itched for something to do, rather than watching others do the work.

Suddenly, a whole group of Galician soldiers fell, overcome by a huge man wielding a gigantic sword. He only wore metal gauntlets, his torso unprotected. From his confidence, size, and deadly skill, it seemed he was not concerned about any fatal injury. Kaie's face paled upon seeing him take out five men with one swing, the urge to do something rising within her, greater than ever. Instinctively, she turned her horse towards the man, wanting to take him down.

Tristen noticed the movement and looked to where she was aimed. "Kaie, don't do anything. Just stay here. Kaie!" His strangled yell rose as she raced off, ignoring him. "Raven, Rosse, make sure that she stays safe. You two are responsible for her," he said, before turning back to the battlefield to direct his generals.

The small amount of caution and fear Kaie had felt since the first bugle slipped from her consciousness, replaced by one singular goal. Self-preservation was not a thought—she was focused on the need to prevent the man from hurting anyone else. Already, he was surrounded by a ring of bodies—killing more men in a singular blow than any other enemy soldier.

Raven and Rosse raced after Kaie, watching as she vaulted off her horse when Scrian soldiers blocked her way. She continued to run on foot, unsheathing her sword and slicing anyone who got in her way, ruthlessly cutting through soldier after soldier. A stony focus slipped over her, keeping her from dwelling on slaughtering the men challenging her. Her sword was sharp and ready, and she was merely the vessel used to wield it. As she ran, she gripped the hood of her cloak to hold it in place. She would not let it fall; she had practiced the entire week with it intact.

The giant soldier noticed her and changed direction, a dull glint in his eye as he continued taking out Galician soldiers. Raven and Rosse pushed their horses even more, trying to stop the inevitable fight from happening. Once all soldiers between Kaie and the giant realized what was happening, they parted like the seas to let the two warriors fight.

As Kaie raced towards the man, she ducked the oncoming attack aiming for her head, causing it to pass harmlessly overhead. She swung upward and slashed part of the man's arm, which was as thick as a small tree, leaving a large gash, before pulling her sword out. Blood began to pour from the wound, but he hardly seemed to notice. Kaie managed to dodge the broadsword twice more, but on his third swing, he ripped part of her cloak and caught her arm. Although the wound was not serious, she knew it would hamper her during the fight. The leather armor that had been provided prevented the injury from being worse. Switching tactics, she moved to hit him from different spots, attempting to wear him down.

The surrounding battle continued, leaving the two to their own confrontation. Their fight for survival had blurred their surroundings, yet heightened their awareness of flesh and the metal that could cause their imminent death.

Raven and Rosse were caught up in the melee, unable to get close enough to help Kaie. They continued their own fight against enemy soldiers, forced to watch as Kaie slashed at the man.

Soon, the soldier was covered in multiple wounds, some more serious than others, but he seemed to be unstoppable, still coming after her with all his strength. His eyes continued to have a dull gleam and Kaie felt unnerved as their gazes met.

He wasn't acting on his own accord.

As she had done with Rosse, Kaie reached out to find the man's consciousness. There was a strange buzzing surrounding his being that grew louder the more she focused. A shiver ran down her back as she remembered Avalon's words—he was being controlled through Calming to fight.

Kaie knew she would have to end the fight soon if she was to defeat him, as her stamina was swiftly running out. She came in for the final blow, but he swung a heavy arm before she could get too close. Falling to the ground to dodge the blow, she looked up as he began to walk towards her, towering over her.

When he raised his arm to finish her off, his broadsword gleaming in the morning sun, her mind reached out to his, attempting to remove the buzzing. For good measure, she jabbed her sword forward into his stomach and dragged it across his abdomen—a fatal blow. He stopped and looked down at his insides seeping out in utter disbelief just as she broke the Calming tie from another Inviver.

"Thank you," he said, his eyes clear as he sank to his knees, his energy sapped. "I've been under their control for so long..."

Kaie watched in horror as his voice trailed off and the dullness slipped back over his face. He leaned forward to grab her hood as he fell, ripping it from her head before she realized what he was doing.

All the men from the enemy battalion and some from the Galician army gasped in surprise, and both Tristen and Raven groaned once they saw that her identity was now exposed.

CHAPTER 29

Across the field, Crevan had been watching the entire fight with great interest and his mouth gaped open in surprise. Silently, he handed the spyglass to Fallon, whose eyes widened before returning the telescope, a smirk twitching the corners of his mouth.

"Looks like I was right," Fallon said, trying to keep the smug smile off his face.

"Quiet," Crevan snarled. "I don't want to hear any of your theories about her."

Fallon quickly wiped the grin off his face, retreating into himself while Crevan began to pace. His commander was angry, and those were the times he became the most violent.

"What are we going to do about this?" Crevan muttered to himself, barely audible. "It would be best to meet the girl as soon as possible, but how?"

***

After the giant's death, Raven and Rosse pulled Kaie back to Tristen. She was barely able to move, her feet stumbling over themselves as she returned to the prince. She was shocked that she killed a man who was under the influence of Calming, and a shiver ran through her as she remembered the countless others she had killed on her way to take him out. Her stomach roiled, and the two brothers stopped so she could vomit. Aira had run off sometime during the battle, so Tristen pulled Kaie onto his horse when she was close enough.

"I told you to stay put," he said in her ear. His voice was gentle. He could tell how shocked she was, but needed her to know what she'd done was dangerous.

After several moments, she registered what he'd said. "I wanted to do something useful, and he was taking out a lot of our troops. It seemed like the right thing to do," she answered, focusing on the horse's mane, running her fingers through it.

He glanced down at her, at her pale appearance. "Yes, but now you're in shock. You are staying with me for the rest of the battle."

"Tristen, he was being influenced to fight," Kaie said. "He didn't know what he was doing."

"What do you mean?" Tristen asked with a frown.

"An Inviver was Calming him," she said. "He—"

Across the field, the bugle rang out three times, to which the Scrian soldiers began to retreat. The Galician cavalry began to follow, pushing their sudden advantage. But the Scrian archers were able to keep them at bay with their poisoned arrows.

Tristen frowned at that latest development. "I don't like the look of this," he said grimly, before also calling for a retreat.

Within minutes, both sides retreated completely to their sides of the field. Watching warily, Tristen spied a man holding a white flag entering the field, approaching the Galician camp.

"I don't believe it. He wants a truce?" Tristen whispered in disbelief. "Sir Shalane!" he called out to the man nearby, and Lorne rode over. "Let the soldier through. No one is to touch him. I'll at least hear what Crevan has to say, though I have a feeling this is a trap."

The man walked through camp and soon was in front of Tristen's horse, unscathed just as ordered. His journey across the battlefield and through camp had given Kaie enough time to put her hood back on, her coloring returning to normal. Raven had managed to find her horse and she was now astride Aira.

When the man bowed to Tristen, the prince ordered, "What is it? I don't want any formalities. What does Crevan want?"

"Your Highness, Commander Crevan wishes to talk with you out at the center of the field. He wants you to bring the girl." The messenger nodded towards Kaie. "You may bring her bodyguards with, if you wish. I will bring your answer back to him."

Tristen looked at Kaie, glancing between her, Lorne, Raven, and Rosse. "I don't like this," he said grimly. "It sounds like a trap."

Lorne nodded in agreement. "Why does he want to meet her?" he asked. "If he truly wishes to have a truce, what does he have to offer?"

Tristen sighed, weighing over the options in his head. "Very well," he said, addressing the messenger. "Tell Crevan we'll meet with him, but he better not try anything. Our archers will have arrows trained on him the entire time."

The man bowed before scurrying back across the field to relay the information to his commander. Galician soldiers watched him warily as he returned, unsure of what message he brought to their prince.

"Kaie, you can go change. We have time," Tristen said. "You're covered in blood."

Kaie looked down, realizing that Tristen was correct. Her stomach churned at the damp clothing that clung to her skin. She rushed off to her tent, Lorne following behind to ensure nothing bad happened.

Once in her tent, she scrubbed at her skin from a small bucket of water before changing into coffee-colored trousers and a forest-green tunic. Her hair had started to fall out of its braid and she fixed it, wishing not for the first time this past week that Farin was there. Finally, she dug through the bag of clothes Farin had thoughtfully packed for her, finding a dark-green cloak. Putting it on, she followed Lorne back to Tristen. Achaius was waiting as well.

"Much better," Tristen said, nodding as he saw her. "Are we ready to go?"

Kaie mounted Aira. "Yes," she said.

"I can help too," Achaius whined, wanting to be part of the action. He had seen Kaie fighting and was jealous that he had been forced to stand on the sidelines.

"No," Tristen said in a voice that declared the conversation was over. "Kaie almost got killed trying to save some men today. I will not have that same foolhardiness happen again." He turned his horse towards the battlefield.

Achaius walked up to Kaie and put a hand on her knee. "Be careful," he said, giving her an earnest look.

Despite not wanting to, a blush covered Kaie's cheeks as she met his eyes. Wordlessly, she nodded and placed her hand over his. Achaius looked shocked, but pleased at the gesture. He took her hand, squeezing it gently in reassurance as he felt the slight tremor that was still affecting her.

"I'll be fine. These four will protect me if it comes down to it," she said with a slight smile. "I'll see you soon."

As the small group left their camp, Crevan and two others left the Scrian side, also on horseback. Crevan rode ahead of his men at a leisurely pace, as if it was a nice afternoon ride rather than negotiations for war.

"I wonder who he's bringing," Raven said, moving his horse protectively closer to Kaie.

"One is Fallon, his advisor, but I don't recognize the other one," Tristen said. "Rosse, do you have any idea?"

"No, but he seems to be around Raven's age," Rosse mused.

Tristen slowed his horse down. "This meeting is not going to be pretty," he said. "Kaie, I think Crevan is going to try and persuade you to join their side."

"What? That's ridiculous!" she exclaimed, her voice rising in pitch. "I would never join them!"

"You say that now, but Crevan will do whatever it takes to convince you," Tristen warned. "Just stay strong and it will be fine. We'll protect you."

Conversation stopped as they were now in hearing distance of Crevan's party. Kaie inspected the Scrian commander, intense dislike curling up from her belly. His tanned face had a scar stretching across one eye, and his aquiline nose and sharp cheekbones gave him a look of mistrust. Black eyes darted back and forth greedily as he took stock of the group before finally resting on her, trying to peer at her face within the cloak.

"Ah, Prince Tristen! So good to see you again," Crevan said grandly as he approached. "Such a nice day, yes?" When Tristen remained silent, he continued, "Well, that was certainly an interesting battle, wasn't it? I never expected your Inviver here to have such a *ferocious* side to her." Crevan smiled widely, and Kaie had to hold back a shiver. He sounded so *proud* of her.

"Say what you want and let's get this over with, Crevan," Tristen said in a low voice.

"Not feeling too friendly today, are we? Very well, I'll start with why I called this little meeting."

Tristen said nothing, and Crevan took his silence as affirmation.

"I wanted to meet your new pet. May I see her face or are you the only one privy to that benefit?"

Tristen's face did not change from its stoic expression, but his eyes revealed his hatred and anger towards Crevan. He turned and nodded towards Kaie, signaling for her to remove her hood. He would allow the enemy commander to take a look at what he could never have.

Before her fingers reached for the hood, Raven moved his horse a step closer to her.

Crevan burst out laughing, and she paused. "Look at him! What do you think I'm going to do, boy? Whisk her away or attack her? What a strange notion you have!"

His laugh was coarse, grating on Kaie's ears, and she tried not to flinch. Her dislike of him continued to grow, and she noticed Raven's hand resting lightly on his sword. His face turned bright red, but he remained silent.

"Well? Am I to see the young lady's face?" Crevan asked again.

Kaie's hands rose once more, and she was able to remove her hood without interruption. As it fell to her shoulders, Crevan's disbelief at her youth was displayed clearly on his face. He quickly schooled his features, but not before everyone was able to see his expression.

"I didn't know that you were having children fight your war for you, Tristen," he said mockingly.

Kaie prickled at his words. In half a year, she would be of age. She was hardly a child.

"To be fair, she did just defeat your biggest soldier," Tristen said. "Just get it out. What do you want?" His bared his teeth, finally showing a fraction of his hatred.

"I have an offer to make the girl, but first I would like to know her name. What is it?" Crevan asked.

"None of your business," Kaie growled.

Tristen shot her a look, but she returned one of her own, pleading with him to understand. She did not want an evil man like this knowing her name.

Crevan's surprise was apparent, his eyebrows raised. "Fine. As for my offer, I know you'll reject it at first, but please let me explain it completely before you interrupt." Kaie remained silent, and he continued. "There's no easy way to say this, so I'll be as blunt as possible. I would like you to join my cause."

Even though Tristen had warned her of this exact scenario, her mouth still fell open in shock. Kaie's ears burned with anger that this commander thought so little of her loyalty that he would offer such a ludicrous idea in front of her own leader.

Crevan chuckled at her expression before continuing. "You would be treated like royalty in my camp, and our Invivers could teach you the unreadable parts of the book that your Invivers have so desperately been trying to keep a secret. There's nothing terrible in that part of the book—it just explains how you can live forever, Cure anyone without consequences to your health, and how you could be on the path to become the greatest Inviver in history. Maeve only wants you to follow the lowly path she's laid out for you. She doesn't want you to surpass her skills. What do you say?"

Kaie remained silent, trying to understand all that he was saying. He was obviously lying. If the Scrian Invivers were able to do all that, they would not need to invade Galicia to obtain their secrets. "I've heard stories about how you abuse your Invivers," she said. "You only want me for my power, while my friends care for my well-being. I won't join you."

Crevan's face turned from openness to anger. He quickly tried to calm down, trying to persuade her some more. After all, it was better when they fought back. It made victory all the sweeter. "I don't know what you think you've heard, but I even brought one of my Invivers to tell you how well we treat them. Haelan, please come forward."

The young man who stepped up looked to be a few years older than Kaie. His brown hair was cut close to his head, and his bright-blue eyes were piercing. He sat stiffly on his horse, dressed in fine clothes, looking as though he would fit in more at a royal court rather than a muddy battlefield. On his chest was an Inviver's brooch that matched Kaie's. A quiet, ominous hum emanated from him and Kaie frowned slightly. Haelan's eyes searched hers, trying to find any source of weakness, causing her to sit taller in the saddle.

A quick and easy smile flashed across his face in response. "It's true," he said, a lilt to his words. "Crevan does treat us very well. At least, better than your commander does."

"You take that back," Kaie snapped, her horse moving forward. "I've heard how your commander tests on you. I've seen the scars."

Raven reached out and grabbed her arm, preventing her from getting too near the trio.

"Prince Tristen is the best commander ever. He treats us all with respect and kindness."

Haelan attempted to shrug nonchalantly, but there was a stiffness to his shoulders. He adjusted one of his sleeves and Kaie spotted a similar injury to Avalon's. "But I know all sorts of things you don't—we have been researching different Curing techniques with great success. I can help teach you, if you'll come with us."

"I don't need your help. I know all that I need to help others," she said, raising her chin proudly. "I know secrets, too, ones you would never understand."

"Like what?" Haelan asked, curious to know what she knew.

"Wouldn't you like to know," she said, a smug smile on her lips. "Unfortunately, they're well-kept secrets. You will never find out what they are."

Tristen could tell she had sparked Crevan and Haelan's interest. *They have no idea what she is capable of.*

"By the way, Crevan, I want to thank you for that little gift you sent me. Almost finished me off, but luckily, Kaie was able to fix me up." Tristen wanted to rub this fact in Crevan's face just a little more.

"No almost about it," Kaie muttered, and Tristen smiled as he heard her comment.

"What did she say?" Crevan demanded, leaning forward as if that would allow him to hear the words she had just uttered.

"She said that there was no *almost* about it," Tristen repeated.

Kaie's eyes widened, not expecting that he would give away what she had done.

"So... you were dead?" Haelan asked, his voice revealing his disbelief. He glanced at Crevan, taking in the greedy gleam in the commander's eyes. This was what he had been searching for.

"Yes," Tristen said, a feeling of power rushing over him as he saw their shocked faces. "But she was able to bring me back to life. I bet none of your Invivers can do that, now can they?"

"It's impossible for any Inviver to do that," Fallon said, his mouth gaping open.

"Trust me, it's possible," Tristen said confidently.

"Then maybe she'd like to repeat the demonstration?" Crevan asked, cruel pleasure dripping from his lips like sticky sap. He looked like a hungry beast, ready to devour its meal.

"No," Kaie said sharply, causing everyone to turn and look at her. "I'm not doing it again. Not as a show."

Crevan looked at her, the greed in his eyes growing. "Is no your final answer? If it is, I can assure you, we will make your life miserable. You don't want me as an enemy. I can find what you hold most dear and take it away. Isn't that right, Fallon?"

Fallon's face fell as he answered sadly, "Yes, it is."

He looked at Kaie, and she noticed the sadness in his eyes, as if he was pleading with her not to test Crevan's rage. Something in his expression made her realize that the man knew firsthand about the black poison that ran in Crevan's veins.

She paid him no heed. "No, I'm not doing it. Besides, you're already my enemy. You don't scare me." Her voice had an edge to it. Clenching the leather reins in one hand, she managed to fend off the urge to spit in Crevan's face.

"Fine," Crevan said coolly, his face resorting back to an eerily neutral expression. "Come, Haelan, Fallon. We are leaving." He turned and headed back to his camp, a dangerous silence falling over him.

Fallon gave Kaie a regretful look before leaving, then shuddered. He did not seem eager to return back to the Scrian camp. If the commander's yelling the day before was any indication of how the man usually was, she assumed the advisor would not have an easy night.

Haelan was the last to go, looking at Kaie strangely as if trying to gauge the truth of the tale. When he saw the truth in her face, he nodded "I wish that it would have worked out," he said sincerely. "I could easily imagine us being friends."

"Maybe," she said. "If you were on the right side."

He gave her a grim smile before following Crevan and Fallon back to camp.

CHAPTER 30

Achaius ran up to the group as soon as they returned. "What did they want?"

"He wanted me to join the Scrian side," Kaie answered wearily as she slid down from her horse, the strain of the conversation finally weighing on her.

"You said no, right?" Achaius asked.

"I'm still here, aren't I?" Her tone was clipped, and Achaius got the not-so-subtle hint that she did not want to talk about it.

They walked over to a nearby fire, where they began to eat with the others. Dusk had already fallen, and Kaie finished her meal quickly, then headed to her tent to sleep. The day's intense physical and mental exhaustion weighed on her.

"What's with her?" Achaius asked his older brother once she was out of sight, interrupting the peaceful crackling of the fire. He turned back to his own bowl of stew, grabbing another spoonful.

Tristen sighed. The day's activities had worn him down as well. "I think it was Crevar's words."

Achaius's head jerked up at his answer. "What did he say?"

"He promised immortality, and he just had this *look* about him when he found out she'd Cured me," Tristen said. He sighed and ran a hand over his face. "I shouldn't have said that she brought me back to life, but I just wanted to rub it in his stupid, smug face."

"You didn't say that you had *died*!" Achaius said accusingly. He had heard the rumors around camp, but assumed they were exaggerated. Even if Kaie was a great Inviver, bringing someone back from the dead was unheard of. His mind whirled at how powerful she was. "Why didn't she tell me? Why didn't *you* tell me?"

"The important thing is I'm alive," Tristen said. "We have more important things to worry about."

"Do you think she believes Crevan's promises at all?" Raven asked.

"No, Avalon has told her how she was treated when under Crevan's command," Achaius said slowly, still thinking about his brother's words. "She wouldn't betray us for someone like him."

"We do need to send people to protect her family. I have a feeling they'll get caught up in this, too, no matter how hard she'll try to keep them out of it." Tristen stood. "Lorne, can you find Barra? I'd rather send someone in person rather than a raven."

"I don't think he's returned from the palace," Lorne said.

Tristen frowned. "Really? He was told to come back right away."

Raven looked up at Tristen. "He said he was going to follow us the next day."

"But that means he should be here several days ago," Raven interjected.

Tristen ran a hand over his face, exhaustion overwhelming him. "We need to send word to the king of this new development, and we'll need to send about a dozen men to Kaie's house to protect her family. That should be enough. Send Ronan. He's a fast rider and can take care of himself. Make sure you stress the importance of him returning here. If he doesn't come back within a week, I'll be forced to send Rosse after him."

"Very well." Lorne turned to send off the messenger, the fact that Barra had not returned weighing heavily on his mind.

***

Around midnight, Raven crept out of his tent wearing a black cloak to cover his face as he quietly maneuvered around camp towards the forest. Carefully picking his way past the trees, trying not to step on any twigs, he trekked deeper into the forest. About a hundred yards from camp, he found another person.

"Are you sure you weren't followed?" the man asked.

Raven nodded. "Yes. Do you want the news?"

"Yes, what happened? I was surprised to get your signal so soon."

"It was an emergency."

Raven and the other man whispered late into the night until dawn came, at which point Raven snuck back to his tent.

***

The next week passed quickly as Tristen and the other generals prepared for the next battle. Kaie spent her mornings in the Invivers' tent taking care of any injuries the soldiers experienced. Anyone who had been shot with poison arrows during the previous battle were directed to her for Curing. Once everyone had been taken care of, Evidian spent time with her honing her Calming ability. No matter how much she tried, the most she was able to Calm at a time remained at ten people, unlike the older Inviver's three hundred.

Afternoons were spent practicing with Raven and Rosse. She was glad that she no longer had to worry about the cloak, and was having fun trying out more dangerous moves with the two men. From time to time, Achaius would join them, but for the most part, he stayed away. Instead, he practiced with the other soldiers.

By the end of the week, with no sign of Ronan, Tristen pulled Rosse aside in the middle of practice. Raven and Kaie remained quiet, trying to eavesdrop on the conversation. Worry overtook Raven's face as they listened to what was going on.

"I need you to go to the palace," Tristen said to Rosse. "Neither Barra nor Ronan have returned and I'm getting worried. If we can't communicate with the palace, then we're sitting ducks here. We'll be forced to retreat and Crevan will have won the border. If you find them, I want you to bring back the culprits responsible for this. Leave tonight when everyone is asleep. I don't want anyone finding out about this." He turned, seeing Kaie and Raven watching them. "I expect you to keep this a secret."

The two nodded, and Tristen slapped Rosse on the shoulder. "Finish practicing. I expect you all in my tent for dinner."

***

At dinner that night, Tristen started the meal by discussing battle tactics with Lorne, and everyone came to find out that the next battle was to happen in a couple days' time, with the focus of gaining control of the hill. Crevan's forces had been banding around that spot the past few days.

"The only reason we got through that last battle was because Crevan had his men retreat so he could talk to Kaie. The sooner we get control of that hill, the better," he said. "The battle will be in a few days, so that gives Rosse plenty of time to get to the palace and back." He turned to Rosse. "I need you to make this plan work—your fighting skills are needed. You'll be leading an elite group of men to take over this hill. If you're not here by the next battle, I will have to forsake my plans until we have a better opportunity."

"Yes, sir." Rosse nodded, finishing his last bite. "Should I leave now? It should be dark enough."

Tristen opened the tent flap, observing the dark night sky. "Wait until everyone is asleep, but you can go get ready," he agreed. He shook Rosse's hand. "Good luck."

Rosse nodded to everyone before leaving. Raven looked after him, longing to say goodbye, but knew that his duty required him to stay behind.

Tristen noticed his wistful look. "Raven, if you want to say goodbye to your brother, you may. Just return here when you're done."

Raven looked at him gratefully before rushing out of the tent, the entrance flap swaying from his swift departure. Kaie watched him go, knowing the sharp pain of saying goodbye to a loved one and never knowing if they would be seen again. Tears pricked her eyes at the thought, and she turned back to Tristen, trying to distract herself.

"I think it's time you two go to bed," Tristen said, seeing her expression.

Kaie stood, knowing it would be futile to fight with Tristen on this matter, if past arguments were anything to go by. Not to mention Lorne would take his side as well.

Achaius stayed put, frowning at his brother. "Why can't I stay up and learn more about our plans?" he asked.

"Because you have had circles under your eyes since the last battle. To bed—*now*." Tristen's voice left no room for argument.

"Come on, Achaius. We can walk back together," Kaie said.

Reluctantly, he stood and followed her out of the tent. Once outside, Kaie grabbed his hand and pulled him further away from Tristen's tent.

"What is it?" he demanded curtly, still peeved at Tristen's dismissal.

"I want to tell you about when I Cured Tristen," Kaie answered. It had been weighing on her to keep this a secret from him for so long.

"He told me you brought him back from the dead," Achaius said, crossing his arms. He was still mad she'd kept this information from him.

Kaie's eyes widened in surprise. "He said he wanted to keep that a secret," she confessed. "I wanted to tell you."

"It slipped out when he was talking about your conversation with Crevan," he said. "So what did you want to talk about?"

"During that last battle, I noticed that we didn't have enough Invivers. I doubt any more will be sent here, so I need to ask you something."

"Yes? What is it?"

"In the cave, after you Cured me and left—" both Kaie's and Achaius's faces blushed at the memory, the darkness hiding their reactions from the other, "—Maeve came in and told me how when you were little, she tried to pass on some of her powers to you. If you want, I could try to do the same. Since no one has brought anyone back from the dead, I wonder if maybe I can do what she can't."

"Really? That would be great!" Achaius exclaimed in an elated whisper. He paused for a moment, trying to think rationally and not get caught up in the thought that he could become an Inviver. "But what about your powers? Would you be able to do the same things you can do now?"

"Maeve said that if an Inviver can share their powers, sharing it with one or two people would be okay. Sharing with many people would diminish my abilities, but if it's just with you, that should be fine. You would use your own energy for Curing and be an Inviver, but you wouldn't be able to surpass my abilities." She bit her lower lip. "It also means that even if this works, I wouldn't be able to Cure you if you get hurt. Invivers can't Cure each other, remember?"

"I remember," Achaius said eagerly, coming closer to her. "But I really want to be an Inviver. I want to give it a try."

"Are you sure?" Kaie questioned, wanting to make sure that he thought about the consequences. In the back of her mind, she knew that Tristen would disapprove of this decision, but Achaius seemed so excited. And they did need more Invivers. Selfishly, she wanted to be the one who could give him this gift, to make him happier than anyone else could.

"Yes, yes, I'm sure," he said impatiently. "Just do it."

Kaie gently took his hands in her own before closing her eyes, breathing deeply in concentration. She took a few minutes to identify and focus on the sounds emanating from both their bodies. When she heard a deeper thrumming coming from her, she sliced off part of it and pushed it towards Achaius. As she exhaled, her chest began to glow through her clothing. The two watched in amazement as the glow passed through her hands and into Achaius's body, where it traveled to his chest. His light was not as bright as hers, but it remained behind when the glowing light passed back to Kaie. As she exhaled once, the glow from their chests began to fade.

"That should be it," she said. "But the book didn't explain any more of the process."

"How will I know if it worked?" Achaius asked.

"It won't work on me, but maybe someone nearby has an injury or something," Kaie said.

"What are you two doing?" Raven's voice came from behind them.

"Raven!" Kaie exclaimed, turning to face him. "What are you doing here?"

"Never mind that," Achaius said impatiently. "Do you have an injury? A cut or something?"

Frowning at Achaius's question, Raven pulled up his sleeve, revealing a small cut. "I got this a couple days ago in the armory," he said. "Why?"

"Shhhhh, just watch." Achaius slowly put his hands on Raven's arm, and as they all watched, he took a deep breath. There was a brief flash of light that faded quickly, but when it disappeared, Raven's cut still remained.

"What's going on?" Raven asked.

Achaius frowned and looked towards Kaie, ignoring the question. "Why didn't it work?"

"You might need to focus more," she said. "Just concentrate on the cut and imagine it fixing itself."

Achaius took another deep breath, staring at the cut. As he focused, a glow emanated from his hands before moving toward the cut. When he breathed out, he could feel the energy flowing from his heart and through his hands. The cut began to heal before their eyes until the glow disappeared and the wound was completely closed.

"Wow," Achaius whispered, raising his hands and looking at them in wonderment. "I can't believe that worked."

"What did you do?" Raven asked, inspecting his arm with wide eyes.

"I was able to pass some of my powers to Achaius," Kaie said, a wide smile on her face. It had worked after all.

"Really? That's incredible! Do you realize the implications of this? Kaie, you could transfer your powers to everyone in this camp and they could Cure themselves. We'd be unstoppable!" Raven's words sped up in excitement.

"It doesn't work like that," she said, shaking her head. "I would only be able to do this a limited number of times before my powers would start to fade. When you have something you can share, it's only a matter of time before it's all gone. Achaius doesn't have the same abilities as me, but he'll still have the ability to Cure some major injuries, like a broken leg or something."

"Really?" Achaius exclaimed. "That's awesome! I can't believe you did this. You're the best!" He hugged her tightly, which, after a moment of hesitation, Kaie returned, her face crimson.

"I better get to sleep. I imagine that Lorne and Tristen will be coming out soon," she said, glad that the darkness hid the color on her face as she pulled away from Achaius. "I'll see you tomorrow." She rushed off to her tent.

"We should head to bed ourselves," Achaius said, watching Kaie run away.

"I'll be back in a bit. I have to talk to Tristen," Raven said. His mind was still spinning.

"Hey, can you keep this a secret? Just for a little while? I want to figure out a way to break this to Tristen without getting Kaie in trouble." Achaius turned to Raven, his eyes pleading.

Raven nodded, and Achaius let out a relieved sigh before heading back to their tent.

Knowing what he had to do, Raven snuck out to the forest again to tell his contact all that had gone on that night—that Kaie had the ability to share her powers.

CHAPTER 31

The day before the next battle, in an attempt to distract from the upcoming bloodshed, Raven challenged Kaie.

"You still owe me an official rematch," he said after she had returned from her daily duties at the Invivers' tent. "No Calming powers this time."

"Is now really the best time?" she asked. Tensions had been high the past few days and she could tell Tristen was anxiously waiting for Rosse to return.

"Why not? It'll help you get ready for tomorrow. There's a lull right now anyway," he said.

Shaking her head at his logic, Kaie unsheathed her sword. A small group of soldiers gathered to watch. Her sparring sessions with Raven and Rosse usually attracted attention all around the camp, and the soldiers relished seeing her acrobatics.

Raven dove at her, and she easily deflected his attack.

She tsked at him. "You're getting to be predictable. You start out almost every fight this way. It's time to change it up."

His smile grew at her comment before he retorted, "I've still got a few more tricks up my sleeve."

Sweat soon beaded on both fighters' brows, and Kaie deflected a blow to her face. Her strength was running out and she would need to end the fight quickly if she was going to win.

"Come on, Raven. Surely you can do better than that," she said, trying to goad him into making a mistake.

"I will say, you've gotten very good at trying to provoke your opponent into slipping up," he said.

Trying to take her by surprise, he aimed again for her face, rolling to dodge one of her attacks. Closer to her now, he was at a better angle to attack her flank, but Kaie was ready, backing up as he approached. She watched his face, gauging his movements by his eyes. Suddenly, his eyes flickered to something behind her and widened in surprise. Taking this opportunity to jump forward and disarm him, she had to stop herself when she realized that his attention was no longer on her. She spun and saw Rosse approaching with a small group of soldiers and a few bound men.

Looking closer at the captives, she recognized them. "Raven, do you know why Revelin and his crew are here?"

"I believe we have just found out who has been ambushing our messengers," he said, turning to a nearby soldier. "Go find Prince Tristen and tell him that Sir Swain has arrived and that he has found the culprits."

The man immediately ran off, and within a few minutes, Tristen joined them.

"Rosse, you've finally arrived," he said. "We have much to discuss." He took in the bound men. "I take it that you found the offenders?"

"Yes. They tried to ambush us on our way back. We found Barra and Ronan too. They had them as captives."

"Did you bring them with you or did they need to recuperate at the palace?" Tristen asked.

"They came. I sent them to the Invivers' tent. They are being seen to now."

"Good. We need them for tomorrow. They're going to be critical to our plan."

"What for?" Rosse asked.

Tristen smiled. "You'll be leading the main ambush, but they'll be leading two smaller parties as decoys. If we can get Crevan's forces preoccupied with Ronan and Barra, it will be the perfect time to strike."

Rosse smiled at Tristen's plan. "Sounds perfect. He'll never know what's coming."

Tristen nodded, turning to go back to his tent. Rosse followed along to continue discussing tomorrow's battle strategy.

Kaie turned back to the small group of soldiers who had accompanied Rosse, and her mouth dropped open once more. "*Farin*?" she asked in disbelief, running over to the other girl and enveloping her in a hug. "What are you doing here?"

"I figured you could use some help," Farin said, smiling slightly.

"But it's so dangerous here!" Kaie exclaimed. "How did your family even allow it?"

Farin laughed. "I can be pretty convincing when I want to," she said. "And I'm not too bad with medicine, even if I'm not an Inviver."

Kaie hugged her again. "I'm so glad to see you. I've missed you," she said. "But this is a battlefield, not the palace."

"I knew that you needed me," Farin said. "Who else can take care of you the way I do?"

"You can share my tent," Kaie said. "I'll show you."

She linked arm with Farin's and walked her to their tent. Though she was filled with concern for Farin's safety, she was immensely happy that her friend from the palace had come to see her.

***

That night, Raven snuck out of his tent to go speak with his contact. Their meeting was brief, but on his way back, he was caught by Rosse.

"Raven! What are you doing out at this hour?" Rosse asked sternly, not happy that his younger brother was out in the middle of the night.

"I could ask the same to you," Raven said.

Rosse crossed his arms, not impressed with his brother's response. He raised an eyebrow.

Raven let out a sigh. "I left my sword by the campfire and had to go get it. I couldn't find it when I went to bed." He was glad that he'd brought his sword for his quick meeting.

Rosse looked carefully at his brother, trying to figure out if he was lying or not. "Fine, but no more of these midnight escapades, understood?"

"Yeah, yeah. All I had to do was find my sword." Raven waved away his brother's concerns. "I'm going to bed now."

"Good. You'll need your rest for tomorrow." Rosse watched Raven walk back to his tent with narrowed eyes.

***

The next day, the battle seemed to be going in the Galicians' favor. The Invivers had rested well the previous night and were able to energize the soldiers. When Crevan's forces were preoccupied with the battle, Tristen signaled for Ronan and Barra's forces to advance towards the hill.

Crevan seemed ready for them, and when the forces that protected the hill were focused on the attack, Rosse led his men for an ambush. As they approached, an entire battalion popped up from a blind spot behind the hill, resulting in catastrophe. Kaie and Tristen watched helplessly as Crevan's men slaughtered Rosse's forces. Tristen called for a retreat, pulling the army out from the battle. Crevan's forces surprisingly did not push their advantage, but they yelled their victory throughout the field.

As their forces returned, Tristen looked angry. "How could he have possibly known that? There's no way that he could have known we would pull such a move."

Kaie was just as confused as he was, but rode to meet Rosse and the small remainder of his men. "Is everyone all right?" she asked.

"Most that are still alive have some pretty serious wounds," Rosse says, holding his slashed and bloody arm close to his body. "You better go Cure them."

"What about you? Your arm looks horrible," Kaie said, thinking that Raven would have her head if she did not Cure his brother.

"They're worse off than me. Come find me after you've taken care of them, but only if you have enough energy," he said, dejectedly heading off towards Tristen.

Kaie turned to the other men, starting to Cure those with the worst injuries. The cacophony of high-pitched noise began to subside as she worked.

Achaius found her half an hour later. "Need any help?" he asked.

"I'm not sure if these are out of your realm or not. Rosse is injured, but I think it looks worse than it is. If you could go Cure him, that would be great," she said, her brow furrowing in concentration over the soldier in front of her.

Achaius nodded, heading off to find Rosse. After looking around for a while, he found the man with Tristen, discussing what had gone wrong with the ambush. Rosse was holding a cloth to his arm to stem the bleeding, but the cloth was soaked, blood dripping from it.

Achaius walked up to the two. "Rosse, I can take a look at that arm if you want. It could get infected if I don't look at it soon."

Tristen looked at his younger brother. "I don't think you can do that much with medicine. We should probably wait for Kaie or another Inviver to come and take a look at it."

"Kaie sent me over. Can I just see it?" Achaius tried to hide his grin, excited about Curing someone else. So far, he had kept his abilities a secret at Kaie's request.

Rosse removed the cloth, offering his arm to the youngest prince. Achaius gently probed the wound, and when he was satisfied with his examination, he focused on the injury, closing his eyes. He breathed out, feeling the energy flowing from his heart to Rosse. As he weakened, he heard a gasp from Tristen and opened his eyes just as the wound disappeared.

Rosse looked at his arm in amazement and flexed it, testing it out.

"How did you do that?" Tristen asked his brother, somehow knowing Kaie had something to do with this.

Not wanting to get her in trouble but seeing no other way to explain the truth, Achaius said, "A few nights ago, Kaie passed on some of her skills to me.

Her abilities haven't diminished, but now I can help the Invivers with some of the injuries here. Isn't that great?"

"But what will happen if you get hurt?" Tristen's voice rose with worry.

"I can Cure it myself," Achaius said confidently.

"But what if it's out of your skill range?"

"Then it would be difficult to Cure the wound," Achaius admitted, but nothing could have prepared him for his brother's rage.

"What would you go and do that for? Are you trying to be foolish? Why would Kaie even agree to do such a thing?" Tristen yelled.

"If I was born an Inviver, I would have the same problem. Since I wasn't, I can now fulfill my dream to be an Inviver. And it wasn't my idea, it was hers," Achaius answered.

"You two should have run this by me first," Tristen said, putting a hand on his brow in frustration. "Now what am I going to tell Father?"

"Tell him the truth. I am an Inviver now and I can work to expand my limits as Kaie has been doing for the past year. It's not a big deal," Achaius said, not understanding his brother's anger.

"But... why... Oh, never mind." Tristen stormed off toward his tent. "When you see Kaie, tell her I want to speak with her," he shouted over his shoulder.

CHAPTER 32

When Kaie came to Tristen's tent a few minutes after he entered, he had not had enough time to cool down. He was scowling as he paced, muttering under his breath. Upon seeing her, his scowl grew and he pointed to a chair. "Sit," he spat out from between clenched teeth. His blue eyes were like ice.

Never before had Kaie ever seen him this angry.

Tristen paced a few more times before stopping in front of her. "Did it ever occur to you to check with me if it was all right to give Achaius Curing powers?" He struggled to get the words out, he was so furious.

For a moment, Kaie was at a loss for words. Even when they'd fought in the past, he had never scared her like this before. "I figured you'd say no before I could explain my reasoning," she said, her voice barely above a whisper.

"Your *reasoning*?" His voice changed to be scarily quiet. "Please tell me, what is this *reasoning* that you have for going behind my back?"

"Achaius has wanted to be an Inviver for a long time," she began. "When we visited the Mists, Maeve told me that when Achaius was younger, she tried to pass her power on to him. I figured if she thought it was all right, then it would be fine for me to try too."

"Is that all?" Tristen raised a hand to his brow.

"Well... no, that isn't the entire reason I did it," she confessed, suddenly frightened to tell him the other reason. It seemed so silly now. She looked away, unable to maintain eye contact.

"Then why did you do it?"

"Why is it so bad when Maeve tried to do the same thing?" Kaie tried changing the subject.

Tristen shook his head. "When Father found out, Maeve got into a lot of trouble. He was so furious, he almost banished her from the kingdom."

"Oh." The magnitude of what she had done finally dawned on Kaie.

"Now what is the reason why you did this? I want the truth," Tristen said, finally lowering his hands away from his face.

Kaie looked away, embarrassed by her reasoning. "He seemed so excited when he Cured me at the Mists," she began, her face flushing at the memory.

"Wait, he's Cured you before?" Tristen's eyes widened at this news, but it did not escape his notice that Kaie was blushing.

"Yes. There is a pool there that allowed him to harness my powers, but use his own energy to Cure me," she said. "Ever since Maeve told me about trying to pass on her powers, I've been thinking about it."

"There's something you're not telling me," Tristen said. More must have gone on in that cave than she was letting on. Something to explain her blushing. "What else happened after he Cured you?"

"He gave me a hug and then he, um..." She trailed off, cheeks turning even more crimson.

"He kissed you, didn't he?" Tristen said. Kaie's behavior made it easy to guess what had happened.

Her eyes flickered to his face before darting away again, and she nodded slowly. "Yes, he did, on the cheek. I was shocked at first, but after that, he seemed to pay more attention to me and looks at me when he thinks I won't notice."

"And you would like it to happen again, wouldn't you?" Tristen's voice turned tender with understanding, upset with himself that he had not seen this coming. His brother's infatuation with Kaie was obvious, but he had not expected her to return his feelings.

She paused for a moment, thinking the question over. "Yes," she finally admitted, still not meeting Tristen's eyes. "But even if he does feel the same way about me, I don't think he would do anything to jeopardize our friendship."

"Probably not," Tristen said. "But over time, he'll see how you feel about him." He reached out and tilted her chin up so she was looking at him. "It's okay to feel this way. It's a part of life. For now, just keep acting the way you usually do and change the way you act towards him slowly. He hasn't had a lot of experience with girls, so you might have to be patient before he catches on."

Kaie nodded. "Farin said the same thing," she said.

Tristen was not surprised that Kaie had found someone else to talk over these topics with, but it still stung a little.

"Am I forgiven?"

Tristen sighed. "You're forgiven," he said. "But I still need to break it to Father in such a way that he won't want to come down here and handle the situation himself. I'll take care of it."

The dismissal was clear.

Kaie left, joining everyone at the fire for dinner, where she listened to Achaius chatter on about his new skills and smiled over her newly realized feelings.

***

"Why do we just sit here waiting for the Scrians to attack? Shouldn't we try ambushing them or something?" Achaius asked one day, bored of sitting around for the past couple days.

"The mountain pass we came through to get here is a direct line to the capital and the palace," Lorne said as he sharpened his sword. "We're protecting the pass from being breached."

"Then why don't the Scrian forces just get more men and wipe us out?" Achaius asked.

Kaie shot him a look, nudging him to be quiet.

"They don't have enough forces to spare to do so," Lorne said, fixing Achaius with a stare. "There are a few other ways through the mountains to our lands, so their forces are spread thin attacking those spots. And," he added, seeing Achaius open his mouth with more questions, "there are only so many men we can enlist for the war. So right now, we're at a stalemate of sorts, trying to turn the tides in our favor."

"So once Crevan's army over there is defeated, then the war will be over?" Kaie asked.

"Yes," Lorne said. "Most of their forces would be wiped out at that point. Not to mention, we'd have a straight shot to their palace as well."

"We're stuck until we annihilate each other?" Achaius sounded bored.

"Come on," Kaie said, standing and offering a hand to Achaius. He was too blunt for his own good and she could tell that Lorne's patience was growing thin. "We can go to the Curing tent and see what we can do there. That will keep your mind off such morbid matters."

***

After dinner several nights later, Tristen ordered Raven to keep watch on Kaie and Farin's tent overnight, much to Kaie's dismay.

"Why?" she protested. "I can take care of us."

"Be that as it may, I don't want to take any chances," he said. "Tonight, there is no moon, and I'm worried Crevan has something planned. This is not a topic up for discussion."

Soon enough, it was bedtime, and Raven went to guard the entrance of Kaie and Farin's tent. "Sweet dreams," he said as they both entered.

"I can't believe Tristen thinks I need a babysitter," Kaie muttered.

Raven laughed at her remark before standing vigil.

After half an hour of tossing and turning, Kaie knew she would not be able to sleep if she could not take a walk to clear her mind of all its buzzing thoughts. Knowing that Raven would never approve of the idea, she quietly slipped on her clothes and put on her hunting boots. As an afterthought, she grabbed her sword and dagger for protection before exiting through the back of her tent, making sure not to disturb Farin's sleep.

Kaie breathed in the cool night air, carefully picking her way across camp. She purposefully avoided the guards and exhaled a sigh of relief when she reached the tree line. Slowly, she walked through the trees until she found a perfect one to lean against, staring at the stars. The cool night wind helped clear her mind.

***

Meanwhile, an elite group of Crevan's men crept across the field, their swords unsheathed. They soon reached the camp, and began to take out the guards, silently ambushing them in the dark. Haelan and part of Crevan's army followed suit while Crevan and Fallon watched from across the field. At that moment, a war meeting Tristen was holding adjourned. As Lorne and Rosse exited, they noticed the fallen guards, their throats slit.

"Intruders! Intruders!" Lorne shouted, raising the alarm.

It was as if an anthill had been kicked. Soldiers rushed out of their tents, swords ready for a fight. Raven heard the alarm and prepared for an attack. This was precisely what Tristen had been worried about.

Haelan navigated through the camp, trying to find the small tent that Crevan had pointed out earlier. Soon, he spotted a tent with Raven standing outside it.

"That's it!" He grinned, knowing without a doubt that this was Kaie's tent. He slowly crept forward, hoping to take Raven by surprise.

His ploy did not work. Raven was on edge and heard Haelan's breathing before he saw the flash of the sword. He turned to Haelan and raised his sword, ready to fight to the death to protect Kaie.

Haelan noticed the change in his demeanor and attacked. Raven deflected the blow, and the next two as well. Haelan soon started to fight with a purpose, trying to find chinks in Raven's defense and slip through them. After a few minutes, Raven was battered, wounded, and tired. A day without sleep had not helped at all. As he lifted his blade once more to defend, Haelan darted forward and hit him on the head with the hilt of his sword.

Raven crumpled to the ground and watched as Haelan entered the tent. "No," he whispered, feebly stretching out his hand as if that would stop the nightmare that was unfolding.

He heard Farin's scream, swiftly cut short, before seeing Haelan storm out of the tent, his face livid. Haelan yanked Raven up by the roots of his hair and brought his face close so they see eye to eye. "Where is she?" he asked from between clenched teeth.

Raven's eyes darted to the open flap of the tent and widened when he saw only Farin's unconscious body. A breath of relief swept through him. Haelan had not killed her after all.

"Must have... snuck out," he whispered weakly.

"To where?" Haelan pulled up on Raven's hair even more.

Raven winced in pain. "No idea. She could be anywhere," he said. In an attempt to keep Haelan's attention preoccupied, he said, "Besides, if I knew, why would I tell you?"

Yelling with rage, Haelan threw him to the ground, beating him with the hilt of his sword until Raven was unconscious and bloody. Looking at the young man's prone body, he felt guilty about his savage act. Kneeling, he quickly Cured most of Raven's wounds, but not enough for the man to awaken.

"No, I'm not like Crevan. I didn't mean to do that. Crevan beats people for fun. I'm not like that," he repeated to convince himself that his commander's brutality had not rubbed off on him.

Looking around, he pulled Raven's unconscious form into Kaie's tent to prevent him from being found and slaughtered by Scrian soldiers, then he proceeded to walk towards the forest, having a general idea of where Kaie would go.

***

Kaie's solitude was broken as she heard sounds of the ambush. She rose, her sword drawn, torn between going to fight or staying away where it was safe, knowing that Tristen would want her to choose the latter. The cries of men reached her ears and she knew that she would not be able to stay still while others were being injured. As she raised her sword, about to head into camp, she saw a figure purposefully heading towards her. Kaie's heart dropped to her stomach once she saw it was Haelan, his sword splattered with blood.

Knowing that he had to have come across Raven—and that Raven had been on the losing end of that fight—Kaie ran further into the forest in hopes of outrunning him until someone could come to her aid. From how Avalon had talked about Scrian Invivers, she did not know what tricks he had up his sleeve.

Haelan saw her run off and sprinted after her. At that moment, a flash of lightning sliced overhead and the skies opened into a downpour. Haelan continued to run after Kaie, but struggled to keep her in sight.

Kaie ran deeper into the forest, beginning to dodge behind trees in an attempt to lose Haelan. Eventually, she hid behind a tree, trying to catch her breath. She tensed, her ears listening for any sound that would give away his position. Over the sound of the rain, she was barely able to hear a twig snap nearby. The low humming she had heard when they first met was barely audible, but she could sense it. Haelan froze immediately at the sound, waiting for Kaie to reveal herself.

Although all her instincts were screaming at her to run, she did not disappoint him. Kaie stepped from behind the tree and faced him, her sword raised in front of her. She looked at him and tilted her head to the side, perplexed as to why he did not immediately attack.

Haelan lowered his sword and threw it on the ground next to him.

"Why are you doing this?" she asked in shock, and his ears strained to hear her above the rain.

Haelan took a step forward, stopping as she raised her sword. He put his hands in the air in surrender. "Relax. I just want to talk to you," he said in an easygoing tone, attempting to get on her good side.

"About what? I can only guess what you've done to Raven or Farin," she said, unable to keep the worry out of her voice for her friends.

"He's fine. Just has a couple cuts and bruises, but otherwise he's fine. He's unconscious in your tent. As for your other friend, I just used knockout powder on her. It's Fallon's special recipe," Haelan explained.

Her eyes narrowed suspiciously. "What did you do?" she repeated. "It takes a lot more than cuts and bruises to knock Raven out. If that was true, I would have knocked him out easily on my own when sparring."

"I may have gotten a little... angry with him. I Cured most of his wounds though," he added hurriedly as she took a menacing step forward. "He just wouldn't tell me where you were."

"So you tried to *beat* the information out of him?" Her voice rose several notes.

"Not necessarily. He honestly didn't know where you were. I had to guess," Haelan said.

"Well, you found me and you dropped your sword. What now?"

"I need to talk to you."

"About what? I won't believe anything you say right now."

He nodded his head. "I deserve that. Just hear me out." He spread his hands pleadingly. "Crevan sent me here to kidnap you. I don't want to, and I don't think you'll do whatever he wants you to anyway. If I don't bring you back, I'm in big trouble. Basically, it's a lose-lose situation."

She frowned, not understanding him. "How's this *my* problem?"

"If I don't bring you back, he'll keep sending men after you—men who won't hesitate to kidnap you. Either that, or he'll find some sort of leverage against you."

"He can't use my family against me. King Torin has already threatened to imprison and kill them," Kaie told him.

Haelan's eyes widened at this fact.

"He hasn't used the threat in a while, but I imagine it still stands."

"What do you have to do to get your family off the hook?"

"Stay here and help win the war. Once the war's over, I can go home. If we lose, I imagine I still wouldn't be able to go home. Your king will probably want to meet me, so the only way I can go home is to win the war."

"How do you know he'll want to meet you?" Haelan was taken aback by her arrogance.

"I can bring people back from the dead," she said, enunciating each syllable. "Or at least to some extent."

"So we need a plan so Crevan won't come after you, and I need an excuse as to why I couldn't capture you."

"Why did he send you in the first place?" Kaie asked. "Surely he has bigger and tougher men than you to kidnap me."

"I'm one of their better Invivers," Haelan said. "He thought I could use my Calming powers on you."

"But Invivers can't use their powers on each other," Kaie said.

Haelan gave her a wry smile. "The other Invivers and I have been fooling him into thinking I can to get out of his punishments," he said. "Obviously, that lie will come out if we don't come up with something."

"I can bring people back from the dead. Surely it isn't beyond the realm of possibility that I can resist your Calming," Kaie said. "And if we're just focused on fighting skills, just say I was too hard to beat."

"Then I'll need to have wounds to show it."

Almost before the sentence left his mouth, Kaie came forward with her sword, beginning to slash at his clothing. She cut his arms and legs, making sure that his sleeves were shredded. She stood back to take a look at her handiwork, and as an afterthought, carefully cut his cheek, leaving an injury that extended from his temple to his chin.

He clutched the stinging wound. "What was that for?"

"He wouldn't believe that we were in a good enough fight if I didn't cut your face. You can always Cure it later. Besides, I'd say it looks believable. Now we just have to smear some of the blood around."

She began to wipe some of the blood from his cut around the rest of his face and all over his clothes. At first, she felt awkward, but knew that she had to make this believable or the effort would be wasted.

"There. I'd say you look like you were in a pretty bad fight."

Haelan looked at her carefully. "If I didn't know better, I'd say you were enjoying this."

She smiled at his comment. "That's for Raven. Now we can start all over again. Fresh slate and everything. I'll still be watching you, so don't try anything else. You'd better head back. It looks like your men are retreating."

They both noticed that the rain had stopped. The rosy pink of dawn peeked over the skyline and Haelan turned to see that she was right.

"Thanks for all of this. I'll make it up to you," he called as he ran to regroup with his men.

Kaie watched him disappear, wondering if it had been a smart move to let him return to Crevan. Just thinking about the different ways that Crevan could make Haelan talk was enough to make her shiver.

Kaie hurried back to camp. Despite exhaustion filling her from the night's events, she was worried about her friends and concern gave speed to her steps. Upon entering her tent, she stopped suddenly, Both Raven and Farin were lying unconscious on the floor.

"Haelan, what did you do?" she whispered under her breath as she Cured her friends.

She put her hands on Raven's shoulders and breathed out. She felt the familiar feeling of energy leaving her and Raven's final injuries disappeared as he opened his eyes. She slumped, so tired from the night's activities, before moving to Farin and doing the same. Raven looked at her and shook his head as his memories came back from the night. Blood remained on his face, yet his cuts were healed and the bruises that had begun forming on his tender skin faded to only a reminiscent ache.

"Haelan! Did he find you?" he asked, slowly rising to a sitting position.

"Yes, he did. We made a sort of truce," she said, helping Farin sit up.

Farin clutched her hands to her mouth in horror. "A truce! What do you mean?"

"He didn't want to capture me so he let me go."

"Did you at least capture him?" Raven asked, his tone biting.

"No, but—"

"You know he beat me senseless, right?" He could not believe that Kaie had let the enemy Inviver go.

"Yes, but I gave him some pretty nasty injuries as well. If you hurry, you could probably borrow Tristen's spyglass to get a look at him before he Cures himself. Now, if you'll excuse me, I'm going to sleep," she said, crawling over to her bundle of blankets.

Farin gave Raven a sympathetic look before placing a blanket over Kaie and leaving the tent. Raven could see that the Inviver was exhausted, and exited the tent to find Tristen to tell him all that had gone on that night.

CHAPTER 33

"What do you mean she resisted your Calming?" Crevan asked Haelan icily, taking in his bloody appearance. If Kaie had not injured the boy badly enough, he certainly wanted to.

"Her powers are greater than we expected. We fought and she trounced me. You see how I look. I was lucky to escape with my life," Haelan said.

"I still don't see how she could beat you," Crevan said with narrowed eyes. "You beat her little bodyguard easily enough and she struggles to beat him sometimes. It should have been easy for you to defeat her."

"I think she holds back in their fights to make them last longer," Haelan said, wincing at the pain lancing through his face. "Can I Cure myself now?"

Crevan looked at him once more, his disgust evident. He wanted the boy to suffer longer. "Fine, go ahead," he said. He tapped a finger against his temple, contemplating how Kaie had resisted Haelan. If she was truly powerful enough to bring people back from the dead and render another Inviver's power useless, surely she would be the key to unlocking immortality. He had been lying when he'd told her what the Scrian Invivers were capable of; they also did not know what the forbidden section of the book contained.

Haelan breathed a sigh of relief that Crevan had bought his story, and his wounds began to Cure. The consequences of being caught in a lie by Crevan were something he did not want to think about.

***

Across the field, Raven managed to see Haelan's wounds through the spyglass before he Cured them. Pride filled him over Kaie getting vengeance on his behalf.

"Kaie really did a number on him," he told Tristen.

Tristen gently took the spyglass from Raven, looking through it. He gave a low whistle as he took in Haelan's appearance. "She sure did," he said. "Probably revenge for what he did to you."

Raven shook his head. "I don't think she knew about that at the time. She practically collapsed from exhaustion when she came back. She said she let him go."

"What do you mean when she came back? Where was she?" Tristen asked.

"She snuck out sometime in the night," Raven admitted, not eager to suffer Tristen's wrath.

To his surprise, Tristen began to laugh.

"What's so funny?" Raven demanded.

"It's nothing," Tristen said, wiping tears from his eyes.

"Obviously," Raven said, rolling his eyes.

"All right, all right. I'll tell you. I'm just surprised that it took her this long to sneak out of her tent," Tristen said.

"I guess it is funny. She really likes to explore," Raven mused. "It's fortuitous that last night was the night that she decided to escape."

"Yeah, it really worked out well for us," Tristen said.

At that moment, Achaius came running up.

"Tristen! Tristen! What happened during the night?" Achaius demanded when he reached his brother. Surprisingly, he had slept through the fighting.

"There was an ambush," Tristen started as Achaius's eyes widened in surprise. "Apparently, it was a diversion so Haelan could kidnap Kaie."

"Is she okay?" The distress in Achaius's voice was apparent.

Tristen recounted what Raven already told him, though he wasn't sure of all the details regarding the truce.

"Well, if you don't know the specifics, then let's go ask her." Achaius began to head off in the direction of her tent, but Tristen grabbed his brother's arm.

"Easy now. She's fast asleep, worn out from last night. Let her rest for a while."

"Fine," Achaius grumbled, but then quickly fell silent as he realized how inconsiderate he was being, especially after everything Kaie had done for him. After a moment, he remembered why he'd initially come to see his brother. "Tristen, I went by the captives this morning and Revelin demands to speak with you."

Tristen's brow furrowed in concern. "Did he say what about?"

Achaius shook his head. "No, but he hinted something about Kaie. That it's important."

Tristen began to walk towards the area of camp where Revelin was being kept captive. "Very well."

At the pen where they were keeping Revelin and his men, Tristen motioned to the guards to let him pass. They stepped aside and he entered. The captives were tied up by their hands and feet to posts that were driven into the ground behind their backs.

Tristen walked over to Revelin's post and untied the rope holding him secure. "Come on, we are going to take a walk," he said.

Revelin's mouth broke into a smile. "To what do I owe this fine pleasure?" he asked, his voice as sweet as honey.

"You know very well why I'm here," Tristen answered, his voice stiff. "Achaius said you wanted to talk to me." Despite Revelin's question, Tristen continued to untie his legs.

"Yes, I do. I'm surprised that boy relayed my message." Revelin followed Tristen out of the pen, rubbing his wrists where Tristen had loosened the rope for more comfort and mobility.

"I'm going to warn you—try anything and the guards will finish you," Tristen advised.

"Don't worry, there would be no point in my escaping," Revelin said. "If I did, my proposal wouldn't happen."

"And what is your proposal?" Tristen asked. He knew better than to trust Revelin, but his curiosity pulled him in.

"We can help each other," Revelin began. When he saw Tristen's impatient look, he continued, "I know some very valuable information about Crevan and his army. How much would it be worth to you?"

"Depends on the information," Tristen said, trying to keep his face impassive, though his heart was beating wildly.

"I also have some other tidbits you might be interested in. As I'm sure you know by now, you have a spy in the camp. I could help weed him out for you." He tapped his nose with his index finger. "I can sniff out a spy from a mile away."

"We don't need your help for that. We can handle that ourselves," Tristen said. "If you don't have any other proposals..."

"Wait, there is one more thing. In exchange for your father pardoning my men and me, I have one more interesting piece of news for you." His voice turned sly. "No one knows this except me."

"And that would be...?" Tristen was growing impatient at Revelin's riddles.

"May we go to your tent for more privacy? I don't want to just tell you in the middle of everyone. Someone might overhear and that would, in turn, cost me my life."

Despite knowing that it was a bad idea, Tristen led Revelin to his tent. Lunch had been laid out on the table. There were platters of grilled vegetables and a whole roasted quail.

"By all means, help yourself," he told Revelin, gesturing to the fare.

Revelin started wolfing down the food. The past few weeks of eating nothing but bread and dried meat had taken its toll on him.

Tristen served some food on his own plate, then began to eat civilly.

After a few minutes, Revelin began his story. "Only you and your family know of my history," he said. "I once was an earl, but I got in your father's bad graces and he stripped me of my title. You know of this, correct?"

When Tristen nodded, he continued, "Years of being a thief has helped me hear secrets that others normally wouldn't know. I admit to being a mercenary for hire, and the king of Scria paid me to waylay travelers on their way to the palace—you know, the men you sent to your father for advice. This worked fine until your general took us by surprise."

"And what does this have to do with your story?"

"Patience, patience. It helps to know all this before I get to the good stuff. When Kaie came to the palace the first time, I was surprised that King Torin wanted a young girl for something. I wasn't sure what, but I had suspicions that she was important for the war. When I came across her again, I knew that Scria would be very interested in her. I tried to capture her so I could take her to their king."

Tristen's fury rose up, and he lunged at Revelin, a knife gripped in his hand. "You were going to take her to him! You would betray your own country and take an innocent girl to that monster, just for a few coins?"

Revelin raised his hands. "Relax. If your brother hadn't been able to run for help, we would have succeeded."

"You're lucky for that. I would have found you and gutted you," Tristen growled.

"At any rate, I didn't get to capture Kaie and I never told the Scrian king about her. I do have some sort of a heart, despite what stories will say about me. Rumors have been floating around about Crevan and what he has picked up about Kaie. The king knows about her now and has instructed Crevan to do whatever it takes to get her on their side. I may have heard that if Crevan's ambush didn't work, he would send some men for her family."

Tristen's heart dropped at this information. "You mean... he'll kill them?"

"I'm not sure, but knowing Crevan, I'd say it's a good possibility."

"How do we stop this?" Tristen said to himself, attempting to figure out a solution.

"I know you have already sent men to her house. If they can't protect her family, no one can. The men Crevan will send will be ruthless," Revelin told him after taking a large gulp of watered-down ale. "It might be worth relocating them elsewhere."

Tristen suddenly became suspicious. "Why are you so interested in helping me?"

Revelin shrugged as he answered. "Let's just say that the Scrian king hasn't been paying me as well lately." He paused. "And Kaie saved my son from Sir Shalane when he brought her to the palace. Even if I'm a thief and mercenary, I do want to pay back that debt."

"She did?" Tristen was surprised. Kaie had not mentioned anything about that. "I didn't see a boy in your group when you were brought here."

"When we started ambushing your messengers, I sent him away," Revelin said. "It seemed too risky. I don't want him to grow up as a mercenary. He's a good kid."

Tristen knew he should not, but he took Revelin at his word. "Fine. I'll let you walk around, but one move out of line and I will personally end you. Your men will still be kept captive in the pen. You do anything to give me a reason not to trust you and it's finished. I don't want you antagonizing Kaie, either, and you can't tell her about the danger her family's in. I don't want her to hear about this at all."

Revelin nodded. "Very well. Shall we shake on it?"

The men shook hands before Tristen called for Lorne to show Revelin to his new tent. The older general was surprised, and looked at Revelin with suspicious eyes, but followed Tristen's orders.

***

Unbeknownst to Tristen, Crevan was already plotting his next plan. "Fallon, you found her family, right?" he asked, licking his lips with anticipation.

"Yes, sir. My sources tell me they live off the forest near Riverton," Fallon answered, feeling sorrow for Kaie's family, knowing what his commander had in mind.

"Do you hear that, men? Near Riverton," Crevan repeated to the group of ten men standing before him. All the men nodded as Crevan continued. "If you can't capture them and get past the guards that the prince has surely placed there, just kill them all and burn everything to the ground. If I can't have Kaie on my side, she can't have her family."

Fallon's eyes widened at his commander's ruthlessness. Though he knew Crevan was cruel, he had not expected him to kill Kaie's family—especially when he was still trying to get her to defect. *Although I suppose this shouldn't surprise me. He did something similar to me.*

"All right, go," Crevan commanded. "Make sure no one sees you." The men left, and Crevan took a step closer to Fallon. "This time, it better go as planned," he warned, taking out his dagger again to hold close to Fallon's left eye. "Or it will end badly for you."

Fallon gulped, nodding slowly. Even if he had nothing to do with the mission's success, it would not matter to Crevan.

Neither noticed Haelan perched behind Crevan's tent, and therefore, neither noticed him sneaking away to the forest.

CHAPTER 34

Around midday, Kaie awakened. Despite the noise around camp, she had been too exhausted and slept through the racket. The first thing she did was immediately change into a fresh set of clothes. Her clothing from the night before was still damp and covered in Haelan's blood—the rain had not lasted long enough to wash it away. Her nose wrinkled. She could not believe she had slept in the dirty clothing.

"I'll have to see if Farin can get the stains out," she muttered. "Otherwise these'll need to be burned."

Raven was waiting outside her tent. "It's about time you got up, sleepyhead," he joked.

"Keeping watch again?" she asked, giving him a wry smile before heading to Tristen's tent.

Two guards were stationed outside and blocked her entry. "He's in a meeting," one said.

Kaie turned back to Raven, an eyebrow raised in question.

"He's speaking to Revelin about something." Raven shrugged, not having answers himself. "Why exactly did you let Haelan go?" The question was blunt, but her actions had been bothering him all morning.

"He's been lying to Crevan and has agreed to help us," she answered. "I think he's also tired of being treated badly."

"Still doesn't seem like a good enough reason to me," Raven muttered.

"You were there the day I first met him," Kaie argued. "He was acting so stiff. It's obvious he's not treated well. Maybe we could be friends."

"Kaie, it's a noble thought, but we are in the middle of a war," Raven said, enunciating each word. "Did it ever occur to you that he was instructed to say that to play on your emotions?" When Kaie shook her head, he continued, "And in the forest, that could have been more of his ploy to get you on his side willingly."

"No, you're wrong," she said, tears entering her eyes at the thought of being tricked. "I could tell he was sincere. He meant every word he said."

"Kaie, think about it. He probably told Crevan everything that happened," Raven said.

"Just because you're older, doesn't mean you know everything." Kaie's face burned that she could not come up with a better response. So she turned and walked away, back towards the forest.

***

Haelan swiftly moved from tree to tree as he approached the Galician camp, attempting to not be seen. A couple hundred yards from the camp, he heard someone crying. He took a quick peek through the branches, astonished to see Kaie crying on the ground, her head in her hands. Despite knowing he would most likely regret it later, he emerged from behind a tree. Her head snapped up as she heard his approach, watching as he took a couple steps forward.

"Kaie, what's wrong?" he asked softly.

She watched him with wide eyes, wiping the tears from her face. "What are you doing here? What if you get caught?" she asked, remaining seated.

"We're far enough away from camp, it should be fine," he said, moving next to her. "So what's troubling you?"

"Nothing," she sniffed. "I'm fine."

"No, you're not. Tell me," he said. "What is it?"

The tone of his concern was so like Tristen's that she almost started crying again, desperate for Tristen's advice.

"Well, it's…" She hesitated, unsure of what to tell him as Raven's comments echoed in her mind.

Haelan crouched down so they were eye to eye. "Come on, you can trust me."

The comment angered Kaie, as her conversation with Raven reeled around in her mind. She pushed Haelan away from her, jumping up. Haelan fell back and remained on the ground, looking up at her as she paced back and forth.

"Can I really trust you?" she asked, her voice echoing her doubts.

Haelan remained silent, feeling that she had to get this out first. He picked up a nearby stick and began to pick at the bark as she continued.

"Why did you let me go? What have you told Crevan? I don't know your reasoning for any of this. You've told me *nothing* about why you're trying to help me," she said in a rush, her hands falling to her hips. "You say you want to help me, but how do I know that your words are true? How do I know that this isn't another trap that Crevan has set for me?"

"Why would he bother setting another trap for you when I could have captured you last night?" he asked. "You seem to know how he treats Invivers. Why would I want to continue working under him?"

"Why don't you just escape?" Kaie asked.

Haelan ripped his sleeve open, displaying a pulsating gash going up his forearm. It was filled with a deep, swirling red liquid, and Kaie flinched as she heard an ominous hum coming from it. Immediately, she felt sick to her stomach.

"Because of this," he hissed.

"What is that?" she whispered.

"After Avalon escaped, he had Fallon put this on the remaining Invivers," Haelan said. "It prevents any Inviver with this mark from getting too far away from the one Crevan has. It drives us mad with pain before killing us."

"How was he able to do that? I didn't think Fallon was an Inviver," Kaie said. The smaller man, while good with potions and experiments, from what Tristen told her, did not seem to have the same aura as an Inviver.

"He's brilliant," Haelan said. "Somehow, he was able to use our blood to harness our powers and twist it so we are stuck. Trust me, none of us would stay unless we had no other option."

Kaie's gaze shifted from the mark to Haelan's face, watching his eyes as he continued.

"Crevan's become obsessed with Invivers," Haelan said. "He thinks we hold the key to unlimited power, to immortality."

"So he really was lying when he said you had already unlocked that power," Kaie said. "But what does that have to do with me?"

He let out a heavy sigh. "He thinks since you brought Prince Tristen back from the dead, that key resides in you."

"What?" Kaie covered her mouth in horror. "That means he's never going to stop trying to get me."

"For now, we've bought you time," Haelan said. "Time to figure out the next move."

"Why did you pursue becoming an Inviver after you discovered your powers?" Kaie asked.

Haelan could see that was the real question bothering her. "I became one because I wanted to help my country. I thought it was my chance to help others. Instead, I've become Crevan's lackey. He makes Fallon and I do all his dirty work. The reason I joined in the first place has become clouded, but now I'm trying to make things right."

"But you said you want to help your country," she said.

"That was before I realized that what they are doing isn't right," he said. "The king is almost as cold-blooded as Crevan. He started the war because he thought Torin killed his own daughter! How ridiculous is that? But I found out the truth behind the princess's death." His voice became melancholy at the thought.

Kaie was interested by this news—she knew how important Catriona was to Tristen. "What is it?"

"It turns out that Crevan wants access to the Mists. If those are under Scrian control, he can take the time to uncover the secret to immortality. He snuck into Galicia to find the location to see if he could break in, but the mist surrounding the place kept him out. On his way back, he came across the princess and killed her," Haelan said. "Then he spread the rumors about the king killing his daughter to misplace blame and instigate the war. So he could take his time getting into the Mists."

"*What*? You mean that all this is Crevan's fault?" Kaie was horrified at the news.

"Yes, it is. Where are you going?" Haelan shouted after Kaie as she raced back to Tristen's tent.

"Tristen needs to know this!" Kaie shouted. "He deserves to know the truth!"

Haelan sighed and shook his head before slowly following her. He would have to wait for the right moment to tell Tristen about Crevan's plan for Kaie's family.

Kaie raced up to Tristen's tent and pushed past the guards despite their protests. She burst in, and Revelin stopped what he was saying mid-sentence.

"Tristen, I need to talk to you," she said, trying to catch her breath.

"Can it wait?" Tristen asked, trying to hide the purpose of the meeting—that he wanted to protect her family from Crevan's schemes.

"I don't think so. It has to do with Catriona's death," Kaie said.

At the mention of his sister's name, Tristen's eyes narrowed. "What have you found out?" he asked, all his attention on Kaie.

"I'm not sure Revelin should hear this. It's none of his business," she said, giving the mercenary a distrusting look.

Revelin stared back at her, not backing down. "Don't worry, I won't tell," he said smiling, knowing that Tristen would not send him away.

"But—"

"Kaie, Revelin has agreed to help us. He has dealt with Crevan in the past and is willing to help us defeat him," Tristen said, cutting her off. "Whatever you have to say regarding this, you can say it in front of him."

Kaie scowled at Revelin, not believing his transformation as Tristen did. "I was talking to Haelan a minute ago and—"

Revelin perked up at the name. "Haelan? Where is he? We need to talk to him."

"I was in the forest and he appeared," Kaie said, not happy at being interrupted. "Anyway, he said that he heard that Crevan was the one who killed Catriona."

Tristen paled at the news. "I knew he was devious, but I had no idea he killed her," he whispered in disbelief.

"If you want more details, I'll bet that Haelan hasn't left the forest yet," Revelin said. "He risked coming here for a reason, and I doubt it was just to talk to Kaie."

Tristen nodded. "Come on," he said to Revelin. "We need to go find him. If we hurry, we might be able to catch him. You stay here," he told Kaie. "I don't want you getting hurt if this gets messy."

The two exited the tent, leaving Kaie behind. She stormed out, watching them head off towards the dense forest. Tristen and Revelin walked side by side, a prince and a criminal—an unnatural pair. Revelin's body exuded rugged strength with his broad shoulders and forceful gait, while Tristen emitted refined power as he walked with his head high.

Achaius walked up to her and turned to see what she was looking at. His mouth dropped open upon seeing Tristen and Revelin walking together.

"What happened?" Achaius asked. "Where are they going?"

"They're off to find Haelan," Kaie said, crestfallen. "They don't want me to get in the way."

"What does Haelan want?" Achaius asked.

"I don't know," Kaie confessed. "He mentioned something about Catriona's death and I came to tell Tristen about it."

"What about her death?" Achaius asked, his expression turning intense.

"Crevan ended up being the one to kill her," Kaie said.

"Of all things! How bloodthirsty *is* that monster?" Achaius shouted, his fury evident. Cruel people were not a surprise to him—he had learned of them from his lessons about past wars. However, feeling the pain of Crevan's bloodlust firsthand hit home.

"Well, Tristen is going to talk to Haelan about it. He just went to the forest to find him."

"Wait, isn't that Crevan's Inviver?" Achaius asked, distress in his eyes.

Kaie looked at him, noticing how striking he looked in the sunlight. The sun glinted off his hair, his dark-green eyes gleaming brightly in his anxiousness.

"Yes, but he seemed to have other things on his mind when we talked," Kaie said, patting him on the shoulder.

"What else did he say to you?" Achaius was anxious to know the details.

"Crevan has trapped all the Scrian Invivers so they can't leave." Kaie's face fell as she repeated what Haelan had said. "And Haelan and the others are sick of his cruelty and how he treats them."

"Do you think he might be trying to trick you?" Achaius asked.

"He showed me the mark. It was ghastly." Kaie shivered. "So I don't think he's lying about that. But it still feels odd that he's willing to help us."

"What *exactly* happened last night?" Achaius asked, his tone bitter. "I know you worked out some sort of truce with him." Anger surged through him at knowing that Haelan was affecting Kaie's emotions.

"Crevan thinks I hold the secret to immortality. Haelan's our best shot at trying to foil Crevan's plans," Kaie pleaded, his anger hurting her. "Even if we're able to hold him off, I don't think Crevan will easily give up."

Achaius suddenly realized how aggressive his tone was and backed off. He could see that he was making her uncomfortable. "I'll protect you from Crevan," he said. "And I know Tristen and Lorne will too."

"I know," Kaie said. "But what if he goes after my family?"

"Tristen's taken care of that," Achaius said. "I know he sent men to guard your family. And your father is a great fighter too."

Kaie smiled. "That's true," she said.

"Let's not worry about him and go the Invivers' tent," he said gently, attempting to move the conversation away from her fears. "I'm sure they could use the help after last night."

***

Once Tristen and Revelin reached the edge of the forest, they started searching for any sign of the Inviver. Haelan spotted them first and whistled softly, hoping they would take the hint to come further into the forest so he would not have a chance of being spotted by Crevan. Revelin's sharp ears heard the whistle and he motioned for Tristen to follow him deeper into the forest. Once they got far enough in, Haelan walked forward from behind a broad tree.

Tristen looked at him, scanning the outlying forest as a precaution. "What are you doing here? Why do you keep bothering Kaie?" Tristen saw no point in beating around the bush.

Haelan looked at Tristen somberly. At first, he'd planned to ask who the unknown burly man on his left was, but decided that Tristen would only bring someone along if he was confident in his trust.

"I come with bad news. Crevan has sent men out for Kaie's family. If they can't capture her family, Crevan has instructed them to kill and burn the house down. I came to warn you so you can take the necessary measures to prevent their deaths from happening."

"Why are you telling me this?" Tristen was curious to know Haelan's reasoning.

"Crevan has trapped all the Invivers under his control and I'm sick of it. I don't want Kaie's life to be ruined like Fallon's was in Crevan's quest for immortality. I have seen the effects up close and I don't want her to turn into something like him," Haelan answered.

"Why are you helping her? Why didn't you capture her last night?" Tristen asked.

The question caught Haelan off guard. Though he had guessed Kaie would have told Tristen, he had not expected the crown prince's bluntness.

"I was serious when I told her I wanted to be friends," he said. "I just don't want her getting caught in the middle of all this. It's not her fight. It's not even my fight, but I'm mixed up in it. We shouldn't even be at war to begin with, but if anything, I just want her to be safe."

"Why?" Tristen pressed.

"I don't know. I... it's complicated. If she can help kill Crevan, then this mark might deactivate," Haelan said, showing them the gash. Both Tristen and Revelin grimaced at the sight of it. "Are you going to send protection to her family or not?"

"We already have," Tristen said, his eyes picking up on Haelan's hesitancy with answering his question. "If they can't protect her family, then Crevan has sent soldiers who are more skilled than any I've ever seen. We sent the best of the best to her house."

Haelan shook his head. "I'm not sure if it will be enough. Crevan got some mercenary friends of his to go. They owe him favors from his previous exploits. They're ruthless."

"I'll be sure to send word to my father. Maybe he'll relocate them," Tristen said. "Now, are you going to continue to help us?"

Haelan nodded. "Yes, I just have to be sure not to get caught."

"We'll find ways to make it work," Tristen said. "Now, is there any truth to what Kaie told me about Catriona's death?"

"Yes, Crevan was the one who killed her," Haelan said, not liking the pain he saw in Tristen's eyes. "I tried to tell my father about it, but he wouldn't listen."

Instantly, Haelan wished his words back in his mouth, but they could not be returned. It was not the right time to tell Tristen about his history, but he knew he would have to explain himself.

"What do you mean?" Tristen asked, looking at Revelin to see if he knew what Haelan was talking about. But Revelin looked equally shocked at the implications of Haelan's words.

"I'm the king's son," Haelan said softly, hoping the quick sentence would not be threatening.

He took a step backward as both men lunged at him. In a fluid motion, Tristen knocked him over, pinning him to the ground. Leaves and twigs poked into Haelan's back in spite of his coat, but he did not writhe or attempt to sit up for fear of angering Tristen further.

"What are you saying?" Tristen growled, feeling like he had been deceived. He would have warned Kaie away from Haelan if he knew that he was the Scrian prince.

"Relax," Haelan croaked out. "I'm not the true heir, just his illegitimate son. The only way I would be accepted into court was as an Inviver. Once my powers made themselves known, my father made sure that I had the best tutors. My brother would have married your sister, not me."

Tristen eased back, his eyes locked on Haelan's face. "What else haven't you told me?" Tristen demanded.

"Nothing." Haelan winced as Tristen pushed down on his chest. "You know everything else about my family. I have an older sister and brother. I was raised in the shadow of my brother, kept away from the rest of my family until I joined the war. Then my father welcomed me back for a month before I had to leave. It was only then that I got to know my sister."

Tristen eased off Haelan's chest. "I guess that will have to do," he said. "What are you hoping to get in return for helping us?"

Haelan sat up, rubbing his sore chest. The Galicians certainly liked using force. "I want to work with Kaie to figure out a way to fix the mark. She's powerful enough that she could get rid of it," he said. "Will you allow her to help me?"

A strong hope stirred in Haelan's heart as he saw Tristen's hardened face return to its former composure. Haelan desperately wished to remove the brand that tied him to Crevan, that allowed the commander to yank him around as he pleased. The day he had been given the mark, he had exhausted himself trying to Cure it off. But Fallon's work was effective. None of the Scrian Invivers had been able to remove it.

"Very well." Tristen nodded, holding his hand out, which Haelan shook gratefully.

"I'll tell you everything I know."

Haelan spent the rest of the afternoon spilling his guts about Crevan's plans, putting his own life on the edge of a precipice where falling would mean certain death.

CHAPTER 35

When Tristen returned from his discussion with Haelan, there was a small group of people waiting for him: Kaie, Achaius, Raven, and Lorne. With a sigh, he ran a hand through his hair before inviting them into his tent.

"What are your questions?" he asked, pouring himself a large glass of wine from a nearby decanter.

"How did your talk go?" Kaie asked, fiddling with her hands.

"We'll be working together with Haelan to circumvent Crevan's plans," he said.

"Are you sure that's wise?" Lorne asked, raising his eyebrows. Though Tristen's decision-making thus far had been sound, he was starting to question these recent decisions. "First you choose to trust Revelin, and now the enemy's Inviver?"

"I know how it looks," Tristen said, taking a gulp of wine. "But in case you haven't noticed, we haven't been making any progress in defeating Crevan's forces. Both Revelin and Haelan have made reasonable offers to turn to our side and provide valuable information. Not to mention, the cost of being caught is death."

"What price is Haelan asking for?" Achaius asked. He noticed how exhausted Tristen looked and knew that having the responsibility of countless lives was weighing heavily on his brother.

"He wants Kaie to help him break the tether that's keeping him and the other Invivers tied to Crevan," Tristen said.

Achaius let out a growl of frustration, causing Tristen to raise an eyebrow.

"What we gain from him helping us is immense. We will try to help him as best we can."

"Don't tell me you're planning to let him get close to her!" Achaius snarled. "He's too dangerous!"

"I agree," Raven spoke up. "He injured me last night. This could be a ploy."

"He told us about the true cause of Catriona's death," Tristen said quietly, a pained expression on his face. "He didn't have to, yet he did. We are to trust him for now."

"What about Revelin?" Lorne asked. "What does he have to gain?"

Tristen sighed, taking another gulp of wine. "There's a spy in our midst," he said, and the tent was filled with gasps. "He has offered to help us find them in exchange for getting his title back—he wants a better life for his son. If he does well enough, I'm going to put him in charge of a small group of soldiers for more secretive operations."

"Couldn't he be lying about the spy?" Kaie asked. Despite how easily she'd forgiven Haelan, she could not forget how Revelin had hurt both Maeve and Achaius.

"It's too coincidental that Crevan was able to ambush us at the hill," Tristen said. "For now, I'm planning to cautiously trust him. We're still going to have Revelin guarded by a few men, but he'll have free range of the camp. He knows that if he steps a foot out of place, he and his men will be killed." Finishing the goblet of wine, he let out another sigh. "If you'll excuse me, I'm planning to retire for the night."

Kaie stayed behind as the others left. "Thank you, Tristen," she said.

"For what?" he asked.

"For deciding to trust Haelan. I've been questioning myself, but it helps to know that you are planning to trust him too." She gave him a hug. "I can always count on you to set my fears to rest."

Tristen watched her leave, shaking his head. "This is going to get a lot more complicated before it gets better," he muttered to himself, sitting down to pen a letter to his father, informing him of Crevan's planned attack on Kaie's family. Maybe they could move her family before the mercenaries arrived.

***

Shortly after midnight, Raven snuck out of his tent again, heading off to speak with his contact.

"Are you sure they think there's a spy in their midst?" the man asked.

"Yes. How many times do I have to tell you?" Raven said impatiently. "Tristen is convinced. Make sure to tell them that. Now, I have to go back before they catch me out of bed and accuse *me* of being the spy."

"Very well," the man said. "I expect you to summon me if anything else happens."

He slipped off into the night like a ghost, leaving Raven questioning if he was doing the right thing.

***

As the weeks passed, Kaie lost track of time, as her skills were needed with a flurry of battles. Crevan kept trying to push his advantage, continually attempting to ambush the Galician camp without giving either side time to rest. But each time, the Galicians were able to fight back, and Kaie's Curing skills made it so the other Invivers had more time to recuperate and use their Calming instead. The Scrians' advantage was starting to slip as the Galician casualties lessened significantly.

Achaius continued to learn Curing mechanics under Kaie's guidance, becoming a great help Curing the wounded. The elder Inviver, Evidian, also helped teach him about Calming, as Kaie's skills were still lacking.

Most days, Kaie stayed up late into the night Curing soldiers while the other Invivers rested up to help with Calming for the next battle. Farin did her best to stay awake to care for her, but usually by the time Kaie came to bed, the other girl was fast asleep.

"Kaie, it's time to go to sleep," Achaius said, trying to rub the tiredness from his eyes. It felt as though there was sand in them and his head ached.

"I can't. I still have ten more soldiers to go," she protested, Curing the man in front of her.

Seeing that she would not leave until all the wounded had been tended to, no matter how small their injury was, Achaius walked towards some who had not been Cured yet, trying to fight off his weariness. Though he was glad he now had the opportunity to Cure, he had never really considered how exhausting the job was.

As he placed his hands on the man's chest in front of him, he heard Kaie say, "What are you doing?"

He turned to look at her. "I'm going to help you so you can get some more sleep."

She paused, considering his kindness. "Thank you, but I can handle it."

Achaius shook his head. "I'm doing this. You cannot do this all by yourself. You've done so much already today. Me helping out with a few more men won't hurt you."

"I'd let him do it, Kaie," the soldier she was working on interjected. His face screwed up in pain as she placed her hands on his broken leg. Earlier that day, he had been trampled by an enemy soldier on horseback.

Though she could see the reasoning, she refused the help. "Achaius, go to sleep. I can handle this on my own. You've done enough for today."

Despite her protests, he Cured the soldier in front of him.

The man gave a sigh of relief as the pain from his bruised ribs was alleviated. "Thank you, Your Highness," he said before getting off the table and leaving the tent. "You'd best let him help," he said to Kaie before exiting.

She let out a huff of frustration, but no longer protested Achaius helping. They soon finished Curing and headed back to their tents.

"Why won't you accept help?" Achaius asked as they walked back.

"I just don't want you exhausting yourself," she said stubbornly.

"It's how I expand my limits," Achaius said. "Are you the only one allowed to exhaust yourself?" He took her hand and gently squeezed it. "I don't want you overdoing it either."

Kaie flushed, but did not remove her hand from his. "Achaius, I..." She trailed off, trying to find the words. She stopped, and he turned to face her. "I'm glad you can Cure now, but it's dangerous here." She lifted her free hand and stroked his cheek. "I don't want you to get hurt."

He placed his hand over hers. "I don't want you getting hurt either," he said in a soft voice, his gaze tender. "You mean the world to me."

Kaie swallowed, trying to speak past the clog that was suddenly in her throat, her chest feeling like it would explode. "I feel the same way about you," she croaked.

Achaius put a hand on her waist, pulling her closer. Kaie stared up at him and let go of his hand so she could fully cup his face. He placed his now-free hand on her chin, tilting her face towards him. Slowly, they approached each other until their lips lightly touched.

Kaie focused on the feeling of his lips against hers, her mind going blank. As the kiss deepened, she felt Achaius's hand moving to tangle in her hair, the hand on her waist pulling her tightly to him. A roaring sound filled her ears as she moved her hands, running her fingers through his impossibly soft hair.

Time slowed as she savored the moment, her attention wholly on Achaius. Eventually, the two broke away to stare at each other. Kaie's eyes were bright and her cheeks were flushed as she looked into Achaius's gleaming eyes.

"I've wanted to do that for so long," he gasped before leaning forward to kiss her again.

Kaie eagerly kissed him back before gently pushing him away. He looked at her in confusion.

"I've wanted to do that for a while too," she said, and a smile crossed both their lips at her words.

When Achaius pressed his lips to hers again, Kaie felt like the world was spinning. She was so happy, and if Achaius had not been holding her steady, she knew she would have fallen to the ground. She loved the feeling of his strong arms surrounding her, not having realized before how muscular he was. Her body was on fire, and everywhere he touched felt like flames dancing.

"We... we need to go to bed," she said, trying to organize her thoughts when they broke away once more.

"And yet I feel like I could stay awake for several more hours," Achaius said, giving her a mischievous smile.

Kaie gave a small chuckle and nodded in agreement. "Be that as it may," she said. "We will have another long day tomorrow."

"And it still won't be enough time with you," Achaius said, giving her a shorter kiss this time. He rested his forehead against hers. "I'm so happy right now. I thought I could only dream about this," he breathed, his voice tight with emotion. He clenched his jaw, trying to rein his feelings back. He did not want to overwhelm her.

"Why?" Kaie asked. She reached up and stroked his jaw, causing him to relax into her touch.

He did not speak for several moments. "You're so smart and talented... and beautiful," he whispered. "How could I hope that you would ever return feelings for a hothead like me?"

Kaie chuckled. "You are explosive at times," she said, "but your passion and kindness towards me are what made me fall for you. You've changed so much from the arrogant prince I first met."

Achaius surged forward and kissed her intensely, as if he could communicate how much he cared about her in one kiss. Kaie gasped at his intensity and kissed him back, wanting to tell him how much she cared about him.

Suddenly, from behind, there was the sound of someone clearing their throat, and the two broke away to see a guard staring at them, his arms crossed.

"Your Highness, I don't think Prince Tristen would like you and Kaie to be out this late," he said, raising an eyebrow.

Kaie flushed and buried her head into Achaius's shoulder while he chuckled. She was mortified that they had been caught.

"Yes," Achaius said. "We'll be going. Good night." He took Kaie's hand and led the way to her tent. There, he kissed her hand before entering his own.

Kaie laid on her cot, a huge smile across her face. Though she had not expected this to happen, she was glad they finally had taken this step.

CHAPTER 36

When there was time, Kaie met with Haelan in the forest about once a week, and the two worked on his mark. After a couple meetings, he finally convinced her that he was a friend and she trusted him.

The day before an important battle, they met up again. Kaie escaped into the forest early, sitting on a tree branch to watch for Haelan in their usual spot. Around midday, just as she was about to give up on him appearing, he ran into view—the ominous hum following him as always. As he approached the tree that she was sitting in, he slowed down and began to look around cautiously, searching for any enemies that might be nearby.

"Kaie?" he whispered, his eyes on the lookout for any clues as to where she was located.

In one smooth motion, she leapt to the ground, her knees bending on impact. Haelan did not jump as she appeared, but his eyes clearly showed his shock at her choice of entrance.

She stood, her voice betraying her amusement. "Surprised to see me?"

He shook his head. "Just a little. You haven't tried scaring me by jumping from a tree before. I suppose it was just a matter of time before you tried that."

"I don't *try* to scare you," she said. "It's not my fault that you aren't expecting me. I have to hide to make sure that no one sees me here with you."

"I thought Tristen made sure that none of his soldiers are wandering in here during our meetings, just in case the spy sees us," Haelan remarked.

"He does, but just because *our* soldiers don't see us doesn't mean any of yours won't. Imagine what would happen if Crevan found out."

He considered that for a moment. "Fair enough."

The two settled on the ground, hidden by the foliage. Haelan pulled up his sleeve, holding it out to her.

"It's been two months that we've been at this, I'm sorry we haven't made much progress," Kaie remarked, once more examining the gash. The thick red liquid constantly looked wet and she always felt squeamish being so close to it. Its low hum was so discordant with the deep sound of the earth that she had trouble focusing.

"Well, I'm sure part of it is Invivers can't Cure each other," Haelan said. "But I was hoping since this isn't just tied to me, we could crack through it."

"It's still tied to your powers, isn't it?" Kaie asked. "You said that the further away you are from Crevan, the more you feel your energy being sapped."

"Yeah, but it's just drawing on my powers," Haelan said.

Kaie closed her eyes and once more focused on finding the deep hum of the earth. Lately, practicing with Haelan, she was able to find the sound more quickly. She allowed the deep sound to wash over her and vibrate within her body, filling up every inch of herself with the pounding beat.

Then she reached out towards Haelan's energy. Reaching out to another Inviver was different than a normal person. She could sense his vibrations, but was unable to adjust them like she usually could. But the gash on his arm was a different story, she could easily sense its sound, how wrong it sounded. Like their previous sessions, she tried molding the hum—pulling and pushing on different areas. Haelan's quick intake of breath let her know it was somewhat working. Usually this caused him some sort of pain.

Kaie placed a hand on the ground, feeling the hum of the earth coming up to meet her hand and moving through it, while also holding on to Haelan's arm near the gash. She guided the hum through her body to release through her hand. There was a bright flash of light from behind her closed eyes, and the discordant humming stopped.

Upon opening her eyes, Kaie was disappointed to see that the gash still remained, the red liquid looking as oozy as ever. As she watched, remnants of the light dissipated through the gash, worming their way into Haelan's arm. After they disappeared, the horrible hum came back.

"It didn't work," she said in disappointment.

"No, but I think that's the closest you've gotten," Haelan said, flexing his arm. "You haven't been able to produce light like that before. And I could tell that for a moment, the tether disappeared."

Kaie flopped back on the ground. "I don't know what else to try," she admitted. "If the sound of the earth won't directly fix it, I don't know what will."

"We can try again another time," he said with a sigh, laying down on the ground next to her.

"Tell me more about your family," she said, wanting to continue where their last conversation had left off. After the Curing attempts, they had been learning about the other.

Haelan took a deep breath. He had been expecting this. "Well, I have a brother and a sister. A couple of months before I had to leave, my father called me to him and I was able to get to know them better. Since I am his illegitimate son, I was able to have a pretty privileged life in the palace, even if I didn't get all the perks that the other two got," he said, shrugging. "I was able to learn a lot about Curing, so it all worked out in the end. My sister and I got pretty close right before I left, but my brother doesn't like me at all. He can't stand the sight of me."

"That's terrible," Kaie said sympathetically.

"It's not that bad," Haelan said. "He's always a jerk to everyone anyway. I'm a threat to him apparently. So I just avoided him. Now, what about your family?" he asked. All he knew was that she had a little sister.

"I haven't seen my father in such a long time, almost six years. Around three years ago, he was sent to lead one of the eastern bases," Kaie said. "I haven't seen my sister or mother in about a year, either, but my sister and I were really close. I made a promise to her before I left." Kaie stopped for a moment, trying to rein in her emotions, fiddling with her necklace. "I promised that I would be back soon and that I'd always be there to protect her. I haven't been able to keep those promises since I've been sucked into this war."

Haelan could see the conversation had upset her and tried to divert her thoughts. "So, how did you find out you were an Inviver? I found out when I was fighting one of the really arrogant warriors in my father's army and he cut me up pretty bad. We had been throwing insults at each other and it went downhill until it looked like my arm would have to amputated. Instead, when I tried to focus on the pain, it started to fix itself up. Surprised everyone, including myself."

"That's crazy. Who was the fighter?" Kaie asked.

"Crevan. Back then, he was a little milder than he is now, but not by much. I still don't like him," Haelan said.

Kaie's mouth fell open in shock and horror. "How did your father still allow him to be in charge of an army?" she asked.

"I honestly don't know," Haelan admitted. "So what about you?"

"I was called to the palace to heal Achaius," Kaie said. "Except it was all a plot to see if I could Cure. The king poisoned him to put him in a bad enough state that I felt desperate enough to unleash my powers."

"He poisoned his own son?" Haelan was appalled.

"Yeah, I was shocked when I found out myself," Kaie said.

"How did they even guess that you were an Inviver?"

"When healing back home, sometimes people got better more quickly than I expected. While my mentor was traveling, I guess she talked about me. Reports eventually made their way back to the palace and they recognized the traits of an Inviver."

Haelan looked around at the late-afternoon sun beginning its descent in the sky. "I should probably head back before Crevan starts to notice," he said, standing to return.

Kaie followed, and they both said goodbye before heading back to their respective camps.

***

The next day's battle was grueling for everyone involved. Tristen had stayed up most of the previous night, ironing out the battle plans with his generals, including Revelin, who had proven himself over the past couple months of being wise counsel. Kaie slept well, prepared for the next day of Curing. For the entire battle, she and the other Invivers scurried about, trying to Cure everyone. At the end of the day, after both sides retreated in another stalemate, she collapsed on the ground in the Curing tent, exhausted.

Achaius walked over to her and helped her back up. "Come on, I'll walk you to your tent," he said, his face betraying his own exhaustion. At her tent, the two exchanged a kiss before Kaie headed inside, collapsing on her cot, and falling fast asleep.

During the night, she had a nightmare of fire. She could smell charred wood and burning flesh as the fire burned everything, with no sign of it weakening. Over the roar of the fire, she heard screams. Though she did not know who or what was making the howls of agony, she broke into a cold sweat, trying to find them to help. Every way she turned was blocked by the fire, an impenetrable wall of flickering red and yellow. She awoke with a scream as the fire crept in closer to overtake her.

Kaie's hair was in a knotted mess around her head, her blankets tangled around her legs. Like in her nightmare, she had broken out into a cold sweat and she panted with fear from the dream.

Farin looked at her in concern. "Bad dream?" she asked sympathetically, while going over to the water pail and dowsing a rag in water. She walked back to Kaie's bed and placed the cool rag on the Inviver's head. "Do you want to talk about it?"

Kaie shook her head, still too overwhelmed with panic. Out of all her dreams, this was by far the worst. She stood, dressing quickly. "I need to go," she said. Before Farin could say anything, she escaped into the cool night.

Panic still rising within her, Kaie began to walk towards the forest. Once she'd broken past the edge of the trees, she began to run. The exercise felt freeing, her legs pumping in a repetitious movement, stretching and contracting with each stride. Even though she did not know where she was going, the running helped distract her from her buzzing thoughts. Kaie ran until her body could no longer continue and she collapsed onto the forest floor, a pounding ache resonating through her feet even though they had ceased hitting the ground.

Exhausted mentally and physically, she fell asleep.

***

After Kaie ran off, Farin wasted no time in going to Tristen's tent. She had to plead with the guards to wake the prince.

"Kaie's run off!" she exclaimed once Tristen came to see her, hair disheveled and shirt unbuttoned.

"What do you mean?" Tristen asked, immediately snapping awake at her words.

"She had some sort of nightmare and ran off," Farin babbled, tears streaming down her face. She was so worried about what danger Kaie could be in. "I asked if she wanted to talk about it, and she just... She's gone, Your Highness!"

"She needs to stop running off," Tristen muttered, putting a hand to his head. "Go have Revelin woken up. He'll be able to track her."

Farin raced off.

Kaie's screams had woken up those in the nearby tents, and Achaius and Lorne came to Tristen's tent in concern.

"We heard screaming," Lorne said. "And Kaie and Farin aren't in their tent."

"Kaie had some sort of nightmare and ran off," Tristen said. "Farin just told me. She's gone to fetch Revelin to track her."

"Where'd she go?" Achaius asked in panic.

"We don't know," Tristen said. "We need Revelin to find her."

"But can you really trust him?" Despite all that Revelin had done in the past two months helping the Galicians, Achaius was still hesitant to trust the man.

"Quiet. Here he comes," Tristen said, pulling on his boots.

Raven came marching up, pushing Revelin in front of him. Farin followed behind the two, her face pale and frightened.

"Farin got me to wake Revelin," Raven said. "What's going on?"

"This better be important," Revelin grumbled. "You woke me up from my sleep."

"It is important," Tristen snapped. "Kaie's run off. We need you to find her."

Revelin's eyes widened in shock. "Let's not waste time then."

"Farin, you stay behind. We'll bring Kaie back," Tristen said. "You can stay in my tent for now if you would like. We'll bring her back here."

"I'll stay behind as well," Lorne said. "In case she returns."

Tristen nodded, turning back to the three remaining men.

Revelin led the group over to Kaie and Farin's tent, following Kaie's tracks around the camp, pausing when he saw them leading to the forest. "This isn't going to be good," Revelin muttered when he saw her hurried footsteps.

"Why? What is it?" Tristen demanded.

"Looks like she started to run. See where the tracks start to get smudged?" Revelin pointed out the footprints.

"Just hurry and find her," Achaius pleaded.

Revelin shot him a look that silenced him immediately. "What do you think she was running from?" Revelin asked Tristen. "It doesn't look like anyone was chasing her."

"She had a nightmare," the prince said.

"Must have been a terrible one," Revelin commented.

He continued to lead them through the forest, the group tripping over underbrush and ducking under branches.

"How did she not fall?" Raven asked as Achaius released a branch too quickly and it smacked him in the chest.

"What are you talking about? She comes here all the time," Achaius said. "She must remember enough to know how to navigate in the dark."

"Hush." Revelin silenced both of them. "Her tracks are slowing down."

Up ahead, under a tree, Kaie was collapsed on the ground. Everyone let out a sigh of relief that she seemed to be uninjured.

"Kaie!" Achaius cried out, running towards her.

At the sound of his shout, Kaie began to stir. "What happened?" she asked as she sat up.

"Farin said you had a nightmare and ran off," Achaius said, kneeling beside her. "You had us worried!"

"Why didn't you stay in camp or tell her where you were going?" Tristen asked, his brow furrowing in concern as he stepped closer.

Kaie shook her head, trying to dislodge the sleep clouding her mind. Her eyes opened wide when she remembered the terrible dream, the fear and panic enveloping her.

"I couldn't stay," she said, her voice suddenly hoarse as she began to tremble. "Something was burning. Everything was consumed with fire. I heard screams, but couldn't do anything to find the people who made the sounds. I was surrounded by the fire."

Achaius pulled her close, surrounding her in his embrace. "It's okay, we're here now. Nothing like that could ever happen. Everything's fine," he said, trying to calm her down.

Tristen and Revelin exchanged a look, not as convinced as Achaius.

"Kaie, let's head back to camp," Tristen said. "It's best if we don't stay in this unprotected area much longer."

By now, the memory of the dream overwhelmed Kaie so much that she began to cry, leaning into Achaius's shoulder for comfort. He tightened his grip on her, his expression full of worry.

"Kaie, it's okay," he said, rubbing her back. He looked to the others for help.

She was unable to speak as the crying overtook her, and the other men watched helplessly as she sobbed. Tristen rubbed the back of his neck, unsure of what to do to help her.

After Kaie was able to calm down enough to speak, she said, "Tristen, I previously had a dream that you died and it paralleled exactly what happened when I came to Cure you. The same thing happened with Achaius. What if this is a similar dream? What if this is actually going to happen?" Tears continued to pour down her face.

Gently, Achaius wiped the tears away, cradling her face in his hands so she was staring into his eyes. "Don't worry, we'll protect you," he said tenderly. "I will do whatever I can to prevent this dream from coming true."

Kaie gave a small smile at his words, leaning forward to kiss him. It was an instinctive motion without hesitation, and Achaius's face flushed that the others had witnessed the intimate moment.

"Thank you," she whispered softly, pulling away.

Achaius dropped his hands from her face in slight embarrassment and stared at her. "Always," he said, shaking himself from his daze. He still felt as though Kaie's lips were pressed against his. He had not expected her to do such an action in front of his brother.

Kaie stood and walked over to Tristen, her cheeks flushing when she realized there had been an audience. When Achaius said those words, she had forgotten everything except him. He had said the words she'd most needed to hear.

"Are you ready to go?" Tristen asked, a small smile on his face. It seemed as though the two had certainly taken a step forward in their relationship.

She nodded gratefully, and the group headed back to camp. On the walk back, Achaius took Kaie's hand, squeezing it to communicate his support. She looked at him and smiled, squeezing back. The rest of the way, they walked hand in hand.

It was early morning when they returned, the tendrils of dawn reaching into the sky. Tristen walked back to his tent alone and sent word of Kaie's dream to his father, warning him to have Kaie's family relocated. The monarch had not previously seen a need to send them away despite numerous letters over the past couple months. This time, the prince prayed that his letter would be enough to convince his father, that Kaie's dream would be enough to justify moving her family.

CHAPTER 37

Several days later, Tristen and Revelin went to the stocks where they had been keeping Revelin's men for the past couple months. Now that Revelin had proved his trustworthiness, the prince was willing to let his men join their side to keep them as part of Revelin's secret battalion. Each man pledged his loyalty to the prince upon the promise that they would be rewarded handsomely should the war end in the Galician's favor.

The two men were in high spirits as they headed to Tristen's tent for lunch. Upon entering, both were surprised to see Lorne waiting. Seeing the look on the captain's face, Tristen stopped short.

"What happened?"

Lorne was sitting at the table, looking at the map before him. His hands were at his temples, a grave expression etched onto his face. As he looked up, his eyes were filled with sorrow. "It's not good, Tristen," he said.

Tristen's heart plummeted. "What is it? Do we need to change our strategy?"

Lorne shook his head. "It seems that Kaie's house was ambushed in the night. Only one soldier survived, and as soon as he sent word to the palace, your father sent a raven with the news." He stood to face Tristen and Revelin, holding out the letter with a shaking hand. "Crevan's men took them by surprise—they were getting ready to go into hiding based on your latest letter. Kaie's father tried to protect her mother and sister, but..." He faltered and closed his eyes before continuing. "They burned everything when they realized they couldn't take her family alive. It's all gone. The surviving guard saw Shayla run into the forest before he passed out, but they've probably found and killed her by now. Kaie will be crushed when she finds out."

Lorne's voice broke over the pain this would cause Kaie, who had become like a daughter to him. The news of his friend's death did not help matters. He could easily imagine how she would feel—he'd felt the same devastation when his own family was murdered.

"Who else knows of this?" Tristen asked. He took the letter and glanced through the contents.

"No one," Lorne said. "I read the letter and immediately came here. What do we tell her, Tristen? How do we break it to her gently?"

"We don't," Tristen said simply, his face stony. At Lorne's news, he'd tamped down all emotion. He had to act like a leader and not let his personal feelings get in the way of his decision. He held the letter over a candle and watched it burn. "We can't risk her falling apart. The only way the war has been turning in our favor is due to her Curing abilities. For the army's benefit, this will remain between us. We'll tell her later, when the time is right."

"You mean at the end of the war," Revelin said, understanding what Tristen was saying.

"You can't," Lorne protested. "You know she'll hate you for this."

"It doesn't matter. She can't know," Tristen repeated before leaving the tent, rushing before they could see the tears threatening to spill from his eyes. He needed to remain stoic until he was by himself. Then he could fall apart.

"I'm so sorry, Kaie," he whispered, looking to where Kaie and Achaius were sitting, laughing with Farin and Raven over lunch. "I did all I could. I just wish I could have done more."

He turned and began walking through camp, reining in his emotions before anyone could see.

***

Haelan watched through Crevan's spyglass across the field. The commander was nowhere to be found, but Haelan stayed alert, not wanting to be caught unaware. Not to mention, he had stolen Crevan's telescope a few days ago when the commander had been particularly annoying. Since then, Crevan had been on the warpath to find it.

He saw Tristen's face and knew that he had heard the news that had spread like wildfire across the Scrian camp. The news of Crevan's ruthlessness did not surprise his troops, but it was beyond his usual cruelty that he'd had the young Inviver's family burned.

Haelan shook his head. "It's only a matter of time before he starts going after Tristen and Achaius to get to her," he muttered, low enough that Fallon, who was standing a few feet away, could not hear him.

Fallon was leaning over one of Crevan's ornate mahogany tables. Suspended in one hand was a flask filled with dark-blue liquid, and in the other was a small vial of a blood-red mixture. Beads of sweat popped out on his forehead as he slowly added the contents of the vial to the flask, turning everything to a sickly green. Haelan's stomach churned, imagining what horrors Fallon was concocting now.

Haelan stood, walking past Fallon. "I'm going for a walk," he called over his shoulder, setting Crevan's spyglass on the table.

Fallon's eyes rested on the item, a small smile quirking on his lips. "Fine. Just be sure Crevan doesn't catch you consorting with the enemy," he remarked casually, writing down the results of his experiment on the parchment in front of him.

Haelan froze in his tracks. "What do you mean?" he asked, turning to face Fallon. The thought to deny Fallon's words completely escaped him.

Fallon finished writing before looking at Haelan through his spectacles. "Haelan, it is my job to be observant. Do you think I hadn't noticed that when you came back from your 'battle' with Kaie that she wasn't injured at all, yet you were completely beat up? You're an Inviver—you should have Cured yourself during that fight. Plus, these past couple months, you've been sneaking off to the forest around the same time Kaie disappears from her camp. It's obvious you've made some sort of truce with them."

"But..." Haelan could not think of a cutting response. His mind flashed to killing Fallon—that would certainly ensure the man couldn't tell Crevan about his duplicity. But then how would he make Fallon's death look like a reasonable accident? Haelan's thoughts swirled as he tried to figure out the best course of action.

Fallon chuckled. "Relax. Crevan won't find out from me. You'd just better hope our spy doesn't let it slip to Crevan. He has been meeting with the spy lately rather than me."

"You're not going to report me?" Haelan was shocked at Fallon's willingness to keep this a secret. Usually, the man was so scared of Crevan that he would let the secret slip at the soonest possible moment.

Fallon shook his head. "I won't tell," he said. "I hate Crevan just as much as you do. Now go. You'd better meet with Prince Tristen to plan your next move."

Haelan nodded, running off towards the forest. After a few minutes, he was able to locate the Galician prince, announcing his presence to not be mistaken for an enemy. "Your Highness, it's Haelan. I see you've heard the news."

Tristen turned towards Haelan's voice, seeing the Inviver emerge from the forest. "What am I to do?" he asked. "Revelin and Lorne know not to tell her, but when she finds out I've kept this from her, she'll be devastated. But if I tell her now, she'll lose her focus and we'll lose the war."

From his words, Haelan could surmise Tristen had decided not to tell Kaie. "I would do the same thing," he said. "Even if she was able to function after finding out, the risk of her shutting down is too great."

"It still feels awful. I don't know how to keep this a secret from her," Tristen said, sitting on a fallen stump.

"It's known all around our camp what happened, but I doubt it would get back to her from our side," Haelan said. "For what it's worth... I'm sorry."

Tristen shook his head. "It's your damn commander that needs to be killed," he said grimly. "And I have no clue how we're going to go about that."

***

Since the nightmare, each night Kaie's thoughts were consumed with the dream as soon as it grew dark. She stared into the flames despondently, while Achaius watched her with growing concern. No matter what he tried, she slipped back into herself, barely responding to him. He put his arm around her and saw a flicker of her old self when she looked into his eyes and smiled. Physical touch sometimes drew her out of her head.

"Wonder what Tristen and them are talking about," Achaius said in an attempt to break the silence. Since late afternoon, Tristen, Revelin, and Lorne had been holed up in Tristen's tent, talking about plans for the next battle.

"Doesn't matter. They'll tell us when we need to know," Kaie said. "I have a feeling there will be another big battle coming up this next week. I should probably go and get some rest." She gave Achaius a quick kiss before standing and heading off towards her tent.

Achaius sighed. Today everyone acted surprisingly downtrodden. Lorne refused to talk to anyone after lunch, his eyes suspiciously red. And before Tristen had disappeared into his tent for the planning session, Achaius had found him behind a tent wiping his eyes. When asked about it, Tristen brushed him off, saying it was none of his business. Not to mention, Revelin was quieter than usual, a somber air about him. But so far, everyone was keeping their own secrets.

"I will find out what's going on," he muttered before heading off to bed.

CHAPTER 38

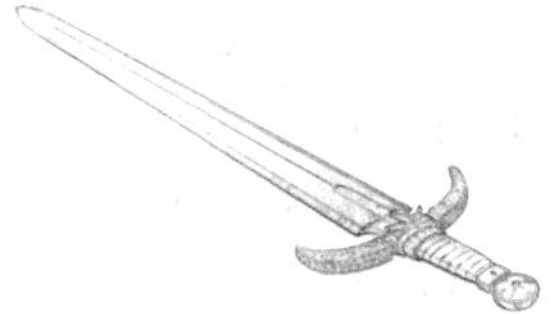

During the next battle, Kaie and Achaius raced around the field, Curing the soldiers while having to fight off their fair share of opponents. Achaius was able to handle himself well, only suffering a few minor cuts and scratches. For the most part, Kaie got away unscathed. At one point, when she leaned down to Cure a fallen soldier, the man's face turned pale.

"Behind you," he whispered.

Kaie turned in time to see Crevan moving towards her. She leapt up and unsheathed her sword, blocking his attack. It seemed this time, he had come to capture her personally, as everyone else he'd sent to do the job had failed. Though his arms rippled with muscle, Kaie managed to dodge his attacks, even giving him a couple cuts, though none were too deep due to his armor.

They continued to circle each other, neither seeming willing to give up. Kaie started to tire as she continued to block Crevan's blows. Tristen was busy organizing his troops, so it took a while before him noticed the fight. When he realized Kaie was beginning to tire, he looked around for Raven, who was nowhere to be found.

Just as Crevan was about to deal a serious blow to Kaie, Achaius parried the attack with his sword. Kaie fell back in surprise, but quickly recovered, coming to his aid to help defeat Crevan. The two of them moved as one in their attacks, overpowering the commander. Crevan began to look around for aid, whistling a clear, shrill tone. A moment later, a few Scrian soldiers joined the fight while Crevan slipped back amongst the ranks.

As Kaie and Achaius fought off the new group of soldiers, Kaie was once more struck by how dull the men's eyes were.

"They're being Calmed!" she said to Achaius. "Someone else is controlling them!"

The two continued working together to defeat the soldiers. It seemed there was more than one person controlling them, as their movements were disjointed and they did not work together as a unit. Kaie and Achaius pushed that advantage with coordinated attacks until there was a bugle call over the battlefield, calling for the Scrians to retreat. The two did not follow the soldiers as they ran back to their own lines. The soldiers had enough wounds that the Scrian Invivers would be busy for a while.

"You saved me just in time," Kaie said, gasping for breath. She sheathed her sword before falling to the ground in relief.

"I saw you were in trouble and I couldn't stay put," he said, sitting next to her. "Although I'm sure to be in trouble now." He looked towards Tristen, who was now staring at the two of them, a look of rage on his face.

"Yes, you are," Kaie agreed as they watched the troops retreat. "I didn't know you were so skilled with a sword. I've never seen you fight like that before. Even when we've sparred, you've never moved like that."

"It's because I don't show off like you and Raven," Achaius said, putting a hand theatrically to his forehead, pretending to be a dramatic damsel in distress.

"We practice," Kaie corrected, laughing at his antics. She leaned against him.

"Whatever you want to call it," Achaius said with a cheeky smile. He kissed her forehead before resting his head on top of hers. "Regardless, I'm glad you're safe."

***

Once they returned to the camp, Tristen gave Achaius an earful on how dangerous his actions had been in facing off against Crevan. Achaius, to his credit, put on the correct expression of contrition, although Kaie could tell that he did not feel bad about his behavior at all.

"You could have been killed, do you know that?" Tristen yelled, continuing his tirade after Kaie had been dismissed. "What would I do then? Just because you can Cure yourself now doesn't mean you should put yourself in danger! You're supposed to stay near the back anyway!"

"Tristen, I think that's enough for now. I'm sure Achaius knows that what he did was dangerous," Lorne said, coming forward and placing a hand on the eldest prince's shoulder.

Tristen looked at Lorne for a moment before turning back to his brother. "Just... just don't do it again," he spluttered before going into his tent.

Lorne gave Achaius a wink. "Thank you," the older captain said quietly before following Tristen.

Achaius quickly escaped to the Invivers' tent to meet up with Kaie. The other Invivers in camp were grateful for the youngest prince—after Kaie, he was able to Cure the most injuries, allowing them to save up most of their energy for Calming the soldiers for battle.

"Kaie, this soldier needs your help," Achaius said as he passed by one of the cots. The injury was too much for him to handle, but the man next to him had a manageable one. "I'll take over this injury. It shouldn't be too hard to finish up."

Kaie moved towards the soldier near Achaius, putting her hands on his arm, around the injury. His arm was so cut and bloodied that it looked like a piece of raw meat. She looked at Achaius, and as she exhaled, the light flowed from her hands to the wound where the flesh began to fix itself, regenerating the destroyed muscle and tissue, while the skin grew back over the arm.

Achaius smiled once she finished, his adoration reflecting in his eyes. Her face warmed under his gaze and she moved quickly on to the next patient before anyone could notice.

Achaius laughed quietly at her before focusing on Curing the soldier in front of him. Just as the light was about to materialize, Kaie appeared next to him.

"No, put your hands closer to the wound," she said, taking hold of his hands and guiding them to the right place. "Remember, the further away from the wound, the more energy it takes to Cure."

Achaius did as she said, but Kaie did not remove her hands from his. She instead rested her head on his shoulder as she observed the light disappearing. Achaius turned his head to look at her, giving her a light kiss on the cheek. Startled, she pulled back, and upon seeing his look of impertinence, she gave him a slight slap on the wrist before moving to help the other patients. The men and other Invivers all exchanged knowing looks. Everyone in the camp knew about the young couple's adulation for each other.

The two spent much of their free time together, enjoying each other's company immensely. The afternoons were filled with whispered conversations and secret kisses where no one could see.

But all too soon, the routine was broken. Only a month after the last one, another vivid nightmare plagued Kaie.

In her dream, she was in the middle of battle. Their forces were outnumbered. She watched one soldier in particular, his wavy blond hair making it easy to spot him. One of Crevan's monstrous soldiers pushed his way through the others to get to him. She tried to run through the soldiers separating them, to protect him, but she could not get to him in time. Forced to watch as the soldier stabbed through his abdomen easily, she pushed past all enemies as the soldier laughed when the young man fell to the ground. With a single stroke, she decapitated the soldier. Her heart pounded as she turned to look at the blond man, knowing who he was.

With a jerk, she awoke before she could see his face, the name of the prince lingering on her tongue.

Farin was looking at her, a concerned expression on her face. "Another nightmare?" she asked.

Kaie nodded. "I need to see Tristen now," she said, standing. Tristen would be able to sort this all out.

Lorne was already waiting for her, having been woken by her screams of terror. He escorted her to Tristen's tent, where Lorne walked in first to wake Tristen, then poked his head out. "You may come in now."

Candles were lit and Tristen was sitting in front of the map of the battlefield. He looked up as Kaie entered. "Lorne said you had another nightmare?" he asked.

Kaie took a shuddering breath, not sure if this nightmare could be stopped. "It was Achaius," she said. Her heart raced with panic.

Tristen nodded solemnly as she relayed her dream to him.

"I'm not sure what we can do to prevent this," she said. "It looks like he's going to die. What's the plan?" She looked at him expectantly, her eyes hopeful.

He paused for a moment, trying to figure out everything in his mind. "Achaius has Curing powers, right? So even if he got injured, he should be able to Cure himself."

"It was really bad, Tristen," Kaie said. "I don't know if he'd be able to Cure this wound. And I can't Cure him if he gets hurt." For the first time, she cursed herself for transferring her powers. If her actions led to his death, she would never forgive herself.

"You could send him away for this next battle," Lorne said quietly. "Until the danger has passed."

"I wish it was that easy," Tristen said with a groan. "But as long as Kaie is here, he refuses to leave, especially after he saved her last time. And we can't afford to send her away. If she was gone, not only would the men's morale plummet, but our casualties would be higher."

Silence filled the tent as they tried to figure out a course of action.

At last, Tristen broke the silence. "The best we can do is keep him towards the back of the battle," he said. "And Kaie, you can be nearby to help."

"Would you have men protecting Achaius too?" Kaie asked, her concern apparent.

Tristen nodded. "Of course. We'll do everything we can to protect him."

CHAPTER 39

Early the next morning, Kaie began to prepare for battle. Her sword and dagger were sharpened, her herbs were ready, and despite the nightmare, she had a good night's sleep. Her senses were heightened and her terror over the dream had lessened. There was a plan in place—a plan that would work. She moved into position to protect Achaius, knowing that once this battle was over, the pit in her stomach would go away.

Swiftly, the fight began, with Crevan's forces changing their tactics from the previous battles. Rather than any sort of formation, they streamed onto the field in a massive crowd of chaos. Despite this, no soldiers approached Achaius, and Kaie was called away from his side to Cure some heavily injured soldiers. Due to the intensity of the battle, the two remained separated, but Kaie kept her eye on him to be sure. By the afternoon, she began to breathe a sigh of relief as the battle seemed to be coming to a close. The disarray of the Scrian forces was working against them.

Then it happened.

She spotted the large soldier barreling through the Galician army as if the men were mere toys. Kaie could see him making a beeline for Achaius.

No, it can't be, she thought.

She tried to wade through the sea of people to reach Achaius in time, knowing deep in her heart that it would be futile. Tristen spotted her movements, cursing himself for his foolishness and wishing he had sent his brother away for this battle. Achaius's stubborn pleas early that morning had swayed his judgment. He'd thought the plan he came up with would be enough to keep his brother safe.

Kaie watched as the soldier stabbed Achaius in the stomach, screaming as she raced forward. The giant of a man laughed as Achaius fell to the ground, not seeing Kaie until it was too late. In her anguish and anger, she sliced her sword at the man, to make him hurt and feel the pain she was feeling. The strength of her fury removed his head cleanly from his body. Before he even hit the ground, she turned to focus her attention on Achaius, whose face had paled. Her heart quickened in fear. As soon as the assassin was killed, Crevan's forces dispersed and were nowhere to be seen. It was as if they had been waiting for Achaius to be taken down.

A couple Galician soldiers picked up Achaius and carried him to a nearby tent. Kaie watched his face the whole time as she followed them. Now that there was the quiet aftermath of the battle, she could hear the screeching sound emanating from him—his injury was very serious.

He gave her a reassuring smile. "I'll be fine," he said, reaching out his hand to hold hers once he was laid down.

Kaie cradled his face in her hands. "Try to Cure yourself. I can't," she said, cursing herself for giving him powers.

His face screwed up in concentration. There was a brief flicker of light, but it faded quickly. "I'm too weak." He gasped from the effort. "I won't make it."

Tristen walked in to hear his words and watched as Kaie broke down.

"Yes, you will," she sobbed. "I need you. You'll be fine. You *have* to be fine." Tears poured down her face.

Achaius took one of her hands and stroked it. "Kaie, you know as well as I do that this wound is too serious if I can't Cure myself."

She shook her head, trying to deny it.

"Don't cry. I can't stand to see you this way," he said.

Kaie gulped, trying to stop the flow of tears.

Tristen stepped forward. "Kaie, maybe you should step outside for a moment," he said, wanting to give her time to regain her composure.

She shook her head vehemently, unwilling to accept what he was saying. "Please don't make me go," she said, her voice thick with tears. "I... I can't go." She clenched the fabric at the bottom of her tunic in her fists. "Please don't make me go."

Achaius reached out and took one of her hands, gently wrapping it in his own. "You don't have to leave," he said gently before groaning as a fresh wave of pain passed over him. His breathing became more labored.

Tristen knelt next to Kaie, realizing how much she needed to stay. She was as unwilling to lose a moment with Achaius as he was.

"Achaius, I... I...." Tristen tried to force out the words, to find a way to tell his brother he loved him. But it felt too *final* and the words refused to come out.

"Tristen, don't," Achaius said, holding up a hand. "I don't want to hear it. If I hear it, I have to face it." His voice broke, and Kaie put her hand over his, clasping it in hers.

"It's my fault," she whispered. "If I hadn't given you the powers..." She could not even say the words as she bowed her head in shame.

"I got to Cure," he said. "Don't you ever apologize for that. I got to live my dream. Even if it was only for a few months. And though our time together was even shorter, it was wonderful."

"But I can't... I can't—" She broke off suddenly, and her head snapped up, looking at him closely.

"What is it?" Tristen asked. "What are you thinking?"

"Since I gave my powers to Achaius, if I Cured him, it would technically be like I'm Curing myself," she said. There was hope.

Achaius looked grim. "I don't think it's going to work," he rasped. "It's already too late." He paused, growing even paler, his breath coming out in rasps. All three knew he would die within moments. The screeching grew shriller in pitch.

As the last breath choked out of Achaius, Kaie put her hands on his chest and took a deep breath before pushing all her Curing power towards him. She screwed her eyes shut, praying that it would work, that death would not be so cruel as to take Achaius from her. A light flashed behind her closed eyelids, so bright that even she was blinded for a moment. Immediately, the sound stopped, leaving silence in its wake. When the light faded, she slowly opened her eyes.

Achaius's wound was gone and his pallor was much improved.

"You... you did it," he whispered, looking at her in wonder as he sat up. He leaned forward and kissed her fiercely.

"I guess I did," she said when he pulled away, relief washing over her. He wasn't dead. "I wasn't sure if it would work."

Tristen hugged her tightly. "Thank you," he said. "You brought my brother back."

Kaie moved to stand and would have fallen if not for Tristen's quick reflexes.

"Careful, you're going to be really tired," he reminded her gently as he helped her stand.

"I know," she said sheepishly. Slowly, a frown came over her face.

"Kaie, what is it?" Achaius asked, moving towards her. His cheeks were flushed and full of life again.

"I feel... different," she said, holding her hands up, trying to figure out what was wrong. "I don't know how to explain it."

Achaius blinked and then looked around. "I feel it too," he said. "I feel more energized, more than I have ever felt before. Like I could do anything!" He turned to her. "Is that what you feel?"

Kaie looked lost and confused. "No," she said. "If anything, I feel the exact opposite."

"What do you mean?" Achaius's look turned to one of concern. He put his hands on her shoulders.

"I feel weak," she said softly.

Inside, she felt drained, as if something was gone, something that she had been with her whole life and was used to, but now had disappeared. Kaie tried to think of what could be missing, but in her exhausted state, her mind was blank.

"That's to be expected. You just Cured me," he said.

Kaie shook her head. "It's more than that." She was at a loss for words. "I don't even know how to explain it. I feel as if part of me is missing."

"But you did it!" Achaius said. "Imagine what this could mean! I wonder if you could Cure other Invivers then."

"Maybe." Kaie said, her mind still searching for an answer. She shook her head. She would have more time to think later when she wasn't exhausted.

"Well, let's go show everyone that Achaius is okay and get dinner," Tristen said proudly. "After today, you both deserve a good meal."

Kaie let out a small laugh. "You just want to show him off," she said. She took Achaius's hand and clasped it tightly in hers. "I'm glad you're alright," she said quietly to him. "I thought I lost you." Tears pricked her eyes.

Achaius cupped her cheek and brushed his nose across hers. "I will stay by your side as long as I can," he said. Once more he kissed her, more tenderly this time.

She closed her eyes, relishing the fact that he was still alive. He was alive and breathing, his heart was beating. That was something *she* did.

They were walking to Tristen's tent when Raven approached them. "Achaius, you're alive!" he exclaimed loudly. Other soldiers turned their heads, and there were whispers of amazement. "I thought your injury was too severe to Cure!"

"Kaie was able to Cure me anyway," Achaius said, putting an arm around her.

Kaie's face flushed at all the attention as soldiers approached to offer congratulations and clap Achaius on the back. She felt as though she was in a fishbowl. More than anything, she wanted to go take a nap.

"Come on, Kaie needs some food and rest," Tristen said over the din of the crowd. "Let's give her a break."

The soldiers quickly dissipated, and they continued to Tristen's tent. Once inside, they discovered a feast waiting for them. Lorne, Farin, and Rosse were already seated. There were exclamations at Achaius's healthy appearance.

"Kaie was able to Cure me," Achaius said to their confused looks.

"That's amazing!" Farin said, clapping her hands.

"You were able to Cure him?" Lorne asked in shock.

"That's unheard of," Rosse said in surprise.

"It's not a big deal," Kaie said, sitting down in her usual seat.

"Oh, Kaie, I got cut during the battle," Raven said, approaching her. "Can you Cure me? I was going to stop by the Invivers' tent, but it's so small, I didn't want to bother them. I'm sure they're exhausted from today."

"So you bother me instead? I'm exhausted, too, you know," Kaie said with a smirk. "Come here."

Raven held out his arm, and Kaie put her hands near the wound, frowning slightly that she was not able to hear the usual sound of injuries. Even if they were small, there was some sort of buzzing. She closed her eyes and focused on Raven's wound. Upon exhaling, she opened her eyes, shocked to see that the wound was still present.

"Is everything all right?" he asked.

Kaie frowned. "I must be more tired than I thought," she said. "Let me try again."

Once more, she was unable to Cure him, and Kaie's face paled as she suddenly realized what happened. She turned to Achaius, a look of panic on her face.

The enormity of what she had done suddenly hit her, and she felt like she was about to faint or vomit. "Please excuse me."

Kaie fled from the tent, running from what she knew to be true—in saving Achaius, she had given up the thing that had meant so much to her over the past years.

Everyone watched her go, confused at her actions. Achaius looked down at his hands, feeling the power coursing through him.

He looked up at everyone. "I don't think Kaie can Cure anymore," he said softly.

"What do you mean?" Tristen asked.

"I think she transferred *all* her powers to me," Achaius said in disbelief. Once the shock wore off, he moved to follow. "I have to go after her," he said.

Tristen stepped in his way, blocking him from leaving. "She seemed pretty distraught," he said. "I don't know if it's the best idea for *you* to go after her."

Farin stood. "I'll go."

"What's going to happen?" Achaius asked Tristen as Farin left. "I have her powers now—but *she's* supposed to stop the war! How is that going to happen if she can't Cure?"

The older prince was at a loss for words, unable to comprehend how this would change the current war plan. "I'm not sure," he finally admitted. "She is the whole reason we even have a chance at winning this war." He thought for a few moments more. "I guess we could switch the plan over to have you take her place, but I don't know what we would do with her. She's an excellent fighter, but without her Curing abilities, I'd be too worried to let her out on the battlefield. We need to send word to Maeve."

"She could always go home," Achaius said quietly, though the idea of having Kaie sent far away pained him.

"No," Tristen said sharply, knowing that Kaie returning home was no longer an option. "I'll send word to Maeve and see what her advice is."

***

Kaie burst into her tent and immediately collapsed on her bedroll, sobbing uncontrollably. The emptiness she felt was a sharp pain, the hollowness threatening to swallow her whole.

When Farin arrived, she was frozen in shock upon seeing Kaie's reaction. After a moment's hesitation, she moved towards the younger girl and knelt next to her, gently rubbing her back while whispering soft words of reassurance. Kaie continued to wail incoherently. After several minutes, her crying softened enough for her to properly form words.

"I've lost my powers. I'm useless now," Kaie said. Her throat throbbed painfully as she tried to swallow some of her screams.

"Hush now, that's not true," Farin argued. "You are a remarkably talented swordswoman. You could easily defeat any soldier in the Scrian army as well as our own."

Kaie lifted her head up to look at her.

"It's true," Farin insisted upon seeing her doubtful look. "You've defeated two of their biggest soldiers without issue."

"Kaie?" Tristen entered the tent. He stopped upon seeing Kaie's reaction. Knowing that this would have a huge impact on her, he sat down across from her.

Kaie looked at him with red-rimmed eyes, tears threatening to fall. Her lip quivered from the effort of keeping her emotions from spilling over. "What good am I now?" she asked, hesitant to know the answer but knowing the topic needed to be discussed.

Tristen could tell that she did not have the emotional capacity at the moment to have such a discussion. "You should come back and eat dinner with us," he said gently. "Everyone has had a long day."

Kaie was too tired to argue, though a knot began to work its way into her abdomen. She felt nauseous, not knowing what was to become of her. Despite knowing she wouldn't be able to eat much at all, she stood and followed Tristen out of the tent. Farin trailed behind the two, knowing it was her duty to take care of Kaie and sensing that she would be needed for the foreseeable future. Farin and Tristen both talked about the summer weather, trying to keep Kaie's thoughts occupied.

Kaie noticed the effort on both their parts, but remained silent, the knot in her stomach growing larger and larger.

All heads turned towards her when she entered the tent, and Kaie's face flamed in shame. She ignored everyone's gaze, keeping her eyes downcast as she went to sit next to Tristen, Achaius already seated on her other side. She remained silent as food was passed around and her plate was filled for her by Tristen.

Achaius felt extremely guilty about possessing Kaie's powers and reached out a hand to comfort her, only to stop when she flinched away. Inane conversation started throughout the group, everyone trying to ignore what had happened earlier that day. Kaie stared at her plate, not touching anything until Tristen gently prompted her.

"Kaie, you really need to eat something."

Conversation immediately screeched to a halt, and Kaie could feel everyone's eyes upon her.

She looked up at Tristen, her face grim. "I'm not hungry," she said.

"You've expended a lot of energy today. You need to restore your strength," Tristen responded, knowing he had to be firm or Kaie would let herself go to pieces.

Kaie's jaw clenched. "What for? It's not as if I'm useful for anything anymore." She stood, suddenly feeling claustrophobic in the tent with everyone.

"Kaie, wait," Achaius said, standing to block her. "I know you're upset about what happened today, but—"

"Move out of my way, Achaius," Kaie said with a scowl, her voice turning deadly.

"Kaie, please," he began to beg.

"Get out of my way," she said, shouldering past him.

"Kaie, I'm sorry about what happened," Achaius said in a last-ditch effort to stop her. "Can't you just talk to me?"

"Haven't you stolen enough from me already?" she asked, tears pouring down her cheeks, her angry façade crumbling completely. She knew it was not his fault she'd lost her powers, but he was the easiest target for her rage.

Achaius paused, mouth agape as he did not know what to say. The tension over the group thickened, and after an agonizing moment, Kaie fled back to her tent. Farin followed not far behind.

The older girl waited patiently as Kaie took a detour to vomit. "There, there," she soothed, rubbing Kaie's back. "It's going to be okay."

Kaie vomited and coughed, a disgusted look on her face from the taste. "How?" she asked. "My powers are gone."

"We'll figure it out," Farin said helplessly.

Kaie only shook her head, but allowed herself to be led back to their tent, where she laid silently in her cot, staring at the ceiling instead of sleeping.

CHAPTER 40

The young Inviver tossed and turned, weak and exhausted from the day's events, but was unable to sleep. Farin slept soundly, the sound of her deep and even breathing filling the tent. Kaie had just switched to lay on her other side when she heard the crunch of a stick outside her tent. Immediately, she froze, a chill running down her spine.

"There's no way they could get into camp," she whispered, knowing all the precautions Tristen had put in place since the last kidnapping attempt. Slowly, she reached for her sword, trying her best to remain quiet.

Soldiers burst into the tent like lightning, their actions quick and efficient. Kaie was barely able to unsheathe her sword before hands were on her, covering her mouth. She tried to fight against their grip, but was too weak, all her remaining energy dissipating.

Farin awoke at the sound of Kaie's struggles, but she, too, was quickly overpowered. The men left her behind, bound and gagged so she could not warn anyone, before disappearing into the night with Kaie.

Raven woke up suddenly, wondering what had roused him from a deep slumber. He listened closely and heard what sounded like muffled screams from outside. He jumped up and grabbed his sword, dashing to Kaie's tent. Taken aback by the sight of Farin tied up with no sign of Kaie, he quickly got over his shock and removed her gag before going to work on her restraints.

"They took her," she gasped, tears running down her cheeks. "They took Kaie." Sobs overtook her frame. "I wasn't able to help. Raven, she doesn't even have her powers. What will Crevan do with her?"

"I don't know, but we need to get Tristen and Lorne," Raven said, jumping up.

There was no time to comfort Farin. To her credit, the girl stood and followed him out of the tent. Swiftly, they woke Lorne and Tristen, filling them in on what had happened.

"I can't believe he kidnapped her right under our noses," Tristen roared, banging his fist upon his knee. "I thought reinforcing our guards would work! Who knows what he'll do with her once he realizes her powers are gone!"

"We'll have to hope she stays safe until we can rescue her," Lorne said calmly, although everyone knew how worried he was. The way he was clenching his fists was enough to tell that he was concerned.

***

Kaie's heart pounded as she was brought to the Scrian camp. Her fighting abilities were weakened and there was no possible way for her to Cure herself. The soldiers bound and gagged her, much like Farin, so she was unable to alert anyone as they rushed past the guards. Two tears leaked from her eyes as she watched her camp growing farther and farther away from her place over the soldier's shoulder. When they got to the Scrian camp, Kaie was taken into a tent where she was unceremoniously plopped on the ground. She winced at the impact.

"It's taken four months, but at last I can speak to you without any of your bodyguards present."

Kaie's head snapped up at the sound of Crevan's voice. He smiled at her brief look of panic before she could control her reaction.

Crevan leaned down and removed her gag. "Is that better?" he sneered, laughing as she tried to move away from him. "You are mine now. You will Cure for *me*," he said softly, threateningly. "Now that the prince is dead and you are gone, they will have no choice but to surrender."

Kaie's expression fell, and Crevan took this as a sign of her defeat. Her words took him by surprise.

"They won't give up," she said softly. "I am no longer important." Her eyes darted around, looking for some kind of escape, when she noticed Fallon, who was standing silently in the corner.

"Join us, Kaie," Crevan said to the poor girl tied up in front of him.

Kaie kept her eyes downcast, not looking at him. She did not respond to him at all, a fact which grated on Crevan's nerves. He liked it when his prisoners put up more of a fight.

"We have much need and use for an Inviver of your caliber," he said, trying a different tactic. "We could help you as much as you could help us. We can help unlock more secrets of your power—secrets you would never dare to dream about."

Kaie's jaw clenched at his words, her heart breaking at the thought of her powers being gone for good. Unlocking any more Curing secrets was no longer in her future, her entire path now upended.

Haelan walked in to hear Crevan's persuasions and took up a place along the wall of the tent. Behind him, the camp was buzzing with the news that Kaie was in custody.

Fallon noticed how quiet Kaie was and how she reacted to Crevan's words. His brow furrowed nervously, knowing something was off, but he could not tell what.

Crevan continued to taunt, plead, and threaten the girl until, at last, she broke.

"I'm not an Inviver anymore, got it?" she yelled, her head snapping to look the commander in the eye, her face filled with fury. She strained against the ropes constricting her and screamed a raw, screeching sound. "I'm not an Inviver anymore. My powers are gone! Gone! They no longer exist! I am of no use to anyone!"

Crevan took a couple steps back as he, Fallon, and Haelan watched as Kaie broke down, releasing her feelings of hurt, despair, and anger in a way she had been unable to before. None of them had expected this sort of reaction. They watched in silence as she screamed, cried, and yelled, most of her words unintelligible. After a few minutes, she had spent her rage and sat limp, breathing heavily. Tears coated her cheeks and she could tell her face was flushed.

Fallon and Haelan watched as Crevan screamed in disbelief, "That's not possible!" The commander took his sword and cut Kaie's cheek. She jumped from the unexpected pain. "Cure yourself!" he screamed when she did not.

Kaie looked at him, her eyes still burning with fury. "This is all *your* fault," she seethed, her tone deadly. "If you hadn't gone after Achaius, I wouldn't have tried to Cure him. This was your doing."

"That's—that's not possible," Crevan stuttered in shock. "You can't use your powers on an Inviver."

"But I did," Kaie said as blood dripped down her cheek.

Haelan went to her and put his hands to her face, Curing her instantly. Her head jerked up in surprise, and her eyes widened when she saw it was him. He watched as shame and tears filled her eyes, knowing that he had heard every word.

"By Curing Achaius, your powers disappeared?" Haelan clarified, confusion spreading across his features.

Kaie nodded silently, letting loose a deep breath as she felt all the anger and hurt slowly vacate her body, leaving behind emptiness.

"Get out of the way," Crevan snarled, kicking Haelan over.

Kaie's eyes followed the Inviver as he stood and moved out of Crevan's line of vision into the shadows, waiting until he was needed.

"You have to be lying—tricking us somehow. No Inviver has ever lost their powers before," Crevan said, licking his lips nervously. He thought for a moment before barking, "Fallon! Go get that concoction ready! If she has any power left in her, she will be bound to me."

Kaie's heart dropped to her stomach as the commander took out a vial fastened around his neck. It was filled with a viscous green liquid, and her stomach turned at the sight of it. From what she heard from Haelan, this vial tied all the Scrian Invivers to Crevan.

He leaned forward and cut her bonds with a single swipe of his blade. "You will belong to me," he said.

***

Tristen jumped up and ran outside as he and everyone else heard a scream coming from the Scrian camp. Crevan's harsh taunts could be heard, but his words were indecipherable at the distance.

"What is he doing? Is he torturing her?" Tristen asked, his face paling. He turned to Lorne. "He can't be." He was begging the older man to correct him.

"He wants to find out something," Lorne said quietly, his hands clenched at his sides. Though it was a terrible idea, the general wanted to storm across the field and save Kaie. But he knew that sort of mission would only cost more lives in the long run. Crevan would be sure to have Kaie well-guarded.

"We need to work out a plan to get her back," Tristen said, clenching his teeth when he heard Kaie cry out again, her voice ringing into the night. He stormed back into the tent, Lorne following closely behind.

***

Crevan dragged Kaie to Fallon's workspace, throwing her once more on the ground. Her head spun.

"Hurry up," he snarled at Fallon, his eyes glowing brightly. The other man was adding different ingredients to a flask, swirling them around slowly. The mixture quickly turned a shade of dark red.

"Almost done," the man said, focusing on the concoction in front of him.

Haelan had followed them, but remained off in the shadows, out of Crevan's notice. Kaie looked to him desperately, and he silently shook his head. He would not be able to interfere and help her.

"Please don't do this," she begged, turning back to Crevan. Maybe she could convince him to change his mind. Somehow.

"Silence!" Crevan hissed. His eyes were glued to Fallon and the flask.

Fallon began to heat the mixture over a fire and Kaie's stomach roiled. She began to edge away from Crevan and Fallon, back towards the Galician camp.

"And where do you think you're going?" A hand encased her ankle and pulled her back. "You are stuck here with us," Crevan spat, his hand still gripping her ankle.

"Let go," she said, kicking her other foot at him. He captured it easily and tied her feet back together.

"If you won't behave, I will bind you up again," he said. "Fallon, how much longer until it's ready?"

"Almost there," Fallon said, watching the flask closely. It was just starting to bubble. "You can prepare her."

Crevan grabbed Kaie's left arm and pulled her sleeve up. Her right hand pried at his fingers, desperately trying to loosen his grip. But he was too strong.

"Haelan, come here," Crevan barked. "Hold her still. We can't have this going wrong."

The Inviver came forward and took Kaie's right hand, pulling it away from Crevan.

I'm sorry, he mouthed when she looked at him in disbelief.

Kaie looked away from him, tamping down the sharp sting of betrayal. Even if Haelan's actions were needed to keep his cover, it did not make her feel any better.

Panic bubbled up in her throat as Crevan pulled a long, thin dagger out.

"Stay still," he warned her. "The less you struggle, the less it will hurt."

She was surprised by the slight tone of kindness in the commander's voice. But all surprise was shattered when he slit the underside of her forearm in a long gash. Searing pain shot through her body, and Kaie let out a scream of pain. Even with how deeply Crevan cut her, she had not expected this level of pain.

Looking down at her newest injury, Kaie noticed a sticky green liquid coating the edges of her wound. Crevan's dagger was coated in something and it burned.

Fallon approached with the bubbling flask, and she began to thrash. Anything to keep that from touching her skin. But Crevan and Haelan held her still.

"Do it," Crevan ordered when Fallon seemed to hesitate.

Fallon tilted the liquid, and Kaie screeched as it touched her skin. It was molten hot and her mind was blank from the pain. She felt it sizzling into her arm. Crevan waited several moments before squeezing the wound. Once more, Kaie screamed as white-hot pain shot through her arm. He released her as soon as the liquid landed in a new vial, capping it immediately.

Kaie collapsed completely on the ground, the cool earth soothing against her cheek. Her arm throbbed with searing pain as it fell beside her. From her vantage point, she saw Crevan staring at the vial greedily.

"At last," he said. "At last, you are tied to me." His gaze darted to hers. "This one is different than the other. You'll have a shorter leash than the other Invivers. You'll never return to your friends again."

Tears pricked her eyes. She could never return home, and she couldn't go back to the Galician camp. And worst of all, she was stuck here with Crevan.

"Don't cry, Kaie," Crevan said with mock sympathy, kneeling next to her. "We're going to be very closely acquainted while you unlock the secrets of immortality for me."

"That's what this is all about?" Kaie asked in shock. "Immortality?"

"I know you have the power to find it," Crevan hissed. "But I will let you rest for tonight. Tomorrow, our work begins." He turned and walked toward his tent, retiring for the night.

Kaie looked down at the gash in her arm, the red liquid Fallon poured on her melded with her skin. Like Haelan's, it was filled with a deep red, swirling liquid. Her stomach still heaved at the sight of it, and she averted her gaze. She would be branded forever by Crevan's experiment. Tears fell down her cheeks.

Haelan knelt next to Kaie and reached towards her. She flinched away. He had helped hold her still.

"I'm sorry," he said quietly with a remorseful gaze. "But I had to do what he told me. Now, let me Cure that for you."

Reluctantly, Kaie held her arm out, and Haelan probed it gently. She sucked in a hiss of pain as he got closer to the gash.

"I know it hurts," he said gently before closing his eyes. There was a moment's pause before her skin began to creep over the edges of the liquid. But they did not knit together completely. Haelan opened his eyes and frowned slightly. "I guess there is only so much Curing can do with a potion like that," he said.

Kaie pulled her tunic sleeve back over the wound, unable to look at it for any longer. "What happens to me now?" she asked, her voice small and frightened. "Even if I can't Cure myself, I'm still tied to him."

Haelan smiled slightly. "I don't think it worked on you," he said. "I don't sense the tether that the rest of the Invivers have. You could still escape."

"What?" Kaie's voice was soft.

"You aren't tied to him," Haelan said. "We just need to figure out how you can escape without getting caught. The good news is Crevan thinks you can't get very far, so you'll be able to surprise him." He reached down and untied the bonds keeping her feet together. "But for now, you need sleep," he said, extending a hand towards her.

She took it, and he pulled her upright.

He led her to his tent. "You can sleep here tonight," he said, gesturing to his cot. "I'll sleep right outside. We'll figure things out in the morning."

Kaie nodded wordlessly as he left, collapsing onto the cot. Sleep immediately came for her.

***

Tristen and Lorne did not sleep that night, instead spending the time outlining a plan for rescuing Kaie. When the morning came, Achaius showed up to Tristen's tent.

"Where's Kaie?" Achaius asked, as he had not seen her around camp. Nor was she in her tent.

Tristen looked at them with bloodshot eyes. "Crevan's men came and kidnapped her in the night," he said in a hoarse voice. The night of no sleep had taken its toll on him.

"What? Then why aren't we doing something?" Achaius demanded, immediately becoming agitated.

"We are currently trying to figure out a plan that would be best for this situation," Lorne said. "We can't act rashly on this or risk losing many lives."

Everyone fell silent as they heard shouts coming from across the field. They rushed outside to see what the commotion was about.

"Is that—?" Tristen began to ask.

"*KAIE!*" Achaius yelled, starting to run towards her.

Lorne snagged the back of his tunic and pulled him back. "Wait for her to come here," he said quietly.

Kaie was sprinting across the field, arms pumping, while the Scrian soldiers were shouting at one another.

"Get her! Get her!" Crevan's screeches could be heard over the noise. "Bring her back here!"

Soldiers streamed onto the field after Kaie, but she had too much of a lead.

"Shoot her if you have to! I just want her alive!"

Arrows began to fire off, but in the panic, several hit other Scrian soldiers who were in pursuit of Kaie. Crevan's singular goal was causing casualties.

Kaie continued to sprint, panting heavily. She had to make it back to the Galician camp.

"No! Not that one!" Crevan shrieked as an arrow made its way towards Kaie. "You idiots, I told you I want her alive!"

Several yards away from the Galician camp, Kaie collapsed to the ground, an arrow sticking out of her back.

Tristen's heart sank—he recognized one of Crevan's poisoned arrows.

"Bring her here!" he ordered.

A couple Galician soldiers ran out onto the field and carefully picked her up, taking her to the prince.

"Take her to my tent," Tristen said, leading the way.

The men laid Kaie upon the prince's bed before swiftly departing.

She winced in pain and let out a groan.

"We're here," Tristen said softly, laying a hand on hers.

"I'm sorry. I couldn't fight them off," Kaie said, her voice raspy. She blinked slowly.

Tristen and Achaius stared at her, unsure of what to make of how sickly she looked.

"That's okay. You're weak right now," Tristen said. She looked at him, and he had to hold back his shock at how dull her eyes seemed. It seemed the arrow that hit her was more potent than the one Crevan had shot him with. It was affecting her more quickly.

Lorne rushed into the tent with Evidian. As soon as Kaie was brought into camp, he had run to fetch the Inviver.

"What happened?" Evidian asked, blanching at the sight of Kaie.

"She's been shot with one of their poisoned arrows," Tristen said. "Can you Cure her?"

"She's an Inviver. I can't," Evidian pointed out.

Tristen let out a heavy sigh. "She passed on all her powers to Achaius yesterday," he said. "She's no longer an Inviver."

"*What?*" Evidian's voice came out as a horrified whisper. "I know she Cured him, but I didn't realize..." He trailed off.

Kaie let out a moan of pain.

"Can you help her?" Tristen asked.

"We need to take the arrow out." Evidian's voice was clipped. "Since we know what the cause is, hopefully we can Cure her."

Kaie moved more on her side for easier access. Evidian gripped the arrow and yanked it out. She screamed in pain as the arrowhead left her back, tears streaming down her face.

"It's going to be okay," Achaius said, kneeling in front of her and taking one of her hands. "Evidian will take care of everything."

The Inviver nodded and placed his hands gently on Kaie's back. She forced herself to remain still, breathing shallowly through the pain. He closed his eyes and breathed evenly. Slowly, a glow surrounded his hands, and Kaie could feel the pain fading away. Evidian frowned slightly, and everyone waited with bated breath until the glow disappeared after a minute, her back clear of any wound.

Kaie's complexion was back to normal and her eyes were bright once again. She sat up as Evidian stepped away.

"That was... odd," he said.

"It took longer than it should have, didn't it?" she asked, nodding in agreement with his statement.

"What do you mean?" Lorne asked.

"Curing poison is usually something that takes seconds, half a minute at most," Evidian said. "This time, it took over a minute. Not to mention, I feel more drained than I usually would after Curing poison."

"Well, it was one of their poison arrows that almost killed me before," Tristen offered.

"Last time, the wound festered due to our exhaustion. Curing it right away should not have taken that long," Evidian said. "But the fact that I was able to Cure Kaie does mean she is no longer an Inviver."

"What happened?" Tristen asked, turning to Kaie. "We heard your screams last night."

Her face fell. "He... *marked* me," she said, pulling her tunic sleeve up. Gasps filled the tent. "He wanted to bind me to him like the other Invivers. I wasn't supposed to make it past the middle of the battlefield with this."

"Why would you risk escaping?" Lorne asked. "That could have meant your death."

"Haelan said he couldn't sense the tether," Kaie said. "Crevan was cocky. He thought that I couldn't escape so he didn't assign any guards to me. I snuck out this morning and ran across the field."

"That was so dangerous," Tristen said, placing a hand on her knee. "But I'm glad you're back."

Evidian came closer to inspect Kaie's mark, frowning slightly as he probed her skin. "While it's true this mark is inert," he said, "I still sense something coming from it. Something ominous." He turned to the prince. "What are you planning to do with her?"

Kaie shifted uncomfortably on the bed. She wasn't ready to hear what Tristen's decision was.

Achaius sat next to her. "How are you feeling?" He reached for her hand.

Kaie dodged him and stood. "I'm fine," she said tersely, moving to Tristen's side. "I'd like to go back to my tent," she said to the eldest prince.

"You may go," he said. "But are you sure you don't want to stay?"

"I'm fine," she repeated. As she passed by Evidian, she quietly thanked the Inviver.

"Why won't she look at me?" Achaius asked the group when she was gone, his voice heartbroken.

"She's still upset at no longer having her powers," Tristen said. "You'll need to be patient with her, Achaius. She'll need time to get used to this."

"I didn't mean to take her powers!" Achaius said. "If I could, I'd give them back to her right now!"

"What are you planning to do with her, Your Highness?" Evidian repeated to Tristen. "Having her at camp is a risk without her powers."

Tristen ran a hand over his face. "I need time to think," he said. "And I have to write to my father."

CHAPTER 41

"For the last time, would you *please* come home with me?" Tristen begged Achaius. He had written his father about the near-death experience and the monarch had insisted that Tristen and Achaius return home immediately. The king made no mention of Kaie or her lost powers. Tristen and Lorne agreed that his silence on the matter meant she had to stay at her post.

"As long as Kaie is here, I'm staying," Achaius said, folding his arms. Ever since she'd lost her powers over a week ago, he had resolved to remain by her side. "Even if you drag me home, I'm just going to come back. You and Father will have to lock me in the dungeons to keep me from returning to her. And we both know he won't do that."

Tristen let out a groan of frustration. He turned to Lorne. "What do I do?"

"You could head back anyway and explain it to your father," Lorne said.

"He's going to be furious." Tristen groaned in frustration, rubbing at the stubble covering his chin.

"And that's why he can yell at Achaius once the war is over," Lorne said.

Achaius rolled his eyes. "By then, he'll have forgotten about all this."

"You better hope he does," Tristen said, leveling Achaius with a glare.

Kaie came up to the group, studiously avoiding looking at Achaius. "Tristen, can you make sure this gets back to my family?" Kaie asked, holding out a letter.

"I haven't written since coming here and they... they deserve to know what happened."

Tristen swallowed down the sudden sadness that filled him. He dared not look at Lorne or the façade would crack. "Of course," he said, pocketing the letter. It felt like a weight was dragging him downwards. "I'll make sure it gets to them."

"Thank you," she said, looking at the ground.

Achaius reached out a hand to her, but dropped it to his side, remembering Tristen's words from before. He had to give her time and space. But he stared at Kaie, willing her to look at him.

Tristen cleared his throat. "I need to get going now," he said. "The newly promoted *General* Shalane will be in charge while I'm gone and taking over my position as commander. I'm not sure how long Father will keep me for, but I hope to see you both soon."

"Goodbye, Tristen." Kaie came forward to give him a tight hug. "Be safe on the journey back."

"Both of you stay safe," he said. "I don't want to hear of any reports of either of you getting injured."

With a small group of soldiers, he departed for the palace.

***

Upon arriving at the palace, Tristen headed straight to his father's study. No matter how much he wanted to delay the conversation, if he put it off, his father's anger would be worse.

"What?" King Torin demanded once Tristen finished speaking, his mouth open in shock. "What do you mean he stayed behind? He almost died!"

"Achaius refuses to leave Kaie's side," Tristen said.

"Why would he do a thing like that?" the king said.

"Surely you're not blind, Father. Anyone can see he loves her." Tristen's tone was filled with admonishment. "And she loves him too. Isn't that enough?"

Torin let out a heavy sigh and sat back in his chair. "I was afraid of that," he said.

"Why are you so against Kaie? You're the one who summoned her here," Tristen said.

"I never expected the two of you to be so drawn to her."

"She reminds me of Catriona, what's so wrong about that?"

"Those memories are painful," Torin whispered. "Every day, I relive her death. The war, that girl, everything. It's all a constant reminder of her." His voice broke. "A parent should never have to bury their child."

"Father." Tristen's voice was full of soft surprise. His father had never shared this depth of emotion with him before.

The king sniffed before his expression changed to the steely neutral look Tristen was accustomed to. "Now that you're back, we can at least move forward with war plans."

"What do you have in mind?" Tristen was unsurprised by the sudden shift.

"I've written to the king of Scria. You leave in a few days to negotiate peace."

"Why now?" He was surprised that his father was finally willing to enter negotiations.

"I've almost lost both of my sons," Torin said. "And I'll be damned if I let my pride risk having either of you taken away from me again."

"Very well. I will do my best." Tristen bowed his head. "And Kaie gave me this letter to send to her family. What should I do with it?" He took the letter from his pocket and placed it on the desk.

His father eyed it with a grimace. "We put it with all the others," he said, taking the letter and walking over to a box on the bookshelf. He opened it and placed the letter inside, atop multiple others.

"What are those?" Tristen's voice was filled with horror. "You never sent her letters?"

"And I've been keeping the ones her family had sent as well," the king said, returning to his desk.

"She thinks they forgot about her!" Tristen said, his eyes burning with anger. "Why would you do such a thing?"

"In case a situation happened where her family was unable to respond back!" the king roared. "If they sent letters and then suddenly stopped, she would have been suspicious. This way, she doesn't know a thing."

"I just... how could you..." Tristen couldn't formulate a sentence. His mind was reeling. "This is going to make finding out about her family's deaths so much worse."

He let out a sob, finally able to release his emotions about the whole ordeal. Kaie was going to be devastated at the end of all this and he shouldered the blame for her pain.

***

Over the next couple weeks, Kaie cried herself to sleep most nights. She felt so empty and lost, wandering around the camp most days, trying to avoid Achaius. Though she knew it was not his fault that he now had her powers, it still hurt that he was able to do what was now gone to her. She knew her silence and distance hurt him, but could not find herself able to push past her own feelings to reassure him.

The mark on her arm was a constant reminder of what had happened to her, the sight always making her stomach roil. On days Kaie did not wear long-sleeved tunics, she covered the mark with a scrap of fabric. She could not stand looking at the gash.

Now she had nothing to do to fill her time, so she stayed out of the way of the soldiers, knowing she could no longer help them. She also gravely disliked the looks of pity they gave her whenever she passed them by. Whispers always swiftly stopped when she was nearby, and she knew they were talking about her.

Lorne continued Tristen's tradition of having everyone at his tent for dinner. Revelin turned into a more valuable ally, as he helped run the camp and came up with battle strategies for the next few fights. He was a welcome addition to the group, drawing everyone in with stories of his escapades. Other than Revelin's theatrical storytelling, meals were quiet with little discussion. Achaius continued to try and draw Kaie into conversation, but she had slipped back into giving him one-word answers. Her gloomy disposition brought the rest of the group down.

Evidian fully took over Achaius's lessons. Mostly, that entailed being in the Inviver tent Curing the injured, but there were other lessons that he imparted on the prince that Kaie had not gotten to yet.

One morning, he took Achaius to the forest. He sat down on the ground. "Join me," he said, patting the spot next to him.

Achaius followed suit, remembering Maeve's lesson from what felt like ages ago. Back when he was able to make Kaie laugh.

"Are you going to have me listen to the sounds of the earth?" he asked skeptically.

"Ah! You know about it!" Evidian was gleeful. "It's a great exercise to realign with the earth and thank Mother Nature for our gifts."

"Last time, nothing happened," Achaius said. "I wasn't able to hear the sounds of the earth."

"What instructions did Maeve give you?"

"To just sit and listen," Achaius said. "There weren't any specifics."

Evidian pursed his lips. "Well, I want you to try something else," he said. "Close your eyes."

Achaius did as he was told, though let out a small sigh. That was how it started last time.

"Patience," Evidian gently reprimanded him. "Take a moment and listen. Then tell me what you hear."

The prince paused and listened. "I hear the wind in the trees," he said. "And the birds calling to one another." He frowned slightly. "I think there's a squirrel nearby running in one of the trees."

"Very good," Evidian said quietly. "Now try and listen past that." He waited as Achaius focused. "Do you hear a humming?"

It took a moment. "Yes," Achaius said softly. He felt as though he could not speak any louder than a whisper. "It's a deep sound."

"What else?"

"It feels like... it feels like it's thrumming through me," Achaius said.

"Keep going. Follow the hum."

"It's... it's in the trees," he said. "It's in the ground." The intensity of the sound coming from the ground made him feel small, insignificant. Like he could be swallowed whole. But at the same time, it was calming. He opened his eyes. "It's everywhere."

"Exactly," Evidian said with a proud smile. "The sound of the earth is everywhere and within us all."

"So what does that mean?" Achaius asked.

"That sound is what we fix when we Cure others," Evidian said. "Injuries or sickness cause the sound within us to become distorted, and we have the power to balance that distortion using our own sound, our own energy."

"But how have Kaie and I been able to Cure others without being able to hear that sound?"

"Being able to hear the sound of the earth helps with fixing it in another person, but there's an innate ability that Invivers have to seek out and fix it," Evidian said. "If there is an invisible wound, seeking out the sound of the earth can help with figuring out where the problem is and using up less energy to repair it. But it isn't necessary to have the skill to Cure someone. Next time you Cure someone, try to hear the earth within them."

"Now how do I realign with the earth?" Achaius asked.

"Listen to the earth and the sound within you," Evidian said, closing his eyes. Achaius followed suit. "Typically, there is a slight imbalance between the frequencies. Focus on having the sound within you match the sound of the earth. And at the end, thank Mother Nature for your blessings."

Achaius settled back and focused on the humming. He could hear a slight buzzing when he listened to the hum within himself and the hum within the earth. Frowning, he tried to make the sounds match one another, but as his consciousness tried to mold the hum within himself, his mind flashed to Kaie. Achaius tried once more, and as he did so, he heard Kaie crying out. His eyes flashed open.

"I can't do it," he said with a gasp, clutching his chest. A dull pain thudded within his rib cage. "If I align my hum to the earth, it'll hurt Kaie."

Evidian watched him carefully. "I suppose it's because your powers were originally hers," he mused. "Maybe the frequencies haven't fully settled within your body yet."

"I need to see Kaie." Achaius scrambled up to head back to camp.

"Achaius, wait—" Evidian tried to stop the prince, but Achaius was already sprinting back.

CHAPTER 42

"Kaie!" Achaius shouted out her name when he saw her. She and Farin were walking through the camp.

Kaie spun to face him, shocked to hear a note of panic in his voice. "What's wrong?" she asked as he ran up to her. She eyed him warily.

"I was with Evidian and thought I heard you yell."

Her expression fell at the mention of Evidian. "What were you two doing in the forest?" She had seen the direction he came from.

"We were listening to the sound of the earth." A smile quirked at the corner of her mouth, and Achaius felt encouraged. "And I was able to hear it this time!"

"Really? What did it sound like to you?" Kaie felt caught up in his excitement, forgetting the devastating loss of her powers. The fact that he could hear the sound of the earth was quite the accomplishment and she was eager to hear more.

"A deep humming. And I could hear it within myself too! Evidian said that I could make the hum frequencies match, but when I tried to, I heard you yell."

Kaie paled. "I did feel a tug from my chest," she said. "But it was brief. I didn't shout though."

"He thinks it's because I have your powers and they haven't settled yet."

At his words, Kaie's eyes dulled and she turned away from him. Immediately, Achaius knew he'd made a mistake. She was pulling away from him once more.

"Kaie, I'm sorry. I wasn't thinking when I said that. I—"

"Enough," she said tonelessly. "I don't want to talk about this anymore."

Achaius looked to Farin, silently pleading with her to step in.

"He didn't mean anything by it, Kaie," she said gently, putting a hand to the younger girl's shoulder. "He was just explaining what happened."

"Every time I see him is a reminder of what was taken from me," Kaie said, pain entering her voice.

"Kaie, please. Tell me what I can do to make it better," Achaius pleaded, his voice breaking. "We were so happy together before. *You* were happy. I'm not asking you to suddenly act like nothing's wrong. I just want to be by your side and help."

She turned back to him, a tear running down her cheek. "But you *can't* help, can't you see that?" she whispered. "I'm no longer an Inviver. A key part of me is missing. Instead, I'm this... this... this *useless thing*." Kaie fell to her knees and began to sob. "I can't help anyone. I'm nothing now."

Achaius knelt in front of her, pulling her to him. She clutched the front of his shirt and cried into his chest. Gently, he rubbed her back. "Despite what you think, you're not nothing," he said. "You mean so much to our friends, your family, and you mean *everything* to me. Having or not having your powers does not define you. You were somebody even before you found out you were an Inviver."

"But I was somebody important with the powers," she cried. "Everyone is counting on me to end the war. I know they all think I have this great destiny. That's all gone now." Her voice turned a heartbreaking whisper. "I feel so lost."

"You tied a lot of your identity into being an Inviver," Achaius said. "So it's not surprising that you feel lost now." He pulled back and wiped away a few of her tears. "But you can lean on others. You can lean on *me*. We're all here to support you."

"But everyone else is so busy picking up my slack," Kaie sniffled. "Lorne and you especially. You're too busy for me."

"We will always make time for you," Achaius said gently. "And you're amazing just the way you are."

"That's right." Farin knelt down too. "And even if you don't have your powers, you're still a wonderful fighter, Kaie. You can still train with Raven."

"Yeah," Achaius said. "You have so many more abilities than just being an Inviver."

Kaie heard their words and knew they were trying to help her, but their words felt hollow. She wanted to believe them both, but instead, words just spiraled around in her head. *Useless. Useless. Useless.*

Achaius stood and helped her up. "Why don't we get lunch?" he suggested.

"Sure," Kaie said with a sigh, mustering up a smile. It felt fake, but Achaius and Farin didn't comment on it.

***

Raven came up to her as they finished eating. "Lorne would like to talk to you about an upcoming battle."

Kaie frowned. "He hasn't asked to see me about anything in a while. Is anything wrong?"

Raven shook his head. "There's just some information we received from Haelan that they want to review with you," he said.

Raven, Kaie, and Achaius walked together to the general's tent.

"Kaie, it's so good to see you!" Lorne exclaimed. The past couple weeks, he had been so busy, he had not gotten a chance to talk with her privately.

"Great to see you too," she said. "Raven said you wanted to see me?"

"Yes. Crevan will be attacking from the forest this time," he said, pointing towards the map. "Our objective is to stop this from happening. However, if we focus all our forces there, then it leaves our camp wide open for an ambush."

Kaie frowned. "You're planning to split up our forces?" she asked.

Achaius smiled at her, proud that she was able to make the connection so quickly. She flashed a small smile back, a warmth filling her heart—maybe she wasn't so useless after all.

"Yes, that's right," Lorne said. "But we also don't want Crevan to realize that he has a spy in his midst if we put all our forces in the forest. I was hoping you,

Achaius, and a group of soldiers could be part of that ambush. Your fighting skills are needed."

"Okay," she said. What Lorne said was right—even if she could not Cure, she could still fight. There were other ways she could help.

When the meeting came to a close and Kaie left the tent, Achaius followed closely behind.

"See? You were quick on your feet," he said, linking arms with her.

"I didn't do anything special," she said, blushing slightly at the compliment. It had been a while since she had allowed physical contact and she could admit that she missed him. The tension between them had disappeared after he'd comforted her. "Besides, I could only make that conclusion based on your history lessons."

"Regardless, you did a great job," he said. "Let's go get dinner. The fires are lit and it's been a long day." They had spent the whole day with Lorne planning for the upcoming battle and he was looking forward to spending time with her. Especially since she didn't seem like she was going to push him away.

"I wonder what the hunters caught today," she wondered aloud.

"Probably quail again," Achaius said.

"Most likely," she agreed. "I can't wait until this war is over and I can go home to have a nice meal made by my mother."

"That sounds nice," Achaius said.

The two drifted into silence, Kaie's thoughts wandered to what would happen to her and Achaius when the war ended. Maybe he would want to come meet her family. Though the fare her mother cooked up was simpler than what was served at the palace, she hoped he would like it. Or maybe he would want to call off whatever their relationship was. Kaie's heart clenched at the thought. Even if she had been standoffish lately, she did care deeply for him.

***

After dinner, Kaie moved next to Achaius, lying her head on his shoulder. "I may not have shown it," she said, "but I've really missed you these past few weeks."

"And whose fault is that?" he gently teased, putting his arm around her. He turned serious. "I know that this whole experience has been a shock and you've been out of sorts. I'm not upset that you blame me for losing your powers. I just hope you don't forget how special you are, with or without your abilities."

"I know it's not your fault I lost my powers," she said quietly. "But I was just so *angry*. And you were the easiest target for that anger."

"I know," Achaius said, kissing the top of her head. "But it's nice to see you happier now. You look more like you did when I first met you—a strong, beautiful young woman."

Kaie turned her face away, glad the darkness hid the sudden blush that painted her cheeks. "Thank you," she said softly, leaning her head on him again.

A sudden feeling of contentment and happiness overcame her for the first time since losing her powers. Kaie let out a heartfelt sigh and soon drifted off to sleep, Achaius holding her close by the fireside.

CHAPTER 43

Within two days, Crevan made his attack, just as Haelan had warned. He sent his forces into the forest, but they were attacked by the well-prepared soldiers that Lorne had put there in the night. In a desperate move after seeing the counterattack, Crevan sent men into the camp, where they once again were met with a formidable and ready opponent. At the end of the day, Crevan had lost a third of his forces before calling a retreat.

Lorne pushed his advantage until a barrage of poisoned arrows took out a battalion. Keeping Crevan at bay was enough for now. The general wanted to ensure he never tried attacking through the forest again.

"How could they have been so ready?" Crevan thundered to Haelan and Fallon.

"I have no idea, sir. Maybe they were just prepared," Fallon offered, consciously not looking at Haelan. He knew who was behind the trap. His only regret was the massive loss of life.

"No! I must have a spy in my camp," Crevan roared.

"Or maybe our spy decided to help his own side for once," Haelan said, trying to lead Crevan off his scent.

He knew that his commander had picked up on a few clues here and there, so it would not take much for him to figure out that Haelan was a spy for the enemy. To Haelan's chagrin, despite sniffing around, he still was unable to figure the identity of Crevan's informant.

"If he did that, I'll murder him! Anyone who betrays me will die!" Crevan shouted, loud enough that some soldiers a hundred yards away looked at him.

"Sir, it could have just been a coincidence," Fallon said.

"No, I don't believe that for a second. It can't just be a coincidence that they were in the forest during that time. When I get my hands on him, he's finished."

***

The Scrian king's response to Torin's request for negotiations was swift. Tristen set off with a small group of guards and dignitaries, arriving at the Scrian palace a week after setting out from Galicia. Everyone wanted to return to Galicia quickly, and the very small entourage of guards his father had insisted sending set a grueling pace.

The Galician prince was welcomed into the throne room to greet the royal family. Upon a regal throne covered in velvet sat the king, Jarlan Scrinan Plutus, his eyes sharply watching as Tristen approached. Wrinkles covered his face and limp, gray hair fell to his shoulders. On his right was a young man with a harsh face, a younger version of the king, while on his left was a young woman with kind, sweet eyes. Tristen was not fooled by her innocent demeanor—he could tell she was watching him closely, judging his every move.

He came forth and bowed to the elderly king. "Greetings, Your Majesty. I am Tristen de Galac, crown prince to Galicia."

"We welcome you, Prince Tristen," the king said in a deep voice. "I hope your travels weren't too tiring?"

"No, Your Majesty. I am ready to begin negotiations immediately," Tristen said.

For the next several days, negotiations occurred. Tristen, the Galician dignitaries, and the king's advisors discussed different ways to satisfy both countries. The king and the crown prince, Cyric Scrinan Plutus, sat in on the negotiations, offering input as well.

When not negotiating with the king, Tristen spent time with the princess, Lillian. The two began to grow closer, talking about their families and interests. To Tristen's delight, she also loved history.

Finally, at the end of the week, Tristen and the king reached a stalemate. Both sides were exhausted from spending all day in stressful conversation, and tensions were at a high.

"I will agree to having Invivers from both countries cross borders to learn from each other as long as they are treated by Galician standards," Tristen said. "There will be no experimentations on the Invivers like what's happening on the battlefield."

"How will I know you'll keep your word?" the king shot back.

"Is that what this is all about? My *word*?"

"Yes. Historically, Galicia has never allowed outsiders to learn from their Invivers. Why start now?"

"I think we could learn from each other and foster our countries' relationships," Tristen said.

"How can I trust that you won't pull another stunt like the one with your sister? Learn our secrets and then cut us off?"

"My *sister*?" Tristen thundered. "You dare suggest that I had *my own sister* killed? If this was a question of keeping my word, what was the point of calling me here if we won't be able to reach an agreement?"

"I wanted to see what type of person you were first, before making judgment." The king sat back in his chair, his hands steepled before him.

"I'll have you know, I loved my sister very much." Tristen pointed a finger at the king. "I had to leave the front lines of this war—where I've been actively fighting off your bloodthirsty commander—to tell my father that my brother had almost been killed. I left behind that brother and someone who is like a sister to me so I could try to find a solution so no one else has to die! If you don't believe me after all that I have had to leave behind, then I no longer see a point in settling this." He turned to leave, his face red with anger.

The king's voice stopped him, the calmness of his tone bewildering. "If I were to believe you about all of this, why would I risk having you find out all our secrets without promise of anything in return?"

Tristen turned, looking back at the king. "You would be learning from us too," he said. "I think now is the time for us to put aside our differences and take the path forward that is the best for our citizens. There is so much to gain for both of us."

"I would need insurance to make sure of an equal exchange of knowledge," the king said, leaning forward. Tristen could tell this was some sort of test, but one to which he did not know the answer.

Lillian spoke up from her place, where she had sat in on the discussions for the past couple days. "I believe I know how to solve this," she said softly.

Everyone turned to look at her, ready to hear what she had to say.

***

"Crevan sure has backed off lately," Achaius commented as he and Kaie looked at the sun setting. It had been almost a week since Crevan made any movement.

"I think he's preparing for another attack. He just needs to figure out a cunning plan and we might be done for," Kaie said tiredly. That day, she had spent most of her time sparring with Raven and gathering herbs. Since she was unable to Cure, she'd decided to utilize her other skills. If the Invivers were too worn out, her medicine might be able to save lives.

"If that's the case, Lorne will be able to come up with something to save us. I have faith in him. He's done well this past month since Tristen left."

Achaius slung his arm over Kaie's shoulder, pulling her closer. She leaned into him, her heart swelling with joy. He bent his head and kissed her gently.

"How was the Invivers' tent today?" she asked nonchalantly. Even if she could no longer Cure and always felt the pang of loss when they discussed it, she couldn't help but ask.

"Same as always," Achaius said cautiously. He didn't want her to dwell on what she no longer had. The prince rubbed his chest, trying to rub away the dull throb that had become more frequent these days. Evidian had noticed and asked him about it, but Achaius had brushed him off. He knew it had something to do with his frequency not being in sync with the earth. The Inviver powers within him were interfering somehow.

"I suppose it's time to give you this," she said, passing over her Inviver brooch. She hoped that this would make up for her earlier anger and symbolize them moving forward. "I'm not an Inviver anymore so I don't need it."

"Kaie, you don't have to do that," Achaius protested. "That's still yours."

"Nonsense," she said, moving to pin it to his cloak. She leaned back slightly, nodding at the placement. "You have my powers, you should have the brooch too." Kaie moved back into his arms, leaning her head on his shoulder.

The sun soon slipped behind the horizon and the night air began to grow chilly. Kaie shivered slightly, and Achaius's arm instinctively grew tighter.

"Even here, past the mountains, there are still cold nights," he said. "It's fall now, which means your birthday is nearing."

"We've been gone from the palace for so long. I miss it," she said wistfully. The past five months felt like an eternity, filled with bloodshed and death. Only quiet moments like these were the bright spots in her life.

"If the war finishes soon, we could head back together," Achaius said gently.

She shifted and looked at him. "What about going home?" she asked.

"Home for me is wherever you are," he said, his eyes shining with the love that he felt. "I would love to return to the palace with you, but if you want to go home to your family, I'd be honored to take you there."

"I... If... when I go back home, there's no one else that I'd rather have come back with me than you," she said, her heart thundering. She wanted to introduce Achaius to her family.

The words spilled out, Achaius not even having time to think. "I love you."

Kaie stared at him in shock, not expecting to hear such a sincere declaration of love. "I love you too," she said, fully realizing her own feelings.

Encouraged by her words, Achaius leaned forward and kissed her fiercely on the lips. For the past few weeks, he had backed off and kept only to chaste kisses. But now that she had said those words, he could no longer hold back. Kaie jumped slightly at the intensity radiating from Achaius, but deepened the kiss, putting a hand to his face. A fire ignited in her belly.

His hands tangled themselves in her hair, undoing her braid while she pulled him closer. They caressed each other, their touch leaving sparks and heat in their wake. When Achaius's hands dipped beneath Kaie's tunic and she felt his fingertips on her skin, she jolted back to reality and broke the kiss, pushing him away.

Kaie's face was on fire, her heart thumping so loud that she was sure that everyone in camp could hear it.

Achaius stared at her with reddened cheeks and ragged breathing. "I'm sorry. I got… carried away," he said. "I was just so happy to hear you say those words."

"They're true," she said, gasping slightly. While their previous kisses had been filled with sparks and fire, she had never felt that level of intensity before. She leaned forward and gave him a quick, chaste kiss on the lips.

"You love me," he said in wonderment. A radiant smile crossed his lips.

"And you love me," she said, moving to lean against him once more.

Achaius took her hand and wove their fingers together. He did not say anything further, only kissed the top of her head, savoring the moment. Despite the cool night, he felt comfortably warm.

The couple stared into the fire, and soon, both were asleep in each other's embrace.

***

At dawn the next day, there was an ambush. Achaius and Kaie were jolted awake by the sound of clashing swords. Kaie saw an enemy soldier coming for them, but she had left her sword in her tent. Noticing that Achaius's was strapped to his waist, she pulled it out, deflecting the attack.

"I'm not letting you hurt him again," she muttered, trying to get a feel for the alien sword.

She soon defeated the soldier and rushed off to her tent, making sure that Achaius followed closely behind. Once she had her own sword in hand, she and Achaius were ready for any opponent that came their way.

The ambush was short-lived, with Crevan's troops dispersing a few minutes later. Kaie and Achaius looked at each other in confusion.

"That was odd," Achaius said, wiping the sweat from his brow. "That was so short."

"There was a reason behind it," Kaie guessed. "That was a diversion. Crevan must have gotten what he wanted."

Raven came running up to them. "Rosse was captured!" he gasped. "They took him. As soon as they had him, they retreated."

"They have Rosse?" Achaius asked incredulously. "Does Lorne know?"

"I don't know. I wanted to find you first to make sure they hadn't taken Kaie as well."

"Like I would allow *that* to happen. I would kill everyone in my path before I let her get taken again," Achaius said fiercely.

Kaie gave him a tender look. "I would be able to defeat anyone Crevan sent, so you wouldn't have to worry," she said, giving him a kiss on the cheek. "I wouldn't allow you get injured just to protect me. I just wonder why they took Rosse."

"Crevan's a twisted, sadistic man. Does he need a reason for anything he does?" Raven spat out.

"So far, he hasn't done anything rash that wouldn't help him win the war," Kaie pointed out. "He's had a reason for everything, including..." She trailed off, a pang in her chest. If he hadn't gone after Achaius, she wouldn't have lost her powers.

There was silence for a moment, but Achaius soon broke it. "We might as well go make sure that Lorne and Revelin know about this," he said, leading the way to the tent.

They burst into the tent together. Lorne and Revelin looked up from the map where they were planning out an attack.

"Do you know that Rosse has been taken?" Raven demanded when they did not say anything.

"Yes," Lorne said calmly.

"And you're not going to do anything about it?" Raven shouted.

"We will not be manipulated by Crevan into taking rash action. When we find out what he wants in return for Rosse, we will discuss our possible options," Lorne said.

"But—"

"Raven, think for a moment. Doing anything impulsive would be foolish. We'd only lose more men. Right now, cool down. If I hear anything, you will be the first to know. Now please give me and Revelin time to plan an attack." Lorne looked back to the map, signaling that the conversation was over.

Raven stormed out of the tent, Kaie and Achaius following close behind. "I can't believe he's not going to do anything!" he fumed.

"I'm sure he has his reasons," Kaie tried to calm him down.

"Reasons? *Reasons?!* I want to tell him what he can do with those reasons. I just want my brother back. He's all I have," Raven said, tears threatening to spill.

Kaie patted him on the back. "And Lorne will do everything in his power to get Rosse back. Trust me, he's thinking up something."

"Yeah, so far, we've won every battle against Crevan thanks to Lorne," Achaius added. "He'll get Rosse back safely."

"I just wish I knew what Crevan wants with him," Raven said.

CHAPTER 44

The entire room was silent after Lillian's suggestion. The king stared open-mouthed at his daughter while Tristen looked mildly amused. After a moment, the king's advisors began whispering amongst themselves, discussing the idea.

The king finally broke his silence. "Why?"

"It's a good idea," she said. "It would be a gesture of good faith on your part and it's not like we find each other repulsive—or at least, I don't think so." She looked at Tristen, who nodded, showing his agreement with her statement. "It's not ideal, but under the given circumstances, it's certainly the best option."

"But... you want to marry him?" The king's voice came out in a whisper.

"It's my duty to our people," she said. "Our people and his people have a mutual need, and being married would strengthen this bond. If you remember, his father was willing to have his daughter marry Cyric. He was willing to make that sacrifice, and now you're not willing to do the same?"

"Lillian, are you sure this is what you want?" The king's voice was desperate. Although Tristen seemed like a kind enough man, he could not imagine sending his daughter over to the kingdom he had fought so desperately against for all these years.

She nodded. "I'm willing to do this if Prince Tristen is."

The king turned to Tristen, silently begging him to turn the offer down. "Would you agree to this deal?" he asked.

Tristen nodded. "Her Highness worded it better than I could have," he said. "We've gotten to know each other over this week, and based on our discussions, it's not like we don't get along. I would be willing to get married immediately."

"The sooner we get married, the sooner the war will be over," Lillian said, walking over to Tristen and taking his hand in hers. "All this worry and death can come to an end." A smile quirked across her mouth. "And to think, I get such a handsome husband out of the deal."

Tristen chuckled and kissed her hand. "I think we'll get along just fine," he said, looking warmly into her eyes.

The king shook his head, knowing that going against Lillian's plan was both futile and inadvisable. "I guess that means we're to have a royal wedding," he said. "We'll begin preparations at once."

***

A week after his brother's kidnapping, Raven snuck out in the night to meet his contact. As he slipped out of his tent to go into the forest, his mind was so heavy that he did not pay attention to his surroundings. He walked over to an older oak tree, where his contact was waiting.

"What is it now?" The man was impatient.

"I need my brother back. I'll do *anything* to get him back. Just tell me what to do," Raven begged desperately.

"I'll have to talk with my leader," the man said. "Don't do anything to compromise our position and I'm sure everything will fall into place. Crevan won't do anything stupid. I will meet with you in one week." He disappeared into the night without another word.

Raven let out a sigh, his stomach still in knots as he began to head back to his tent, but Revelin ambushed him, pushing him against a tree.

"What was that all about?" he asked.

He had noticed the young man sneaking about and followed him into the forest. Raven was so unfocused that he had not noticed.

All possible answers were gone from Raven's mind. "I... I..."

Revelin grabbed the front of Raven's shirt, dragging him back to camp. "I knew I smelled a rat. Lorne will have a hard time with this, but he'll get over it. I thought I knew you better. I had you pegged for a loyal man. You know, the kind who would try to help out his friends and family any way he can."

"I'm not the spy!" Raven gasped out.

Revelin snorted. "Yeah, right. Save your excuses and stories for Lorne. He'll sort through them soon enough." When they arrived at Lorne's tent, Revelin thrust Raven in before entering. "Lorne, I have found your spy," he announced triumphantly.

Lorne looked up, surprised to see Raven as he took in Revelin's words. He removed his glasses and set down the paper he had been reading.

"Lorne, I swear I'm not the spy," Raven said, his eyes pleading to be believed.

"Revelin, you can let him go now," Lorne said, looking back down to the paper in his hand. "I'm sure if he decides to run off, you'll be able to catch him before he gets too far."

Revelin did as Lorne commanded, but kept a watchful eye on Raven.

"Raven, how about you sit down? Once I'm finished reading this letter from King Torin, I want you to tell me what this is all about," Lorne said as he continued to scan the paper.

"You got a letter from the king?" Revelin asked in surprise.

"Yes. Why?" Lorne asked, still not looking up from the letter.

"I thought he hadn't sent word since calling Tristen back," Revelin commented.

"Tristen got called to an audience with the Scrian king a couple weeks ago," Lorne said, to which Revelin and Raven exchanged an astonished look. "It seems they are trying to negotiate terms to end this war. The king wants me to keep an eye out for Tristen returning safely." Lorne finished scanning the letter, folded it up, and put it in his breast pocket. He looked back and forth from Revelin to Raven. "Now, what's this all about?"

Revelin started. "I caught him talking to some stranger about what has happened with Rosse. Then the figure just disappeared into the forest. I think they've had these little meetings since Raven arrived."

Lorne turned to Raven. "Is this true? Have you been meeting with someone and telling them about our plans?"

"Yes, but—"

"See? I told you!" Revelin crowed triumphantly.

"Raven, why have you done this? I'm sure that this isn't as it seems, but the evidence mounting against you certainly portrays you as the spy. Please explain yourself," Lorne said softly, his eyes showing his disappointment at this news. He had recruited Raven and Rosse himself.

"I'm not Crevan's spy," Raven said vehemently. "Before we came here, Maeve pulled me aside. She wanted me to tell her about Kaie's progress and anything else that happens during the war. As you can imagine, Maeve is not able to travel very well, so every couple weeks or so, her messenger comes here or I send a message back to the palace requesting to meet early with him. Then I tell him what's going on and he reports back to Maeve. That's all there is to it, I swear."

"If this is true, then why haven't you come to Tristen or me to talk about this matter? Has it occurred to you that maybe we would like to give some input as to what Maeve hears?" Lorne asked.

"Maeve wanted our correspondence to remain secret. She said that if Kaie ever found out, it might inhibit her growth as an Inviver," Raven said.

"Very well. I guess we'll have to leave it at that, but next time, Revelin is going to the meeting with you to make sure that your story is true," Lorne said. "Now off to bed, both of you. We are going to have a long day tomorrow. From the way the king's letter is worded, we might hear some news tomorrow of this war ending. I personally look forward to that. And if not, we might hear news from Crevan as to what he wants in return for Rosse."

***

Only half of Lorne's prediction came true the next day. Crevan himself personally approached the Galician camp alone, holding a white flag of truce. Soldiers alerted Lorne immediately and he was waiting for Crevan at the edge of camp, Revelin by his side. One look at Lorne's face and Revelin knew this would not be a pleasant conversation. Lorne's face was cold and impassive, while Crevan's broke into a cruel smile.

"I have a proposition for you," Crevan said, his voice betraying how much he was enjoying this.

"And what would that be?" Lorne asked.

"I will trade you your... well, I don't know what he does for you, but I'll trade him for someone else."

"Depends on that someone," Lorne said.

"Oh, now don't be coy. You know *exactly* who I'm talking about." Crevan's grin widened. "I heard her powers were transferred to someone else. But I still want Kaie."

Revelin was overcome with the urge to pound the smirk off his face, barely managing to hold back. His skin crawled, thinking about how he used to be on Crevan's payroll.

"You can't have her." Lorne said coldly, crossing his arms. "Tristen told you no then, and I'm telling you no now."

"It would be a shame for something to happen to my prisoner. I believe one of your soldiers is *very* attached to his older brother." Crevan took a slim dagger out of its sheath, beginning to clean it.

"Raven would agree that Kaie's life is more important than Rosse's in this war," Lorne spat out, fists clenched.

"Very well. I see there's no reasoning with you," Crevan snarled, his good humor gone. "I will be in touch after you've seen one of my demonstrations. I will get every ounce of information out of that man that I can."

Lorne leaned forward. "That will never happen. Rosse's loyalty to his country is too great. He will never tell you anything."

Crevan smirked, his eyes darting to something behind Lorne. "We'll have to see. I can be pretty persuasive." He fingered the dagger again before sheathing it. Loudly, he called out, "Kaie, it's such a shame we leave on opposite sides. You would be wise to make the right decision before it's too late. If you come with me now, I will spare your friends."

Lorne's eyes closed in chagrin. Achaius and Kaie had approached once they found out Crevan was at camp. "Go," he forced out through clenched teeth.

"I'll see you soon," Crevan hissed before leaving.

"What was that about?" Kaie asked, coming up alongside Lorne to watch Crevan's departing figure.

"He's heard news that your powers have gone to Achaius, but still wants you," Lorne said, his arms crossed.

"He thinks I hold the secret to immortality," Kaie said. There was a quiet thought in the back of her mind that even if she lost her powers, Crevan still thought she was useful. She was filled with a mixture of pride and disgust.

Achaius put an arm around Kaie, pulling her close. "I would never allow him to take you," he whispered into her ear.

She grabbed his hand, squeezing it tightly. "He has something planned," she said quietly, trying to fight the sense of foreboding rising within her.

"Did he say that he was willing to trade Rosse for Kaie?" Raven's voice came from Lorne's left, and the general silently cursed his luck. Anything Crevan said would poison the boy's mind.

"Yes, it's true," Lorne said after a pause. "But it is not going to happen. Kaie is far more important to the war effort than Rosse," he said tersely, not cutting corners to spare Raven's feelings.

"How can you say that?" Raven asked angrily. "He's helped plan countless attacks against them!"

Lorne glanced at Kaie and Achaius. "You and I can discuss this in my tent," he said quietly, firmly.

Raven stalked to Lorne's tent without a response, muttering under his breath.

Lorne held up a hand with Kaie and Achaius moved to follow. "This is a conversation for just me and him," he said. "I'll see you two at dinner."

Trailing after the young man, he calmly entered the tent. Raven was standing at the table, refusing to sit down. Lorne took a seat.

"What I said earlier is true and you know it. Maeve surely told you why it's important to keep tabs on Kaie, and now by extension, Achaius. Even I figured it out before I left. If you need me to explain it, I will, but deep down, you know I'm right."

Raven sat across from Lorne. "She didn't tell me anything. What are you talking about?"

"You're familiar with the Inviver book with the prophecies inside?" Lorne asked, to which Raven nodded impatiently. "The Invivers have been waiting for the chosen Inviver to end the worst bloodshed. All the kingdoms have searched for this Inviver since this prophecy was written. At the beginning of King Torin's reign, he sent out some soldiers to find the Inviver, as all kings had before him. I've had my suspicions about Kaie since she arrived at the palace due to Maeve taking such a special interest in her."

"You think Kaie's the chosen Inviver?" Raven asked in disbelief.

Lorne nodded. "One of the characteristics of the chosen Inviver is they can pass their powers on to others. Before we left, Maeve confirmed my suspicions and told me to keep an eye on Kaie. This is why we can't give Kaie up to Crevan. The prophecy states that if the chosen Inviver is on the side of evil, then the world will be plunged into darkness. If Crevan gets his hands on Kaie, he'd be unstoppable. Right now, his only focus has been on acquiring Kaie, rather than focusing properly on strategy—that's part of the reason why we've been able to win so frequently. But if he got Kaie, he would essentially have access to her powers through Achaius."

"What do you mean by that?"

"You've seen the two of them together, how attached they are. Wherever Kaie goes, Achaius follows. Pretty much everyone in camp has noticed at this point. They have a betting pool on whether the two will get married. If anyone made a threat towards Kaie, Achaius would go berserk."

Raven nodded, knowing that what Lorne was saying was true. He had been enjoying having a tent to himself, now that Achaius had been sleeping outside most nights. In talking with Farin, he also knew that Kaie never returned to her tent at night anymore.

"When's your next meeting with Maeve's contact?" Lorne asked. "I'll be going instead of Revelin."

"I can send word for us to meet tomorrow night," Raven answered. "Aren't you worried about leaving Revelin behind? What if *he's* the spy and this has been a cover the whole time?"

"Tristen trusts him, and so do I," Lorne said. "And Tristen relayed some of their conversations to me. Revelin doesn't want to be at the losing end of this war, and whatever side has Kaie's powers is going to win."

"Sounds awfully cocky for the leader of the army," Raven said with a smile.

"Achaius now has the ability to defeat the Scrians. Maybe not single-handedly, but he has us to help. With him on our side and Crevan distracted by Kaie, we are an undefeatable combination. Please keep this a secret," Lorne said, dismissing Raven.

Lorne was left alone with his thoughts on how to keep everything from falling apart before having the chance to deal the final blow.

***

Announcements about the royal engagement quickly went out, along with notices to the generals of the Scrian and Galician armies to stop fighting, stating the war was over. Despite the notice, Crevan refused to back down.

"Sir, the king has ordered us to stop fighting. Why do you persist?" Fallon asked, scared of the answer. Crevan had grown increasingly crazed over the past weeks.

"We must crush the Galicians to gain access to the Mists or Kaie," Crevan said, his eyes wild as they roved over the map.

"But the mark didn't work. She doesn't have her powers anymore," Haelan said. Crevan's obsession had grown continuously over the past few weeks.

"No, that's not it," Crevan said. "She's still trying to trick me. She somehow was able to Cure herself and disable the mark. The king might be weak enough to let such a prize go, but not me. We must defeat the Galicians and learn their secrets."

Fallon and Haelan exchanged a concerned look. If Crevan wouldn't listen to the king, who would he take orders from?

CHAPTER 45

The Galicians remained on alert after the announcement came out, seeing that the Scrians were still conducting business as usual. Lorne held a meeting in his tent to discuss their next steps, baffled by Crevan's behavior.

Haelan burst into the tent halfway through the meeting, having sprinted through the forest. "Crevan refuses to give up. He's still focused on Kaie," he gasped, trying to catch his breath. "He's gone absolutely crazy. He's convinced she still has her powers. No one can reason with him." He paused. "Well, not that we could before, but it's gotten much worse."

"Sit down," Lorne said. "We were discussing ambushing your camp to retrieve Rosse. If you can tell us where he is being held, we can attempt to rescue him."

Haelan shook his head. "It's no use. Crevan has him tied up at the very back of camp. There's at least a hundred men guarding him. Crevan doesn't want to take the chance of losing him. Here." He pointed to the very back of the map. "He's only a hundred yards from Crevan's tent."

"Then our plan can't fail. We must take out all their soldiers if we are to save Rosse," Kaie said.

"When?" Haelan asked, seeing the determination on everyone's faces.

"Two nights from now," Lorne said.

"You should do it tomorrow," Haelan recommended. "Crevan is planning to interrogate Rosse tonight, then discuss his answers tomorrow. If he survives the night, Crevan will give him a short reprieve."

"What do you mean *if* he survives?" Raven spat out.

"His methods are... It's not going to be good," Haelan admitted, having seen firsthand what his commander had done to get answers out of unwilling participants in the past. "He won't allow me to Cure Rosse until he's passed out from pain, and only then, it's to continue the interrogation."

"And you're just telling us this now?" Raven shouted.

"He spontaneously planned it today," Haelan shot back. "He has announced that tomorrow, he'll be running the men through drills, so they'll be too tired to put up a fight, and his generals will be preoccupied discussing Rosse's answers."

"What about Fallon? Or the other Invivers?" Kaie asked. Haelan had told her long ago that the advisor had been silently helping him slip away to meet with the Galicians.

"I can give them some warning. Fallon'll find an excuse to sneak away," Haelan said. "And I'll make sure the Invivers are out of camp for your ambush." He paused. "I could ask them to Calm the soldiers to put them in a deeper sleep to make it easier for you."

"Then it sounds like tomorrow is our best opportunity," Lorne said. He turned to Achaius and Raven. "For this, I want you two to stay behind with Kaie." He raised a hand as all three began to protest. "Kaie and Raven, you two will be in charge of shooting flaming arrows at Crevan's tent and leading the aerial assault to take out any enemy soldiers from afar. Achaius, you'll be staying behind to protect Kaie. In case anyone gets past the volley of arrows, she needs to stay alive. Now out. I need to finish conversing with the other generals." He waved his hands, signaling for them to leave.

Once outside, Raven grabbed Haelan's collar. "Everything you said better be true," he threatened, allowing his hand to linger on the hilt of his sword.

Kaie stepped between the two, pushing Raven away. "Haelan has risked his life countless times to help us," she said. "He wants to end this as much as you do."

"Crevan's gone crazy," Haelan said. "He's gotten so much worse than before. I need to head back before he notices I'm gone. Good luck tomorrow." He raced off into the night, finding his way back to camp.

"I can't believe we're still fighting even though the war is over," Kaie said. "Not to mention, Tristen's getting married."

"That's the most surprising part," Achaius said. "Even though he'd do anything to protect our country, I didn't expect that." He let out a yawn. "We need to get some sleep. Big day tomorrow."

The trio split up, Achaius and Kaie heading to their usual spot by the fire while Raven went to his tent. As they settled against each other, Kaie's mind slipped back to when she was captured. A shudder ran through her and her right hand trailed to her mark. Bile rose as Kaie's fingers made contact with the torn skin and she swiftly pulled away.

Achaius noticed and intertwined her fingers with his, bringing them to his lips for a kiss. "You're safe now," he murmured, his eyes heavy with sleep.

"I know," Kaie said, leaning her head against his shoulder. "But the mark still disgusts me."

The prince kissed the top of her head. "You're still beautiful," he said. "And soon all this will be over."

Kaie nodded and stared into the fire, allowing the flickering flames to lull her to sleep.

***

Kaie was jolted awake by the sound of a seemingly inhuman scream coming from the Scrian camp. She moved closer to Achaius, shuddering at the sound.

"What do you think is happening?" she asked fearfully, wiping the sleep from her eyes.

He tightened his arm around her. "Remember, Haelan said that Crevan was going to interrogate Rosse tonight. I think that might be happening now."

The two stood, walking towards the edge of camp, eyes straining to see anything in the darkness. Another scream echoed across the field, continuing infrequently to break the silence it left in its wake.

Kaie faintly saw a glow appear across the field. "He's torturing Rosse, then having Haelan Cure him when he passes out to torture him some more," she whispered, horrified. Though Haelan had mentioned it, seeing it firsthand was shocking.

Achaius pulled her away from the sight. "Come on, try not to think about it," he said.

Raven rushed past them on their way back to the fire. Kaie managed to catch his arm before he was out of reach and pulled him back.

"There's nothing you can do," she said helplessly.

"Is it Rosse?" he asked, his eyes wild with worry.

"We think so. Regardless, you can't go bursting into that camp all alone. They would kill you," she said. "The best thing to do is get revenge tomorrow when we shoot the arrows."

"I want to be the one to shoot first, understand?"

Kaie nodded in agreement. "Let's do that," she said. "Now come away. Try to get as much sleep as possible."

The rest of the night was filled with infrequent screams, interrupting any sleep they tried to get. Shortly before dawn, the screams stopped for good, leaving a heavy silence behind.

***

The following night, everything went as Haelan had predicted. All the Scrian soldiers immediately went to sleep, Crevan having drilled them to the point of exhaustion, while Crevan and his generals went to his tent to plan their next attack. Shortly after they entered, Lorne and his men moved in. They crept along the camp, sneaking into tents, taking out soldiers as they went.

Finally, Raven and Kaie shot their flaming arrows upon Crevan's tent, causing everything to erupt into pandemonium. Unlike Crevan's previous ambush, the Scrians were sluggish, unable to put up a fight against the Galicians. The Invivers had done an excellent job dulling their senses.

The tent burned quickly, but Crevan managed to escape at the last minute while his generals burned inside. Screams filled the air as Lorne and his men made their way further into camp. About half an hour after the start of the ambush, Lorne and his men returned with Rosse, who was slung across Lorne's back, unconscious. Thankfully, they had taken no casualties that night.

"You got him!" Raven exclaimed as he began to inspect his brother once Lorne set him down on the ground.

Rosse's face was unrecognizable, his body severely injured, blood seeping through his clothes. Many bones looked to be broken as well. Raven turned to Achaius, his eyes begging the prince to Cure his brother.

Achaius came forward and got to work. Closing his eyes, he focused on Rosse's frequency, easily finding the high-pitched hum. He frowned slightly at how unsynchronous it was with the earth, but was able to find the areas that needed the most help. He Cured the gravest injuries first, on Rosse's torso and head. Then he moved to the broken bones and the minor injuries. Everyone remained quiet as they watched him work. At last, when he was done, Rosse was still unconscious.

"What's wrong? Why isn't he waking up?" Raven asked.

Achaius shook his head. Despite doing his best to realign the frequencies, there was still an underlying buzz. "He's been too traumatized. Crevan did a lot to him. He won't wake for a few more hours." Achaius looked to Lorne, seeing a strange expression on his face. "What's wrong?"

Lorne instructed a few men to keep watch on Rosse while motioning the group to follow him into his tent. He dropped his bloody armor on the ground before beginning to pace in circles, muttering under his breath. After a few more minutes, both Revelin and Haelan entered.

"Lorne, what is it? What have you found out?" Kaie asked softly when it did not seem as though he was going to speak.

He looked up, his expression grim in the lantern light. "Rosse is the spy," he said.

"What?" Raven jumped up. "How could you say that?"

"Crevan's parting words were that he hopes we enjoy getting our traitor back and that he has been extremely helpful these past months," Lorne choked out.

"That doesn't prove anything!" Raven shouted.

"This was the first time Crevan has actually been taken by surprise. He didn't know anything about this attack like he has in the past," Lorne said. "What if that was because Rosse was already in their camp, so Crevan didn't have his inside man?"

"That's... that's ridiculous!" Raven spluttered.

"Based on Fallon's description of the spy, it sounds like Rosse," Haelan said softly.

"Revelin, did you have any idea? Back when you ambushed him?" Lorne asked.

Revelin thought for a moment. "We ambushed him on his way back to camp. Crevan has other mercenaries on his payroll, so one of them could have caught him and made an offer he couldn't refuse." He looked at the commander. "The offer did not come from me or my men."

"Then we'll have to wait until he wakes," Lorne said grimly.

CHAPTER 46

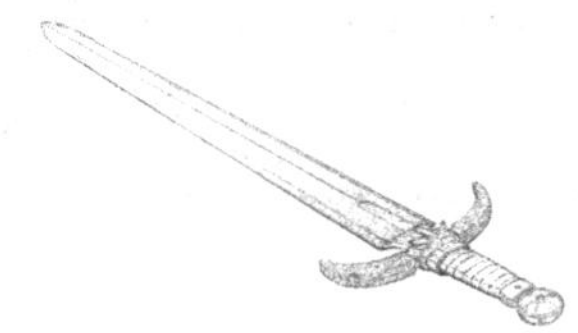

It was not until the next morning that Rosse awakened. He was swiftly brought to Lorne's tent, where Raven was already waiting.

Rosse gave his brother a wan smile, still exhausted from his injuries. "Thanks for coming to get me, Lorne. It means a lot," he said as he sat down.

Raven scowled at him.

"What is that for?" Rosse asked, frowning slightly.

"You know very well why," Raven retorted.

"Crevan said something interesting as we escaped with you," Lorne said, maintaining his composure. "I want to know if there's any truth behind it."

"I will, if you tell me what you're talking about," Rosse said innocently.

"He said you were the spy!" Raven shouted, standing to yell at his brother. "Is it true or not?"

Rosse was taken aback by his brother's fury. "Yes, it is," he admitted softly after several moments, looking at the floor.

"Why?" Lorne asked. "Why would you betray us like this?"

"Crevan threatened to kill Raven if I didn't comply!" Rosse shouted. "I couldn't let that happen so I agreed to help him. Trust me, I didn't want to, but I had to for Raven's sake."

"Do you realize how many men have died because of what you've told Crevan?" Lorne asked.

Rosse nodded miserably. "I know," he said. "But Raven's the only family I have left. I couldn't let him be killed because of me. Crevan's men ambushed me on my way to the palace and gave me his proposition. Once I agreed, they disappeared. Then when Revelin's men tried to capture us on our way back, I thought I could cripple Crevan by taking out his most valuable mercenary."

"Why did he capture you?" Lorne asked.

"He thought I had betrayed him, let you know about our deal. He wanted to punish me for that. I didn't tell him anything else, though. Not even that Haelan has been helping us. I've kept some things from him," Rosse said, holding out his hands.

"I can't believe you'd do this," Raven said in disgust.

"I did it for your benefit," Rosse argued.

"So? I mean nothing to the war. You shouldn't have done that," Raven said, standing to leave.

"Raven, wait," Rosse said desperately. "You're my brother, and I wanted to protect you. Can't you see that?"

"You're no brother of mine," Raven said before leaving.

Rosse looked after him sadly.

"In light of these events, we need to discuss your punishment," Lorne said, to which Rosse's face fell. "You will be tied up and we will be keeping a close eye on you. Once we finish the war, you will be sent back to the palace as a traitor. You know the punishment for that."

"Death." Rosse nodded. "I know you're only doing your duty, but you can't know how sorry I am."

"It's too late for that," Lorne said, a sad expression on his face. "Come on, I'll take you to the posts."

***

"Raven, how are you taking this?" Kaie asked in concern as she and Achaius watched him pace back and forth angrily. News of Rosse's betrayal and subsequent punishment had spread throughout the camp.

"How could he do this?" Raven fumed.

"To whom? You or the country?" Achaius asked.

"Me... everyone... Ugh, I don't know!" Raven grabbed his hair in frustration, letting out a howl.

"He did it to protect you. You would have done the same for him," Kaie said.

"I would not have betrayed my country, my friends for just one person!" Raven growled.

Kaie walked over, placing her hands on Raven's shoulders to prevent him from pacing. "I mean, you would have done anything to protect him," she said. "You know, deep down, he only did it to protect you."

Raven shrugged her hands off. "He shouldn't have done it," he said. "The penalty for a traitor is death. You both know that."

"Ahhhh." Achaius nodded in understanding. "You just don't like him putting himself in the position to protect you when it meant he would die. You don't like feeling that responsibility," Achaius said.

"It wasn't his decision to make. I can protect myself!" Raven said, his voice rising in pitch.

"But it was his decision. You're upset because you feel he doesn't trust you to take care of yourself," Kaie insisted. "But Raven, listen to me. He did it because you're his brother and he loves you. He just wanted to protect you, like you want to protect him. What's wrong with that?"

"Because now his decision doesn't allow me to protect him!" Raven shouted, his eyes filling with tears. "He's the only family I have left and now he's going to get taken away from me and there's nothing I can do about it," he whispered.

"And so now you're going to give him the cold shoulder instead of trying to work it out?" Achaius asked. "Wouldn't you rather be on good terms instead of spending what might be his last days angry at each other? Trust me, it's not worth it."

"I'll think about it," Raven said as he walked away.

"I'm worried about him." Kaie turned to Achaius. Her eyes were sorrowful, knowing what it was like to argue with a sibling and feel that guilt.

"He'll learn to forgive Rosse and they'll go back to being as close as they were," Achaius said confidently.

***

The Scrian king looked at the letter in his hand in disbelief, his eyes practically popping out of his face.

"What is it?" Lillian asked, seeing her father's strange expression.

"Crevan isn't backing off. He's still fighting," the king said incredulously.

"What?" Tristen exclaimed. Lillian put her hand gently on his arm and he immediately calmed down. "I knew he was crazy before, but this is insane. What did he say?"

"That I'm weak and unfit to be a ruler. He's planning on defeating the troops you have at the border before storming the capital and will then come home victorious." The king's hand shook at the obvious sign that Crevan was unwell.

Tristen shook his head. "I should have guessed that this obsession with war would lead him this far," he muttered.

The king frowned. "What are you talking about?"

"He killed my sister so that you would think that we broke the treaty and go to war with us. He wants access to the Mists," Tristen explained.

"I had no idea about that," the king said. "We must send someone down there to stop him immediately!"

"The only way you could get him to stop is to kill him," Tristen said. Lillian's hand tightened on his arm, and he turned to her. "It's true. I've seen his ruthlessness firsthand. He had one of my siblings killed and tried to kill the other. He must be stopped."

She nodded, understanding his logic. "It just seems so sudden," she said. "I want you to make sure that your personal feelings aren't clouding your judgment."

He leaned down, kissing her cheek gently. Over the past week, since the announcement of their engagement, they had grown exceedingly close.

"Don't worry. I plan out my actions and think about the consequences. Perhaps we can go try to reason with him directly and see where that leads."

"It's worth a try," she said.

"Before you two go anywhere alone, I want you married," the king said.

"Don't you trust us to be proper?" Lillian asked her father, aghast at his insinuation.

Tristen added, "We can even bring a chaperone with us. But we can't delay dealing with Crevan. He's too dangerous to be left alone."

The king pondered the suggestion. "I suppose that will have to do," he said after a long pause.

"And once the war is over, we can have a proper wedding to celebrate." Tristen turned to Lillian. "How does that sound?"

"Sounds perfect," Lillian said as her eyes sparkled.

***

To everyone's surprise, Maeve visited the Galician camp. Kaie ran to the elderly woman when she saw who had arrived, enveloping her in a hug. To her dismay, the elderly Inviver looked even more frail than she had six months ago.

"Maeve! What are you doing here?" she asked. Anxiety filled her. Surely Maeve knew she had lost her powers and that Achaius had them now.

"For your eighteenth birthday, I had to do something big," Maeve said with a smile.

"Thank you. It's so nice to see you." Kaie paused. She didn't want to see the disappointment in Maeve's eyes. "I don't know if you heard, but..."

"Relax, my dear," Maeve said, putting a hand to Kaie's cheek. "I know about everything. We'll get it all figured out. But I needed a break from the palace monotony. It was getting too cold there for these old bones so I decided to come past the mountains where it's warmer."

To Kaie's shock, Brayan had come to the camp as well. He was holding the reins of Maeve's horse. "What is *he* doing here?"

"Brayan's my newest apprentice," Maeve said. "A month after you left, his powers manifested."

"Really?" Kaie's mouth dropped open.

The physician shrugged, remaining silent.

"Now, I need to speak with Lorne," Maeve said once the pleasantries were out of the way. "Achaius, could you direct me to his tent?"

"Follow me," Achaius said, offering Maeve an arm as he guided her through camp.

"So you're an Inviver now?" Kaie asked Brayan. "How have you been adjusting to the change?" Even if the physician had been harsh in the past, now that he was an Inviver, maybe they could get along.

He crossed his arms. "It's interesting enough, I suppose," he said. "Though I was surprised when she mentioned coming here to further my training. She thinks that battlefield experience will help." He let out a sigh. "But I would have rather stayed back at the castle."

"The battleground does provide a lot of good experience," Kaie said.

"Easy for you to say. Everything comes naturally to you," Brayan said. "Or at least, it did."

"That's a horrible thing to say," Kaie said, aghast. She took a couple steps away from him. It seemed the physician still didn't like her.

He shrugged. "Well, it's true. I'm not going to dance around your feelings just because you gave your powers away." He yawned. "I'm going to put the horses away and then go to sleep. For an old woman, she sure rides the horses hard. I'm exhausted."

"See you later," Kaie muttered in confusion as he walked off.

***

Maeve interrupted a meeting when she walked into Lorne's tent. "I'm here. What is so urgent that I had to drop everything to come?" she snapped.

Revelin looked at her in surprise, seeing her steely gaze. "I'll go," he said, exchanging a look with Lorne. "I can see you two have a lot to talk about." He left quickly.

"Why did I have to leave the palace and drag my current student down here with me?" Maeve asked, her hands on her hips.

"There's a problem," Lorne began.

"And that is?" Her tone was clipped. She was tired of beating around the bush.

"The war should be over, but Crevan hasn't stopped fighting us. He's going against his king's orders," Lorne said. "I know Kaie is the chosen Inviver and she will end the war, but she passed her powers on to Achaius. I thought if you came, you could help shed some light on the situation."

"I don't know how I can help," she admitted. "I just know that she's the chosen Inviver. Everything I know has come from the book. It didn't mention anything about her fully transferring her powers to another."

"Then maybe the first Inviver should have been more specific," Lorne muttered.

"I *am* the first Inviver!" Maeve snapped.

Lorne's eyes widened.

"I just wrote what I was instructed to. Mother Nature did not tell me specifically what to do when I found the chosen Inviver, she just told me to write it in the book."

"She told you?" Lorne's tone was skeptical.

"I was sent dreams, like the ones Kaie has," Maeve explained.

"How have you lived this long? Hasn't the king realized how old you are?" Lorne asked, too distracted to focus on the main topic of conversation.

"If you're as knowledgeable in our history as you say you are, you'd know that the unreadable parts of the book have closely guarded secrets—one of which *is* immortality," she said. "When I was in the service of the original king of the first Invivers, he wanted us to find a cure for death. I found the way, but he was not worthy to live forever. He was cruel. As the generations have gone on, the kings have grown mellower. I believe Torin has his suspicions, but he hasn't said anything and I haven't told him. Each king just assumes I was a nursemaid to his father and have been blessed with good health. It's not hard to fool them and they rely on me for advice. I'm too useful for them to want to poke around into my history and risk me leaving court."

"Why do you stay in their service if there is a risk they will force you to give them the secret?" Lorne asked.

"I needed to remain to teach the chosen Inviver," Maeve said. "After Kaie, I might just allow myself to die. The ritual doesn't last forever, and it needs to be redone after a normal person's lifetime. Now that the chosen Inviver has been found, there's no reason I should stay."

"What if Kaie's children are Invivers? Would you stay to teach them as well?"

"She's more than capable of teaching them after I'm gone," Maeve said. She let out a weary sigh. "I'm just so tired."

"You wouldn't stay to keep on the tradition and make sure everything unfolds as it should?" Lorne pressed. For so long now, Maeve had been orchestrating things behind the scenes. She was the leader of the Invivers, not to mention the kings kept her as a close confidant.

"Who am I to say what should or shouldn't happen? After the war is over, I don't know what the future holds. With Kaie being the chosen Inviver, I know the possibilities of what could happen," Maeve said. "For now, I can guide Achaius through what she was supposed to do, but that doesn't mean it will all turn out all right. Human nature can be unpredictable."

CHAPTER 47

On her eighteenth birthday, Kaie awakened as dawn arrived. She slowly got up so as to not disturb Achaius, deciding to take a walk to stretch her legs. After quick contemplation, she brought her sword along with her, knowing she would never hear the end of it if Achaius or Lorne knew she had snuck off without her weapon.

Across the field, Crevan spotted her movements through his spyglass. Lately, he had barely slept, keeping his eyes glued to the Galician camp to watch Kaie.

"Haelan," he called loudly, causing the young Inviver to stir from his spot on the dewy ground where he had collapsed from exhaustion the night before. "Go find Kaie."

"What?" Haelan shook his head to fight off sleep, unable to figure out how to get out of capturing her this time.

"I don't want you to capture her, just see where she's going. The opportunity may present itself to recapture her," Crevan said. "Go!" he barked suddenly, causing Haelan to jump.

Haelan rushed off towards the forest, looking back to watch Crevan for a moment. The commander continued to watch the other camp for a few more minutes before disappearing into his tent. Despite the fact that Kaie had lost her powers, Crevan was still obsessed with her. Haelan had noticed over the weeks that the crazy look in Crevan's eyes had begun to grow wilder.

As his legs sprang across the forest floor, sleepiness was soon erased from Haelan's body as he searched for Kaie. His noisiness gave him away, and when he finally spotted her, her hand was on her sword, staring in his direction. Once she saw him, her body immediately relaxed.

"It's just you," she said in relief.

"Crevan saw you leaving camp and wants me to follow you," he said. Kaie frowned as he continued. "He's still focused on capturing you."

Kaie's frown deepened. "I had another dream last night, but it wasn't quite a nightmare, so I didn't pay much attention to it. Plus I don't have my powers anymore so I didn't think it meant anything. Crevan issued a challenge for me to fight him, saying it would just be the two of us. It didn't really seem like something that would happen."

"Aren't you worried?" Haelan asked when she did not seem to have much of a reaction to this news.

"I could always turn his challenge down. Nowhere does it state I have to actually fight him," Kaie said, shrugging. "Besides, it's my birthday. I don't want to dwell on that unpleasantness."

"What are you doing in the forest so early?" Haelan willingly changed the topic of conversation.

"I just wanted to take a walk," she said.

The two walked in silence for a bit, listening to the sound of the animals waking up. By the time Haelan walked her back towards camp, she turned to him.

"The others are planning a nice meal for tonight," she said. "You should come."

"I'll see what I can do," Haelan said before heading back to Crevan. Depending on the commander's whims, he might be able to sneak away.

Once Kaie entered camp, she saw Achaius waiting for her. As she approached, he came forward to give her a kiss.

"Happy birthday," he whispered in her ear.

"Thank you," she said. She took note of his big grin. "What's going on?"

"Nothing important," Achaius said, a mysterious smile playing on his lips.

"Come on, tell me," Kaie said, holding Achaius's hand. "I can't stand waiting. The suspense is killing me."

"Well, I certainly wouldn't want you to die from suspense," he said dramatically. "Here." From behind his back, Achaius pulled out a high-quality black cloak embroidered with emerald leaves.

"It's beautiful!" Kaie exclaimed as she took in the craftsmanship, knowing that this cloak would keep her much warmer than her old one. "Thank you so much!" She gave him a hug before putting it on.

"The surprises have just begun. There's a special dinner planned for you tonight," Achaius said when she took his hand.

"We already talked about that," Kaie said with an impish grin. "So that's not a surprise."

"Then you'll just have to wait and see," he said.

***

Dinner that evening was an over-the-top affair, as much as it could be on a battlefield. Achaius walked Kaie down a candlelit path to Lorne's tent where all their friends were waiting: Lorne, Farin, Raven, Maeve, Revelin, Haelan, and Brayan. All of Kaie's favorite foods were laid out on the table. The camp chefs had done their best to cook to the standard of the palace, serving roasted pheasant and beef, roasted potatoes and vegetables, and a fruit tart. A couple musically inclined soldiers were playing their instruments for the group, reminding Kaie of when they had celebrated the end of her Inviver training.

Conversation flowed freely and Kaie's heart felt light for the first time in a long time. She was able to laugh without care, touched that so many people cared for her. Tristen's missing presence was glaringly obvious, but the others were able to make up for his absence.

In the middle of dinner, Crevan's voice echoed across the field. "Kaie! I want to speak with you!" he bellowed.

Kaie and the others walked to the edge of camp, where they saw Crevan standing in the middle of the field.

"I have a proposition for you," Crevan announced. "I will fight you one on one, just the two of us, no interference from either side. Whoever wins, the other side immediately forfeits. This would be a fight to the death, a final end to this. Isn't that what you and your friends want? I am offering it to you if you will just fight me. What do you say?"

Kaie looked at the others in shock. "Did he just say that? He's willing to end this?"

"But it could mean your death!" Achaius exclaimed. "Surely you can't be serious!"

"I'm not going to fight him," Kaie reassured Achaius. She turned back to Crevan. "Thanks for the offer, but I'm going to have to decline," she shouted, the wind carrying her words to the commander.

Upon hearing this, Crevan's face turned purple with rage. "The rules of engagement state that you must accept the challenge!" he yelled. "You must fight me!"

"And rules were made to be broken," Kaie called back. "I know this is just a trap you want me to fall into, but I won't let you get rid of me that easily. Think up a new plan. Now if you'll excuse me, I have a birthday celebration to get back to."

She turned her back on him, heading back to Lorne's tent, with Achaius and the others trailing behind. She sat back down.

"I can't believe he said all that," she said. "It could be the answer to ending this fight..."

"Kaie, you are *not* going to fight him," Achaius said. "I know you're a brilliant swordswoman, but there's still a chance that he could kill you. And that's not a chance I'm willing to take."

"Don't worry," she said, kissing his cheek. "I won't be fighting him. It's too dangerous."

"Good," Achaius said as she served herself a slice of fruit tart. "I don't want to lose you because of some spur-of-the-moment decision."

After they finished dinner, the musicians led everyone back outside, where they began playing a lively tune with some other soldiers. To Kaie's surprise,

Achaius took her hand and twirled her around the fire. Laughter and clapping filled the air as other soldiers began to dance with each other, the atmosphere light, even though everyone's mood was slightly dampened by Crevan's challenge.

A few hours later, as the festivities began to die down, Kaie let out a yawn.

"I'm going to bed," she said as she headed off towards her tent.

Achaius was shocked. "Are you going to your tent?" he asked. For the past month, they had spent their nights outside together.

She turned back to him. "Yes, I don't want to sleep outside tonight. I just kind of want to be alone right now."

He nodded. "Okay. Come find me if you have trouble sleeping or need to talk."

Kaie came over and kissed him tenderly. "Don't worry, I'll be fine. Thank you for the lovely evening. I know you planned the dancing."

"I thought you would enjoy it. I'll see you in the morning," he murmured before she left. He watched as she walked off, then turned to the others. "That was unusual," he commented.

"Not really," Raven said. "She's wanted to be alone before. Maybe she's finally over losing her powers. That was the happiest I've seen her in a while."

"If she wants to be alone, maybe I should find somewhere else to sleep tonight," Farin said, looking in the direction Kaie went.

Raven scooted closer to her. "If you wanted, you could stay in my tent," he said, causing Farin to flush at the comment.

Achaius looked between the two, his mouth dropping open in shock. "You two are together?" he asked.

Farin giggled before nodding. "With Kaie sleeping outside with you, we've had the opportunity to get to know one another." Raven's hand moved to hold hers.

"Congratulations," Achaius said. "I'm happy for you two, and I know Kaie would be too."

"We'll tell her soon," Farin said. "She's just been so preoccupied lately, we haven't had much time to talk."

***

Crevan stormed back to his camp, soldiers rushing out of his way, not wanting to ignite his obvious wrath. Everyone had heard Kaie's staunch refusal and now Crevan was looking for blood. Shortly after stomping into his tent, his bellow could be heard. "Haelan! Fallon! Get in here! We have much to discuss!"

Fallon raced into the tent where Crevan was waiting. "What is it, sir?" Fallon asked, nervously cleaning his spectacles.

"She refused to fight me. I need to come up with another plot to get her to agree to the challenge. When I defeat her in combat, I can take her once more." Crevan stumbled over his words in his anger.

"I thought you wanted to kill her? Isn't that what you just said?"

"That's an excuse," Crevan said. "I know she wants me dead. I just want her beaten to the point of unconsciousness so I can get ahold of her again." He paused in his pacing. "Where's Haelan?"

"Somewhere around camp, I would imagine," Fallon said with a shrug. "Or spying on Kaie as you ordered him to."

Crevan's attention was gone once more, focused on Kaie. "Well, I'll just have to wait until something else comes along. Looks like it will have to be spur of the moment," he said, grinning maniacally. "Excellent. I've always loved a challenge."

He continued to mutter to himself while Fallon watched him, filled with worry and fear.

CHAPTER 48

The day before their entourage left the Scrian capital, Tristen could not find Lillian anywhere. He wanted to review the itinerary with her one final time. As far as he knew, this was the first time she was leaving her home and he wanted to ensure she was fine with leaving. After all, it had only been a few weeks since they'd first met and he would not fault her if she wanted to back out of their upcoming marriage, now that she'd had more time to think about it. When Tristen stopped by her rooms, he knocked softly. A maid opened the door, her expression blanching when she saw it was him.

"Is Princess Lillian in?" he asked, taking note of the maid's reaction.

The young woman nodded silently, opening the door to let him in. When he entered, she stood off to the side, pointing to a room further inside. As Tristen approached the doorway, he noticed that the maid made no move to follow.

To his surprise, Lillian was pacing her room, muttering to herself, her fingers crumpling a handkerchief. Clothes were strewn about the room, her trunk haphazardly thrown together. Her eyes widened when Tristen knocked on the doorframe and entered the room, mouth falling open as her cheeks flushed.

"I didn't expect you to see me like this," she said, her hands moving to cover her face in embarrassment.

"This wasn't how you pictured our courtship?" Tristen asked softly. He tried to tamp down the disappointment at her clear display of turmoil. Maybe she was having second thoughts after all.

Lillian let out an unsteady laugh. "Not necessarily," she said. "And I never expected to depart so suddenly. But I'm not unhappy with the arrangement." She took a few steps towards him. "What about you?"

"I appreciate that you're doing this to help broker peace between our two countries," he said. "I know this isn't what you expected, but I'm glad to have found my future queen here."

"Do you think your family will like me?" she asked, face flushing further at his words. She moved to put more dresses in her trunk, to occupy her hands.

"Of course they will. You're everything they would hope for in a queen," Tristen said. He paused when Lillian gave him a tender look. "How do you feel about getting married in Galicia? I know you always expected to have your wedding here."

"Where we get married doesn't matter to me," she said. "But I want you to know that I'm so glad you decided to go through with this, even though you didn't have to. I'm still surprised you agreed."

"It's for the best for both of our kingdoms. How could I refuse?" Tristen asked, giving her a teasing smile. "Besides, I get the better end of this deal with such a smart and beautiful wife."

Lillian softly laughed. "And I get such a handsome husband," she teased. Her eyes drifted back towards the doorway. "But you should get going. My maid seems to be worried that your presence will cause rumors."

Tristen glanced back and saw the young woman standing silently, watching them. "Then I will take my leave, Your Highness," he said, taking her hand and kissing it.

"Thank you for coming to see me. It helped my nerves," Lillian said.

Tristen gave her a tender smile. "My pleasure."

***

Letters arrived at both camps announcing the news of the royal couple's visit. The recipients took the news very differently.

Achaius ran through camp, waving the letter high above his head. "Tristen and Lillian are coming! They'll be visiting in a few days!" he shouted.

"That's amazing!" Kaie exclaimed. "I can't wait to see Tristen. It's been so long."

"Once he's here, this fighting should come to an end. I can't wait," Achaius said, enveloping her in a hug.

The reaction on the Scrian side was the opposite. Crevan paced inside his tent alone, letter in hand. Bloodshot eyes and mussed hair were the main indications that he had not slept the past few days. No one was aware of the dangerous path Crevan's thoughts were taking as he continued to deliriously talk to himself.

***

When Tristen and Lillian's entourage arrived at the battlefield a couple days later, heading towards the Galician side, they were attacked by a group of Scrian soldiers. Though they had their own guards to protect them, they were nothing compared to Crevan's forces.

"What's going on?" Achaius asked in confusion as the Galicians watched the attack in stunned silence. "Why are they attacking their own princess?"

"Must be another one of Crevan's plans," Maeve said, pursing her lips.

"We have to help them," Kaie said, sprinting across the field to help Tristen and Lillian. It was obvious this was another one of Crevan's attempts to continue the war.

Achaius, Raven, and Lorne followed close behind, swords drawn and ready.

Kaie reached the attacking soldiers first, beginning to mercilessly fight her way through them. To her surprise, only Lillian's horse and guards were being targeted. The others swiftly followed behind her, fighting back as well. Suddenly, the soldiers retreated and Kaie could see Crevan yelling at his men.

She pulled Lillian's horse forward, moving them safely across the battlefield. Tristen and his men followed once they saw Lillian headed towards safety. When

Kaie turned to look closer at the princess, she saw various wounds bleeding profusely. As the other men rode up, she helped Lillian down from the horse, walking her to the Invivers' tent. The others from the fight began to follow, Tristen leading the way.

"Crevan ambushed as we approached. His men were only interested in hurting me. They didn't care about the others," Lillian said, tears escaping from her eyes as Kaie encouraged her to sit down. She was shaking like a leaf.

Tristen walked over, placing his hands gently on her shoulders. He murmured comforting words to her.

"It's going to be okay," Kaie reassured her before stepping aside so Achaius could Cure the injured princess.

"Thank you," Lillian said as the injuries and pain disappeared.

Tristen draped a blanket over her shoulders with some quiet words of assurance before enveloping Kaie and Achaius in a warm hug. "It's so good to see you two," he said. The past few months of not seeing them had been tough, always wondering if they were safe. "I missed you."

"We missed you too," Kaie said, returning the embrace.

"But we've been taking care of everything in your absence," Achaius said. "Crevan's schemes have been getting more difficult to guess. He's so unhinged."

"This whole problem with Crevan is ridiculous," Tristen said to the room in general. "I don't know what to do about it."

"I do. I'm going to fight him," Kaie said grimly, her eyes narrowing.

"Kaie, he could kill you! You can't even Cure yourself!" Achaius exclaimed.

"He's right. Just think about this for a moment," Tristen cautioned.

"I don't care. He's bullied us long enough. And now he's tried to kill our future queen, making it look like we did it. He's gone too far. He needs to be stopped." Kaie pushed her way past Achaius to exit the tent.

She strode to the center of the field, facing the Scrian camp. Crevan watched with great interest as she began to shout, "Crevan, you said you wanted to fight one on one. Well, here I am! It's time to end this once and for all!"

Crevan smiled wickedly. "Excellent," he hissed before shoving the spyglass at Haelan and unsheathing his sword. "Wait here," he ordered all the men as he began to head out to the battlefield. "Once this is over, we will finally be victorious."

"What if she beats you?" Haelan asked, unable to hold his tongue. He had been following Crevan's eager strides.

Crevan saw the hopeful look on Haelan's face and his expression turned into rage. "You want them to win, don't you?" he shouted as he punched Haelan to the ground. As Haelan collapsed from the blow, Crevan stood over him, his sword point touching the Inviver's throat. "Don't even try to get up, you traitor. I'll deal with you after I beat your precious friend." He whirled around and continued to his fight with Kaie.

"She will defeat you. She's better than you think," Haelan called after him, trying to bait him.

With a yell of rage, Crevan raced back, kicking Haelan in the head and leaving him unconscious. "That's what you get for talking back to me. When I get back, you'd better listen. Fallon!" he barked, and Fallon came forward. "Make sure no one helps him. I want him to remember this lesson."

"Yes, sir." Fallon gulped.

"Now it's time to deal with the other nuisance."

Kaie watched Crevan emerge from between the tents of his camp, her hands tightening on the hilt of her sword as she moved anxiously from foot to foot. As Crevan approached, getting closer and closer, she noticed how crazed he had gotten in the past weeks, with his bloodshot eyes and oily hair. Without a doubt, she knew she could win.

His mouth curled up into a sneer. "So glad you decided to come to your senses. This makes it much easier to keep you in my grasp."

"My skills have improved since I've arrived," Kaie said as they began to circle each other. "Don't be so sure you'll win."

"I will be the victor," Crevan said emphatically. "You could always forfeit and save yourself the pain."

"Never," Kaie breathed. "I will never join you."

"You have chosen your own demise," Crevan said with a dark chuckle. "Just like your foolish family."

Kaie stumbled back at his words. "What do you mean?" she asked, her face pale.

Without an answer, Crevan lunged forward. Kaie was too shocked by his words to lift her sword up in time, barely deflecting his attack. He scraped his sword against hers, getting close to her face.

"I killed them," he said, his eyes gleaming as he watched her face fall. "You have nothing waiting for you. Did your *precious* friends not tell you?"

Kaie pushed him away, a tear falling down her cheek. "You're lying!" she shouted, aiming her sword at him, which he easily deflected.

"They burned alive!" he shouted ecstatically, pushing her to the ground.

She let out a sob, realizing that her fiery dream had been true. Her chest felt as though a weight was pressing on it, but she knew she had to kill Crevan. If what he said was true, he'd killed her family.

Scrambling to stand, Kaie was able to block his attack once more, a steely resolve encompassing her. She would make the bastard pay for all the pain he had caused.

Crevan noticed the change in her and began to test her defenses before beginning his assault by jabbing and savagely thrusting his sword forward. Knowing she had to focus, Kaie needed to push the thoughts of her family out of her mind if she was to survive.

The sword flicked forward and Kaie dodged just in time as it swung inches away from her neck. Crevan's speed was faster than she'd anticipated—he was able to recover quickly from her blocks, continuing to slash his way forward while she moved to the defensive, trying to evade the blade that would swiftly bring her death.

But her speed advantage did not last. Crevan's sword cut deeply into her arm. Kaie gasped at the pain, wishing she was able to Cure it. Crevan pushed his advantage and she fell to the ground. Her arm throbbed as she brought her sword up just in time as Crevan slashed downwards.

In an attempt to injure him, Kaie aimed for his leg, managing to cut him, though the wound was not as serious as hers. But the distraction gave her time to catch her breath as he staggered from the cut.

She lifted her sword quickly as Crevan turned, ready to continue the fight. As the sun rose in the sky, both fighters dripped with sweat as their bout continued. By that time, both were so covered in blood that those watching could only imagine how they were able to see. Crevan continued to bring his sword down on Kaie's, trying to weaken and finally defeat her. Yet she still managed to hold her sword up even though her arms burned. Each time he beat down harder and harder, she tried to move back without much progress. Though each was giving the other injuries, the fight was far from over.

Every fiber in Achaius's being cried out each time Kaie was injured, but he held back, knowing that this was her fight. He stood by, watching helplessly as she continued to be bruised and battered. She held her own better than anyone else would have been able to, but everyone could tell that if she did not finish the fight soon, she would be killed. He tried to focus solely on the fight, but there was a screeching sound in the back of his mind and the thudding ache had returned to his chest.

Achaius fell to his knees, his hands digging into the earth. The deep hum reached out to him, telling him something. He frowned, trying to decipher the message. As the sound of swords clashing rang at the same pitch of the sound inside him, his fingers dug deeper into the earth. The pain was becoming unbearable.

As the sweat dripped down Kaie's face, she felt exhausted. Chancing a glance at the ring of people, she saw Achaius kneeling on the ground looking ashen. He gave her a wavering smile before grimacing once more in pain. With her attention unfocused, Crevan lunged forward, cutting her dominant arm deeply.

Kaie let out a cry as she backed away from the commander, glancing briefly at the wound. She would not be able to hold out for even a minute longer. The injury was too deep. She needed to end the fight, to take out Crevan so he could no longer hurt any of her loved ones. As he shifted, there was a glint from the vials hanging around his neck—the ones that tethered the Invivers to him.

With a swipe upwards, she aimed for Crevan's neck. He was able to dodge, but the string holding the vials around his neck was severed, causing them to fall to the ground. Kaie jabbed forward and stomped on the vials when she was close enough. The liquid seeped into the dirt.

"*NO!*" Crevan roared, his face twisting into a look of rage. His eyes darted to her once more. When he brought his sword down, she allowed Crevan to knock her sword from her hand. Pulling out the dagger she had hidden in her boot ever since her kidnapping, she lunged forward, raking it across his stomach.

Crevan gasped in pain, but continued to stab his sword towards her, unwilling to admit defeat. Kaie rolled to the side, barely dodging the attack. The wound in his stomach gushed blood, but he did not seem to care. Kaie knew that until he succumbed to the wound, she would have to keep fighting him. He was not going to stop while breath remained in his body.

Crevan staggered forward, stabbing his sword time and time again towards her. Kaie rolled out of range until she'd put enough distance between them to stand. Shooting pain lanced through her arm, but she raised her dagger, ready to finish the fight. There was a moment of doubt before she steeled her resolve.

She could do this.

As Crevan approached, she allowed herself to be impaled by his sword as he drove it deep into her abdomen. She gritted her teeth through the pain as she stabbed her dagger into his heart. At last, he sank to the ground, his bloody sword stuck in her body.

"No, it can't be," he whispered, his face paling as blood leaked through his shirt. "You can't beat me. I'm the more experienced fighter."

Everyone from both camps watched as he fell face-first to the ground, the life gone out of his cruel eyes.

Kaie wobbled away from him on unsteady legs as the blood loss caught up to her. She fell to the ground, her hands barely able to hold her up from total collapse. With great difficulty, she pulled Crevan's sword from her body.

The Inviver powers within Achaius were screaming at him to do something, the shrill sound becoming deafening. With a gasp, he released the building energy. He could sense Kaie's power traveling through the earth to return to its rightful owner. At last, the pain and sound vanished, replaced with a deep exhaustion.

Kaie sensed a burst of energy fill her, as if she was electrified. Her entire body felt as though it was vibrating. But that did not take away from the agonizing pain radiating from her wounds. She gasped as the pain began to intensify, her vision spotting.

"Kaie!" Achaius cried out as he stood and raced towards her.

Kaie looked up, seeing his approach. "I did it," she whispered so softly that Achaius had to strain to hear her, her face pale. "He's gone. He can no longer hurt anyone."

Achaius took her face in his hands. "Kaie, listen to me. You need to Cure yourself. You have your powers back now. If you don't, you'll die from blood loss and no one can help you."

Her face grimaced in pain as she tried to concentrate.

Achaius watched in concern as her breathing grew shallower. "Kaie, you can do it. I know you can," he said, helpless to do anything.

Tristen joined them, kneeling on the other side of Kaie. "Why can't you Cure her?" he asked Achaius.

"I was able to pass her powers back," Achaius said. "Please, Kaie."

Kaie tried to concentrate, but the world spun before her. She could feel the glow at her side as she willed her body to Cure itself.

Before blackness overwhelmed her, she whispered to Achaius, a tear trickling down her cheek, "I tried so hard, but in the end, it didn't matter. He killed my family. I'm all alone."

CHAPTER 49

A splitting headache greeted Kaie when she finally regained consciousness. Opening her eyes and looking around, she recognized her room at the palace.

"How did I get here?" she whispered. She still felt dazed, and everything spun slightly when she shifted. Any movement caused stabbing pain behind her eyes.

"We brought you here after you fainted," Achaius said, sitting to her right in a plush armchair. She had not noticed him until now. "You've been out for a week. Your body continued to Cure itself after you passed out."

She looked at him, her mouth dry. "Is it all over?"

He nodded, reaching out to stroke her cheek. "I thought I'd lost you. It was the scariest moment of my life."

Kaie put her hand over his. "What happened?" she asked.

Tristen's voice came from the doorway. "The Scrians immediately surrendered. Crevan was the only one who wanted to continue the fight," he said. "They all headed back to their homes while we came here. Lillian and I have been working to get the kingdom back on its feet, and Father has been passing his duties to us. After all this, we can start a peaceful reign."

Tears entered Kaie's eyes as she suddenly remembered Crevan's words, her memories of the final fight coming back to her. "He said he killed my family," she said. "You said you sent men to protect them!" Anger rose in her at Tristen's treachery. He had lied to her.

He came to her bedside, kneeling next to her. "I'm so sorry," he said, his expression tortured. "But the men we sent weren't enough to protect your family. We were even working to relocate them when they were ambushed. When we received word of their deaths, I made the decision that the truth be kept from you. I hold all the blame here." His voice turned to a whisper. "I'm so, so sorry."

"You used me," she said, a tone of betrayal in her voice. "You only wanted to keep me focused on the war! I was just a tool to you!" She leapt out of bed, ignoring the pounding pain in her head. She closed her eyes briefly to fight off a wave of nausea.

"Kaie, you shouldn't get up yet," Tristen said, reaching out a hand when she stumbled. "You're still recovering."

"Don't touch me!" she wailed, backing away from him on unsteady feet. Her gaze darted to Achaius. "Did you know?"

"I did not," he said. "I only found out afterwards, like you."

"Who else knew?" Kaie screeched at the Tristen. "Who knew and lied to my face?" She retreated to the doorway, her hand holding her steady against the frame. "Did Lorne? Raven?"

"Kaie, please, you're still recovering," Tristen said, trying to deflect the question. He took another step towards her, trying to calm her.

"He was just trying to protect you," Achaius said. Tristen had told him everything after she had passed out. While he had been angry for Kaie, he knew why his brother had made the decision.

Kaie let out a heartrending, guttural scream, collapsing to the ground. "They died months ago and I just find out now?" A horrible thought filled her and she looked up at Tristen through tortured eyes. "Did... did they actually ever get my letters? Or was that a lie too?"

Tristen hung his head. "My father ordered that they be intercepted." He looked at her with shame-filled eyes. "I'm so sorry."

"Who else knew?" she repeated. "Maeve had to have known, too, didn't she?"

Tristen could only shake his head, unable to answer her question directly. "We just wanted to keep you safe. It seemed the only way at the time."

"You're wrong," she shouted, her voice hoarse, clogged with unshed tears.

She stood and raced down the hallway, away from the man who had broken her trust, one she considered family. Being in the same room as him was unbearable. His presence was now a constant reminder of all she had lost.

"Kaie!"

"Wait!"

Tristen and Achaius yelled behind her, trying to catch up with her.

Kaie ran through the hallways, attempting to lose them before ducking into an empty room to catch her breath. Her vision spun as the rush of adrenaline left her. She let out a sob when she realized that she had unknowingly run to the history room. It had remained untouched since they left over six months ago, dust settling on the furniture and books.

She walked towards the closest bookshelf, looking at the titles of the tomes she had spent hours studying with the two brothers. She had been so happy at the opportunity to learn more than what her life had originally offered her. A wave of grief overwhelmed her. If she had returned home, none of this would have happened, and she missed her family desperately. Shayla would still have her whole life ahead of her, her mother's soft presence would be a comfort, and her father... she would have been able to see and remember his face again.

Soon, Kaie's legs shook and she collapsed to the floor, her body worn from being pushed too hard so soon after waking. Tears spilled down her cheeks as she sobbed, the bottled-up pain of her family's deaths spilling forth. She knelt on the ground, her forehead to the carpet, screams of rage and anguish escaping her already-raw throat.

As her energy waned, Kaie slumped against the floor, completely spent.

***

After a while, a figure entered the small library, gently picking her up and carrying her back to her room. Kaie's eyes could barely open, but once in the hallway, she was able to take note of the face of the person carrying her.

"I don't want to see you," she rasped, closing her eyes once more.

"I know." Lorne's voice was gentle, his strong arms supporting her.

Tears leaked past her eyelids. She missed her father. She would never see him again. Lorne's face would be all that she could envision when she thought of him now.

"Everyone is searching for you."

"I don't care," she said tiredly. "You all lied to me. You *used* me."

Lorne was silent the rest of the way to her room, where he set her down on the soft, pillowy bed. He settled in Achaius's now-empty chair after telling Farin to call off the search, that Kaie had been found.

"I knew you wouldn't forgive us," he said softly, and Kaie opened her eyes to look at him. "It was a chance we were all willing to take, so you wouldn't be devastated and allow Crevan to win. He would have used your grief against you, to turn you to his side. To use your grief for his vile purposes."

Kaie bit her lip, knowing that Lorne spoke the truth. "I was such a fool," she said, her voice breaking. She should have known Crevan would find some way to kill them. She had failed her family.

He shook his head, tears in his eyes. "No, you weren't," he said. "We're the ones who failed you."

"It hurts so much," she said weakly, putting a hand to her chest. "I have no family left."

He placed a hand on hers, squeezing gently. "You are still surrounded by people who love you. We will be your family now," he said, a tear falling down his own cheek.

Kaie had never seen the general cry before, and it brought her a small sense of comfort that he seemed to be hurting as badly as her.

"Even though we messed up, we still love you."

Knowing that he was right, Kaie nodded, though it did not lessen her pain. She knew Tristen and Lorne truly cared for her and loved her. If she had found out about her family earlier, Crevan would have won and their deaths would have been for nothing.

She saw movement in the corner of her eye and looked up, seeing Tristen standing in the doorway, his cheeks wet with tears.

The crown prince remained still, waiting for her to break the silence first. She held out a hand, gesturing for him to come closer, and he slowly walked to her bedside.

"I promise I did everything I could," he whispered, kneeling once more next to her, resting his forehead against her outstretched hand. "We sent men to keep them safe, but it wasn't enough…" He trailed off, tears falling down his face.

"I know," Kaie said gently, and Tristen's head shot up to look at her. "I know you did your best, Tristen. I'm still angry, but that…" She took a shuddering breath and pushed past the painful lump in her throat, tamping the burning anger down. "It will get better with time. I need time."

Lorne was right—she still had people who loved her, people who were her family, even if they were not blood related. If she pushed them all away, she truly would have no one left.

"I can give you time," Tristen promised. "I will do everything I can to make it up to you." He set a bound stack of letters on her bed. "These are from your family," he said. "I know it's not enough, but… I thought it might help."

Kaie's clasped the small stack in her hands, tears spilling as she read her mother's handwriting on the envelope. *Our dearest Kaie.*

"I think she also needs time to rest, Tristen," Lorne said gently, standing to leave. "She's used up a lot of energy."

"We'll be here when you want to talk, okay?" Tristen said, looking at Kaie with wide eyes. "We'll always be here."

"And I'll be here," she said weakly, her energy completely sapped. Even if she wanted to devour the words written to her, her body would not allow it. Before Tristen and Lorne left the room, she was fast asleep.

***

The next day when Kaie awoke, Farin was sitting in the chair by her bedside, knitting. She looked up as Kaie stirred, then handed her a glass of water, which the Inviver eagerly gulped down.

"How long have you been here?" Kaie asked, handing the glass back.

"A few hours now," Farin said, continuing her knitting. "Prince Achaius was at your bedside all night. Do you want me to get someone else for you?"

Kaie shook her head. "Not yet," she said. "How... how have you been? It feels like ages since we last talked like this. Things got so busy on the battlefield."

Farin smiled gently at Kaie, her hands pulling at the yarn in her lap. "Things have been good," she said. "I met someone while we were out there."

"Really? Who?" Kaie sat up in shock, a smile spreading over her face. She was glad Farin seemed happy.

"It's Raven." Farin blushed, a giddy smile on her lips. "We are planning on getting married soon. I'll be leaving the palace in a few months."

Kaie's head spun. It seemed awfully fast to her, but she was happy for the two of them. "That's... amazing," she said, tongue-tied at the news. "I'm so happy for you."

"We didn't think we'd be getting married so soon," Farin admitted. "But things... kind of happened." She held up what she was knitting and Kaie could make out the start of a baby booty.

"You're expecting?" she whispered, her hands covering her mouth in shock.

Farin nodded. "We're so excited," she gushed. "He's planning to get a house in the capital near my parents and we'll be living there instead of at the palace."

"Farin, I'm so happy for you," Kaie said, getting up to give her friend a hug. "And what perfect timing! The war is over and there's no more conflict. A perfect time to start a family!"

"While it wasn't expected, it all worked out," Farin agreed.

There was a light knock on the door, interrupting their conversation. Farin got up to answer it, allowing Achaius to enter.

He looked at Kaie, his expression brightening once he saw she was awake, before falling slightly, remembering yesterday. "Good morning," he said hesitantly.

"Good morning," she responded, giving him a small smile.

Encouraged, he walked towards her and sat on the edge of her bed. Kaie reached out and took his hand, squeezing it gently.

"I... I'm sorry I wasn't able to help," Achaius said slowly, trying to find the words. All night, he had been thinking over what to say. He had not slept, as he knew he needed to get this right. "And I'm sorry about what my family has done to you—what they have kept from you. I want to protect you. I don't want you to be hurt." He let out a long breath. "I know I cannot protect you from everything and you need to get through some things yourself. The only thing I can do is be there to support you through them, and I will be by your side if you'll let me."

Tears filled Kaie's eyes, and Achaius became alarmed.

"I'm so sorry," he said in a rush. "I knew I'd say something wrong. I—"

Kaie squeezed his hand tighter, silencing him. She shook her head. "That was the perfect thing to say," she said. "There *are* things I need to do myself, but knowing you'll be there for me takes a lot of weight and pressure off of my shoulders."

She pulled him closer, giving him a kiss. Achaius's hands tangled themselves in her hair as he kissed her back, keeping her close. Keeping his distance had been torture. As soon as she had opened her eyes yesterday, he'd wanted to smother her in kisses.

Farin cleared her throat, and the two sprang away from each other, forgetting that she was in the room. "I'll get your breakfast," she said, looking at Kaie before turning her gaze to Achaius. "I expect you two to be on your best behavior while I'm gone."

Kaie let out a laugh, while Achaius's face flushed in embarrassment.

"Does this mean I'm forgiven?" he asked hopefully.

"You were never in trouble," Kaie said. "You didn't know what happened."

"So Tristen's still in trouble?"

"I'll get over it eventually," she said, tangling her fingers with his. "But for now, the pain is still fresh."

"They're planning a banquet in a month, to celebrate the end of the war *and* Yule, and give you time to recover so you can join in the festivities," Achaius said quietly. "Then Tristen and Lillian will be getting married in the spring. Afterwards, we could go to your hometown and do a ceremony for your family. If you want."

She looked at him, her eyes glassy once more at his thoughtfulness. "I would like that very much."

CHAPTER 50

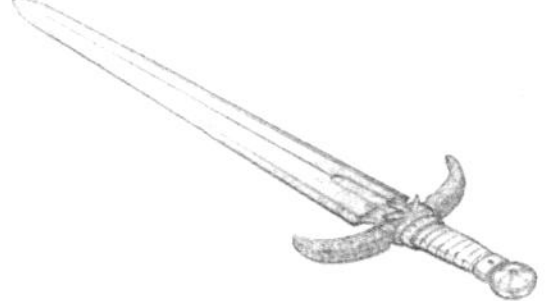

Kaie stared at the gash in her arm. The liquid was no longer a swirling red, but had instead turned to a dark, dull burgundy. While the liquid did not seem to be alive, it was still unsightly. At least her stomach didn't roil each time she looked at it anymore.

Avalon entered the room as Kaie poked the gash and let out a heavy sigh.

"What's wrong?" she asked, coming to sit next to the bed.

"I just wish I didn't have this," Kaie lamented. She pulled her sleeve down so she did not have to look at the mark any longer. "It's so ugly."

The older Inviver gave her a sympathetic smile. "It's proof that you survived what you've been through," she said. "Coming out of war unscathed is a next-to-impossible feat. But you *survived*."

"I know," Kaie said. "But Crevan marked me. I don't like seeing that constant reminder."

Avalon gently took Kaie's arm and pushed her sleeve back up. "Be *proud* that you defeated Crevan," she said. "Let this show that you overcame what he did to you." She pulled her own sleeve up to reveal the scar encircling her wrist. "I have a similar reminder."

"Can't I just try to cut it out and then Cure myself?" Kaie asked. "Make most of the reminder go away? I've got my powers back, so surely I can get rid of this."

"You can't Cure scars like this since the wound has already healed itself. There's nothing else for your body to do," Avalon said, shaking her head. "And you're still recovering, so creating a new wound to Cure is not wise."

Kaie's eyes filled with tears, and Avalon squeezed her hand gently. "I know you don't want feel like he still has power over you, but Kaie, you endured and lived! And he's gone!"

"I still dream about him," Kaie admitted softly, embarrassed that the commander still had power over her, even in his death. "Nightmares of him giving me this, of him coming back and using it against me... It's horrible."

"Those mental scars won't go away immediately, I know," Avalon said. "But as time goes on, those will fade. I still have nightmares about him sometimes too. It's normal."

"Really?" Kaie asked, a tear slipping down her cheek. "Because I feel like I'm broken. I'm weak, have this ugly *thing* on me, and he is still in my head. I hate it."

"You're recovering," Avalon said. "That is to be expected. You need to take your time. Progress isn't linear, and you might have setbacks as you go." She moved to give Kaie a gentle hug. "Be patient and gentle with yourself. You've been through a lot."

"I'll try," Kaie said. She would need to remind herself to be patient with her recovery.

"I'm here if you ever need to talk," Avalon said. "If your memories become too much, it might help to talk with someone."

"You're not going to return to Scria?" Kaie asked. She'd thought that now that the war was over, Avalon would return to her homeland.

Avalon shook her head. "I'm not planning to," she said. "Maybe in the future, I'll be part of the group of Invivers that visits Scria to share knowledge, but for now, I'm going to stay here. I've made a home for myself in Galicia."

***

Kaie spent her time slowly regaining her strength, and by the end of the second week, was able to resume her usual activities. There were a few setbacks with her recovery, and she kept Avalon's reminder in the back of her mind. She had to be patient and gentle with herself.

After getting approval to move about the palace, she spent time with Lillian, bonding with her immediately. Kindness and compassion radiated from the princess, and Kaie could see why Tristen had fallen in love with her.

Tristen gave Kaie a wide berth, giving her the time and space she'd requested. If she entered a room he was in, he would quietly slip out. Kaie noticed and felt bad, but it was too soon to forgive him. Lorne's presence was noticeably absent as well. He no longer joined the royal family for meals and only entered the palace when meeting with the king or Tristen. The rest of his time, he spent outside with the troops, and Kaie sometimes watched him running them through drills. Even if the war was over, it was not the time to slip into complacency.

Spending time with Lillian and Achaius helped—they took her mind off her grief. Though frequently when she was alone, she would pore over the letters from her family, reading their words over and over. They had written to her weekly, it seemed, based on the number of letters she had from them. She had missed so much—for Shayla's birthday, their parents had taken her to one of the nearby towns for their market; her mother's illness had been steadily improving with a constant supply of medicine; her father had started a small garden plot in their yard; and their Yule was lonely without her. The stories she read were a balm to her heart. With each letter, they had always sent their love and reminders of how proud they were of her.

When her feelings grew overwhelming, Kaie would find a quiet alcove to cry in, still overcome with the loss. On more than one occasion, Achaius found her and patiently sat with her until she calmed down. He murmured comforting words to her and rubbed her back. Each time helped to ease her grief, if only for a small while. He never rushed her and never asked about her tears, always waiting until she was ready to talk.

A month after Kaie regained consciousness, the banquet was held a few days before Yule, and all the Galician soldiers were invited. Farin dressed Kaie in a turquoise dress with golden embroidery across the bodice and skirt, braiding her hair into a coiled bun.

"You look stunning," she said to the Inviver, stepping back to admire her handiwork.

"You're coming to the banquet, too, aren't you?" Kaie asked, looking at Farin.

"Yes. I need to go get ready now. I'll see you in a bit." She squeezed Kaie's shoulder before leaving the room.

A little while later, Achaius came to Kaie's room to escort her to the banquet. "You are breathtaking," he gasped when he saw her.

Kaie blushed at the compliment. "You look very handsome yourself," she said.

Achaius was wearing a matching outfit, and Kaie guessed that Farin had coordinated their outfits on purpose. He wore a gold-embroidered turquoise tunic with a white jacket and shiny black boots.

They walked towards the ballroom arm in arm and Achaius pushed the door open. Immediately, Kaie could see the room was filled with familiar faces. It seemed that everyone already arrived.

She turned to Achaius. "Are we late?" she asked.

Achaius shook his head with a smile, leading her inside.

The room burst into applause and cheers as Achaius led her towards where the king was seated. Even King Torin was standing and clapping for her. At a table to the right, she could see Lorne, Raven, Farin, Avalon, Maeve, and Brayan.

Kaie curtsied when they were close enough and the cheering began to die down. Everyone wanted to hear what the king was going to say.

"Kaie Durac, you have served your country well," King Torin began. "You have exceeded our expectations and brought down a highly dangerous man all by yourself."

"I had help." Kaie could not stop herself from interrupting.

"Regardless, it was *you* who killed Crevan," the king continued. "Because of this, I would like to reward you. Ask for anything, and if it is in my power, I will give it to you."

Kaie paused, thinking her request over. "I would like to have a formal ceremony for my family," she said softly. "I want to see if there are any remains and have them brought here to be buried." She looked to Achaius. "And I would like Prince Achaius to come with me when I go."

The king saw the tender look that passed between the young couple and recognized the immense love they had for each other. Lorne had notified him of their relationship, but seeing it in person was another thing entirely.

"Of course he may go with you. A proper funeral will be arranged," he said. "Is there anything else that you wish for?"

"Am I able to stay here?" Kaie asked, her voice uncertain. She had no home to return to, and if the king said no, she did not know where she would go.

"You will always have a place here," King Torin said, nodding. "Please come forward."

Kaie stepped forward and knelt.

King Torin took an ornate sapphire ring off his own finger, holding it up for all to see. "With this ring, I give this young woman, Kaie Durac, the position of ward of the crown. From this day on, she is outranked only by the royal family. She will be protected and provided for until her dying day."

At this proclamation, everyone in the room bowed to her.

Kaie looked around in horror. "Oh, no one needs to bow to me," she said as the king handed her the ring. "I don't deserve this."

"Yes, you do," King Torin told her. "You deserve all of this and so much more." In an uncharacteristic moment of kindness, he squeezed her hands and whispered, "I am so sorry for your loss."

Tears pricked Kaie's eyes as she stepped back next to Achaius, who took her hand, leading her to the table where the others were sitting.

As they sat down, the king raised his voice once more, making another announcement. "I have more news to share," he said. "I will be passing the throne to my oldest son and heir, Tristen de Galac, and his bride-to-be, Princess Lillian Scrinan Plutus, on their wedding day."

Tristen stepped forward in shock. "Your Majesty, it's too soon. You can wait before making such a monumental decision. You aren't thinking clearly," he said.

Torin patted his son on the back. "It is time for me to step down," he said. "And we have a few months to prepare you to fully take over my duties."

Tristen bowed his head in respect as he clasped his father's hand. "I will not disappoint you."

"I know you won't," Torin said. "But for now, we have a celebration to commence. Our enemy is dead and we have Kaie and all these brave souls to honor."

The meal began, with conversation sprouting up throughout the room. Kaie was seated between Achaius and Brayan, with Lorne, Maeve, Raven, and Farin sitting across from her.

Brayan turned to Kaie. "I told you everything came easily to you. You beat Crevan without an issue."

"You wouldn't call being seriously injured and unconscious for a week after fighting him an issue?" she asked incredulously.

"Not exactly, but it was obvious to everyone you would beat him," Brayan said. "We all knew you could do it."

"Thank you," Kaie said, surprised by the first compliment he had ever given her.

"You beating him does say something about how much your skills with the sword have improved," Raven said. "Remember our first lesson where I beat you without a problem? I doubt that could happen now unless I got very lucky."

"Give yourself some credit. I think you could," Kaie said, giving him a smile.

"I somehow doubt it," Raven said. He looked towards the main doors of the room, his smile quickly fading.

Kaie looked as well and saw that two guards were bringing in Rosse, his hands bound behind his back, head bowed.

Tristen's face paled upon seeing his old friend being brought in. "Why are you bringing him here now?" he demanded. He had been told of Rosse's betrayal when they had returned to the palace.

"This man was a spy for the Scrians and revealed our plans to Crevan," the king announced, his voice booming over the hall. Immediately, all conversation ceased. "Tristan, you will decide his fate. I figured that it is best for you to make a decision now rather than wait. Doesn't he deserve quick judgment?"

"Don't we deserve to celebrate without having a death sentence?" Achaius muttered under his breath.

"I'm guessing your father wants to see how Tristen will handle this situation now that he's going to be king soon," Lorne said quietly to the prince.

With tortured eyes, Tristen turned back to Rosse. "What do you have to say for yourself?"

Rosse bowed his head instead of looking into Tristen's eyes. "I have no excuse for what I've done. Everything I did was my decision. I should have come to you when Crevan approached me about this, but he threatened my brother's life. Surely you understand why I did what I did. I was scared for Raven. It was my responsibility to protect him! Please, Your Majesty, please understand."

Tristen looked over to Raven, who was watching his brother with tears in his eyes. "A traitor is a traitor," Tristen said softly. "The punishment is the same for all traitors, no matter if their treachery was done with good intentions. I wish I wasn't in charge of your punishment, Rosse. Really, I do." He unsheathed the sword from his side, walking over to Rosse.

The entire room was silent, somber tension falling over the crowd.

Raven jumped from his chair. "Your Majesty, you can't! He did it to protect me. Take my life instead of his!" he shouted as tears ran from his eyes.

Farin pulled Raven back to his seat. "You know he has to do this," she said, her eyes mirroring the pain on Raven's face. "He has to prove that he will be a just king."

"But Rosse is all I have left," Raven said. "Who else will I have after him?"

Farin put a hand on his cheek, wiping away a tear. "You have me and our little one," she said quietly. "We will be here for you."

Tristen watched the exchange, but continued walking towards Rosse. Rosse watched him coming, his eyes filled with regretful understanding. He bowed his head as Tristen stopped before him. Everyone watched in silence and disbelief as Tristen raised his sword above his head. No one could believe that this gentle man was willing to kill one of his closest friends. Tristen took a deep breath to steady his nerves as he made his final decision.

Rosse flinched as the sound of Tristen's sword hitting the ground clanged throughout the room. He raised his head to see Tristen turn his back.

"I will pardon you this time, but if you betray me again, I will not be so forgiving. You may continue to be in the guard, but you are stripped of you rank. Your responsibilities will be to train the recruits as Lorne has done. Despite your treachery, you have played a part in winning the war. Now go change and join us at the celebration."

Rosse got up, bowing before leaving.

Kaie turned back to the meal and saw that Raven was shaking. "What's wrong? Tristen pardoned Rosse. There's nothing else to worry about."

"I didn't expect him to do that. I thought that Tristen was going to kill him," Raven said. "Excuse me, I have to go." He got up, rushing from the room after Rosse.

"That was odd," Brayan said as he watched Raven leave.

"What would you do if your brother just got pardoned for betraying the country? Wouldn't you be emotional?" Kaie asked.

"I guess, but I wouldn't let my emotions take over," Brayan said while shrugging.

Kaie shook her head at his attitude, which always rubbed her the wrong way. "Try to imagine how he's feeling and sympathize with him instead of making judgments," she said as she turned back to the meal.

The rest of the day passed in a blur as many people congratulated Kaie on the victory. She nodded and smiled politely, but Achaius could tell that she was tired. As she talked to a group of soldiers, Achaius came up behind her, taking her by the elbow.

"Excuse me, but I will have to steal this lovely lady from you," he said.

The men nodded as he led her from the room and onto the terrace, overlooking the snow-covered garden. Achaius draped Kaie's cloak over her shoulders. "Tired?" he asked as he faced her at the railing.

She nodded. "Extremely. I wasn't expecting all these people." She looked at the ring the king had given her. "I wasn't expecting *any* of this."

The prince pulled her into a hug and she rested her head on his chest. For a few minutes, they stood in silence as she listened to the beating of his heart.

"But more than anything, I want to go home. I need to see what happened." She looked up at him.

He looked into her green eyes, giving her a brief kiss. "We'll go there as soon as you want."

"Can we leave right after the wedding?" she asked. "It'll be spring then and easier to travel." Traveling through the snow and cold would be difficult, not to mention finding lodging during the journey.

Achaius nodded. "Absolutely. Anything you want."

CHAPTER 51

Wedding and coronation preparations began after Yule, with everyone scrambling to get everything ready within a few months. It had been years since the palace had hosted such an elaborate event. The Yule celebrations could not compare to the extravagance of a royal wedding. Servants worked from early in the morning to late in the evening to get everything set for the big event.

A few weeks later, Farin and Raven had a small wedding ceremony, with Kaie, Achaius, Rosse, and Lorne in attendance. The couple was radiantly in love and could hardly keep their eyes off each other the entire day. Afterwards, they left to their home in the capital that Raven had bought recently. Farin tearfully let Kaie know earlier that week that she was not going to be returning to work. Though Kaie was sad that she was not going to see her friend every day, she was thrilled that Farin was getting her happy ending.

One morning, when Lillian and Kaie were walking through the greenhouse together, the princess said, "Kaie? I have an important question to ask you." She bit her lip and wrung her hands.

The Inviver turned. "What is it, Lillian?" She was surprised at how nervous the princess seemed.

"I was wondering... you can say no if you wish, but... I was wondering if you would be my bridesmaid?" Lillian asked. "I'm afraid I don't have any sisters and

I don't have anyone else that I could ask. I feel like we've become close and I was hoping you would say yes."

"Lillian, I would love to!" Kaie said, embracing the other woman. "I'm so honored that you would think of me."

"I know Tristen thinks of you like a sister, and I do too," Lillian admitted softly.

Kaie's expression fell at the mention of Tristen. His actions still hurt, even if she loved him.

Lillian immediately realized her error. "I'm so sorry. I didn't mean to," she said hurriedly. She had heard about the conflict from Tristen and was usually conscious about not mentioning him to Kaie.

"It's okay, it's okay," Kaie said in a rush. "I know you didn't mean to bring him up." She let out a sigh. "But you are marrying him. You can't avoid talking about him around me forever."

"I know, but I don't want to make you feel uncomfortable," Lillian said. "If you don't want to be in the wedding because of everything that has happened, I understand."

"No, I still want to be your bridesmaid!" Kaie said, aghast at the suggestion. "And despite everything that has happened, Tristen is like a brother to me. Being included to support you two is such an honor!"

"If you're sure," Lillian said. "You can let me know if you change your mind at any time."

Kaie placed her hand on the princess's. "I won't," she promised. "But thank you for considering my feelings."

The rest of the afternoon, the two walked among the flowers, discussing wedding preparations. Kaie could see how much Lillian loved her fiancé and knew that the two would do a wonderful job leading the kingdom.

Upon returning the palace, Kaie ran into the one person she had barely seen since returning to the palace.

"Tristen," Kaie said in surprise.

He looked equally shocked to see her, immediately stopping. He stared at her silently for several moments, as if drinking in the sight of her, before turning around to go in the opposite direction.

"Tristen, wait," she called out.

The soon-to-be king paused, before turning around. "Yes?" he asked, his voice hoarse. Kaie could see tears in his eyes.

"Lillian asked me to be her bridesmaid today," Kaie said quietly. "I said yes."

Tristen nodded. "That's good," he said. "I know she was looking forward to asking you. Thank you for agreeing. I know it means a lot to her."

"I'm not doing it just for her, you know," Kaie said, taking a few steps forward to close the distance between them. "I'm doing it to show my support for *both* of you."

A sob escaped Tristen's throat, and he wiped away tears.

Kaie stood still, lost as she watched him break down. Seeing how much their distance affected him, how much his actions affected him, made her realize how heavy the weight was upon his shoulders. After a moment's pause, she stepped forward to embrace him.

Tristen clutched her tightly as he shook, his body wracked with sobs. "It means so much to hear you say that," he gasped out, when he could finally speak. "I thought... I was so afraid that you wouldn't even want to attend."

"Of course I want to attend my brother's wedding!" Kaie said indignantly. Once more, she was shocked at how he was willing to do anything to atone for what he had done, even if it meant allowing her to skip his wedding. "No matter how mad I am at you, I want to be there to celebrate you!"

Tristen wiped his eyes before pulling her into another hug. "I know you need more time, but I've missed you. Thank you."

"I've been reading their letters," Kaie said softly. She felt Tristen grow rigid at her words. "It still makes me angry—and sad—that they were hidden from me. And that I wasn't able to learn about their deaths when it happened." She pulled back slightly. "But I understand why you did it." Tears now entered her eyes. "I just wish it didn't have to come to that."

"I know," Tristen said. "I wish I made another decision too." He reached out to wipe the tears from her cheeks.

"Achaius and I will be going back to my home after the wedding," she said. "And after that, I want to do a formal funeral for them." Kaie wanted to wait until after visiting home to hold the ceremony. A small part of her was holding out hope that everyone was wrong and her family was fine. Going home would make her fully accept their deaths.

"Whatever you want, it's yours," Tristen promised. "We'll follow your lead."

"Thank you," Kaie said. "I do still need time, Tristen." A wry smile quirked her lips. "But I don't think you need to run the other way when you see me anymore."

Tristen kissed her forehead, enveloping her in another hug. "Take all the time you need," he said.

***

The morning of the wedding was a bright spring day with fluffy, white clouds in the sky. Everyone in the castle was up bright and early to get the royal family ready for the celebration.

Farin's replacement, an older woman named Lina, helped Kaie get ready. Lillian had picked out a light-pink gown embroidered with roses for the Inviver. After Lina helped her get ready and did her hair, Kaie went to Lillian's rooms to help the bride prepare.

"Oh, Lillian! You are breathtaking!" Kaie gasped when she entered the room.

Lillian was already in her dress, which was fitted, with a white lace bodice, and fell in voluminous folds to the floor. A long train was pooled around her feet as her maids were doing her hair. Torin had gifted her a diamond necklace and tiara from the family treasury that were sitting on a table off to the side.

"You look lovely too," Lillian said, beaming at Kaie through the mirror.

"Are you excited to get married?" Kaie asked, pulling up a chair right next to the princess.

"Excited, but nervous," Lillian admitted.

"Are you upset that your father and brother couldn't come?" Kaie asked softly.

"A little, but Haelan's presence more than makes up for it," Lillian said.

The Scrian king had come down with an illness a month ago that the Invivers had been unable to Cure. True to Tristen's word, a few Galician Invivers had gone to examine the sickly king. Prince Cyric had stayed behind to run the kingdom in his father's stead, but Haelan insisted on attending the wedding. The Inviver had arrived earlier in the week and was going to walk Lillian down the aisle.

The maids continued to do Lillian's hair while the two chatted until the princess's long, raven hair was braided into an updo off her shoulders. Kaie stood and placed the tiara upon Lillian's head before fastening the necklace around her neck.

"You look beautiful," she whispered. "Tristen won't be able to keep his eyes off you."

Lillian blushed at the compliment and inspected herself in the mirror. "Thank you," she said to the maids, dismissing them.

Kaie glanced at the clock on the mantel, eyes widening as she had not realized how much time had passed. "We should head down to the carriage," she said. "We need to head to the cathedral."

Lillian stood and waited for Kaie to gather her train so they could head downstairs together. Their carriage was waiting for them, though the men had departed a few minutes prior. The wedding was to be held at the capital's cathedral, a few minutes' ride from the palace.

"This is really happening," Lillian said once the carriage set off. She wrung her hands nervously as they passed through the roads lined with people.

"It's going to be a wonderful wedding," Kaie said, placing her hands on top of Lillian's. "And you get to marry Tristen."

A soft smile crossed Lillian's lips as she thought of her groom. "That's true," she said. "Tristen will be there."

All too soon, the carriage came to a stop outside the grand cathedral. Stone spires reached high into the sky with stained-glass windows overlooking the city.

Kaie disembarked first and gathered Lillian's train once more. Together, the two walked into the cathedral.

Haelan and Achaius were waiting for them, holding bouquets of roses and lilies for Kaie and Lillian to carry down the aisle.

Achaius came forward and kissed Kaie chastely on the cheek. "You look beautiful," he whispered to her.

"Thank you," she said softly, taking the bouquet from him.

Haelan approached Lillian, handing her the bouquet. "I'm so happy for you," he said. "You couldn't ask for a better husband than Tristen."

"Thank you," Lillian said.

Music began to play from the main chamber and Kaie took Achaius's offered arm so they could walk down the aisle together. When the doors opened, she sucked in a breath, surprised at how many people were in attendance. The entire room was filled with both Galician and Scrian nobility and all eyes were now on her and Achaius. Her cheeks reddened at the attention and she barely noticed Achaius nudging her down the aisle.

"Just ignore them and remember to smile," he said softly, lightly pinching her hand to bring her focus back.

Kaie turned to look at him as they walked, taking a moment to register his words. He prompted her with a smile, one that she gladly mirrored. Then she turned to look at Tristen, who was beaming at her. He was shifting slightly on his feet and she could tell that he was anxious to see Lillian. At last, the two were at the front of the cathedral and Achaius escorted her to her spot on the left before walking to stand next to Tristen. Kaie turned her attention towards the back of the cathedral, where Lillian would enter.

There was a swell in the music and Lillian made her appearance. Kaie chanced a glance at Tristen to see his reaction, surprised to see him holding back tears. He was enraptured, his gaze never leaving Lillian's face as she and Haelan progressed down the aisle until at last, she was at his side. He took her hand and kissed it.

The two approached the dais where the head priest was standing, ready to proceed with the ceremony. Kaie tried to focus on his words, but her eyes were captured by the colorful stained-glass windows, depicting the history of Galicia. She could even see a panel dedicated to the creation of the Invivers.

Her attention snapped back in time for Lillian and Tristen to exchange vows, her heart bursting at the tender look Tristen gave his bride before at last kissing her. Applause erupted throughout the room.

Torin came forward, a servant by his side carrying two crowns on a pillow. "I have an announcement to make," he boomed, holding his hands up. Everyone quieted at once. "Now is the time for Galicia to have a king *and* queen once more. Over these past few years, the crown prince has shown remarkable strength and diplomacy. It is time for me to stand down as king so he can usher in the future. Today, I am officially relinquishing my title over to my son, Tristen de Galac and his new bride, Lillian de Galac."

Cheers filled the room at his declaration.

Tristen and Lillian knelt before Torin, their heads bowed.

Torin took the first crown off the pillow, a tall golden crown with emeralds and diamonds studded throughout it. "I now declare Tristen de Galac the next king of Galicia, to honor and to protect its lands and its people. Tristen, do you accept this responsibility?"

"I swear to do my best for Galicia and its people," Tristen said, his voice ringing loud and clear. At his words, Torin placed the crown upon his head.

Picking up the next crown, a smaller version of the one on Tristen's head, Torin turned to Lillian. "And I now declare Lillian de Galac the next queen of Galicia, to honor and protect its lands and its people. Lillian, do you accept this responsibility?"

"I swear to do my best for Galicia and its people." Lillian's words were more wavering than Tristen's, but her voice was clear. Torin placed the crown atop her head.

"I now present to everyone, the new king and queen of Galicia!" Torin announced.

At his words, Tristen and Lillian stood to face the congregation. Cheers erupted once more. Tristen leaned forward and kissed his wife again before escorting her back down the aisle. Everyone in attendance was invited back to the palace to celebrate the wedding as well as the coronation.

Achaius came to escort Kaie back to the carriages. "That was a wonderful wedding," Kaie said once they were on their way back.

"You seemed pretty distracted during the ceremony," Achaius said, holding her hand. "What were you thinking about?"

"I've never been in a cathedral before," Kaie said. "I got sidetracked by the stained glass. It was beautiful."

Achaius chuckled. "Well, I hope when it's time for us to get married, you'll actually pay attention to the ceremony." He flushed as soon as the words left his mouth, suddenly realizing what he had said.

Kaie's cheeks reddened at his words. "Do you want us to get married?" she asked, her voice soft. They had not really discussed their future together.

He rubbed the back of his neck. "Well, not *soon*. We're still young," he said. "But yes, sometime in the future when we both think the time is right, I'd like for us to get married. What about you?"

"Is that an official proposal?" Kaie asked, quirking an eyebrow. Her heart felt so light.

"Of course not!" Achaius said indignantly. "When I propose, you'll know it!"

Kaie let out a laugh, taking his face in her hands. "I love you so much," she said before kissing him.

The two did not break apart until they arrived back at the palace.

CHAPTER 52

Two days after the wedding, the couple prepared to head to Kaie's home with the well wishes of those closest to them. Kaie had insisted that no additional guards accompany them for faster travel, and after much hesitation, Tristen agreed. Both she and Achaius were talented swordsmen, and now that the war was over, there should be no reason for concern.

Before they left, Tristen stepped forward, wrapping her in a hug. "We will be waiting for you," he said. "Whatever you find, we are all here for you."

"Thank you, Tristen," Kaie said, squeezing him tightly. Apprehension filled her as she tried to mentally prepare for the journey ahead.

The two set off on their horses, traveling the whole day until nightfall, then stopped at an inn. Kaie spent the time telling Achaius stories of her childhood, of fond memories of her family. Achaius enjoyed hearing her talk, and felt honored that she was willing to share these emotional memories with him. She had told Achaius a little bit when she'd shared their letters with him, but now she was sharing stories he had never heard before.

Dinner was a quiet affair as they listened to the boisterous noises of the inn's visitors laughing and telling stories. Kaie didn't feel much like talking and just observed the people. Achaius watched her, the way her eyes flicked from person to person.

"This is all due to you," Achaius whispered to her, leaning in close. "No one would be this happy if it wasn't for you."

Kaie's face flushed and she kissed him lightly. "Thank you," she said.

The following night, they camped under the starry sky as they let the horses rest. They laid next to each other beside the fire, Achaius's arm wrapped around her.

"I'm a little scared to get there tomorrow," Kaie admitted quietly as they stared at the stars.

Achaius turned to her. "Why is that?" he asked.

She remained quiet for several moments. "I just... Nothing is going to be there. I know that, and yet I'm hoping I'm wrong. Part of me expects to see my house still standing, my family inside waiting for me."

"I'm here for you," Achaius said. "I will do what you want me to do. You're in charge with how we do things."

Kaie snuggled deeper into his embrace. "Thank you," she said, giving him a soft kiss. "With you by my side, I know I can get through tomorrow."

***

As the forest and town where Kaie's home resided came into view, she felt a sense of urgency rise up. Without warning, she spurred Aira onwards, towards the well-worn paths she knew so well.

"Kaie, wait for me!" Achaius shouted as he urged his horse to follow her, trying to keep her in sight as they galloped through the village, ignoring the open-mouthed stares of the villagers.

When Aira began to slow, navigating carefully through the villagers, Kaie dismounted, continuing on foot. She ran towards her house, her feet knowing every step of the way. The sun was beginning to set, throwing shadows over the trees. Her feet beat against the ground as she ran into the thicket near her house. All that was left was a big hill, and that knowledge spurred her on. She was so *close*.

Sprinting over the hill, her heart feeling like it would burst, she came to a sudden halt. Tears streamed down her face and she let out a scream at what used to be her home. She knelt where the front door used to be. In her absence, the land had begun to take over the burned remnants, fresh growth covering the ground. Standing, she walked through the house until she was sure that there was no way that her sister or parents had survived.

Taking one last glimpse at the house, she headed back towards the thicket, where she collapsed on the ground, her body wracked with sobs. Though she had known there was no chance they could have survived Crevan's massacre, the little hope she'd had that everyone had been mistaken was now destroyed.

Achaius came up to her, the horses in tow, and he sat on the grass next to her. "I'm sorry," he said softly. "It must be difficult for you."

Kaie nodded wordlessly as tears fell down her face.

Achaius pulled her close, kissing the top of her head. "I'm here," he said softly. "I will always be here."

"I'm sorry for leaving you behind," she said. "But I just needed to see for myself. Alone."

"You have nothing to apologize for," Achaius said. "I understand." He looked at the darkening sky. "We might as well spend the night here. In the morning, we can decide what to do."

Kaie nodded, watching as Achaius began to build a fire. As he cooked dinner, her ears perked up, hearing something that sounded strangely like her sister's voice.

"Did you hear that?" she asked Achaius, who was focused on the roasting meat in front of him.

"Hear what?" he asked.

Then the sound came again from the trees.

"Kaie? Kaie, is that you?"

Kaie looked to Achaius, who nodded. "That time, I heard the voice," he confirmed.

At his words, she jumped up, running towards the forest, towards the voice. "Shayla? Where are you?" she called out, trying to find her sister in the darkness.

In the ruins of the house, she saw a girl walking around, looking at the wreckage. The girl suddenly spotted Kaie, running to her. When she got close enough, she enveloped Kaie in a tight hug.

"I missed you," Shayla said, looking up at her older sister, tears streaming down her face.

"Oh Shayla, I missed you too," Kaie said, clutching her sister close. "I didn't mean to be gone this long. I'm so sorry I wasn't here sooner."

Achaius walked up to see the two sisters hugging, before returning to the fire to give them privacy.

After several more minutes, Kaie pulled back to inspect her sister.

"You've grown, you're so tall now! Your hair is longer too," she said, her face breaking into a smile. Kaie's expression faltered slightly as she saw a pain and sadness that had not been present previously in her sister's eyes. She had been through so much for one so young.

"You've changed too," Shayla said with a grin. "You're so pretty now."

Kaie pulled her sister close again, mussing her blonde hair affectionately. "Thanks. It's good to know I was so hideous back then," she said with a chuckle.

"No! You were pretty then, but much more now," Shayla protested.

"It's so good to see you," Kaie said. "I was only told about the fire a few months ago. They said you all died," Kaie said, her expression turning grim.

"Only I escaped. The men came out of nowhere, Kaie. Father and the guards tried to stop them, but it was no use. Mother sent me out the back door when she saw the torches, but when I saw the flames, I ran back. It was terrible," Shayla said, her voice quivering at the memory.

Kaie held her tighter as if that would make the memory disappear, remembering her own fear from the fiery nightmare.

"When I saw they were gone, I ran further into the forest. It was so scary listening to the men who attacked. They were so happy with what they had done. After that, I stayed in town with a family who took me in. Why did the men attack? We didn't do anything."

"To try and get me to do what their commander wanted," Kaie said. When she saw Shayla's confused look, she elaborated. "I was sent to Carthan Valley, to the front lines of the war."

"Why didn't you write to us and tell us that?" Shayla asked, her tone accusatory. "We wrote to you every week, but you never responded!"

"The king intercepted my letters," Kaie said, her voice quivering with anger. "I didn't find out until after the war that he was keeping your letters from me and preventing mine from reaching you."

"But why?"

"Because of something like this happening." Kaie gestured to the burnt house. "If I had suddenly stopped receiving letters from you, I would have fallen apart and we would have lost the war." She buried her face into Shayla's hair. "I promise I would have come back if I had known."

"What about that commander? Will he send more men to finish the job?" Shayla shivered.

"No, I took care of him once and for all. He won't be sending anyone to hurt you anymore. We won the war," Kaie said. "But I do have someone I want you to meet though. He's very special to me."

Shayla followed her sister, and as they approached the thicket, she moved closer to Kaie, apprehensive as to whom Kaie was referring to. The two saw Achaius sitting by the fire, waiting for them.

"Shayla, this is Achaius," Kaie said with a smile. "And Achaius, this is my sister Shayla."

"He's the prince you went to save," Shayla gasped, recognizing his name. As Achaius stood, she immediately curtsied.

"Shayla, you don't need to curtsy to me," he said, motioning for her to rise. "It's not necessary."

"But you're the prince," Shayla protested.

"Shayla, trust me. When he says you don't need to do something, you don't have to," Kaie said, as she looked at Achaius with a tender expression.

Shayla looked between Achaius and her sister, her eyes seeing everything. "You love each other, don't you?" she asked, wanting confirmation.

"Yes," Kaie said, surprised at how observant her sister was.

Achaius walked over to the sisters, giving Kaie a light kiss on the cheek before saying to Shayla, "And I love your sister very much."

Shayla suddenly shivered in the cold. Spring was here, but winter did not want to give up its hold just yet.

"Oh Shayla, come closer to the fire," Kaie said, pulling her sister toward the warmth. She draped her cloak over the smaller girl's shoulders.

The two sisters sat down next to each other while Achaius sat across from them, finishing cooking dinner.

"Are you going to marry my sister?" Shayla asked him bluntly.

Kaie's face turned crimson at the question.

"We've talked briefly about it," he said, taken by surprise, looking to Kaie. "But we want to wait a while. We're not in a rush. Would you be okay with her marrying me?"

Shayla nodded. "I think you both really love each other," she said. "And you protected her, right? When she was at war?"

Kaie nodded. "Yes, he did," she said.

Dinner was soon ready, and the three began to eat the pheasant Achaius cooked. The bird was juicy and delicious, just what everyone needed after a long, emotional day.

After eating in silence for a while, Shayla asked, "Kaie, where are we going to live now that you're home? The people who took me in, they don't have room for the both of us."

"Won't they be concerned that you're out here in the dark?" Kaie frowned. What sort of guardians were taking care of her sister?

Shayla shook her head, a mischievous grin on her face. "I snuck out when I heard you were seen riding through town," she said. "But we can't stay there and there's no open housing in town. What will we do?"

"I've made a home at the palace," Kaie said. "And I've been told I have a permanent place there. I'm sure the offer would apply to you as well."

"It definitely would," Achaius confirmed. "Tristen wouldn't want you to leave her behind."

"Shayla, how does that sound?" Kaie asked her sister.

"It sounds better than just wandering, trying to find a home," Shayla says. "But are you sure it would be all right?"

"Trust me, any family of Kaie's is now part of the royal family and under our protection," Achaius said. "She has been granted this protection personally by the king."

Shayla turned to look at Kaie, shocked.

"It's true," Kaie said, showing off the ring Torin had given her. It was too big for her so it was hanging on a chain around her neck. "This ring signifies my new position as ward of the crown."

Her sister's eyes were wide as she looked at the ring. "It doesn't matter where we live as long as we're together." She moved closer to Kaie.

"Then we'll leave in the morning to go to the palace. Trust me, Shayla, you will love it there," Kaie said as she put her arm around her sister. "But right now, it would be best if we get some sleep. It's going to take a couple days to get there."

Kaie stayed awake for a while, her eyes trained on Shayla's sleeping face. She could not believe that her sister was still alive. The aching hole that had been present ever since she had regained consciousness lessened just a little bit.

***

Before they left town, Kaie made sure to thank the family that had taken Shayla in. They insisted that the three stay for breakfast, and after a hearty meal, they set off for the palace with Shayla and Kaie both riding Aira.

"Shayla, this will be a new beginning for both of us," Kaie said to her sister. "From now on, I will always be there to protect you. I broke my promise last time and I don't intend to break it again."

"You didn't break it. I knew you would be there when I needed you," Shayla said. "The winter was hard for that family and they told me that they weren't sure how long they would be able to house me. And then you showed up, racing through town. Everyone was talking about it and I came to find you. You did keep your promise."

"Even though we don't have Papa and Momma—you, Achaius, and I will be a little family. All of us together. You'll see. Everything will work out," Kaie said as she looked over to Achaius.

He smiled at her words, holding out his hand to her. She took it as they began the journey back to the palace.

***

A few days later, they arrived back at the palace. Tristen was the first to welcome them back and gave Kaie a hug, which she returned with enthusiasm. Lorne, Lillian, and Haelan followed closely behind.

"Who is this?" Tristen asked, spotting Shayla on Kaie's horse.

"It's Shayla," Kaie whispered, tears in her eyes. "Crevan's men somehow missed her."

Tears entered Tristen's eyes as he bit his lip. He had not been a complete failure after all. "Can I meet her?" he asked, his voice quiet.

Kaie helped Shayla down off the horse. "Shayla, this is King Tristen. In my time here, he's become like a brother to me."

Shayla curtsied. "It's nice to meet you, Your Majesty."

Tristen bent down so he and Shayla were eye to eye. "Shayla, after what your sister has done for our country and for me, you don't have to curtsy or call me by any titles. Do you understand?"

"Yes." Shayla nodded solemnly.

"Now, I have one important question for you, and I want you to take this answer very seriously. I'm sure Kaie and Achaius have discussed this with you, but I want your honest answer. Can you do that for me?" Tristen asked gently.

"Sure," Shayla said.

"Good." Tristen put his hands on her shoulders. "Do you think you could live here in the palace with all of us and learn to accept us as your family?"

Shayla looked at Kaie and Achaius and the others surrounding them, seeing the love in all their eyes. She smiled wide. "I already have."

ACKNOWLEDGEMENTS

This story has been over fifteen years in the making, and I am so pleased to finally share it with the world.

My writing journey began in seventh grade, when we took time in class to write short stories. However, I didn't fully tap into my creative side until senior year of high school, when I enrolled in a creative writing class. My teacher, Miss P., had us listen to excerpts of music and craft short scenes inspired by them. One of those musical pieces sparked the idea that would eventually grow into this story.

I wrote about a girl running toward something, only to come across the burnt remains of her family home. After class, I found myself eager to continue exploring her story—who was she, what had happened, and why was she so important? For the remainder of that school year, I wrote every night, printing pages to share with friends over lunch the next day. By the end of the year, I had completed the first draft.

In the years that followed, I explored other stories but always returned to this one, refining and reimagining it bit by bit. It wasn't until the last two or three years that the manuscript changed dramatically from its original form, yet remains deeply meaningful to me. I'm proud of the final result and grateful to those who helped shape it along the way.

First, thank you to Miss P., for the original prompt that brought this story to life and for creating a classroom environment where I felt safe and encouraged to share my writing. Though it took me much longer to share this particular story with others, the memory of your support made that process easier.

To my high school friends—Charlotte M., Kate W., Sarah B., Jenny H., and Meg M.—thank you for reading those early drafts, talking through ideas with me, and offering unwavering encouragement. Your friendship and feedback were invaluable.

To my college friends—Kathryn M. and Alyssa M.—thank you for the countless Friday nights spent in the computer lab, blasting Disney music while working on our creative projects. Those moments were filled with laughter, creativity, and support and I'll always treasure them.

To Ashley C. —thank you for your thoughtful feedback and constant encouragement. Your enthusiasm for my writing has always been a highlight of the editing process.

To Solomon H. —thank you for your honest, unfiltered critiques. Your insights pushed the story to new levels, and I'm sincerely grateful.

To my wonderful editor, Jess McKelden—thank you for your sharp editorial eye and insightful suggestions. Your guidance helped me shape this story into its best version.

To my SEESTOR, Hannah L.—thank you for your spot-on (and hilarious) commentary. Your sense of humor and steadfast support are constant sources of strength and motivation.

To my parents, John and Valerie—thank you for nurturing my love of reading and encouraging my imagination from an early age. Your support laid the foundation for my creative life.

To my grandparents, Richard and Marty—thank you for sharing your own stories and favorite books with me. Your influence helped spark my love for language and storytelling.

And finally, to my husband, Zach—thank you for your unwavering love, support, and belief in me, even when my own confidence wavered. You have been my rock throughout this journey, and I couldn't have reached this milestone without you.

About the Author

Kendall Lesperance has loved fantasy from a young age. Since high school she has dreamed of publishing one of her numerous stories for people to enjoy. Kendall is a business analyst and lives in Wisconsin. Publishing *The Inviver* is a dream come true, having worked on it for over fifteen years.

Visit her at www.kendall-lesperance.com

www.ingramcontent.com/pod-product-compliance
Lightning Source LLC
Chambersburg PA
CBHW011314310726
48973CB00011B/2913